The Ferret Was Abraham's Daughter

The Ferret Was Abraham's Daughter

Fred Urquhart

WITH AN INTRODUCTION BY
ISOBEL MURRAY

Kennedy & Boyd
an imprint of
Zeticula
57 St Vincent Crescent
Glasgow
G3 8NQ
Scotland.

http://www.kennedyandboyd.co.uk
admin@kennedyandboyd.co.uk

First published in 1949 in London by Methuen.
Text Copyright © Estate of Fred Urquhart 2011
Introduction Copyright © Isobel Murray 2011

Front cover photograph © Kim Traynor 2011
Back cover photograph from Fred Urquhart's own collection
Copyright © Colin Affleck 2011

ISBN-13 978-1-84921-093-5

ONE chapter of this novel appeared originally as a short story, 'Barbara of Shalott', in the *New Statesman and Nation*, and I wish to make the usual acknowledgements to the Editor.

Introduction

When I first heard of Fred Urquhart, perhaps in the sixties, it was as a fine but neglected short story writer. The short story was, as it often seems to be, out of literary fashion, and so was Urquhart. If anyone had suggested that he deserved a major place in Scottish fiction because of his portrayal of women in fiction, I'd have wondered, and if anyone had suggested, as I am suggesting here, that he created one of the most astonishing female figures in a Scottish novel, I'd have shaken my head, privily. When I came to read some of his stories, I did so with great pleasure, particularly those set in the North East of Scotland, having heard his name justly linked with those of Lewis Grassic Gibbon and Jessie Kesson. He had also published novels, but I did not come across them. Now I find myself urging today's readers to read a pair of his novels, published in 1949 and 1951, while in no way wishing to disparage this master short story writer. The novels are *The Ferret Was Abraham's Daughter* and *Jezebel's Dust*. Urquhart told Hugh Macpherson in 1992 that the two novels were:

> Really one long story about two Edinburgh 'good-time' girls who cavorted around with Poles, Free French, and every man they could lay their hands on. One of them became a GI Bride, while the other went to gaol for stabbing her Polish lover.[1]

Ideally, he wanted 'a one volume edition of the two books as they're one long novel.' Indeed, he went on, 'I had always hoped to write a third volume, about Lily's life after she comes out of gaol, but other things. . .' If he had, I have little doubt that Lily's character would have been drawn in similar detail to Bessie's, and that the author could have contrived some sympathy even for this all-time gold digger.

i

The most significant happening in Urquhart's lifetime was the Second World War. He was twenty-seven as it was brewing, in the Edinburgh bookshop where he worked, already himself the published author of his first novel, *Time Will Knit* (1938). He explained to Alan Bold: 'I was greatly influenced by Mrs Woolf at that time, and my one desire was to write inner monologues in Scots.' [2] That novel was based loosely on his grandfather and his family. These generations had to cope with the First World War, and the grandfather here is socialist and pacifist, stern and uncompromising in his anti-war stance, while his children vainly try to come to terms with or without it as it overwhelms them. Fred Urquhart was already a pacifist. When the Second War began, a tribunal sent him to do agricultural work near Laurencekirk in the Mearns. The stories he wrote of his time there are marvellous.

The war was inevitably a major topic in his life and for his work. War as a capitalistic enterprise, inimical to the workers, is an undercurrent almost everywhere, part of an even wider argument about the disadvantages suffered by the working-class, in life generally, in education, in career choice. One line echoes throughout much of Urquhart's fiction: 'I/he/she never had a chance.'   In short stories, which found a ready market then in literary magazines, before he collected them into volumes, he celebrated civilian life in wartime, and his major topic was the way girls and women celebrated the new and exciting opportunities afforded them. These arose from the influxes into the cities of foreign servicemen, soldiers or sailors, Norwegian or Polish or American, and the bizarre encounters and relationships that resulted. In Urquhart's stories the speed with which the beglamorised girls fall in love forever and then move on serially to the next uniform is a recurring topic. The same phenomenon is identified by Muriel Spark in *The Girls of Slender Means* (1963):

The May of Teck girls were nothing if not economical
. . . .
'I thought you said she was in love with the boy.'
'So she was.'
'Well, wasn't it only last week he died? You said he died of dysentery in Burma.'
'Yes I know. But she met this naval type on Monday, she's madly in love with him.'
'She can't be in love with him,' said Nicholas.
'Well, they've got a lot in common she says.'
'A lot in common? It's only Wednesday now.'[3]

This new 'freedom' occurred in fact even more than in fiction. John Costello has a factual social history of what happened to young civilian women (or often girls), which gives a bleak impression of their lives and possible futures, whether in the USA or in Britain. For many, family pressures were lightened or lifted, while entrancing foreign soldiers from many nations filled city streets with smart uniforms, showy manners, glamour, and ready money. Some girls married, as Lily McGillivray did, for the government allowance paid to soldiers' wives, and some of these, like Lily, soon forgot their husbands. (She found reading his letters too much of a chore.) The 'good-time girl' had a heyday, and a number of predictable outcomes followed. There was a steep rise in illegitimacy, and the number of divorces was set to rise, as the infidelities under the unnatural pressures of war rose too. Costello details the great variety of girls faced with illegitimate – and often unwanted – babies:

Some were adolescent girls who had drifted away from homes which offered neither guidance nor warmth and security. . . . There were decent and serious, superficial and flighty, irresponsible and incorrigible girls among them. There were some who had formed serious attachments and hoped to marry.

There were others who had a single lapse, often under the influence of drink. There were, too, the 'good-time girls' who thrived on the presence of well-paid servicemen from overseas, and semi-prostitutes with little moral restraint. But for the war, many of these girls, whatever their type, would never have had illegitimate children [4]

And at the same time there were still families like John Guthrie's in *Sunset Song*, where the father would dictate, whether out of religious principle or pure selfishness, that his wife submit to serial pregnancies, to her physical detriment or even death.

The short stories paved the way for Bessie Hipkiss, the extraordinary central figure of this novel, the Ferret of the title, both typical and one of a kind. Their titles are almost enough: 'I Fell For A Sailor', the title story of his very first collection, as early as 1940 has a Bessie-type figure falling for a sailor who loves her and leaves her, as the last line tells us, with 'the photograph and a scare'. (Bessie, as readers of *Jezebel's Dust* will discover, hasn't even the wit to realise she might be pregnant when she is five months gone.) 'The Last G.I. Bride Wore Tartan', published in 1947, presents the last of the 'good-time girls' who developed the ambition to become married to American servicemen and go West to live in plenty. Ironically, this is to be the eventual outcome for Bessie too. In these stories of seductions and predators, as in the novel, the presentation is generally allowed to speak for itself, with no narrative intervention pointing the reader to judgment, but there is more in the novella '*Namietnosc* – or The Laundry Girl and the Pole'. 'In abnormal times one should expect abnormal feelings...' The laundry girl is worlds away from the war, in a cinema with Jan, watching *The Grapes of Wrath*, when there is an air-raid. The narrator intervenes with a suggestion of a socialist reading of the war:

Although they in their way were starving too: as much driven and harassed as the people in the film. It is because the Netties and Jans are like this that films like *The Grapes of Wrath* must be made to show why wars like this happen. [5]

Again:

In hundreds of places in Britain young couples were sitting, listening to this promise of a better world [a popular song]. Listening as some of their parents had listened to the promise held out in the popular songs of twenty-five years before. None of them ever thought that for one couple for whom the world would glow with gold and glory a hundred couples would never live under any skies but skies of grey. Or if they thought about it, they imagined that they would be the fortunate couple.

In this story, Nettie again has 'a scare'. She panics, and vows everlasting celibacy, but as soon as the scare is over she hurries back for more of the same.

I see *The Ferret Was Abraham's Daughter* as a fine example of narrative, dialogue and comic genius, almost, as it were, the end product of all the war stories. The cinema has the same prominence in the lives of the characters, the same influence on the girls: the girls outside the cinema are described as 'shoddy caricatures of the glamorous girls on stills'. The coming of the Blackout is crucial to most of the activity: 'They are having the time of their lives in the war'. Girls who would never have thought of going near a pub are plied with unaccustomed drink, as in Jan's successful seduction of Nettie.

In the novel, Urquhart presents civilian Edinburgh in the months before and after the start of World War Two. Tenement life and community, Co-op van, Insurance man and air-raid shelter are combined with cinema, drink and the only too liberating Blackout. Add to these the absence of father figures away at the front, and the opportunities for women when children are evacuated to the country, and it is easy to see how Bessie's 'Steppy' can come to run away with her Pole in the next volume when her new marriage has hardly begun. It is all unerringly depicted, with a cast of local women like Dirty Minnie and Mrs Moore superbly characterised with animated gossipy, chattering and suggestive dialogue.

The Hipkiss family is economically sketched in. They are credible, just, as individuals, and can also be seen as typical figures. Pa is a petty tyrant of the old school, a prime example of male chauvinism, a man of unthinking selfishness. He is neatly compared in the title to Abraham, the Old Testament patriarch. For him, it is a man's world. If he is in the mood for sexual intercourse, his ailing wife must necessarily risk yet another pregnancy. If he wants to stay up half the night after he comes home from the pub, then Bessie, who sleeps in the sittingroom, must read in her bed, or listen to his radio. If the younger children annoy him, he will blame Ma and Bessie, and confuse by contradiction any attempt to discipline them. In Genesis chapter 22, Abraham was tested by God, and ordered to offer his son Isaac as a burnt offering. He was richly rewarded for his obedience, and willingness to sacrifice. Pa Hipkiss is a mere caricature of Abraham, with no faith worth speaking of, except in himself, and secondhand stories he gets from students in the pub. No one has to inform him that if his wife dies Bessie must devote her life to bring up his children – it is in this sense that Bessie, 'the Ferret', is Abraham's daughter.

Bessie has unconditional love for her mother, despite the latter's constantly making use of her. She does not resent Ma's demands. She gives up her cinema outings to mind the children. Ma's is a short part in the story, ailing and fearful of the birth of the child she is unwillingly carrying.

She lost her last baby with great suffering. This baby lives, for a few weeks, but Ma dies, trusting Bessie to take care of the children.

These two are a lively and unattractive pair, squabbling and competing over everything from sweeties to stories. Jenny is the insistently loud one, threatening Bad Words, or wizzies on the floor. This critic feels Bessie is heroic to the extent that she looks after them and refrains from physical violence. And the baby, understandably, she cannot take to; she is truly tempted to murder, but the child dies of natural causes.

Bessie herself is more than a type, even an exaggerated one. She has individual obsessions, such as her hatred of her surname Hipkiss, which schoolmates mock. She will go so far as to abandon the first man to whom she promises eternal love, when she discovers that his surname is Smellie. She is at the centre of it all, dominating our attention, an extraordinary figure. Bessie is fourteen and a half at the start, fifteen and a half at the end. She shares in the general man-mad, cinema loving fads of girls – and women ! – of the time, but usually has to have someone to follow, such as Lily McGillivray. She is non-assertive to a degree, and is regularly described by others as 'vacant', and her reply to most words spoken to her is a giggling 'Och away!' Nonetheless, Urquhart contrives to make her an extraordinary and credible individual. There is very little narrative guidance in the novel, but there is one notable exception. After we have met her at home with her often tiresome family, and also experienced a long and vivid example of her day dream of being a lost European Princess, we have this astonishing detailed analysis, which seems to become more condemnatory as it goes on. It all turns out to be true, but arguably it is Urquhart's achievement to win the reader's support for this supremely ungifted heroine:

> She had no ideas about what she wanted to be. Her
> father and Miss Aitchison said she was to be a teacher,

so she accepted that uncomplainingly. She was not clever enough to reason it out within herself. If she had been, she would have known that she hadn't enough brains to be a teacher. She had no head for mathematics, geography, science or any of the other subjects, even in their simplest forms. All she was really gifted with was a good imagination, and it was this imagination as shown in her school essays which had made Miss Aitchison insist to Bert Hipkiss that he allow Bessie to stay on at school. If Bessie had been clever enough to be honest with herself she would have known that what she really wanted was to spend her life day-dreaming. But actually she was rather stupid. In many ways she did not even have the low cunning of some of her contemporaries at school or in the neighbourhood. She had a simplicity which verged at times almost on the moronic. Her life was bound up with her mother and the fantasies she wove for herself and the children, especially those she wove for herself. In some vague way she was dissatisfied with her life and environment, but she knew no way of changing it unless by escape into day-dreams. She knew no other life, except the ones she read about in novels or saw on the films. (30-31)

This analysis does not come as a complete surprise, after we have endured first her chaotic, put-upon life at home, with an unhappy but still manipulative mother and her demanding younger siblings, and second, a long account of her favourite dream, being a somehow wronged Princess of France and elsewhere, and what will happen when she and her family come into their own again. Her life accommodates these clashing concepts, especially before men become her chiefest interest. At the end of the very first chapter:

The heralds were announcing her: 'Her Royal Highness, Madame Elisabeth, Duchess de Bourbon-Parma, Duchess de Guise, Duchesse d'Orleans. . . '
    She opened the door.
'Is that you, Bessie?' her mother shouted. 'Take Jenny to the lavvy, will you? She wants to do a wizzy.' (3)

In her dreams she benevolently transfers her parents and siblings into French royalty, and in chapter 6 her well-named neighbour Dirty Minnie turns up for the Coronation. She restrains herself from calling out, but

made up her mind that as soon as she got to Notre Dame she would send a footman to the Place de la Guillotine and tell Minnie to come up to the Louvre at night for a feed of fish and chips. She would do Minnie proud while she was in Paris. (23-4)

These efforts to reconcile her two worlds in dreams are striking. She hates the noise her father makes when eating soup: 'Heavens, she wondered, what would happen when they went to Paris and had soup at banquets?' (66)
Each of these extended day-dreams is worth savouring at length, noticing the poor materials of the girl's imagination, nourished by films and cheap novels. Her ideas are pitiful, tawdry, and yet clearly immensely attractive to a Bessie anxious to escape the everyday. And yet often she reduces herself to tears by the power of her feelings. In an essay on how his writing began, entitled 'My Many Splendoured Pavilion', Urquhart admitted having things in common with Bessie when he was a young man. There was 'my love affair with the cinema – the most dazzling colour (apart from sex) in the pavilion of my youth', and 'I was teeming with all kinds of far-fetched dreams from being the lost heir to an Italian dukedom to bowing deeply to the applause in a great theatre in New York.' [6] Bessie is never seen as less than human, or as unworthy of our attention, even when we are encouraged to laugh.

The whole story covers only a year: Ma's pregnancy and death, the coming of the baby, Bessie going to work, Pa's bringing home 'Aunt Mabel', the children being evacuated, Pa's marriage to Aunt Mabel, and Bessie's decision to leave home to work for spiritualist Mrs Irvine. A crowded year. It insistently reminds me of another Scottish novel, reputed to be the nation's favourite, *Sunset Song*. I do not know whether the similarities and differences of the two heroines are deliberate, but they are striking. Urquhart could be deliberately shadowing his distinguished predecessor for contrast. Gibbon and Urquhart choose strangely adjacent situations. In a short time, when the heroine is in her teens, Chris's mother kills herself because she is desperately afraid of another ordeal of childbirth: she has already, like Ma Hipkiss, suffered a stillbirth. Her husband's demands have been as heedless as those of Pa Hipkiss. Jean Guthrie also kills her twin babies, it has been suggested this is in order not to burden Chris with their care. Bessie's mother is equally and rightly afraid, and she does die in childbirth, with the baby only surviving her for a few weeks. But she has left Bessie in what we might call a no-choice situation: she is to leave school and her father's unrealistic ambitions for her education, to care for Billie and Jenny, and all depends on her sense of love and duty, and the expectations of others. Chris, on the other hand, loses her father too, after a grim ordeal, and is left to choose for herself between the world of school and education, possibly becoming a teacher, or to go back and work her land: either is easily within her grasp. Bessie never really had any chance of being a teacher, or any strength of mind to make a real decision. Chris is capable of acting – and living – on her own, of accepting bleak realities and surviving alone: Bessie is weak, dependent always on other people and incapable of surviving in solitude. Chris is said to be the nation's favourite literary heroine: Urquhart reminds us of weaker vessels who 'never had a chance.'

Notes

1 Hugh Macpherson, 'Fred Urquhart' in *Scottish Book Collector*, vol 3 no 3 February/March 1992, pp 27-30.
2 Alan Bold, *Modern Scottish Literature*, 1983, p 210.
3 Muriel Spark, *The Girls of Slender Means*, 1963, p 95.
4 John Costello, *Love, Sex and War: Changing Values 1939-45*, 1985, pp 276-7.
5 Fred Urquhart, '*Namietnosc* – or, The Laundry Girl and the Pole', *The Clouds Are Big With Mercy*, 1946, pp 53, 57.
6 Fred Urquhart, 'My Many Splendoured Pavilion' in Maurice Lindsay, ed, *As I Remember: Ten Scottish Authors Recall How Writing Began for Them*, 1979, pp 164, 170.

PART I

1

THE FERRET was delivering her evening papers. She scurried
in and out the entries in the tenements, banging at doors, running up and down the stairs, shouting greetings to people she
knew. 'Ony guid murders in the paper the night, Bessie?' a
voice called from an upper window.

The Ferret looked up. Fat Mrs. Moore was leaning on her
elbows on her window-sill.

'Ay, there's one,' Bessie cried. 'Mrs. Moore, number eleven
Goldengreen Street, has been discovered at the foot of the hole
she's diggin' for her air-raid shelter. It says it's not known
whether a witch or Hitler done it. Her head's been battered in
and her toe-nails cut off, and there was a snake wound round
her neck——'

'Hey you, Bessie Kiss-ma-hip, are ye goin' to deliver our
paper the night or the morn's mornin'?' Lily McGillivray
shouted from her entry.

Bessie Hipkiss flushed. She hated her name, but never so
much as when somebody shouted it rudely like this. She felt
that it was her father's fault. Her mother's name was Campbell, and she had her mother's sandy-reddish hair and hazel-
green eyes. But she had her father's snub nose and her father's
big mouth. At school her name was a burden. She preferred
the nickname 'The Ferret'. Whenever the other children cried
'Bessie Kiss My Hip' or worse, she would say indignantly: 'My
name's Bessie Campbell.' But it made no difference. The hated
name was something she could not get rid of; she realized it
was something she would have with her all her life, like her
big mouth and her snub nose. She hated it so much that she
could not bring herself to write it. In her exercise-books she

I

could never get any further than Bessie Hip . . . The other children knew this, and it made them goad her even more. And they never lost an opportunity to point it out to anybody in authority.

Even the teachers, Bessie felt, were not above making remarks about her name. Not that any of them ever said anything as bad as their pupils; it was just the tone of voice when they said it sometimes. That was what first made her so fond of Miss Aitchison. Never in any way did she ever make Bessie feel that the name was funny.

It started the first day Miss Aitchison came to the school. Their previous English teacher had set the class an essay on 'What I would do if I were alone on a desert island'. Miss Aitchison had corrected these, and she was handing back the exercise-books. She was reading through the list of names: 'Marjorie Johnson . . . George Cook . . . Annie McIntosh . . . Bessie Hippy . . .' She looked about, but nobody came forward to claim this exercise-book. Most of the children giggled, and everybody looked towards the thin little girl with the worried face and the reddish hair in the third back seat. 'Bessie Hippy?' Miss Aitchison said again.

The thin girl rose, glowering at the others.

'Is this your book?' the new teacher said.

The girl muttered something.

'This is a very good essay, Bessie,' Miss Aitchison said loudly and distinctly for the benefit of the rest of the class. 'It's much the best essay here. It shows some imagination.'

Ever since then Bessie had adored Miss Aitchison with an adoration second only to her adoration for her mother. Now at Lily McGillivray's raucous shout she was on the point of shrieking back when she remembered what her mother would have said. 'Suffer in silence, Bessie,' she always said. 'The Lord sees and understands. He wouldn't like you to add anything to other people's crimes by answering back in the same way. Always turn the other cheek, like Jesus did Himself.'

And so she did not say what she'd have liked to say to Lily McGillivray. She handed the paper to her in silence, then she hurried on to the next entry. But she seethed with fury.

Some day, she told herself, some day Lily McGillivray and all the others like her would pay for their impudence. I'll show them all yet, she promised herself. One day when I'm the Duchess of Bourbon-Parma I'll come back here and I'll show that McGillivray where she gets off. I'll come in a big black car—a long Rolls Royce with white leather seats and the Bourbon crest in gold and diamonds on the doors, and when the car stops one of the footmen—his name 'll be Alphonse and he'll be awful good-looking—will hop out and open the door, and then I'll get out and I'll stretch out my arms wide and I'll say: 'Ah, ze old home, ze home of my cheeildhood! Parbleu! eet ees steel ze same. Ah, ze many happee days I 'ave spent 'ere in my youth. Vonce—do you know, Princess de Lamballe—vonce I used to deleever ze papeers in zese streets. Yes, eet ees so! I vos a—vat do you call eet?—a newspapeer girl.'

In this way, by the time Bessie had delivered all her papers and was climbing the stairs to her own home she had forgotten all about Lily McGillivray. She put one slender white hand on the banisters, and with the other she held up her long black chiffon velvet train. She was walking beside the Ambassador from the Court of Spain up the white marble stairs of the Louvre to the court where her father, the King of France, was holding a levee. The heralds were announcing her: 'Her Royal Highness, Madame Elisabeth, Duchess de Bourbon-Parma, Duchess de Guise, Duchess d'Orleans. . . .'

She opened the door.

'Is that you, Bessie?' her mother shouted. 'Take Jenny to the lavvy, will you? She wants to do a wizzy.'

2

BESSIE's father was having his tea before going to work. He was a waiter in a public-house. 'Hurry up with the News,' he cried, 'and let's see if auld Neville has sold us another pup.'

3

Bessie flung the paper on the table beside him. 'Now Jenny,' she said. 'Come on with me.'

Jenny stuck out her lower lip. She was a small, wiry child of three with little sharp eyes and a tow of black hair. 'No,' she said.

'But ye're wantin' to do a wizzy, aren't ye?'

'No,' Jenny said.

'Come on with me like a clever wee girl,' Bessie said. 'Come on before ye wet yer breeks.'

'No,' Jenny said.

Bert Hipkiss lowered the paper. 'Go on, ma wee hen, do what Bessie tells you. Go on and show us all how clever ye are.'

'No,' Jenny said.

Her father made a funny face at her. 'Do I like you?' he said. 'I don't think I do!'

'I'll hit you,' Jenny said, raising her hand. 'I'll throw a stone at ye.'

'Oh, but you wouldnie do that,' Bert said.

'I would sut,' Jenny said. 'I'll kill you. I'll get a witch to come and put ye in a pot and boil ye into wee, wee bits.'

'Come on, Jenny,' said Bessie.

'No.'

Bessie sighed and leaned forward to pick her up, but Jenny kicked and struggled. 'I'll kill you,' she shouted. Then suddenly she quietened down and looked around cunningly. 'I'll say a Bad Word,' she said.

'Jenny!' Bessie was shocked.

But Bert Hipkiss picked up his paper and said: 'Go on to the bathroom like a good wee girl and then ye can say as many bad words as ye like. We don't care.'

'Really, Bert Hipkiss,' his wife cried, moving in slowly from the kitchenette. 'How can ye ever learn the bairn the way to behave if you will insist on saying things like that to her? . . . Jenny!' she screamed. 'Do what ye're told or I'll smack yer bottom for ye. Go on now! At once!'

Jenny howled at this, but Bessie ignored the howls and carried her away, shouting: 'Come on for a wizzy! A wizzy! A wizzzeeeEE!'

4

Bert sighed with resignation and gave Jenny a conspiratorial wink as she was being carried out. He picked up his paper again, but after a few seconds he was forced to say: 'Margaret, I wish you'd learn thae bairns to go to the bathroom without the whole neighbourhood havin' to know about it. It aye turns into a sort of public procession.'

Mrs. Hipkiss leaned heavily on the table. She was far gone in pregnancy. 'It's all very well for you to talk,' she snapped, 'sittin' there on your backside readin' your paper. But if ye had them on yer hands all day like me ye wouldnie be so keen on all yer fancy methods. What that little bitch needs is a good smacked bottom, and one o' thae days I'll give it her. Repressions or no repressions! . . . Repressions!' she cried. 'You and yer bloody repressions! You and yer fancy ideas that ye get from daft books and thae silly students that come into the pub!'

'Well, I don't see why all this fuss should be made about a simple matter like going to the bathroom,' he said. 'It's you that's to blame for it all. Learnin' the bairns to parade themselves. They've no natural modesty at all.'

'Och, ye're just a prude,' she said. 'But you're not so prudish about other things. Like yon day last summer when ye had Jenny out in the go-car and ye let her take off all her clothes in the Botanic Gardens.'

'That was different,' he said. 'The sun was good for her.'

'It was nut,' she cried. 'It was downright indecent, that's what it was.'

'There's nothing indecent about nakedness, Margaret. But it's all this paradin' about goin' to the bathroom that gets me down. Ye make it seem dirty. It's obscene, that's what it is,' he said.

'Och, you and yer big words!' she screamed. 'If I had some o' thae students here I'd cut their bloody throats!'

'Come on and get yer tea like a clever wee girl,' Bessie said, putting Jenny on a chair at the table. 'Wait till I get your feeder.'

'I dinnie want my feeder,' Jenny yelled. 'I dinnie want my tea.'

5

'Come on, my wee pet.' Bert leaned towards her. 'Sit in and take your tea.'

'No, I dinnie want my tea.'

'What do you want then, duck?'

'I want to be bad,' she yelled. 'I'm goin' to be BAD.' She slipped from her chair. 'I'm goin' to say Bad Words, and I'm goin' to take off my breeks and do a wizzy on the floor. I'm goin' to do a lot of wizzies.'

'You sit in your chair at once, young lady,' her mother said. 'Or I'll learn ye!'

But before anything could be done, Jenny had pulled off her little red knickers. 'See!' she cried, pulling up her dress. 'See! I'm goin' to run downstairs and shout Bad Words at everybody. At you and you and you and at Mrs. Finlayson and at Mrs. Moore and—and everybody!'

'Jenny Hipkiss, you get back in yer chair or I'll smack yer bottom till it tingles,' her mother shouted.

'Come on, my wee hen,' Bert said softly. 'You show your mammy what a nice wee lassie you can be sometimes.'

Bessie lifted the struggling Jenny and placed her on her chair again. She bent to put on her knickers, but Bert said: 'Oh, leave those damned things until after the bairn's had her tea. That elastic must be tight on her wee legs.'

'Where's Billy?' Mrs. Hipkiss shouted. 'Billy! BillEE!'

'He's down in the back-green, Ma,' Bessie said. 'Will I go and get him?'

'No, I'll just shout out the windy.' Mrs. Hipkiss lumbered to the kitchenette window and opened it with a bang. Bert closed his eyes as if in pain. 'Billy!' she screamed. 'Billy! BILLY! Where are ye, darlin'? Come and get yer tea!'

Bert tried to read his paper, but he could not concentrate for the noise his family were making. Mrs. Hipkiss kept shouting at Jenny. Bessie ran backwards and forwards banging down dishes and clattering her heels on the worn linoleum. The front door slammed, and Billy stumped in, glowering. 'What are we gettin' for our tea?' he shouted.

Bert put down his paper. 'Can you not come in a bit more quietly?' he said. 'And why can't you come in for your tea in time without havin' your mother bawlin' out the window and lettin' the whole neighbourhood know? Wash your hands and then sit down.'

But Billy pulled out a chair and sat down. He was a sullen, dirty-faced child of five, with three of his front teeth missing. 'Hurry up and gie's ma tea, Ferret-face,' he shouted to Bessie.

'Go and wash your hands when you're told,' Bert said quietly.

'You shuttup,' Billy said. 'Hurry up wi' my tea!' he yelled. 'The gang are buildin' a boat and they cannie get on till I go back.'

'Go and wash your hands at once,' Bert said, even more quietly. 'Or you won't get any tea.'

Billy made a face. 'Ach, awa' and boil yer head!' he shouted. 'Whae's feared for you?'

'I'm not sayin' you're feared for me,' Bert said. 'I'm just telling you to go and get your hands washed.'

'Billy!' Mrs. Hipkiss screamed. 'Go and do what yer father tells ye. Go on now, or I'll gie ye a scud on the lug.'

Billy scowled, but he went into the kitchenette, shouting: 'They're no' dirty. They're no' near as dirty as Jackie McGillivray's and he hasnie washed his hands since Sunday.'

Bert sighed. He made a point of never lifting his hands to his children. But Mrs. Hipkiss had none of what she called his new-fangled ideas. She kissed and cuffed indiscriminately. 'Ye're far too soft wi' them,' she jeered now. 'A good hard slap on the jaw's the only thing Billy would understand.'

'Ay, and if I raised my hand to yer darlin' wee pet ye'd be up in arms at once like a cock at a grossit,' Bert said. He rose. 'Well, I must away to my work. Ta-ta, ma wee doo,' he said, bending over Jenny. 'You'll be a good girl now, won't you, until I come back?'

'No,' she said.

7

3

As soon as Bert had gone his wife relaxed behind the pot of fresh tea that Bessie had put on the table. 'Well, are we all ready?' she said. 'Are yer hands clean, Billy? Who's goin' to say the Grace? Billy?'

He looked coy. 'No. Jenny.'

'No. Billy,' said Jenny.

'We'll not quarrel about it,' Mrs. Hipkiss said. 'Bessie 'll say it tonight.'

'No, me,' Billy said. 'Me wants to say the Grace,' he said in a very lispish, childish voice. 'Me says it best.'

'All right then,' his mother said. 'But before ye say it, Jenny 'll put on her knickers. Little ladies don't sit at table with their bare bottoms showin'.'

'But the lastic's hurtin' my legs,' Jenny said, opening her eyes wide in an injured way.

'Ye're just a wee haver,' Mrs. Hipkiss said. 'It's not hurtin' your legs at all.'

'Daddy said it,' Jenny said firmly. 'Daddy said it.'

'It's just because he said it,' Mrs. Hipkiss said. 'Ye'd never have thought about it if that soft mark hadn't put the idea into yer head. Put yer knickers on at once,' she shouted. 'I will not have you sittin' at my table with your bare bottom showin'. It's not decent. Bessie, put on her knickers at once.'

'Now then, Billy darlin',' she said after Bessie had managed to hustle the struggling Jenny into the knickers. 'We'll all close our eyes and you'll say the Grace.'

He simpered and folded his hands on his plate. 'All close yer eyes now,' he said. 'C'mon, Jenny Hipkiss, ye're lookin'. I'll no' say it if ye look.'

'Jenny!' Mrs. Hipkiss shouted. 'Close yer eyes at once.'

'Lord bless our food,' Billy said, then he stopped. 'What comes next, mammy? I cannie mind.'

8

'Goodness me!' Mrs. Hipkiss said. 'What a bad memory ye've got! A big boy like you should be able to remember the Grace by this time. Lord bless our food,' she prompted. 'For Jesus' sake, amen.'

After tea Mrs. Hipkiss said she had a sore head and she thought she'd lie down. 'Will ye wash the dishes, Bessie, and put the bairns to their bed when it's time?' she said.

Bessie could not keep the look of disappointment off her face. 'But, Ma——' she said.

'Oh, were ye wantin' to go out?' Mrs. Hipkiss sighed. 'Ah well, I suppose I'll just have to manage myself then. My head's awful sore, but I'll maybe manage. I'll take two-three aspirins and maybe that 'll help. Where are ye goin'?'

'I wanted to go to the Rialto,' Bessie said apologetically. 'It's Robert Taylor and Joan Crawford. But it's all right,' she said. 'It won't matter. I'll stay at home.'

'No, no,' her mother said. 'I'll manage fine. I'll just take the aspirins and maybe they'll put the headache away. I'll easy manage. Away you and enjoy yersel'. I'll take the aspirins and then if the bairns would just be quiet for a wee while I'd maybe lie down. It's such a splittin' headache. It just came over me all of a sudden at tea-time. If only I could get half an hour's peace I'm sure I'd be a' right. I've been on my feet all day. But away you go to the picters and enjoy yersel'. Dinnie fash yersel' about me. I'll be all right.'

'Och no, Ma,' Bessie said. 'I'll bide at home. Is yer head awful bad?'

'Well, it could be worse,' Mrs. Hipkiss said, sitting down beside the fire. 'It's been worse manys and manys a time. But it's awful sharp. You know, it just hit me all of a sudden. Just after yer father went away. I'm sure it was all that argy-bargyin' with him that brought it on. And of course, I aye hae headaches just before I hae a baby. But awa' ye go to the picters. I'll just sit here for five meenits and hope for the best. I'll just hae to grin and bear it like I've done often before.'

'No, no, Ma,' Bessie said. 'You sit there and rest. I'll easy bide at home. I can go to the picters another night.'

'Well, if you would, that would be fine,' her mother said.

'It's really not so sore, it's just a sort o' sickness. It'll maybe be better in a wee while.'

Bessie hurried on with the clearing of the table and the washing of the dishes. By the time she'd finished it was half-past six. Jenny kept hanging at her heels all the time, whining: 'Tell me a story, Bessie,' and screaming when Bessie said she hadn't time.

'Bessie, can ye no' keep that bairn quiet?' her mother shouted. 'Every yell she gie's goes right through my scalp like red-hot needles.'

'Now, Jenny, be a guid wee lassie,' Bessie whispered. 'Mammy's got a sore head. If ye're no' guid I'll have to put ye away to yer bed.'

'I dinnie want to go to my bed,' Jenny yelled. 'I want to go to the picters wi' you.'

'But I'm no' goin' to the picters.'

'Ye are sut,' Jenny cried. 'I heard ye tellin' Mammy.'

'For God's sake, bairn, shuttup!' Mrs. Hipkiss shouted. 'My head's like to split. Bessie, if ye've finished the dishes, I think ye'd better take her to the picters with you.'

'But it's half-past six. By the time we get out it'll be long past her bed-time.'

'Och, that doesnie matter,' Mrs. Hipkiss said. 'If only ye'll take her away out o' ma road. See and be back and have her in her bed, though, before yer father comes hame.'

'All right, Ma,' Bessie said.

4

THE FERRET didn't want to take Jenny to the pictures. She was going with two other girls. But she thought she'd better make the best of a bad job. Poor Ma, she needed a rest.

'Ach, what did ye want to bring *her* along for?' Mabel Brown said when Bessie and Jenny got to the Rialto. 'She'll be a right nuisance.'

'I will nut,' Jenny said. She went behind Bessie and, looking round at Mabel, she made a face. 'I dinnie like you,' she cried. 'I'll spit on ye!'

'C'mon,' Mabel said, going towards the pay-box. 'But listen you, Bessie Kiss-ma-hip, you keep that bairn beside you and as far frae me as she can get.'

They weren't long in the picture-house before Jenny said she wanted a wizzy. It was almost time for the feature film to start, so Bessie hurried her to the Ladies and tried to get back to their seats as quickly as possible. But the film had started by that time. 'You're a damned wee nuisance,' Bessie hissed, shoving Jenny into her seat.

She could not enjoy the film because of attending to the child, but Mabel Brown and Nessie Porteous did. They were raving ecstatically about it when they came out at a quarter to ten. 'Wasn't Robert lovely?' Nessie said. 'Gosh, I could fall for him in a big way! That bit at the end where he stood at the gate waitin' for Joan Crawford—oh jings, it was super!'

Mabel and Nessie would have dawdled, speaking about the film, but Bessie hurried them on. 'I want to get hame afore ma father comes in frae his work,' she said. 'He'd raise the roof if he kent that Jenny was out at this time.'

'Och, what's all yer hurry?' Mabel said. 'Let's stop at the Chipper. I want to show ye last week's *Cynthia's Circle*.'

'I want chips,' Jenny cried.

'Well, you're not gettin' chips,' Bessie said.

'I want chips,' Jenny said. 'If I don't get chips I'll say Bad Words. . . . I'll tell Daddy we were at the pictures,' she said.

Bessie sighed. 'All right, you'll get chips—and I hope they choke you!'

A horse-drawn fish and chips van stood every night at the end of Goldengreen Street. A small crowd was gathered in front of it, waiting for Alfie, the owner, to dish out their penny-worths and twopennyworths. Alfie, a small man with a bald head and a perpetual frown, was leaning against the stove, poking occasionally at the chips in the frying grease.

'What are ye waitin' for, Alfie?' a big, stout woman shouted.

'I could have had the tatties planted and gathered and peeled by this time.'

'Planted where, Minnie?' Alfie winked at the crowd. 'In yer hair? There'd be plenty o' soil there, I bet.'

'G'out, ye impiddent brute!' she said, laughing. 'I'll have ye know that my hair was washed only last week. And that's more than can be said about yours!'

'That's got him, Minnie,' a man said.

'LadEES and GentleMEN,' he shouted. 'Walk up, walk up and see the greatest show on earth. An all-in wrestling match between Dirty Minnie on my right and Clean Chips Alfie on my left. Roll up and see the show!'

'Ten to one on Dirty Minnie!' somebody shouted.

The crowd laughed and jostled each other good-naturedly. 'Ten to one?' Dirty Minnie cried. 'My Christ, I'd have thought you'd have laid smaller odds than that on me!'

The three girls and Jenny stood under a lamp-post a few yards from the chip van. Mabel took a folded paper out of her pocket, and they all crowded round to read it, but they kept looking warily towards the van to see that they didn't lose their turn. 'What's Titania sayin' to it this week?' Bessie said.

They turned to a page headed 'Take Your Troubles to Titania'. ' "Worried working girl".' Bessie read aloud. ' "Dear Titania, I am earning only twenty-five shillings a week, but my mother insists on me paying her a pound a week for my board. That only leaves me" . . . Ach, what's the next one?'

' "Two schoolgirls," ' Mabel read, and she giggled. ' "We are two schoolgirls, aged fourteen, and we want to ask your advice, dear Titania. Funny things are beginning to happen to us . . ." '

'The silly bitches!' Mabel said with a guffaw.

'Ooooh!' Jenny cried. 'You said a Bad Word.'

'Aw, you shuttup,' Mabel said. 'If ye dinnie shuttup I'll throw ye into Alfie's van and he'll take ye away and leave ye with the show folk.'

' "Funny things are beginning to happen to us." ' Nessie

sniggered. 'That's right! Are funny things beginnin' to happen to you, Bessie?'

'I dinnie think that's funny at all,' Bessie said, moving towards the Chipper. 'C'mon, or we'll lose our turn.'

'All right then, sniff!' Mabel said. 'Ye're surely turnin' awful proper in yer auld age!'

Bessie stood in silence beside Dirty Minnie, waiting for her turn. The big stout woman leaned down and winked at Jenny. 'Hello, Toots, ye're out late the night!'

'I'm not Toots,' said Jenny.

'How's yer ma, hen?' Dirty Minnie said. 'Has she no' piggit yet?'

'No,' Bessie said.

'Three twos, please,' she said, stepping forward to the counter. 'And a sixpenny fish supper.'

As soon as she had got the warm, greasy parcel of fish and chips, Bessie took Jenny's hand and hurried her away. She did not answer when Dirty Minnie shouted: 'Good night, hen! Tell yer ma I'll be up to see her one o' thae days.' Nor was she going to speak to Mabel and Nessie, who were capering with two boys slightly older than themselves under the lamppost. But they shouted: 'Adios, Ferret, adios!'

'Adios,' she said. And she hurried on, hauling Jenny along behind her, saying: 'C'mon now, hurry up! We must get hame before Daddy comes in.'

5

MRS. HIPKISS was sitting beside the fire with her feet on the fender. She was leaning eagerly over *The People's Friend*, and it was only when Jenny threw herself upon her, crying: 'D'ye ken what we saw, Mammy?' that she showed she was aware of them. 'So ye're back?' she said. 'Was it a good picter?'

'Ach, it wasnie bad,' Bessie said. 'I've seen Robert Taylor in picters I've liked better.'

13

'And were ye a good wee girl?' Mrs. Hipkiss asked Jenny.

'Yes,' Jenny said meekly. 'I was awful good, wasn't I, Bessie?'

'I dinnie ken aboot that,' Bessie said, smiling.

Billy was lying at his mother's feet, dressed in his pyjamas. 'What way did ye not take me, Ferret-face?' he said pugnaciously. 'Ye'll have to take me the morn.'

'I'd be fond,' Bessie said. 'Who would take a wee snottery-nosed cratur' like you to the picters?'

'Mammy would, wouldn't ye, Ma?'

'Yes, son, I would.' Mrs. Hipkiss smiled fondly at him.

'How's yer head, Ma?' Bessie asked, leaning over her.

'We—ell, it's a wee thing better,' Mrs. Hipkiss said slowly, puckering her brows a little to show that it was still there. 'I still feel it, though. It comes and goes. I wonder if ye'd get Jenny ready for her bed and away before yer father comes in? I just feel I havenie the strength to manage her.'

'I dinnie want to go to ma bed,' Jenny shouted. 'I want chips.'

'Ye'll get some chips in your bed,' Bessie said soothingly. 'I'll bring them to ye.'

'No, now!'

'No, after ye're in bed,' Bessie said, and without more ado she picked up the little girl and carried her away to the bathroom.

'I want Mammy to tell me a story,' Jenny screamed. 'I want a story! I want a story! If ye don't tell me a story I'll get out o' ma bed and I'll do a wizzy on the floor and then I'll run outside and down the stairs and—and——'

'And what?' Bessie said, pulling off Jenny's clothes, regardless of her struggles.

Jenny gulped. 'And then—and then I'll go and stay wi' Dirty Minnie and I'll learn to say more Bad Words and more Bad Words. I'll shout up at the windy and SWEAR at ye,' she said solemnly. 'But if Mammy tells me a story I'll be good.'

Bessie lifted her and placed her in the basin. There were three large pots of aspidistras in the bath. Mrs. Hipkiss was always raging at her husband because he did not cultivate

14

their plot at the back of the tenement. 'If we just grew some nice flowers,' she often said. 'Pansies and Wall-flower and Sweet William and things like that—it would be such a treat for me.' But Bert never did anything about it. Mrs. Hipkiss tried to foster her passion for flowers by having plants in pots all over the house. They were always needing water, and the bath was always filled with two or three of them. 'Every time I take a bath,' Bert always complained, 'I have to wade through a bloody shrubbery to get it.'

'Spread out yer legs,' Bessie said to Jenny, 'and let me get the dirt washed out from atween them. Really, I never saw such a dirty wee lassie!'

'How are ye gettin' on?' Mrs. Hipkiss leaned heavily against the lintel of the door. Billy stood beside her, rubbing his cheek against her thigh. 'Tell us a story, Mammy,' he said. 'About a tiger that crept through the jungle and met a little girl and chewed her head off.'

'No, about a witch!' Jenny screamed, almost falling out of the basin in her excitement. 'A story about a bad, bad witch that eats little girls. Only, not me! Not me! I'm a guid wee girl, amn't I, Mammy?'

'Sometimes,' her mother said.

She sat down on the edge of the bath and stroked the leaves of the nearest aspidistra. 'I'll have to put thae pots back in their place,' she said. 'They've had plenty o' water by this time. I've been goin' to do it two-three times, but I've just never felt like it.'

'I'll put them back as soon as we've got Jenny in bed, Ma,' Bessie said.

'Will ye, dear? That would be fine. Get them back in their places afore yer father comes in and starts to rave aboot them.' Mrs. Hipkiss sighed. 'They're bonnie plants, but oh dear, they're no' the same as a garden. I wish yer father was as fond o' flowers as me. He wouldnie leave that back-green like a midden then.'

'On and on and on with the story!' Jenny cried.

Mrs. Hipkiss sighed again. 'Well, once upon a time there was a wicked witch called Witch Blacknose and she lived——'

'Ach, no' aboot a witch,' Billy said with disgust. 'Aboot a tiger.'

'Well, just a minute. Have patience,' Mrs. Hipkiss said. 'Witch Blacknose lived in a wee cave in the middle of a dark, dark forest, and there were snakes in the forest, and wolves and tigers and funny creeping things. But Witch Blacknose wasn't afraid o' them because she was a magic witch. She wasn't in the least bit afraid o' tigers. In fact, she had a pet tiger of her own. She kept it chained up in a corner of the cave, and it was a great big tiger with fierce red eyes like hot coals. Its name was Jeremiah, and at nights when it was dark and stormy Witch Blacknose used to go out riding on Jeremiah's back, looking for little children that had got lost in the wood, and she used to take them home and put them in a cage and feed them up till they got fat. Every day she poked her long skinny fingers through the bars of the cage to feel if they were getting fatter, and as soon as she thought they were fat enough she would take them out and put them in her big black pot and boil them alive. Then she would invite her friends, Witch Whitenose and Witch Rednose, to supper and they would play cards and then they would have a great feast. First they would drink the soup the body was boiled in, then they would eat the fingers and the toes that had been fried in oil——'

'What kind o' oil?' Billy said. 'Olive oil?'

Jenny said nothing. She sat on the water-closet seat with her mouth wide open, letting Bessie dry her.

'Yes, olive oil,' their mother said. 'Then after they'd eaten all they wanted, they threw the scraps to Jeremiah and he gobbled them all up. Then after a while the three witches got on their broomsticks and sailed away up among the clouds to spy out the land and see if there were any more lost children to bring home and put in the cage. . . .

'Now, Jenny,' she said. 'Are ye ready for yer bed? Come on then, like a guid wee lassie!'

But Jenny braced herself against the lavatory-seat. 'No, I want another story. That's not a good story. I want a LONG story!'

'That's a long enough story. It's the only story ye're goin'
to get tonight, anyway. I'm tired. C'mon, get away to yer
beds, both o' ye.'

'Ach, just another wee story,' Billy wheedled. 'Aboot a lion
this time and a brave sailor.'

'No,' Mrs. Hipkiss shouted. 'I will nut. I'm tired.'

'Just one more story,' Jenny said, opening her eyes wide and
looking pleadingly at her mother.

'Ye little bitch!' Mrs. Hipkiss screamed. 'I'll ring yer ears
for ye if there's another murmur out o' ye. Come on!' She
swooped upon Jenny, lifted her up and staggered away to the
back room with her. 'I never saw such aggravatin' bairns,'
she cried hysterically. 'There, get into yer bed at once!' And
she flung Jenny on top of the bed. 'Get under thae blankets
at once afore I skelp yer bottom for ye.'

Jenny started to howl, but she scurried beneath the bedclothes when her mother leaned forward, hand raised, shouting: 'Do ye want it? Do ye want it?'

Bessie carried in Billy astride her back and dumped him
beside Jenny. 'Now lie down and be a guid wee boy,' she said
softly. 'Mammy's tired. Go on, lie down, and I'll bring ye
through yer chips.'

'I'm exhausted,' Mrs. Hipkiss was shouting as she went
back to the kitchen. 'I'm fair exhausted wi' thae bairns. Yer
father doesn't know what it is to have to try to cope wi' them.
It's all very well for him to have all his fancy ideas about what
children should be told and what they shouldnie be told, but
he never does anythin' about them himself. Leaves it all to
me, and then gets on to me when he thinks I'm no' doin' the
right thing. I'm fair scunnered wi' them.'

'They've made ma head bad again,' she whined, sitting
down on the stool in front of the fire, crouching with her head
in her hands. 'Bessie, ye might pour me out a wee nip o'
whisky. Hurry up now, afore yer father comes hame!'

'Ach, it's only half-past ten,' Bessie said. 'He'll no' be hame
for half an hour yet.'

'Eh, but that was fine.' Mrs. Hipkiss wiped her lips with the
back of her hand. 'It's handy sometimes yer father bein' in the

17

trade! Hurry up and wash the glass, Bessie, and put it away
afore he comes. And gie me ower ma chips. They'll help to put
the smell awa'!'

Bessie did as she was told, then she took chips to the children,
who were fighting, screaming at the pitch of their voices.
'Now, be quiet, both of you,' she said. 'If ye're no' sleepin'
before Daddy comes home there'll be a fine howdyedo.'

'I want to see Daddy afore I go to sleep,' Jenny said.

'Well, Daddy 'll no' be wantin' to see you,' Bessie snapped.
'Lie down, like a good girl. Daddy would be furious if he kent
that ye'd been up so late. If there's another sound out o' ye
I'll—I'll—I don't know what I'll do!'

'Bessie!' Jenny spoke earnestly in a stage-whisper. 'Bessie,
bring me a drink o' water.'

'I'll do nothin' of the kind. Water at this time o' night! Lie
down and go to sleep at once.'

'I wanna drinka water!' Jenny howled.

But Bessie shut the door and went to the bathroom to take
the pots out of the bath. Jenny and Billy screamed for a while,
then there was silence.

6

BESSIE was in bed when her father came home at half-past
eleven. She slept on a put-u-up in the living-room. She hated
it because she could never get to sleep until long after her
father came home and had gone to bed, often after a quarrel
with his wife. Until recently she had slept in the same bed as
Jenny and Billy, but her father had said it was unhealthy.
'She's over fourteen now,' he said to Mrs. Hipkiss. 'It's no'
fair either to her or the two wee yins to cramp them.'

Every night she was forced to lie in bed and read because
she could not sleep with the light on. Tonight she was reading
Alexandre Dumas' *Marguerite de Valois*. Her mother, crouching
over the dying fire, was reading one of the *Cynthia's Circles*

that Bessie had brought home from the cinema. Neither of them heard Bert until he was standing in the middle of the living-room.

'Christ, what a poor fire!' he shouted.

Mrs. Hipkiss looked up and gave an exaggerated start. 'My, what a fright ye gave me! I never heard the door.'

'Ay, it seems like' it,' he said. 'Sittin' there like a Craw Nancy at a blackout fire! What kind o' fire do ye call that to have for a man when he comes home tired after a hard day's work?'

'But it's late,' she whined. 'It's not worthwhile puttin' on more coals at this time o' night.'

'No, but it's worthwhile holdin' out your hand for my pay every Saturday night,' he said. 'Come on, put on some coals for God's sake!'

'But, Bert, we'll just be goin' to our beds.'

'Beds! I'm just in. Surely to God a man has a right to sit at his own fireside for a wee while after he comes home from his work.'

'But Bessie wants to get to sleep. She has to be up early to go with her papers. A growin' lassie like her needs a lot o' sleep.'

'It doesn't look like it just now,' Bert said. 'What's that you're readin'? A lot o' trash about kings and queens as usual! It's high time you read somethin' sensible, my lassie.'

'But Miss Aitchison said I should read this,' Bessie said, holding the book against her chest.

'Well, all I can say is I'm surprised at Miss Aitchison, I aye thought she had more sense,' Bert said. 'She must be daft to tell you to read a lot of muck like that.'

'She is not daft,' Bessie cried.

Her father stopped in the middle of taking off his jacket. 'Another word like that out of you, my lady,' he said, 'and I'll draw my hand across yer jaw.'

Bessie lay back sulkily. Tears were pricking her eyelids. Who did he think he was speaking to, anyway? Saying that about Miss Aitchison who was far cleverer than he would ever be. What was he, anyway? Just a waiter in a pub. He thought because he learned a lot of nonsense from those Bolshie students who came into the bar that he knew everything. But he was wrong. Miss Aitchison knew far more than he would ever know though he lived to be a hundred. The best thing really would be for him to kick the bucket . . . though he'd better not do that just yet. Not until after he became King of France, anyway. Gee, it would be fine if they arrived to-morrow morning. . . . Just as she was going away to school. . . .

She was going downstairs with her case in one hand, holding Billy with the other, and just as they came out of the entry a great big Rolls Royce drew up and a man with a tile hat got out, and when he saw them he got down on one knee on the pavement, not minding that it was dirty and all dog-pish, and he took her hand and kissed it and cried: 'Votre Altesse Royale, Madame Louise-Elisabeth, Duchess de Bourbon-Parma, Duchess de Nantes, Duchess de Guise. . . .' And then the Town Council came down hell for leather, and the Lord Provost with his tile hat, and they all got their photos took with him and the Lady Provost—Bessie had seen her doing her shopping once or twice at Greenacre, a little wee cratur' with a black hat and a string of pearls—and then a telegram came from the King, inviting them to go and bide in Holyrood Palace. She got the chance of sleeping in Mary, Queen of Scots' bed in the room beside the room where Rizzio was murdered, but she said: 'No thanks, not on your life!'

No, she didn't say that. She said: 'Ah non, non, I preefaire zees leetle bed zat ze Princess Elisabeth have slep' in. 'Er name is Elisabeth, too. So!' And Jenny slept in the bed that Princess Margaret Rose always slept in. And they had a hell of a fine time in Holyrood, eating ice cream and chips and strawberries, as much as they liked without their mother always having to shout out about the price. And they got photographed every-where with the Lord and Lady Provost and the Duke of Buccleuch and Will Y. Darling, who showed them the sights of the city.

'Ah, Edinburgh eet ees veree beautiful,' the Duchess de Bourbon-Parma said. 'But eet ees not so belle as ma belle Paree. Ah, 'ow I long to return to ma belle Paree!'

And then they got on a special train for London, a train that had been all newly painted with the French Fleurs de Lis, and there were red carpets down at the station. And there were photographers to take their photos so that the *Edinburgh Evening News* could put great headlines: 'Bourbon Royal Family leave for their Kingdom after their long Exile'. And that night in Goldengreen Street and the other streets where she delivered in Calderburn some other lassie or laddie would be delivering her papers. And there were thousands and thousands of people seeing them off, waving and cheering as they drove in their Rolls Royce down the carriage drive into the Waverley Station. And all their friends from Calderburn were driven in motors behind them, and they all got on the platform. Mrs. Moore and Mrs. Winter and Mrs. Finlayson and—well, yes, even Dirty Minnie. The Duchess de Bourbon-Parma waved her white-gloved hand languidly to Dirty Minnie as the train slowly steamed out of the station. 'Good-bye, Minnee!' (Adieu, adieu, you mean) 'Adieu, Minnee, adieu! Ve return now to our countree.' And the Queen of France wept as she leaned out of the window and shouted good-bye to fat Mrs. Moore, her own special pal.

Tears were running down Bessie's cheeks as she became overcome with emotion at her mind-picture, but she hid them under the bedclothes. It would be a terrible wrench for her mother to leave Mrs. Moore. Could they not maybe take Mrs. Moore with them to Paris? She could be made a Lady-in-Waiting and given a title. The Countess d'Orleans. No, that wouldn't do. That was a royal family title. Countess de Montmartre. Ay, that was it. That would suit Mrs. Moore fine. The only trouble was Mrs. Moore's old man. Something would have to be done about him. Maybe they could poison him before they got started. . . .

'The long-exiled Bourbon royal family arrived in London this evening on their way to Paris to take over their kingdom. They were accompanied by the Countess de Montmartre, newly-appointed Lady-in-Waiting to Her Majesty, Queen Marguerite. The Countess, whose husband died in mysterious circumstances last week, wore long widow's weeds.'

The papers would be full of them. They'd wipe even auld Hitler off the map for a while. They would meet him, of course—but not yet. They'd meet him after they got to Paris. She would meet him in Switzerland maybe when she went to ski. The Führer photographed with Her Royal and Serene Highness, Madame Marie-Elisabeth, Duchess of Guise, eldest daughter of the King of France.

But that wouldn't be until after the Coronation. . . .

Madame Royale of France came down the great staircase of the Louvre. She was wearing a green gown and a green velvet train. Marie Antoinette's famous diamond necklace that Count Cagliostro had pinched for her was around her milk-white neck. A tiara of diamonds bound her red-gold hair—that hair that was to become famous throughout Europe during her lifetime, that hair that once, before Madame Royale came into her inheritance, earned her the nickname of Carroty Ferret. Six steps behind her came the Duchess d'Angouleme, clothed in white tulle. She had on a diamond tiara, too, but a smaller one. (Though, mind you, they'd really need to do something about Jenny's hair when they got to France, it was that stiff and wiry.) In the hall below she saw her father, Robert I of France, in his coronation-robes, leading the Queen towards the great doorway. Madame Royale held her dress up with one hand, while with the other she twiddled with the famous diamonds. As she reached the bottom steps her parents went outside. There was a great roar of applause and cheering from the mob without. The Countess of Montmartre came bustling towards her. Her tiara was on a bit squint. Madame Royale reached up and gave it a tweak, saying: 'Really, Mrs. Moore—I mean Countess—you must get your maid to dress you more properly.'

'I'm that nervous, ducky—I mean yer Royal Highness,' panted the Countess. 'Ye'd think it was me that was goin' to be crowned and no' yer puir pa.'

''Ave courage, cherie,' Madame Royale said gallantly. 'Allons, mes enfants!' And she swept forward through the ranks of the bowing footmen, followed by Mrs. Moore and Jenny and the Dauphin.

The crowds howled with excitement as she swept out of the doorway and entered her carriage. She leaned forward and motioned to the coachman with her white-gloved hand. He cracked his whip and the six white horses began to prance across the courtyard. Glancing back, Madame Royale saw the Countess and the two Royal Children get into their carriage, which began to follow hers.

As the carriages came out of the gates, the crowds surged forward to see her, but the mounted policemen kept them back. Madame Royale sat up stiff and straight as a poker. Remember, cherie, a Princess of the Blood Royal does not lounge. She bowed haughtily from side to side, keeping her hands clasped in her lap. There wasn't going to be any of this hand-waving stuff with Elisabeth de Bourbon-Parma. Not on your life. She would always remember that she was descended from a long line of kings, not a commoner who had been raised to royalty by marriage.

Paris was mad with joy. 'Vive le roi! Vive le roi!' People screamed themselves hoarse with excitement. The coronation of George VI in London that she'd seen on the pictures had nothing on this. Apaches twirled in the streets, with knives in their mouths. People were even climbing up the lamp-posts to get a better view. Later in the day the lamp-posts would be used to hang Bolshies on. The guillotine was ready for these Communists in one of the main streets, and the old women with their knitting had taken their places already to wait for the tumbrils. They waved their knitting as Madame Royale's carriage passed and cried: 'Vive Madame Royale! Vive Elisabeth de Bourbon-Parma!' One of them was awful like Dirty Minnie. . . . In fact, it was Dirty Minnie come all the way to Paris to see the Coronation!

Madame Royale was going to leap up and yell: 'Yoohoo, Minnie!' but she remembered in time that she was of the Blood Royal of France, and she restrained herself. She contented herself with giving an extra-special bow and smile towards Minnie. And she made up her mind that as soon as she got to Notre Dame she would send a footman to the Place de la Guillotine and tell Minnie to come up to the

Louvre at night for a feed of fish and chips. She would do Minnie proud while she was in Paris.

The carriage stopped before the steps of Notre Dame. The horses tossed their heads proudly and pawed the ground. The crowds cheered. A line of footmen and soldiers and mounted policemen held them back, and Madame Royale walked up the red carpet to the door. The Archbishop of Paris was there to meet her. 'Welcome, my daughter,' he said as she knelt down before him, and he placed his hand on her head and blessed her. Then he led her down the nave through all the French aristocrats in their jewels and Orders and all the ambassadors right to the altar where her father was sitting on his throne, waiting to be crowned. She sat down on a littler throne, just a wee thing behind him and her mother, and she waited there patiently until the Countess of Montmartre and the royal kids came in. Then the Archbishop stood up on his hind legs in front of the altar and he said a prayer. And he prayed for the salvation of France and thanked *le bon Dieu* for sending their king back again after his long exile. And then they all crossed themselves. And then the Archbishop got down to business. He took the great gold and jewelled crown from the Bishop of Orleans and he put some oil on her father's head and he cried: 'Robert de Bourbon, I now crown thee King of France and Emperor of the French Colonies Overseas. Arise Robert le premier!'

And her mother was crowned and then she was crowned and then Billy and Jenny, and then her father took her mother's hand and they walked slowly down the aisle, and she and the kids and the Countess of Montmartre followed them, and all the great French families and the ambassadors followed them, and as they went out to meet the shouting crowds the bells of Notre Dame pealed forth. . . .

Big Ben was striking twelve!

'What are ye needin' the News for?' Mrs. Hipkiss whined. 'Ye'll waken the bairns.'

'I haven't heard the News the day,' Bert said. 'Surely to God a man can listen to the News in his own house!'

Bessie shrouded her head with the bedclothes and tried to

go on with her fantasy, but she could not help hearing the announcer.

'Oh, God!' Bert shouted. 'Oh, God, the bloody bastards! They've gotten Madrid! It's all U.P. with us now.'

'What are ye needin' to swear for?' Mrs. Hipkiss said. 'I'm sure their auld Spanish Civil War doesnie concern us.'

7

O N Sunday there was the usual uproar in the Hipkiss house. Every Sunday this started when Bessie began to get the children and herself ready for Church and Sunday School. Although Mrs. Hipkiss did not often go to Church herself, being usually pregnant, she insisted that the children go. 'The minister likes to see them there,' she always said to her husband. 'They aye help to fill up a seat and swell the congregation.'

'Fill up a seat! I help my God!' Bert would say. 'If that's all your religion means to you, then all I can say is it's bloody high time ye stopped havin' it. Fill up a seat! . . .'

'It's criminal,' he said this morning. 'Sending the bairns to sit for an hour and a half to listen to auld Wallace ravin' his stupid auld head off. It's bad enough sendin' them to the Sunday School to listen to a lot o' dirt about bein' meek and mild and ye'll inherit the earth without makin' them sit on thae bloody hard seats in the kirk forbye.'

'It's far too long for puir wee Jenny to sit,' he said.

'It's nothin' o' the kind,' Mrs. Hipkiss shouted. 'It's high time she learned to sit still on her backside. You'd think sometimes she had a wasps' bing in her bottom the way she keeps wrigglin' about.'

'Good God, woman, you can't expect a bairn of three to sit mi'mooed. If she did there would be somethin' wrong with her.'

'Will ye kindly stop swearin'?' his wife cried. 'Remember this is the Sabbath day and none o' the rest o' us in the hoose are heathens even though you are.'

'A heathen? So I'm a heathen, am I?' he shouted. 'Just because I want the bairns to be brought up sensible.'

'Sensible?' she shrieked. 'If ye ca' a' thae daft notions ye get frae thae Bolshie students sensible, then I have another name for them.'

'Well, it's better to get daft notions as you call them than to try to get somethin' for nothin' frae that bloody auld woman, Wallace. Sendin' the bairns to the kirk just to see what ye can get frae the Women's Guild and this and that charity. Charity!' Bert shouted. 'Aye puttin' on a poor mouth and havin' a lot o' bloody auld wives comin' nosin' around among yer business. I'm fed up with it all, Margaret, and the quicker ye learn that the better.'

Bessie scurried about, getting the children and herself dressed, pretending not to listen to her parents quarrelling. She whisked Jenny and Billy into the back bedroom out of earshot, but it was difficult in such a small house to keep them from hearing. When you could hear the Finlaysons next door shouting at each other, you could hear everything so much more plainly in your own house, the walls were so thin. Billy, of course, was all ears. He kept trying to get into the living-room beside his mother and father, but Bessie prevented him. 'You bide here,' she hissed. 'Mammy and Daddy dinnie want to be bothered wi' the sight o' your ugly face.'

'Yah, ma face is no' as ugly as yours,' he jeered. 'Ye should see yersel', Ferret. You'll never be a glamour girl.'

Bessie thought it best to disregard this, so she said: 'Would you like to be a glamour girl, Jenny?'

'No,' Jenny said.

'Are ye sure, hen? Wouldn't it be fine! Henry Hall and his Band with Jenny Hipkiss. Are ye sure ye wouldnie like to be a glamour girl?'

'No, I just want to be puir wee Jenny that shouldnie be made to go to the kirk,' Jenny said. 'I'm no' goin', Bessie. The seats are far ower hard for my bottom.'

'Ach, ye're just a haver,' Bessie said. 'C'mon and get your coat on.'

'I'm not goin',' Jenny said, hanging back and refusing to

put her arms into the red corduroy coat that Bessie was holding out for her.

'Put yer arms in thae sleeves at once and less o' yer nonsense,' Bessie cried. 'Your ears are ower-long, my lady! If ye dinnie put yer arms in at once I'll give ye a good clout.'

'I'll say a Bad Word if you don't watch out,' Jenny said.

'Put your arms in!' Bessie shouted. 'If we dinnie hurry up we'll be late.'

'Mind, I'll say a Bad Word in two ticks,' Jenny said.

Bessie seized the child's arms and forced them into the coat. 'There,' she said, giving Jenny's red tammy a tweak, and standing back to see the effect. 'That's you ready, anyway.'

Jenny glared at her. 'P.E.E.,' she shouted.

'Jenny!' Bessie cried in a shocked voice. 'Bessie doesnie like you when you say things like that.'

'I dinnie care,' Jenny said. 'I'm not playin' wis you.'

'Stinky Bessie!' she called, going behind a chair for safety.

Bessie sighed and held out Billy's coat for him. 'C'mon, you,' she said. 'Get this on and let's get away. We're late enough as it is.'

'Me's good, isn't me, Bessie?' Billy said, allowing her to button his coat. 'Me's a good wee boy, and I'll get a sweetie, won't I? Yah!' he shouted, making a face at Jenny. 'You winnie get a sweetie to sook in the kirk. Fee fi fo fum, I smell the smell of Jenny Hipkiss!'

'The bairns 'll be brought up to be good Christians as long as I'm alive,' Mrs. Hipkiss shouted, banging the living-room door behind her. 'So ye can put that in yer pipe and smoke it!'

'Well, are ye all ready?' she said. 'Here, Billy, put yer cap on straight like a guid wee boy. I'm sure I don't know what the Reverend Mr. Wallace would think if he saw ye with it like this. Now, have ye all got yer collection pennies?—and clean hankies?'

When they returned their father was reading *Reynolds's News* and Mrs. Hipkiss was leaning against the gas-cooker, stirring a pot of stew. 'Dinnie blame me if this is burnt,' she shouted to her husband as she began to ladle it on to plates.

'If ye want yer meals properly cooked ye should keep a civil tongue in yer head.'

Bert did not answer. He sat silently throughout the meal, and as soon as it was finished he took Jenny and Billy out for a walk. He did this every Sunday afternoon.

Bessie washed the dishes, then she sat down at the window of the living-room beside her mother. She loved Sunday afternoons, for these were the only times she could really be alone with her mother. Even when the children were in bed and she and her mother were sitting before the fire at nights, Bessie never felt that they were completely alone; one of the children was always liable to get up and disturb them. But on Sunday afternoons when Bert and the two little ones were walking in Inverleith Park or round the new housing scheme at Pennywell, Bessie and Mrs. Hipkiss knew that they would have a clear two or three hours undisturbed. And it was then that they had their heart-to-heart talks.

Bessie had her school-books on the floor beside her and an exercise-book on her knee, but she was not actively prepared to do her home-lessons. The books were just an excuse for sitting there. She chewed her pencil and watched her mother.

'Put on the wireless, Bessie,' Mrs. Hipkiss said. 'We might as well have a tune while we're sittin'.'

It was one of the great sorrows in Mrs. Hipkiss' life that the kitchenette was not at the front of the house. 'There's nothin' to see at the back,' she complained continually. 'Who wants to look out at the back-greens and other folk's washings? Whoever planned the houses should have kept the women in mind. They should have known the puir housewives would hae to spend most o' their time in the kitchenette and that they'd want to see out and see what was doin' in the street. It's easy seen it was some fool o' a man that designed them.'

Often to satisfy her curiosity Mrs. Hipkiss brought her kitchen chores into the living-room and did them at the window, but it was never a satisfactory method. 'I'm fair tied to that gas-cooker,' she would moan. 'I cannie see why that bloody architect couldnie have put it in the livin'-room.'

'If I hadnie a man and bairns that were aye needin' fed,'

28

she often said, 'I'd be able to spend all my time at this windy. I'm fair jealous o' Mrs. Moore and Dirty Minnie that can spend most o' their time hangin' oot their windies. They ken far more about folk's comin's and goin's than I do.'

But on Sunday afternoons she was in her element. She could sit at the window and look out for as long as she liked. They were on the top flat, and the window was an advantageous one. Goldengreen Street was a short street between Goldengreen Crescent and Harrisfield Avenue. Most of the inhabitants of Calderburn, who were making for the tram terminus at Harrisfield Square, passed along it, so Mrs. Hipkiss seldom missed anything. If she opened the window wide and leaned out on her elbows like Mrs. Moore and Dirty Minnie she could see down the hill into Harrisfield Square, and beyond that she could see the funnels of the ships in Harrisfield Harbour and the wide stretch of the Firth of Forth and the coast-line of Fife. But it was only occasionally, when Mr. Hipkiss was safely away to work, that she did this; Bert was always furious when he saw her opening the window and leaning out. 'Letting your vulgar curiosity get the better of you,' he said.

'It's funny Mrs. Moore hasnie been up to see me for two-three days, hen,' she said now. 'The auld bitch, if she'd been wantin' anythin' she wouldnie hae been long in comin' across at the toot.'

'There she is at her windy now,' she said. 'Inquisitive auld bitch, she doesnie miss much. But I'm damned if I'm goin' to wave across at her. I'll just let on I dinnie see her. I'll try and keep ahint the curtains. Mind you, ye cannie blame Mrs. Moore.' Mrs. Hipkiss shifted her chair so that she could see without herself beeing seen. 'Yer father's aye that rude to her when she comes. I'm fair affronted sometimes at the things he says to her. If ony other man said the like o' thae things to me I wouldnie be long in sloshin' him one."

Bessie chewed the end of her pencil and frowned at the open exercise-book.

'But I'd better stop talkin' and let ye get on wi' yer lessons,' Mrs. Hipkiss said. 'Have ye much to do, hen?'

'Och, no' very much.'

'I just hope it'll all get ye somewhere,' Mrs. Hipkiss said. 'It doesnie seem right a big lassie like you havin' to spend all her time doin' so much book-learnin'. Mind you, I'm all for books masel'. I like nothin' better than a good story. But all this dirt ye get at the school—where's it goin' to lead to, that's what I want to know? Of course, it'll be fine if ye're able to go ahead and be a teacher like yer father and Miss Aitchison want, but it seems such a waste o' time. Ye'd be far better away from the school. Ye could either get a nice job or help me at home here. Patterson the grocer's needin' a lassie to serve in the shop. Ten shillin's a week. It's no' bad, mind ye. Would ye no' like that better than bein' at the school, hen?'

'I dinnie ken,' Bessie said, wriggling her shoulders in time with the music being played on the radio.

'I'm sure ye must be fed up wi' the school,' Mrs. Hipkiss said. 'I ken I was. I was glad to leave when I was fourteen and go and work in a biscuit factory. I thought I owned the world the week I brought hame my first pay. And here you are nearly fourteen and a half! Of course, if ye can manage to be a teacher it 'll maybe be all right. Do ye think ye'll like to be a teacher, hen?'

'I dinnie ken,' Bessie muttered.

She had no ideas about what she wanted to be. Her father and Miss Aitchison said she was to be a teacher, so she accepted that uncomplainingly. She was not clever enough to reason it out within herself. If she had been, she would have known that she hadn't enough brains to be a teacher. She had no head for mathematics, geography, science or any of the other subjects, even in their simplest forms. All she was really gifted with was a good imagination, and it was this imagination as shown in her school essays which had made Miss Aitchison insist to Bert Hipkiss that he allow Bessie to stay on at school. If Bessie had been clever enough to be honest with herself she would have known that what she really wanted was to spend her life day-dreaming. But actually she was rather stupid. In many ways she did not have even the low cunning of some of her contemporaries at school or in the neighbourhood. She

30

had a simplicity which verged at times almost on the moronic. Her life was bound up with her mother and the fantasies she wove for herself and the children, especially those she wove for herself. In some vague way she was dissatisfied with her life and environment, but she knew no way of changing it unless by escape into day-dreams. She knew no other life, except the ones she read about in novels or saw on the films. She'd been brought up in a back street near the Cannongate and when she was ten the family had moved here to Calderburn to the Corporation's new slum-clearance tenements. It was only by becoming a teacher, getting some kind of job or by marriage that she could get away from it. And she was neither ambitious enough nor clever enough to reason this out. It was just a vague feeling. She was happy enough to sit like this with her mother, dreaming her dreams. Some day something wonderful would happen and then all would be well with the world and Bessie Hipkiss would come into her own. Though, of course, she would not be Bessie Hipkiss then, but somebody entirely different.

'Please tell me that you love me, oh pulease, say you're not pretending, say the happy ending, and PLEASE tell me that you looove me true,' she sang with a Bing Crosby record.

'Eh, it's fine to sit and listen to the wireless in peace,' Mrs. Hipkiss said. 'Without yer father or the bairns aye nag-nag-naggin'. Yer father's a perfect scunner, aye wantin' talks and the News and a lot o' dirt like that. I dinnie see why he winnie sit and listen to a nice bit o' jazz like decent ordinary folk. But it's politics, politics, politics all the time wi' him. I could crown him and his auld politics sometimes.'

'Why did ye marry him, Ma?'

Mrs. Hipkiss looked at her with surprise. 'Why, Bessie, what a like thing to say!

'Ye shouldnie speak aboot yer father like that, Bessie,' she said.

'Well, I——' Bessie blushed. 'I was just wonderin',' she said.

'Sometimes I wonder myself.' Mrs. Hipkiss shoogled herself into a more comfortable position, pressing her plump shoulder against the window-pane, forgetting that she didn't want Mrs. Moore or any of the other neighbours to see her.

31

'I mean . . .' Bessie began. 'I mean, it's the name,' she burst out. 'Did ye no' think it was funny? I mean, when you met him first, did ye not . . .'

'Och!' Mrs. Hipkiss shrugged. 'I never thought aboot it much, I must say. I suppose it did strike me as kind o' queer, but after all I wasnie thinkin' aboot his name when I took up wi' yer father.' She giggled. 'I met him at a dance. He was a right fine-lookin' felly, I can tell ye, in those days. A real smasher. All the lassies were after him, but I got there first.'

'Hipkiss,' she said slowly. 'Funny I've never thought about it. I daresay I did ask Bert at the time, but he tellt me it was an English name, so I thought that explained a lot. Yer granny and grandfather were English, ye ken. They came frae the Midlands somewhere.'

Bessie knew this already. It accounted for much of her day-dreaming about being an exiled Bourbon. Her father never said anything about his parentage, and Bessie suspected this was because he did not know a great deal himself. What could be more possible than that the Bourbons had settled in the Midlands after the French Revolution and taken a simple name like Hipkiss? In fact, it was more than possible. It must have happened. After all, there was the little Dauphin who was supposed to have died in the Conciergerie prison, but who was also supposed to have escaped to England and then disappeared. The little Capet. . . . Yes, the little Capet had come to a Midland village and he had fallen in love with a pretty girl and married her, and after they were married he had taken her name, Hipkiss, thinking it better than his own. He had been so much in love with her that he had never paused to think what a funny name it was. And of course, being French, poor soul, he wouldn't have been able to see how queer it sounded, anyway. . . .

'Mind you, I'm not sayin' anythin' against yer father, Bessie,' Mrs. Hipkiss said. 'But—well, he's been a right flighty sort o' cove in his day. I've had to keep my eye on him.'

'I'm just tellin' ye this,' she said after a long pause, 'I'm just tellin' ye this because—well, I dinnie mind tellin' ye, hen, I'm a bit feared about havin' this bairn.'

'Aw, Ma, ye're nut!' Bessie cried.

Mrs. Hipkiss sniffed self-righteously. 'Ay, I'm a wee bit scared. I had a terrible time that last time eighteen months ago when I—when I lost it. After all, Bessie,' she said, 'ye're auld enough to hear about thae things now. Ye cannie aye be kept in the dark. I had a terrible time,' she said, 'and I'm fair dreadin' havin' this yin.'

'Och, Ma, ye'll be all right,' Bessie cried.

'Ah well, we'll see, we'll see,' Mrs. Hipkiss said. 'There's Dirty Minnie awa' oot wi' her pal, Big Maggie Burns,' she said. 'Fancy her out walkin' on a Sunday! She's more need to bide at hame. I'll warrant ye could stir her house wi' a stick.'

'Gosh, Minnie's got on a new coat,' she said, craning her neck to get a better view. 'And no' before time either! Her auld one was that stiff wi' dirt it could have stood up itself. And I wouldnie be surprised if it could have walked by itself, too!' Mrs. Hipkiss sniffed. 'What a ticket for soup Minnie is in this one. It's far ower tight for her. Look at the way it's stretched across her muckle dock. If she bends it'll burst.'

'I'm just tellin' ye this, Bessie,' she said. 'In case onythin' happens to me. If it does, well—I want ye to look after the bairns well, Bessie. Dinnie let them forget me. I want them to be right brought up. I dinnie want yer father to upset them wi' ony o' his daft nonsense. I want them to be brought up like guid Christians.'

'Aw, Ma, but nothin' 'll happen to ye,' Bessie said.

'Ye never can tell,' Mrs. Hipkiss said. 'It's in the Lord's hands.'

Bessie traced her pencil along one of the lines of the exercise-book. She remembered the last time her mother had been going to have a baby and the commotion there had been. Mrs. Moore and other neighbours had bustled in and out, pushing her and the children out of the way. Their faces had been anxious and there had been much muttering amongst themselves. She still remembered hearing Mrs. Moore say: 'She's no' strong enough for all this, poor soul. One every year. Her man should be bonnie and ashamed o' bringin' this on her.' And she remembered how ill her mother had been for weeks afterwards.

33

'Mercy, there's a ring at the bell!' Mrs. Hipkiss cried. 'Who can this be for ony favour!'

It was Dirty Minnie and Big Maggie Burns. 'We just thought we'd take a bit run up to see ye, ducks,' Minnie said to Mrs. Hipkiss. 'Seein' ye're no' able to get out thae days we thought we'd come in and gie ye all the news.'

'My, Minnie, what nice ye're lookin',' Mrs. Hipkiss said. 'I saw ye out the windy and I was just sayin' to Bessie "There's Minnie wi' a new coat on. How nice she looks." It sets ye lovely,' she said.

'Ay, it's no' bad.' Minnie looked down with satisfaction at her ungainly figure. 'It's a braw coat, although it's masel' that says it.'

'Ye look real elegant, Minnie,' Big Maggie said, sighing as she lowered herself on to the sofa. Like Minnie's her face hadn't felt soap and water for days. She wore a rakish green velvet hat with an osprey. Her lank straggly hair brushed the dandruff on the shoulders of her soiled fawn coat.

' Ay, a guid face sets the dish-clout!' Minnie laughed. 'I've had a right sad time wi' my lodgers ower the head o' this coat! They were tellin' me afore I came out that I'd be catchin' a man wi' it!'

'Well, better late than never, Minnie,' Mrs. Hipkiss said.

'I dinnie ken,' Minnie said. 'I've come all this length wi'oot gettin' married, and I dinnie think I'll bother now.'

'Still, chance is a good thing!' Big Maggie laughed. 'We're just on our way up to Princes Street now to have a parade along to see what we can nab! And how are ye keepin', hen?' she said.

'Doin' away,' Mrs. Hipkiss said. 'Doin' away. I havenie much to complain about. Bessie here's a great help to me.'

'Ay, she is that.' Minnie scratched delicately with a dirty forefinger under her blue felt hat, knocking it a little more to the side. 'I see ye're busy at yer lessons, hen. Are ye aye stickin' in at school?'

'Ay,' Bessie said, wishing the two middle-aged women had not come in and disturbed her talk with her mother.

'That's the dabber!' Minnie said. 'There's nothin' like a good eddication.'

'That's what I've just been tellin' her,' Mrs. Hipkiss said. 'My word, I wish I'd got such a good eddication when I was young. She's gettin' a wonderful chance if she just sticks in.'

8

THE next afternoon when she left to deliver her newspapers Bessie's mother told her to call and tell Mrs. Moore she wanted to see her. 'And ye might look in at Aggie Renton's, too,' she said, 'and ask her if she'll give me back the baby's shawl. She'll surely have finished wi' it by this time. Her bairn's nearly six months auld. I'll have to get it washed and cleaned afore the baby comes.'

'Tell yer ma I'll come across the night, hen,' Mrs. Moore said when Bessie delivered the message. 'I cannie come the now, I have ma auld man's tea to get ready. He'd raise the bloody roof if I wasnie here to attend to him.'

As she was going up Aggie Renton's stair, Bessie met Lily McGillivray coming down. Lily was all dolled up, a scarlet felt hat stuck on the back of her peroxided hair and her lips reddened. 'Hya, Ferret!' she cried gaily. 'Comin' on the randan with me?'

Bessie gaped. Lily was only six months older, and she had left school only a year ago. But already she was a young woman: far, far ahead of Bessie in looks and dress and experience. She worked in the despatch department of a large bakery in the city.

'Gee, what a swell ye are!' Bessie could not prevent herself from giving voice to her admiration.

'Like my get-up?' Lily pirouetted to show it to better advantage, smoothing her new blue coat at the hips.

'It's lovely,' Bessie said. 'Gee, I wish I could get a coat like that.'

'Och, cheer up,' Lily said. 'Maybe ye will when ye leave school and get a job and a pay of yer own. I'm going out with a boy,' she said. 'An awful nice felly. He works in the bakehouse. Gee, but he's swell. He's takin' me to the picters and then we're goin' on to the Pally dee Dance.'

'Ye're surely finished early the day?' Bessie said.

'Ay, this is my week on the early shift. I finish at three. It's all right. But it's not so fine in the mornings. I start at half-past six. I've got to go up with the workmen's car. But it suits me all right this week because Billy's on the early shift, too.'

'Gosh, I wish I was you,' Bessie said. 'But I'll have to stay at the school until the summer-time onyway. Ma faither says he'd like me to stay for another year, but I dinnie ken about that. Though Miss Aitchison says that, too. She says I should bide on and see if I cannie win a bursary to the university and be a teacher like her.'

'Och, to hell wi' that!' Lily said. 'What's the sense of bidin' at the school all yer days? Be like me and get a job and get some fun to yersel'. Who wants to be an auld wife of a school-teacher, onyway? Ye'd be gey daft if ye did.'

Bessie sighed. 'Well, I dunno. . . . Miss Aitchison says . . . Och, but I'll have to get on wi' my papers. Cheerio, Lily, see and enjoy yersel'!'

'You bet I will! Trust me, Ferret! Cheerio!' Lily clattered downstairs, her too-high heels tapping triumphantly on the stone steps.

Bessie knocked at Mrs. Renton's door, and while she was waiting for an answer she thought about what Lily had been saying. Maybe Miss Aitchison and her father were right—it was the only thing they seemed to agree about—but she didn't know whether it was a good plan or not. In a way it would be fine to be a teacher. Folk would look up to her. They'd say: 'Fancy the auldest lassie Hipkiss bein' a teacher. It takes her, doesn't it? Who'd 'a' thought it to look at her that she had brains?' Still, at the same time she wished she could leave school and earn some money of her own. Like Lily. Look at the good time Lily seemed to be having. Going out with boys and being all dolled up. And with lipstick on, too.

36

'Please, Mrs. Renton,' she said. 'I've come for the baby's shawl that my mother lent you a while ago.'

'The baby's . . .' Mrs. Renton stood with her mouth wide open. 'Oh ay, the baby's shawl! Well, now . . .' She stepped back, scratching her head. 'I wonder what I did wi' it? I wish yer ma had gien me more warnin'. Is she awful desperate for it?'

'Ay, she's expectin' next month,' Bessie said.

'Dear, dear, is it as near her time as all that? I didnie think it was for two-three months yet.' Mrs. Renton inclined her body towards her kitchen door and yelled: 'Mamie! Are ye there, Mamie?'

'Ay, what is it?' a voice called.

'Here's Bessie Hipkiss wantin' her mother's baby's shawl. Do you ken where it is?

'Just a minute, dear,' Mrs. Renton said to Bessie, and she backed quickly into the kitchen before Mamie could shout an answer. Bessie leaned against the door-post. She strained her ears, but she couldn't hear what Mrs. Renton and Mamie were saying to each other. They seemed to be arguing about something. 'I will not,' Mamie shouted. 'Ye can tell her yersel'. Wantin' me to do yer dirty work for ye!'

Bessie advanced a foot into the passage, leaning forward, but she could not make out any more. She sprang back suddenly when Mamie catapulted out of the kitchen as if she had been pushed violently.

'Oh, Bessie,' she said, gulping. 'Ma mother says she's awful sorry, but would ye tell yer ma that she lent the shawl to Mrs. Whitten in number seven, the top flat. If ye go along there ye'll get it.'

And before Bessie could say anything Mamie Renton shut the door in her face.

'A bairn's shawl?' Mrs. Whitten in number seven said. 'A bairn's shawl. Are ye sure Mrs. Renton sent ye to me?'

'Ay, she said she lent it to you. My mother lent it to Mrs. Renton six months ago. It's a white shawl. My granny gave it to me when I was born.'

'A white shawl?' Mrs. Whitten wiped her nose with the

37

end of her apron. 'But what would I be wantin' wi' a bairn's shawl for? I'm sure my last bairn's nearly eight, and I'm no' likely to hae another, thank God!'

'Well, Mamie Renton said her mother lent it to you.'

'Mamie Renton's a liar,' Mrs. Whitten said. 'Or her mother is! You can tell her that frae me. I'm sorry, but I havenie got it,' she said, going in and shutting the door.

Bessie stood and looked at it for a few minutes. Really, some folk were the limit. Shutting a door in her face—in the face of Madame Royale of France! 'Vile voman!' she hissed in a loud whisper. 'You shall pay for thees!' And she shook her fist at the closed door. Then, looking about quickly to see that nobody had either seen or heard her, she turned and ran downstairs.

9

'B U T what can hae happened to the shawl?' Mrs. Hipkiss cried. 'I swear I lent it to Aggie Renton. I couldnie have lent it to onybody else, could I?'

'No, hen, I mind o' ye lendin' it fine,' Mrs. Moore said. 'I mind the night Aggie came round and asked if she could get it. It was just at the end o' August and we'd been at the picters. It was the night we saw Norma Shearer in *Marie Antoinette*. It was an awful hot night and I was sittin' here wi' ma feet in a basin o' water. Do ye no' mind, I said to ye: "If that's yer man at the door he'll wonder what the devil I'm doin' sittin' here like this." And ye said: "It cannie be him. He would use his key." And while you went to the door I ups wi' the basin o' water and padded through to the kitchenette in ma bare feet. I mind it fine, just the same as if it had happened yesterday. I was fair annoyed when ye came in wi' Aggie Renton. I hadnie got ma feet right dried and they were awful uncomfortable in ma shoes.'

'Ay, you're right,' Mrs. Hipkiss cried. 'I mind now. I

wonder if she really did lend it to Mrs. Whitten or if she's lost it. Or pawned it maybe. I wouldnie put it past her, the bitch!'

'Now, now, hen, take it easy,' Mrs. Moore said. 'The shawl 'll turn up all right. I'll go round to Aggie Renton's masel' and see what's really happened to it.'

'I'll come wis you,' Jenny said, looking up from the floor where she was playing with Mrs. Moore's message-bag.

'No, hen, I'll be quicker masel',' Mrs. Moore said.

'I'm goin',' Jenny said, jumping up.

'No, hen, you'll be better here. It's dark outside now.'

'Ay, the witches 'll get you,' Mrs. Hipkiss said.

'I'm no' carin',' Jenny said. 'I'm goin' with Mrs. Moore.'

'You're bidin' here,' Mrs. Hipkiss snapped. 'It's high time ye were in yer bed, onyway.'

'I'm no' goin' to ma bed,' Jenny shrieked. 'I'm goin' with Mrs. Moore.'

'Well, Mrs. Moore's no' goin' with you, ducky! You bide here and do what yer mammy tells ye.'

'Ay, if you're a good girl I'll maybe tell you a story,' Mrs. Hipkiss said.

'A long one?' Jenny looked cunningly at her mother. 'A long one out of your mouth?'

'We'll see,' Mrs. Hipkiss said. 'Now c'mon and get ready for yer bed.'

'No, the story first,' Jenny said.

'Me wants a story,' Billy cried. 'Me wants to sit on Mammy's knee and hear the story.'

'It's high time ye were stoppin' speakin' so bairny, my man,' Mrs. Moore said, picking up her bag and making for the door. 'What would the other wee laddies at the school say if they heard ye speakin' like that? Me wants a story! A big boy like you speaking like that!'

'Och, he only speaks like that at hame,' Mrs. Hipkiss said, taking him on her knee. 'Don't ye, son? Ye just speak like that to yer mammy, don't ye?'

Billy looked coy and hid his face against his mother's bosom. 'Me likes Mammy best,' he lisped. 'Me doesn't like Mrs. Moore.'

39

'I'm sure Mrs. Moore's worried about it,' Mrs. Moore said. 'Well, I'll away and see Aggie Renton, hen. I'll no' be long afore I'm back. Ta-ta the now!'

'On and on and on with the story!' Jenny said as soon as the door had closed upon Mrs. Moore.

'Well, it's just goin' to be a wee one,' her mother said. 'Bessie's waitin' to put ye to bed, aren't ye, Bessie? It's high time a wee lassie like you was in bed.'

'It's not time me was in bed, isn't it not?' Billy said. 'Me's a big boy.'

'Ay, but you're goin' to yer bed, son,' Mrs. Hipkiss said, stroking his hair. 'Bessie's goin' to put ye both to bed while Mammy has a rest, aren't ye, Bessie?'

'Well, I have my home lessons to do,' Bessie said. 'But I suppose——'

'Och, ye'll easy manage to put them both to bed,' her mother said. 'It 'll no' take ye long.'

'On and on and on with the story!' Jenny cried impatiently.

'Well now, once upon a time there was a wee lassie called Cinderella,' Mrs. Hipkiss began.

'Och, not Cinderelly,' Billy cried. 'I want a story about lions and tigers and—and whales!'

'I want a story aboot a witch!' Jenny cried.

'Well, have patience,' their mother said. 'Well, this wee lassie called Cinderella lived with two very ugly, ugly sisters and they were right bad to her.'

'Uglier than Bessie?' Billy asked.

'Och, Bessie's a bonnie lassie,' Mrs. Hipkiss said.

'She is nut,' Billy said. 'She's got a face like a ferret. I heard the other laddies say it. She's no' bonnie at all.'

'All right then,' his mother said. 'They were uglier than Bessie. Terrible, terrible ugly. And they were awful bad to Cinderella, and one day . . .'

Mrs. Hipkiss soon became carried away by her own eloquence, and the children sat, enchanted. At Billy's suggestion she substituted a whale in a bowler hat for the traditional fairy godmother, and many and weird were Cinderella's adventures until Mrs. Hipkiss began to wind up:

40

'You should 'a' seen the ugly sisters' faces! They were right mad. "It must be a mistake," the fat one said, and she rushed forrit and tried to haul the slipper offen Cinderelly, but just then there was a terrible loud noise in the chimney, and the Whale came tumblin' down the lum in a cloud o' smoke. "Hands off the beef!" he cried. "That slipper belongs to Cinderelly. If ye don't stop touchin' it I'll no' marry ye." So everything ended happily and Cinderelly married the prince.

'Now, c'mon,' she cried. 'It's time ye were both away to bed!'

'I dinnie want to go to ma bed,' Jenny cried, putting her hands on the back of her neck, her elbows sticking out pugilistically. 'I want another story!'

'Me wants to hear what happened after they were married,' Billy sniggered. 'Go on, Mammy, tell us!'

'Come on, it's time ye were away to yer beds,' Bessie said, rising from the table. 'Mammy's tired.'

'I'm not goin' to ma bed,' Jenny howled.

Mrs. Hipkiss sighed. 'Well, I'll just tell ye what happened the day they got married,' she said. 'There was a great feast at the palace and they had all sorts of lovely things to eat. Ham and eggs and oranges and bananas and fish and chips and beer and sherry and fancy cakes and——'

'Sweeties!' Jenny cried, her eyes narrowing with vicarious enjoyment.

'And sweeties,' Mrs. Hipkiss said. 'And the fat ugly sister ate and ate and ate until she nearly burst. And the Whale was sittin' beside her and he said: "Ye shouldnie be so greedy." But the ugly sister just laughed and said: "Better belly burst than good meat spoilt!"

'Now,' she said, 'that's the end. C'mon, get away to yer beds like good bairns.'

There were more howls at this. Bessie helped her mother in the struggle, but even against both of them the children were almost superior. It was only the arrival of Mrs. Moore that turned the tables in the go-to-bed cause. Mrs. Moore was waving a very dirty baby's shawl.

'I've got it!' she cried. 'I hunted all round Calderburn, but

I've got it! About a dozen different folk hae had the loan o'
it since Aggie Renton.'

10

"WHAT the hell's this?' Bert Hipkiss cried when he came in
shortly after eleven o'clock.

Mrs. Hipkiss was sitting beside the fire. A chair was drawn
close to her, and on it was a basin of water. Lackadaisically
she was washing the baby's shawl while talking to Mrs. Moore.

Mrs. Moore rose in a great hurry when she saw Bert. 'My,
is that the time?' she cried. 'I must awa' hame or ma man 'll
think the polis have nabbed me for loiterin'!'

'Oh, I don't think he need worry much about that,' Bert
said.

'No, he'll be sittin' by the fire readin' his poetry,' Mrs.
Moore laughed. 'I never saw such a man to read poetry. Burns
and Wordsworth and a lot o' dirt like that. I often say to him:
"Well, if you understand all that muck, I don't." Wastin' his
time when he might be doin' somethin' useful to the garden
or takin' some o' the water out the air-raid shelter.'

'What about the supper?' Bert said, turning his back on
Mrs. Moore. 'You might have had it set instead o' plowterin'
about here with that basin o' water. What's the idea of washin'
clothes at this time of night, anyway?'

'Well, it was that dirty I just felt I had to get it washed at
once,' Mrs. Hipkiss whined. 'It was in an awfie mess, wasn't
it, Mrs. Moore? You'd think every bairn in the toon had worn
it. Oh, are ye for away, dear? Well, cheerio, and thanks a lot
for findin' the shawl for me. It'll put ma mind at rest.'

'Ta-ta, hen!' Mrs. Moore said. 'Cheeribye, Mr. Hipkiss!
Cheeribye, Bessie!'

'That woman's het at hame,' Bert said as soon as Mrs.
Moore had closed the door behind her. 'If I was her man I'd
put my foot down—hard!'

'Ye might take that basin into the kitchenette and empty it,' Mrs. Hipkiss whined, shaking out the shawl after wringing it. 'It's no' very clean yet, but it'll have to do the night. I must wash it out the morn again. Really, what a mess it's in. This is the last time I'll ever lend anythin' to anybody. They never give ye it back the way they got it.'

'Oh, hang it up, for God's sake!' Bert cried. 'And let's get our supper. I haven't had anythin' to eat since tea-time. Never had time for a bite all night. We've been that busy.'

'Hm, surely folk have plenty to spend on booze,' Mrs. Hipkiss said. 'Spendin' all their money on it, and like enough their poor wives and bairns are starvin' for want o' meat.'

'How do you ken?' Bert snapped. 'You don't need to complain, anyway. You aye get plenty o' money to buy your meat and clothes. And plenty o' booze into the bargain! You've been at it again, you and that fat bagsy auld Moore woman. The smell o' yer breaths near knocked me down when I came in. You'd better lay off it, Margaret, now that the bairn's so near at hand.'

'Well, I had a sore head,' Mrs. Hipkiss said. 'I just took a wee thimbleful. My head really was that bad I could hardly bear it. I had to gie Mrs. Moore a wee half just for company like.'

'Ay, just for company like!' he jeered. 'Ye never miss an opportunity!'

'If you'd had my sore head and had had to put up wi' thae girny bairns all night you'd have been driven to it, too,' Mrs. Hipkiss cried. 'It's all very well for you to talk so sanctimonious —comin' hame here after dishin' out the stuff all night. I bet ye've poured a good lot down yer ain thrapple since tea-time.'

'Well, what if I have? What if I have? I can carry it, and that's more than can be said about you.'

Bessie lay silent in bed, listening to them. It was the same every night. God, how she hated her father! She wished she could get away from it all; away from the eternal nagging and quarrelling. She wished she could go to London. Or to Paris . . . or Nice . . .

She had a lovely villa which had been built specially for

43

her above the city, overlooking the deep blue Mediterranean. Tourists used to come and stand in front of the gates, and the guides would point it out to them. And when she was out driving in her long white car the people in the streets would cheer and cry: 'Vive Madame Elisabeth! Vive Madame Royale!' And she would bow and smile and wave her thin white hand, watching the sunlight catching the diamonds on her rings, making them sparkle. . . .

11

IT was snowing. It was a drab, grey March day, and the little flakes had just started. Bessie stared out of the classroom window at a flock of little birds that had settled on the bare branches of a tree. They were thin skeleton branches, etched against the dull greyness of the sky. Like the Japanese print that Miss Aitchison had once shown them, Bessie thought. And the little birds were like black roses growing on the tips. . . .

A motor back-fired in the street, and at the sound the birds rose and fluttered in the air. Like a fountain spraying . . . each spray was a little black jewel. . . .

'Bessie!'

'Bessie Hipkiss!'

Miss Aitchison smiled sarcastically at Bessie's guilty blush. 'Why should Bessie Hipkiss alone be privileged to watch the snow?' she said to the class. 'Let us all fold our arms and we will all look out at the snow for ten minutes.'

Bessie folded her arms with the rest of the class and looked out at the tree. But its magic had gone. It stood there now, stark and cruel, like a cross. She felt the other pupils' hatred against her. They were saying to themselves: 'Teacher's pet! She's fairly copped it this time!' Why, oh why had she not paid attention and listened to Miss Aitchison speaking about

The Merchant of Venice instead of staring out at the old tree? It was only an ordinary tree, anyway, and she'd seen it hundreds of times before. Oh, Miss Aitchison, why did you do that? It was so beautiful. . . . Why had you to go and spoil it like this? You know that I love to listen to you, that I'd rather listen to you than to anybody else. But, Miss Aitchison, it was something I couldn't help. I had to look at the tree instead of listening to you doing Portia's speech . . . and now all the girls 'll crow like anything. They'll say Kiss-ma-hip's got it in the neck at last! Oh, Miss Aitchison, why did you do it?

The headmaster came in and whispered something to Miss Aitchison.

'Bessie!'

She started, wondering what she had done wrong now.

'Come here, m'dear,' the headmaster said, 'I want to speak to you.'

Bessie was aware of the curiosity of the class as she went up to the two teachers. Mr. Black took her gently by the arm. 'Come along with me, m'dear.' Miss Aitchison looked after them with an odd expression as he led the girl into the corridor.

'I'm afraid I've got bad news for you, Bessie,' he said. 'Your father has just phoned, and he wants you to go home at once. Your mother—your mother isn't very well.'

'She's no' dead?' Bessie put her hand up to her mouth, as much shocked at having lapsed into the Doric before Mr. Black as at the news.

'No, no,' he said quickly. 'But I think you'd better hurry home. Your father seems to want you.'

All the way home in the tram she kept wondering what was wrong. Her mother had seemed a bit funny that morning. She hadn't got up, and Bessie had made breakfast for herself and the children. She had not wanted to go to school, but her mother had insisted. 'I'll get up in a wee while,' she had said. 'I'll be all right. I just feel tired the now. I didnie sleep well all night.'

The doctor's car was standing at the entry when Bessie reached home. She saw it when she came up the hill from

45

Harrisfield Square, and she started to run. Jenny was kneeling on the running-board, tracing her forefinger amongst the dust on the door.

'You come off that car quick!' Bessie cried. 'What will Doctor Henderson say if he sees ye?'

'He'll say a Bad Word,' Jenny said, without looking up from the marks she was making.

Bessie lifted her and set her down on the pavement. 'You run into the back-green and play there like a guid wee girl,' she said. 'What are ye doin' outside, anyway?'

'Mrs. Moore said I could play here,' Jenny said. 'She said I wasnie to get in the hoose because I shouted and made Mammy's head sore.'

Mrs. Moore was hustling about the kitchenette, heating water and filling basins. 'Yer puir ma!' she wailed when she saw Bessie. 'She should 'a' stayed in her bed, but she would get up, and then she got dizzy and fell—and it's brought the baby on ower quick. A guid month afore it's time.

'Here, Bessie,' she cried. 'Ye might make some tea for yer puir pa and see if that 'll no' keep him quiet. He's been goin' about here like a hen on a hot girdle ever since it happened. I wish to God he'd gone away to his work.'

'How could I, woman?' Bert said, looking up from the sofa where he was sitting with his head in his hands. 'How could I with her lyin' in there like that?'

'Well, ye might dae somethin' to help,' Mrs. Moore snapped. 'Instead o' sittin' there like a weepin' willy tree.

'You make some tea, lassie,'' she said. 'We could all do with a cup.'

They were drinking the tea when the doctor came out of the bedroom. 'Nurse wants you, Mrs. Moore,' he said. 'You'd maybe better go in, too, Bessie.

'It's a boy, Mr. Hipkiss,' he said. 'But . . .'

He started to whisper, and Bessie caught no more as she followed Mrs. Moore into the room.

She was horrified when she saw her mother's face. It was a dirty grey against the clean white pillow that Mrs. Moore must have put on the bed before the doctor came. 'Ay . . .

Bessie . . .' she whispered. 'It'll no' be long now, lassie. Ye'll
. . . ye'll look after yer faither and the bairns, won't ye, hen?
. . . Promise me ye'll look after them . . . when I'm away. . . .'

'Oh, Ma!' Bessie wailed, and she flung herself on the floor
and buried her head among the bedclothes. 'Oh, Ma! Ye're
no' to dee, Ma! Ye're no' to dee!'

After a few minutes the District Nurse lifted Bessie by the
shoulders and led her out. 'You mustn't take on like that,
girl,' she said more sharply than perhaps she intended. 'You're
not helping your mother in any way. Better go and bring the
other children. Your mother would like to see them.'

Billy had just come home from school and had joined Jenny
on the running-board of the doctor's car. 'Come inside,' Bessie
called. 'And see and not make any noise—or I'll skin ye both
alive. Be as quiet as ye can, mind!'

'Ye've been greetin', Ferret-face,' Billy jeered. 'What have
ye been greetin' about? Did the maister gie ye the strap at
the school the day?'

Bessie did not answer. She took each child by the hand and
half-led them, half-dragged them upstairs. Silently she pushed
them into the living-room in front of her. Bert looked up in a
dazed way from the sofa where he was crouching. He was
going to say something, but he swallowed and looked away.

'Is that the bairns?' Mrs. Moore came quickly out of the
bedroom. 'Come on, ye'd better hurry up. Ye'd better come,
Bert. She's near awa' wi' it, puir lassie.'

Bert rose and shambled ahead of them, crying: 'Oh, Margaret, Margaret, my bonnie Margaret!' Mrs. Moore put out
her hands to grab the children's, but Billy pulled back.

'Me wants a piece,' he said. 'Me's hungry. Me wants a piece
on butter and jam. And sugar!'

'Will ye stop it!' Mrs. Moore cried. 'You and yer me wants
this and me wants that! Can ye no' speak right? If ye dinnie
stop it, my man, I'll rattle yer lugs for ye.'

She seized him by the shoulder. 'Come and see yer mammy
when I tell ye,' she said. 'And if there's one word out o' ye,
I'll . . . I'll murder ye!'

Bessie leaned against the door-post, watching Mrs. Moore

47

hustle the two little ones into the room in front of her. *Ye'll promise me, Bessie, ye'll promise me ye'll look after them. . . .*

'Oh, Ma! Ma!' she screamed, and she turned and hid her face against the lintel, beating with futility on the wall with her fists. Realization of what lay ahead had dawned upon her.

From somewhere a baby was wailing unheeded, and from the bedroom there came rasping, death-like chokes. . . .

PART II

1

'ON and on and on with the story, Bessie!'

Bessie Hipkiss sighed. Really, those bairns were the limit. Little Jenny thought she had nothing else to do but tell her stories. 'I'll hae to get Daddy's dinner ready first,' she said. 'I'll tell ye another story after that.'

'No, now!' Jenny said.

Bessie rose and went to the sink and filled a basin with water. 'After dinner,' she said, putting some potatoes into the basin.

'No, now!' Jenny said, putting down her brows and sticking out her small under-lip. 'Tell me the story now, or else——'

'Or else what?' Bessie said wearily.

'Or else I'll hit the baby!' Jenny looked to see if this had made any effect. But Bessie was quite used to her little sister's tactics; she placed the basin of potatoes on a small table in front of the living-room window and went to fill a pot with water. If possible, she always worked at the front of the house, overlooking the street. Jenny came over and kicked the leg of the table when Bessie started to peel the potatoes. 'Tell me a story, Bessie, or else—or else I'll do a wizzy on ma breeks!'

'Oh, ye wouldnie dae that, would ye?'

'I would sut!' Jenny's eyes gleamed as maliciously as the eyes of a child of three and a half could gleam. 'I'll do it right now!'

'A' right,' Bessie said wearily. 'I'll tell ye while I'm peelin' the tatties.'

Jenny stood for a second, then seeing that Bessie was beaten, she went back and lay down on the rug before the fire. 'Go on,' she said.

'Well, once upon a time there was a bad little girl called Jenny McSquirt. . . .'

'Not me!' Jenny cried. 'Not that story! Anuzzer one!'

Bessie dropped a potato in the pot, making the water splash. 'Well, once upon a time there was a tall, tall girl called Barbara McTurk, and Barbara McTurk was seven feet high. She was so tall and so thin that she could easily have come through the keyhole.'

'Our keyhole?'

'Be quiet,' Bessie said, 'or ye'll no' get ony story.'

Jenny scowled, but was silent. She began to pick at the hem of the rug, watching to see that Bessie wasn't looking. Her small face was serious.

'Well, Barbara McTurk lived on an island, in a castle on the island, and the castle had four grey walls and four grey towers. And Barbara McTurk lived in the tallest tower. It was seven storeys high, and you got to the top storey by a narrow, narrow stair. And the island was called Shalott, and Barbara McTurk was called the Lady of Shalott. Well, Barbara McTurk lived on the top storey and she never looked out of the window. She sat all day at her spinning-wheel, weaving a web that was made of all the colours of the rainbow. And in front of her hung a mirror, and in the mirror she could see all the people that passed down the road leading to the town of Camelot. Well, Barbara McTurk was very, very lonely and she wanted to look out and wave at the people that were passing, but a wicked witch had put a spell on her——'

'What's a spell, Bessie?'

'Be quiet or ye'll no' hear the story,' Bessie said. 'Well, Barbara McTurk got more and more fed up wi' bein' shut up in that tower where she couldnie see onybody, only the folk in the mirror. And so she thought she'd take a bit keek oot o' the windy. So she did. And do you know what she saw?'

'You tell me,' Jenny said without looking up from the hole she was boring in the rug.

'Well, you leave that rug alone,' Bessie said, lifting the pot of potatoes and putting it on the gas-cooker. 'Well, do you know what she saw? She saw a knight riding along the bank of the river. And the knight's name was Sir Lancelot, and he was a great big fat man with a round red face and a steel helmet on his head like the Air-Raid Warden's. He was riding a great muckle cart-horse, and it couldn't go very fast because Sir Lancelot was such a heavy man. He weighed twenty-three stone. And as he rode along he was singing, and with every word his ginger moustache blew up in the air in front of his eyes. He was singing. . . . Do you know what he was singing?' Bessie asked, hoping to get a few seconds' peace while she looked out of the window at Lily McGillivray and Mamie Renton capering with two sailors at one of the entries in the tenement opposite.

'You tell me,' Jenny said.

'No, you tell me,' Bessie said, watching Lily McGillivray knock off one of the sailors' caps and run into the entry.

' "Run, Rabbin, Run"!' Jenny cried, jumping up with excitement. 'Was that what he was singin', Bessie?'

'Ay, that's what he was singin': "Run, Rabbit, Run"! And as he was going along a rabbit ran out in front of him, and so he drew his revolver, and *bang!* he shot the rabbit. And he said to himsel': "That'll do me grand for supper the night." '

'Just a minute!' Jenny cried, going to the door. 'I'm away for a wizzy!'

Bessie leaned against the sill and looked out of the window. She sighed, feeling envious of Lily McGillivray and Mamie Renton down there with the sailors. Some people had all the fun! What fun did she ever get looking after this house and her father and the kids? It was three months now since her mother had died, and since then she seemed to have spent all her time cooking and mending the bairns' clothes and putting them to bed and telling them stories. She was right fed up. Sometimes she thought she'd go away and get a job or something. But of course, her father wouldn't let her. He thought she should want nothing else but to keep house for him and the bairns. She wished she was back at school again, listening to Miss Aitchison. Or even delivering her newspapers. That had aye been better than being cooped up here day in

51

and day out in this damned house with these yelling bairns. She had aye seen something when she was out with her papers, but of course her father had made her give up that job when she started to keep the house. Oh, if only her mother hadn't died and she had been able to go on being at school and had studied to be a teacher like Miss Aitchison had wanted her. . . . She wondered if Miss Aitchison had anybody in her class now who could write essays as well as she'd been able to write them. Oh, it had been right fine at school. . . . *Out flew the web and floated wide, the mirror cracked from side to side* (Miss Aitchison threw her arms wide) '*The curse is come upon me,*' *cried the Lady of Shalott. . . .*

'On and on and on with the story!' Jenny lay down again on the rug, kicking her heels in the air.

Bessie turned from the window and began to lay the table. 'Well, where were we?' she said. 'Oh, ay, Sir Lancelot was ridin' down to Camelot.'

'Tell me aboot a lion, Bessie! I want ye to tell me aboot a lion!'

'A' right,' Bessie said wearily. 'A great big roarin' lion came along and when it saw Barbara McTurk it made a dive at her. And poor Barbara McTurk let oot a yell when she saw the lion and ran into the tower and up the stairs. And the lion ran after her, roarin' and howlin'. And poor Barbara McTurk was fair oot o' breath by the time she got to the top storey, and when she got there she wondered what she was goin' to do. She thought she would hae to jump oot the windy and save herself frae the lion. But she didnie need to do that. Do ye know why?'

'You tell me,' Jenny said.

'Well, do ye mind that I tellt ye that the stairs got narrower and narrower as they got to the top o' the tower? Well, the lion stuck in the top storey and it struggled and struggled so much that it choked and died. And so there was poor Barbara McTurk stuck on the top storey, no' able to get doon the stair because o' the dead lion. Well, she didnie ken what to dae. So she put her head oot o' the windy and stretched her neck as far as it would go—three feet—and she cried: "Help,

murder, polis!" And Sir Lancelot was ridin' along and he
heard her. So he made his horse go faster and they jogged
along wi' Sir Lancelot bumpin' up and doon like a sack o'
tatties on the horse's back and his gas-mask bobbin' up and
doon until they came to the tower. Well, Sir Lancelot was so
fat that he couldnie get off the horse, so the horse had to kneel
down and Sir Lancelot rolled off. And a' the time poor Barbara
McTurk kept howlin' oot o' the windy: "Help, murder,
polis!" But Sir Lancelot cried up to her: "Hold fast, gentle
maiden, and I shall be with you in a trice." '

'What's a trice, Bessie?'

'Be quiet and listen to the story,' Bessie said. But she paused
and had another look out of the window. Lily and Mamie
Renton had gone away with the sailors. Bessie sighed and
watched a vegetable cart move slowly down the street. 'Well,
Sir Lancelot began to run up the stairs, but he was that fat
that he puffed and blew. Still, he kept at it, for he was a great
trier. And as he got near the top he pulled oot his revolver
ready for any emergency. "I'm comin', I'm comin', fair lady,"
he kept shoutin'. But as he just got to where the lion was——
Do ye know what happened? Well, he stuck! For Sir Lancelot
was even fatter than the lion. And so there he was, and there
was the dead lion just six inches in front of him. Well, Sir
Lancelot wriggled and wriggled, but he couldnie free himsel'
and he couldnie reach oot and touch the lion. They were both
stuck, and poor Barbara McTurk kept her long neck stickin'
oot o' the windy, howlin' at the pitch o' her voice. Well, a
night passed and a day, and they were still stuck. But Sir
Lancelot was gettin' hungrier and hungrier, and as he got
hungrier he began to get thinner. He started to shrink. And
as the second and the third days passed he shrunk and shrunk
until at last he was able to wriggle forrit until he could touch
the lion's tail. He got a grip o' it and he tried to pull, but he
was still stuck so fast he couldnie manage it. Well, another day
passed and another, and poor Sir Lancelot was near dead o'
starvation and poor Barbara McTurk was near black in the
face wi' yellin' and wi' wonderin' where her gallant hero had
gotten to. And so at last a week went past, and then one day

53

Sir Lancelot had shrunk so much that he was able to wriggle free, and he pulled and pulled at the lion's tail until it fell right back on top o' him and they both tumbled doon the stairs and Barbara McTurk was free!'

'And that's the end o' the story,' Bessie said, lifting a potlid to see that the mince wasn't burning. She looked at the clock. It would soon be time to lift the baby and give him his bottle.

Jenny sat up on her hunkers. 'That's not a nice story,' she said. 'Tell me another story, Bessie. On and on and on with the story!'

2

BESSIE snibbed the bathroom door carefully and looked to see that the keyhole was still filled up with the wad of newspaper she had put in when she'd discovered Jenny peering at her through it. She took a packet of Woodbines from the pocket of her overall and lit one. Recently she had taken to smoking, but so far only in secret. She did not dare to buy her cigarettes from the Store Van, for then the other women in the street would have known and it would have been all over the place like wildfire. 'Fancy that glaikit lassie, Bessie Hipkiss, smokin'. At her age! If I was her father I'd skelp her backside till it tingled.' And so she filched money from the housekeeping money and bought the cigarettes in shops where she wasn't known.

But I'm getting right fed up with it, she thought as she inhaled deeply and then looked at herself in the mirror to see if she was bringing the smoke down her nose in the proper fashion. Those bloody old women in this street are a proper menace. Aye interfering and sticking their noses into other folk's business. They've had a right royal time ever since my mother died. If it's not Mrs. Moore telling me how to bath the baby, it's Mrs. Finlayson telling me the best way to make an apple dumpling. There's aye some bloody auld nosey-parker

54

dotting out and in here, trying to run the house for me. I cannie get a minute to myself. I'm fed up with knocks at that door. . . . It was hopeless to pretend she was out, for a close watch was kept on her comings and goings. Anyway, all the women knew that she couldn't go far because of the baby. She could not even go down to the back-green to hang up the washing without either Mrs. Finlayson or Mrs. Winter popping her head out of the window and shouting: 'Bessie, that's the bairn greetin'. Ye'd better go up to it at once. I'm sure there's something far wrong wi' the puir wee soul. Are ye sure ye've changed his nappie this last wee while? Ye ken that bairns o' that age need constant attention.'

Oh, Christ, there was somebody banging at the door now!

'Bessie! Bessie!' Mrs. Moore shouted through the letter-box. 'Bessie, are ye there?'

'Ay, I'm comin',' she yelled, throwing her cigarette into the w.c. and pulling the plug. She waved her arms wildly to try to dispel the cloud of smoke, then she opened the window and rushed to the door.

'Mercy, Bessie, what a time ye've been,' Mrs. Moore said, bustling past her, carrying a covered dish at arm's length in front of her. 'I began to think ye must have left on the gas by mistake and that ye were all gassed. Gosh, the pictures that passed through my mind as I stood there! I pictured you and Jenny and the baby all lyin' dead and me havin' to run and get the polis to come and break in. And worst o' all I wondered what I would tell your puir pa when he came home. Ye didnie half gie me a turn,' she said.

'I was just in the lavvy,' Bessie said. 'I came as quick as I could.'

'I thought Jenny had maybe turned on the gas,' Mrs. Moore said. 'She's such a little imp o' Satan. Ye'll have to keep yer weather-eye on her, Bessie. She's just at the age for gettin' into all kinds o' mischief. This is a pudding for yer dinner,' she said. 'It's ready, but ye'd better put it in the oven for ten minutes to heat before the time.'

'Oh dear, I've made a puddin',' Bessie said. 'I've a jelly and custard.'

55

'This is baked rice wi' raisins in it,' Mrs. Moore said. 'This is far more substantial and 'll do ye far more good than jelly and custard. There's no *body* in jelly and custard, and what thae bairns need is some *body* to fill them out and make them grow.'

'But the jelly and custard's ready,' Bessie said.

'Well, ye can gie it to the bairns for their supper,' Mrs. Moore said, implying that it wouldn't really matter if Bessie flung it in the rubbish-can. 'They'd better have the rice for their dinner. That pink jelly 'll no' fill you up very sore,' she said. 'I thought when I saw ye buyin' the packet at the Van the other day that it was just a waste o' guid money.'

'But the bairns like jelly,' Bessie said. 'And so do I.'

'It's not a question o' likes or dislikes,' Mrs. Moore said. 'It's a question o' *filling* and what's best for ye. The quicker ye learn that the better, Bessie. It strikes me that ye have a lot to learn yet as far as housekeepin' is concerned. And how's the wee man the day?' she said, bending over the pram. 'What about a wee smile then! Come on, just a wee smilie!' She cluck-clucked and tickled the baby's toes. 'Will I kittle yer wee tootsies for ye then! Come on, smile!'

But instead of smiling the baby started to cry. And you couldn't blame him either, Bessie said to herself, seeing that muckle red face bending over him.

'Oh, mercy me! Mercy me!' Mrs. Moore cried. 'Has he got a wee pain then? There's somethin' far wrong wi' that bairn, Bessie,' she said. 'He doesnie seem to thrive at all. None o' the rest o' ye were ever as sickly as this. Of course, it's to be expected the way he was born, but still . . . Are ye sure ye're attendin' to him properly, Bessie?'

'Of course, I do everythin' the Nurse tells me. I cannie do any more. I cannie help it if he's aye ill.'

'Well, dinnie jump doon my throat,' Mrs. Moore said. 'I was just askin'.'

'It's a pity he's no' thrivin',' she said. 'I wonder if a ticky cod liver oil in his milk wouldnie be a good thing? I think I'll get a bottle for him when I go up the town this afternoon.'

'He gets his orange juice from the Clinic,' Bessie said. 'The Nurse said that should help him.'

'Orange juice! Tcha!' Mrs. Moore said. 'A fat lot o' good orange juice 'll do him. I've no time for thae modern notions. I'm sure neither you nor Billy nor Jenny got orange juice and ye're all healthy enough. Well, I must awa' and get my auld man's dinner set,' she said. 'He'll be in the now like a roarin' hyena.'

'Bessie,' she said, with her hand on the door-knob. 'Do ye no' think ye should buy a kilt for Billy? Yer puir ma aye wanted him to hae a kilt. He'd set it lovely. He's got nice wee firm legs on him. And a kilt's quite economical,' she said. 'Ye can aye let it down as he grows.'

'Och, we cannie afford it,' Bessie said.

'Havers!' Mrs. Moore said. 'Ye could afford it fine. Look at thae cheap dirt o' trousers ye bought him only last week. They're almost through in the backside already. It was just throwin' guid money away. That would never happen wi' a kilt.'

'But he couldnie wear a kilt to play wi',' Bessie said. 'He could only wear it on Sundays.'

'He could wear it to the school. What's to hinder him, I'd like to know!'

'Och, the other laddies would laugh at him.'

'Nonsense!' Mrs. Moore said. 'And what if they did? It would just be jealousy. No, no, ye must get him a kilt. Yer puir ma had set her heart on it, and if she'd lived I'm sure he would 'a' had one by this time.'

'Ach, we'll see later on,' Bessie said weakly.

'Later on nothin',' Mrs. Moore snapped. 'Ye'd better see about it now. Get the deed done! That's aye been my motto. I'll price the kilts for ye when I'm up town this afternoon. I'll let ye know about it when I bring the cod liver oil,' she said.

Bessie shut the door with a vicious little bang behind Mrs. Moore. Really, it was a bit thick. What right had Mrs. Moore to keep coming and shoving her dirty neb in here? Cod liver oil and kilts! It was too much. Was she supposed to be running this house, or was it Mrs. Moore who was running it? What between Mrs. Moore and her father she was nearly turning daft!

She looked at Mrs. Moore's rice pudding, resisting an impulse to throw it in the fire. Ah well, she thought, I'll just eat the pink jelly and custard myself this afternoon if I can get the house to myself for a while. And she carried them into the bedroom and placed them carefully on top of the wardrobe where Billy or Jenny wouldn't be likely to see them. She would have a right good feed to herself when she got rid of them all. It was a good thing Jenny hadn't noticed her making the jelly; she'd shut the child out of the kitchenette while doing it. But it was a damned nuisance. After this she wouldn't be able to buy packets of jelly at the Van for fear of Mrs. Moore. She'd have to get them somewhere else.

As for that kilt. Really, Mrs. Moore had a nerve. They couldn't afford it. But Mrs. Moore knew she had played a trump card when she said her mother had set her heart on it. Cunning auld bitch! You'd think the bairns were hers the way she carried on. Would she have been so keen if she'd had any bairns of her own? When was Billy going to wear it, anyway? Their mother had wanted it for him to wear to the Kirk and Sunday School. But they hadn't been at the Kirk for months. She just couldn't make it. She couldn't go herself because she had the baby to look after, and of course her father wouldn't take the bairns. He hadn't even gone to the Kirk the Sunday after her mother was buried like any other respectable body. Nor would he look after the baby and let her go. It was a pity Mrs. Moore wasn't a Kirk-goer or she might have taken the two wee ones. Her father and she had had many a row about it. Bessie had wanted to send the children by themselves or to get a neighbour to take them, but Bert had put his foot down. 'They're better at home,' he said. 'They'll learn far more good here than they'll ever learn listening to auld Wallace.' And he'd been terrible rude to poor Mr. Wallace when he'd called to see how they were keeping. Mr. Wallace had asked if he could help in any way and had suggested that he get some of the ladies of the congregation to look in and see if they could help, but Bert had said: 'Keep your bloody charity. You and your kirk have been the ruination of Scotland. Putting a lot of daft ideas into folk's

58

heads. My bairns are goin' to grow up into sensible folk that
'll have no use for superstition and bloody cant.'

Fancy saying that to the minister! Bessie clenched her hands
and she wailed soundlessly: 'Oh, Ma! Ma! I'm glad ye
weren't here to hear. . . . Oh, Ma, it's awful difficult. . . .'

3

THE baby was starting to cry again.

'Damn that bairn,' Bessie said, banging a pot of mince down
by the side of the fire. 'It's aye greetin'.'

'Oh, you said a Bad Word!' Jenny cried.

'What if I did?' Bessie said irritably. 'Ye might give the pram
a wee push back and forrit, hen, while I make the pudding.'

She glanced to see that Jenny was doing as she was told,
then she hurried on with her preparations for yet another day's
dinner. Try as she might she could not become fond of the
baby at all. Although both Jenny and Billy irritated her at
times, she was fond enough of them. She never stopped to
analyse it, but she knew she was fond of them and would have
done anything for them. But the baby . . . No, that was a
different kettle of fish! She could never become fond of the
baby. Every time she looked at it she remembered her mother's
grey face on the pillow. Sometimes she felt when it was wailing,
as it was wailing now, that she would have liked to smother it
with that pillow.

'Jenny!' she cried. 'Don't rock the pram so hard. Ye'll
capsize the baby.'

Though it wouldn't matter much if she did, she thought.
It would be the best thing that could happen. The kid was
aye ailing, and the District Nurse was never away from the
house. Bessie was expecting her at any moment now. This was
just about her time. She always came when everything was in
a muddle; the dinner being got ready and the kids crying and
herself looking like nothing on earth. . . .

Bessie glanced out of the window. Ay, there was the

Nurse's car in front of Mrs. Moore's entry. And there was Lily McGillivray again with that sailor. That was the third day running she'd been with him.

Wonder who it is? Bessie thought, going to the mirror. Wonder if it's the chap she was going with in the bakery? Will he have joined the Navy? Or is it somebody else she's got a hold of? Gosh, Lily's the boy to get the lads! Wish I could take a leaf out of her book! 'Love 'em and leave 'em, Hippy,' she had said to Bessie. 'That's me!'

Bessie wet her fingers and smoothed her eyebrows. For a few seconds the wetness made them blacker, then they relapsed again into their sandy tinge. She licked her lips, wondering. Maybe if she got one of those eyebrow pencils . . .

She combed her hair and gave her face a rub with her handkerchief. There! She looked a bit more presentable for the Nurse coming. Not that it mattered a damn about the Nurse, but the old bitch had said to Mrs. Moore that really there was no need for the Hipkiss girl to look such a sight even if she had her father and the three children to look after. And Mrs. Moore had said: 'If I was you, hen, I wouldnie give her any cause to make such remarks. Ye're a nice-like lassie when ye like to tosh yersel' up. And ye're no' a bairn ony longer. Ye might as well begin to make the best o' yer looks while ye can.'

As if Madame Royale of France cared what the canaille of a District Nurse said! Oh, but things would be different when they got to France. She would have all sorts of things then. Beautiful clothes, jewels, diamonds, furs, silk dresses. . . . She would be the most beautiful woman in Paris. The most beautiful woman in France. And the most powerful. She would be virtually the Queen. . . .

'Can ye no' make that bairn stop greetin', Jenny?' she cried. 'It's continual girn's gettin' on my nerves.'

'I think he's got a wee sore belly,' Jenny said in an old-wifish tone.

'He'll have a wee sore backside if he doesnie shuttup,' Bessie said. 'There's the door!' she cried. 'This 'll be the Nurse. I hope to God it's no' one o' thae other interferin' auld wives.'

60

'And how is the wee man today?' the Nurse said, lumbering towards the pram on tiptoes, her head forward and her shoulders bent. She always seemed to spring a little with every step. She was a large woman with a round red face, which had fairly long grey whiskers sprouting around her chins and lower jowl. As she pulled back the cover to look at the baby, Bessie glanced enviously at her gold wristlet-watch. She often wished she had the courage to say like Jenny: 'Let me try on yer watch, Nurse!'

'Oh now! There, there, there!' the Nurse cried to the howling child. 'Has he got the tummy-ache then? Is his little tum-tum hurting him then? He doesn't look at all well,' she said, after examining him. 'I must get Doctor Henderson to come in and look at him. Are you sure you're doing exactly what I told you, Bessie?'

'Of course.'

'You're sure you're boiling his milk?'

'Of course,' Bessie said.

'You always do it in a clean pan?' the Nurse said. 'An enamel pan, remember! You're sure you always give the pan a good scouring?'

'Of course,' Bessie said.

'I really don't know what's wrong with him at all,' the Nurse said. 'If you're following my instructions I don't see why he should be like this. Of course, he's always been a very weak baby. But I don't think there's anything organically wrong with him.'

You and your big words, Bessie thought. What between you and your see that the pan's clean and Mrs. Moore and her give him some castor-oil, hen, I'll soon be driven crazy. I wish to God the bloody kid would kick the bucket. . . .

'I'll ask Doctor Henderson to look in this afternoon,' the Nurse said. 'I must fly just now. Goodness! Is that the time already? My dinner 'll be waiting for me on the table. I'll have to rush or Mrs. Stout 'll be sending out the Flying Squad, wondering what's keeping me!'

Bessie gave the pram a vicious little rock before she went into the kitchenette to boil the milk for the baby. Are you sure

61

you always boil the milk in a clean pan? After she'd near scrubbed the tips of her fingers off scouring the pan, and then this was all the thanks she got!

She took down the pan and looked at it. She hadn't had time to clean it after boiling the milk the last time, and the inside was sour and thick with scum. More elbow grease . . . and she'd likely scrape her nails into the quick, just when she was wanting to let them grow long and pointed like Ginger Rogers'. . . .

She held the pan under the hot-water tap, but she stood with her hand on the tap, not turning on the water, staring into space. . . .

It would be the quickest way to get rid of the baby. They might all get some peace then from its continual wailing. And after all, nobody could blame her. The baby was ailing, anyway.

Of course, they would discover it hundreds of years after this when they read her Journals. The Journals of Madame Elisabeth Louise Charlotte, Duchess d'Angouleme. . . .

Secretly Madame Elisabeth took the tiny phial from her wide black lace sleeve and, holding it by the tip in her long, white, be-ringed fingers, the scarlet nails flashing as if already dipped in blood, she poured the green evil-smelling liquid into the milk in the golden pan. Her large eyes darted from side to side, though there was nobody in the tiny turret-room of the old grey palace but herself. She started when the red velvet curtains shook with a sudden gust of wind. 'Ma foi!' she gasped, and she put her hand quickly to her throat, clutching at the rope of pearls round her slender neck. Then furtively she stirred the liquid with a long golden spoon which had the Bourbon Lilies engraved on the handle. . . . Then swiftly she poured the milk for the young prince into a crystal bottle, and she smiled—a slow, dark, lascivious smile. . . . A few hours later the infant prince was dead. Madame Royale had paved the way for her own succession to the throne of France. . . .

Horrified at what she had done, Bessie lifted the almost boiling pot from the cooker and poured the milk down the sink. 'Ma foi!' she cried, and she rushed to the mirror.

62

She stood for a few seconds with the empty pot dangling in her hand. Her red hair was a bit mussed, but her eyes looked much the same as usual. 'Murderess!' she hissed at her reflection, then she stepped back and crossed herself.

'What are you doin' that for, Bessie?' asked Jenny.

'Shuttup, I'm makin' the Sign of the Cross.'

'What do you do it for?' Jenny said.

'Just because,' Bessie said. 'Little girls should ask no questions and they'll be told no lies.'

'I want to do it,' Jenny said. 'What do you do? Is this it?'

'If ye watch the next time ye go to the picters you'll see how to do it,' Bessie said angrily. 'Get out o' ma road! I must get the baby's milk boiled.'

She scoured the pan until her fingers were sore and her nails were grated. There was a hot flush on her cheek-bones. Heavens, if she had done it . . .

4

' I WANT ma dinner, Ferret-face!' Billy cried, rushing into the kitchenette.

'You'll get your dinner when I'm ready,' Bessie said. 'I'm feedin' Baby just now, and he's a lot more important than you. Now be quiet, you're disturbin' him.'

'What do I care!' Billy said, and he bent down and made a hideous noise with his tongue against his teeth at the baby.

'Billy Hipkiss! I'll clout ye! Get away out of here till I cry on ye that the dinner's ready. Baby's got to be fed first. He's very ill.'

'Well, if he's ill, I'm hungry,' Billy cried. 'Gie's a piece! If ye dinnie, I'll take one.'

'You keep back from that table, Billy Hipkiss,' she threatened, half-rising from her chair, clutching the baby against her. The infant let out a wail because for a moment the bottle was taken away from his lips. 'Ssh! Ssh!' Bessie whispered soothingly.

'Lookit what ye've done!' she said to Billy. 'Ye've made him greet. I'll tell Daddy on ye when he comes in.'

'Clipe!'

Billy darted back when Bessie made as if to put down the baby. 'Mind, I'll come and cuff ye,' she said. 'See if ye cannie be quiet for a wee while. Ye'll have to wait till Daddy comes, anyway, before ye get your dinner.'

Billy went to look at what Jenny was doing with a pile of old papers in the corner beneath the window. 'What are you playin' at, Rat-face?' he asked.

Bessie sighed and resettled the baby. She hitched her stool nearer a chair on which an open book was lying. 'There, ma wee doo! There, there, there,' she muttered to the child, while she skimmed quickly over a page until she reached the place she had been at when Billy interrupted her. But after she had read a few lines her eyes became blank and she sank into a reverie. . . .

While she nursed the infant prince, Madame Royale of France read Dumas' famous novel *The Count of Monte Cristo*. The Dauphin and the Duchess of Chartres were playing at the other end of the great hall. The table was set for lunch, but the King was late. Madame Royale had dismissed all the footmen except one faithful old retainer. This old man stood at the top of the great staircase, watching like a faithful hound for his royal master.

'He comes, Your Highness, he comes! The King has returned from the chase!'

Robert the First of France entered the great hall briskly.

'Well, Bessie, how's the bairn now?'

'Och, he's no' well at all, Da,' she said. 'He keeps on greetin'. The Nurse was in, and she says she's goin' to send the Doctor this afternoon.'

'Hell, again!' Bert said, sinking on to the sofa. 'He's never away from this house. Here, I'll take him, Bessie, while you dish the dinner.'

Thankfully Bessie handed over the child and the bottle and went into the kitchenette.

'Have ye asked Mrs. Moore to show you how to make soup yet?' her father shouted after her.

'Aw, I forgot!' she cried.

'I wish you'd get her to show you. I miss a plate of soup. Your mother was a dab hand at makin' soup. I wish she'd learned ye to make it. . . .'

Bessie did not listen to him. You and your old soup, she said to herself, taking a pudding-dish from a shelf and banging it on the table. You'll not get soup as long as I'm cooking for you, my man. I'm for none of it. You and the noises you make when you're eating it. You're just like a pig in a trough. It's a wonder to me that my mother put up with it all these years. And anyway, me and the bairns like pudding, and puddings we're going to have as long as I'm the cook here. I will not get Mrs. Moore to show me how to make it. I could make it fine if I liked. But I don't like. So you can put that in your pipe and smoke it. And if Mrs. Moore comes in here again, like she did yesterday, with a big bowl of soup, I'll clash it in her face. 'That's a wee sup o' soup for yer puir pa, Bessie. I ken he misses his soup, so I thought I'd make an extra big potful. There's plenty there for you and the bairns, too.' Oh, I could have murdered her! And then he goes and says: 'Thank you, Mrs. Moore, it's real kind of you. I just wish you'd show Bessie sometime when you have time how to make it.' After all the things he's said about Mrs. Moore when he used to quarrel with Ma. . . .

Bessie shut her eyes tightly, trying to forget what had happened afterwards.

'Ummm, this soup looks good,' her father had said, sitting at the table, rubbing his hands together. 'Come on, you two bairns, sit in and we'll see who'll be finished first.'

Sitting opposite him in the place she'd sat in ever since her mother's death, Bessie was careful not to look directly at him. She always looked at the wall behind him. She tried not to listen to the noise he made with every spoonful. 'Ummm, this is good soup,' he said every now and then. 'It's no' as good as your mother's, but still, it's no' too bad.'

She was so irritated at the noise he made that she was extra

65

careful not to make any noise herself. She sipped genteelly at every spoonful, careful to allow not even a gurgle to escape from her. She sat tense, every nerve on the alert. Heavens, she wondered, what would happen when they went to Paris and had soup at banquets? Her father would need to be trained in table-manners before then. But who would do that? She knew that she dare not say anything to him. If she made the slightest bit of criticism he would fly up in the air.

'Gosh, this is grand,' he said, holding out his empty plate. 'I'll take another plateful, Bessie.'

He belched, putting his hand on his chest and raising his eyebrows in comic surprise at Jenny.

'Well, my wee doo!' he said. 'How are you getting on? Sup it up now! See, Daddy's at his second plateful already! Sup it up and you'll grow big. This is the stuff to stick to your ribs. How're you gettin' on, son?'

'I'm near finished,' Billy said. 'Look! I'm further forrit than Jenny, amn't I?'

'Ye are nut!' Jenny cried. 'I'll be finished first! I'll be finished before everybody! I'll be finished before everybody else in the world!'

'Ye will nut!' Billy said. 'I'll be finished first, won't I, Da?'

'No, me!' Jenny cried.

'Aw, be quiet, both of you!' Bessie shouted, suddenly glad to vent all her pent-up irritation on somebody. 'Eat it up and make less noise or ye'll no' get any more dinner. Billy, you take your elbows offen the table and make less noise with your soup.'

'Aw shuttup, Ferret-face!' Billy said, putting out his tongue. 'I'm no' makin' as much noise as Da!'

'But he's a man and can make as much noise as he likes,' she said. 'You're just a wee shaver, and——'

'Who says I'm makin' a noise?' her father cried.

'Bessie said it,' Jenny said, opening her eyes very wide and gazing solemnly around.

'I never did anything of the kind,' Bessie said. 'I only said to Billy——'

'Criticize me, would you, ye young bitch!' Bert shouted.

66

'If there's any more of it I'll clash this plate of soup in your face. Sittin' there and havin' the audacity to criticize your own father!'

'I never,' Bessie stammered. 'I never said——'

'So you'd call me a liar next, would ye?' The veins on Bert's forehead were standing out. 'I've a good mind to skelp your backside for you, big and all as you are. Criticizin' me that brings in the money that keeps us all! By God, my lady, I've had just about enough of this. Don't think I haven't noticed the way you've been carryin' on lately. Tryin' to be so laddie-da and fine and cockin' out yer wee finger when ye drink yer tea! I'll not have it.'

'I never——'

'Shuttup!' Bert roared. 'Another word and I'll clip your bloody ear for you.'

'Oh, you said a Bad Word!' Jenny cried.

Bessie pressed her hands against her cheeks. They were burning now at the memory even hotter than they had burned yesterday. And as she poured the pudding into the dish she hoped that there would be no scenes like that today.

Her father had laid the baby back in his pram and was bending over it. The child was wailing again.

'Is there nothin' that 'll keep him quiet, Bessie?' he said.

'I don't think so. He'll just have to greet.'

'I wonder,' Bert said, sitting at the table, 'I wonder, Bessie . . .'

'Ay?' she said.

'I was wondering,' he said. 'I was wondering if maybe we shouldnie get a housekeeper. I mean—well, there's a lot of work here for you. It's too much for a lassie that's not fifteen yet. I was wondering if maybe we shouldnie get a woman that would be able to cope with things. Somebody that would have more experience. . . .'

Bessie gave the pram a final rock and sat down at the table. 'Sit properly on yer chair, Jenny,' she said. 'Ye might hitch her chair in a wee thing, Da; she's too far from the table.'

'There, my wee doo! There you are now!' Bert said. He

took his plate of mince and potatoes from Bessie. 'Well, Bessie, what do you think?'

'I don't know,' she said. 'I dinnie want another woman here. I dinnie think my mother . . . But you ken best, Da. You'd better do what ye like. We're not gettin' on so bad. The bairns wouldnie like another woman to come here. . . .'

'Me doesnie want another mammy,' Billy howled. 'Me just wants Bessie.'

'Stop saying "Me doesnie want this" or "Me wants that",' his father cried angrily. 'A great big laddie like you bein' so bairny! Can you not speak properly?'

'Me doesnie like you,' Billy snivelled. 'Me just likes Bessie.'

'Stop it!' Bert cried.

'Now, stop it, Billy,' said Bessie. 'You do what Daddy tells you, like a good boy. It's silly for a big laddie like you to talk so soft. Here, wipe your nose and eat up your mince.'

'Have you not got a hankie?' Bert said.

'Here, wipe your nose on this.' Bessie took the corner of her apron and wiped Billy's nose and eyes. 'Now, come on and eat your dinner like a good wee man.'

'I'll be finished first if he doesnie,' Jenny said, looking across the table at Billy with a superior air. 'I'm a good wee girl, amn't I, Daddy? I'll get the biggest helpin' o' puddin', won't I?'

'Bessie, I wish you'd see that these bairns had hankies,' Bert said. 'It's disgustin', this business of wipin' their noses on whatever's handiest at the time. There's no need for it.'

'Oh dear! That bairn!' Bessie cried, starting up and giving the pram a rock. 'There he goes again!'

'Look, I'll attend to him while you dish out the pudding,' her father said.

'Do you want plums, Billy?' Bessie asked, holding the spoon over the dish.

'You bet your life, kid! I want a lot now, Ferret-face. I want more than anybody else.'

'Don't be greedy, Billy,' said his father.

'He shouldnie be greedy, shouldn't he not?' Jenny said. 'I'm not greedy, amn't I not? I'm a good wee girl.'

68

'You are nut a good wee girl,' Billy cried. 'You did a jobbie in the back-green yesterday, then you covered it up with ashes so that nobody would see and somebody would tramp on it.'

'Billy! I'll clip your ears for you if you say things like that again!' Bessie sniffed angrily and pushed her hair out of her eyes. 'Da, I wish you'd speak to Billy. He's aye swearin' and sayin' dirty things. He's teachin' Jenny a lot of ill.'

Her father didn't answer. He held out his plate. 'Is there any more pudding?'

Bessie handed back his plate. 'Now, who wants to scrape out the dish?' she said. 'Billy?'

'No, me! Me!' Jenny cried.

'You've got plenty there to keep you goin',' Bessie said. 'You've got a lot of plums there to eat yet. Watch the stones now! It would be a terrible job if ye swallowed one, wouldn't it, Daddy? It would grow and grow in yer tummy and then you would turn into a plum tree. Branches would come out at yer ears and yer nose, and yer arms would turn into branches, and each finger would be a little branch and you would grow and grow and grow, and the little birds would come and sit on your branches, and——'

'And the roots would come out at yer bum!' Billy cried.

'Oh, Da!' Bessie wailed. 'Listen to that! Can ye no' speak to him?'

Bert pushed back his chair and lit a cigarette. 'I wish you'd stop tellin' those bairns such a lot of trash,' he said. 'You're just filling their heads with a lot of damned nonsense.'

'Ach, I have to do somethin' to keep them quiet. They're aye pesterin' me for stories.'

'Well, if they must have stories I wish you'd tell them something decent. Not all that muck about witches and turning into trees and fairies and rubbish like that. Tell them something sensible.' He rose. 'Now I'm away to have forty winks. I'm not needing to be back at the pub till five. So if you'd waken me in time for my tea at four. . . . And see and keep thae bairns quiet, Bessie! I hardly got any sleep last night for the baby greetin'. If the doctor comes you'd better give me a shout.'

Bessie leaned her elbows on the table and cupped her face in her hands, staring into space. Jenny and Billy were arguing about the amount of plums they had eaten. 'I had a hundred,' Billy cried. 'See the stones! There's a hundred stones there, isn't there, Bessie?'

'Aw shuttup,' Bessie said. 'Can ye not give me five minutes' peace?'

She closed her eyes. It was all very well for her father to moan about not getting enough sleep because of the baby, but what about her? She hadn't had any sleep either. And she had had these bloody kids on her hands all day. And now she had the dishes to wash and God knows what else to do. . . .

'Oh hell!' she cried, starting up at the raucous braying of a horn in the street. 'There's the Store Van!'

5

B Y the time Bessie got down to the street with her basket and the Store Book, about half a dozen women had collected at the rear of a large red van with Edinburgh United Co-operative Society in huge letters on its side.

'Hurry up, hen!' Mrs. Moore called. 'Hurry up, or ye'll miss yer place in the queue!'

'How's the baby the day, Bessie?' asked Mrs. Winter, a serious-looking little woman with a squint and thick-lensed glasses. Her dark hair was cut in a fringe across her forehead, and it was usually so long, touching the top of her glasses, that she had to hold her head back slightly in order to see.

'Och, he's no' well at all,' Bessie said. 'The Nurse is goin' to get the Doctor to come in this afternoon.'

'Did ye gie him castor-oil like I tellt ye, hen?' Mrs. Moore said.

'Ay,' she said.

'Now, I wouldnie gie him castor-oil,' Mrs. Winter said. 'I'd gie him Syrup o' Figs. I aye give that to mine.'

'Well, I think castor-oil's better,' Mrs. Moore said. 'I'm a great believer in it. Whenever ma auld man has a sore guts I make him take a good big spoonful o' castor-oil and it aye does the trick.'

'Works the oracle, ye might say!' Dirty Minnie laughed.

'Oh, is that the polite word for it?' Mrs. Moore grinned. 'Did ye learn that frae one o' yer lodgers, Minnie?'

'Next, please!' the vanman shouted.

'Oh, it's ma turn, isn't it?' Mrs. Moore said. 'My goodness, Andy, it's no' like me to be so backward in comin' forward!'

'Who's he got with him the day?' Dirty Minnie said to Bessie, craning her neck to see into the dark interior of the huge travelling-shop. 'Whoever it is seems to have got lost away back there among the biscuit-tins.'

'It's Wee Darkie the day,' Mrs. Winter said. 'What a time he's takin'.'

'And him a Boy Scout, too!' Dirty Minnie said. 'I aye thought they learned them to be quicker in the scouts.'

'He gets my goat, he's that slow,' Mrs. Winter said.

'He's a bonny Boy Scout,' Minnie laughed. 'Pity the laddies under him! I doubt he'll lead them all to destruction! Hurry up, there!' she called. 'What are ye playin' at in there behind the scenes? Hurry up, or I'll come in there beside ye, and I'll soon make ye shift!'

'Ye'd better come out, son!' Mrs. Moore called, laughing. 'She means business! Her three lodgers dinnie keep her busy enough, so she's got time to spare for you!'

'Ach, leave the laddie alone!' the vanman said. 'You women, you're that impatient! The laddie 'll be here in a jiffy. He's just gettin' the biscuit-tins put into order. Surely you're not all in such a great hurry. You've got all day in front of you! Am I no' capable of dealing with you all?'

'It would take a *man* to deal with me!' Minnie laughed.

'Next, please!' Andy cried.

Bessie handed him her Store Book, for the other women motioned her to go before them. They were in no hurry, despite their remarks; as far as they were concerned this was a social occasion and they were determined to make it spin

71

out as long as possible. Besides, they were all interested in seeing what Bessie was going to buy.

'Two pounds o' sugar,' Bessie said, watching Andy write it down. 'And a pound o' butter, and a pound o' cheese, and—goodness, what else was it I wanted?'

'Maggie Ann, dear,' Minnie said.

'Ay, a pound o' margarine,' Bessie said.

'Ye're needin' soap, hen,' Mrs. Moore said. 'I noticed that yesterday when I was in.'

'No, it's Minnie that needs the soap!' Mrs. McIntyre said. 'Isn't it, Minnie?'

'Soap?' Minnie giggled. 'What kind o' stuff's that? I don't think I've ever seen it in ma life!'

'Ay, you'd better gie me two cakes o' soap,' Bessie said. 'And a pound o' sago and a packet o' Creamola custard.'

'What aboot barley, hen?' Mrs. Moore said. 'Ye'd better get some and some lentils and I'll make soup for yer puir pa.'

Bessie drew her brows down slightly, but she said nothing; she watched Andy write down the items Mrs. Moore said.

'Ye're lookin' tired, Bessie,' Dirty Minnie said kindly. 'I doubt it's ower much work for ye keepin' house for yer faither and the bairns.'

'Ay, she's thin and peaky-like,' Mrs. Moore said. 'It's far too much work for a growin' lassie. Mr. Hipkiss was talkin' about gettin' a housekeeper. I must speak to him about it again. They need a woman in that house, especially wi' the baby bein' badly.'

'That's a fine job for you, Minnie!' said Mrs. McIntyre, giving Bessie a nudge with her fat elbow. 'How would ye like Minnie for a second mother, m'dear?'

'Och, her and me would get on fine, wouldn't we, ducky?' Minnie laughed. 'Or would ye rather have Big Maggie? Here she comes slitterin' along like last week's washin'!'

Big Maggie Burns wore a dirty brick-coloured felt hat pulled far down over her brows, and a worn leather coat which had been split at the seam down the back into a large V. Her brown, weather-beaten face creased into a broad grin as she joined the other women.

'Late as usual, Maggie hen!' Minnie said. 'Did the Van disturb yer Beauty Sleep?'

'Ay, I thought it was the Last Trump!' Big Maggie said. 'What a noise ye made, Andy! Did ye think ye were Gabriel blowin' his horn?'

'Ye didnie half make a din,' Mrs. Winter said plaintively. 'I thought the war had broken oot and that the sireens had started.'

'Well, it'll no' be long now!' Mrs. Moore said. 'Did ye hear the one o'clock news? Auld Hitler wants the Polish Corridor now!'

'I wish he'd come and polish ma corridor for me,' Dirty Minnie laughed. 'I'd soon polish him off!'

'What a chance it would be for ye, Minnie, when he was on his knees,' Mrs. Moore said. 'My word, if I catch you bendin'!'

'Ach, there'll be no war,' Mrs. McIntyre said.

'Next, please!' Andy shouted.

Although she had got her messages, Bessie was in no hurry to go inside. She did not like any of the women, but it was better to listen to them, she felt, than to go into the house and listen to the baby crying and the children quarrelling. She leaned against the railings.

The above photograph of Madame Royale of France leaning on the balcony of her villa at Nice was taken just after Her Royal Highness returned from Switzerland where she had a meeting with Herr Hitler and Signor Mussolini. It is not known what took place at the meeting, but the Princess' Lady-in-Waiting told our special correspondent that Madame Royale had been instrumental in solving the problem of peace in Europe for many years to come. It is rumoured that the lovely French princess will marry shortly. There are numbers of eligible young men, including a famous film-star, but we are pinning our bets on a certain Spanish prince. . . .

'Hya, Bessie!'

'Oh, hello, Lily! Are ye no' workin' the day?'

'No, I'm havin' a day off.' Lily McGillivray leaned against the railings beside her. 'You look as if you were havin' a day off yersel'!'

'What a hope!' Bessie said. 'I've got piles and piles o' work waitin' for me. I'm just havin' a breather, wonderin' what I'll fly at first.'

She looked enviously at Lily. 'Goodness! You look just like Alice Faye. You look great!'

'Thanks!' Lily simpered and touched the red studs clipped on to the lobes of her ears. 'Like my ear-rings? The boy-friend gave me them.'

'They're lovely.'

'It's about time you started to wear ear-rings, Ferret,' Lily said. 'You should doll yersel' up a bit now that ye're no' at the school.'

'My faither would kill me!'

'Ach, what does it matter about him! It's up to everybody to make the best o' themselves.'

'I tell ye there'll be no war,' Mrs. McIntyre cried, picking up her bag of messages. 'The Germans are ower feared to go to war. That Hitler's just a bluffer.'

'And I say there will be a war,' Mrs. Moore said. 'But I daresay we could argue till we were black in the face and it wouldnie make ony difference. Puir folk like us have no say in the matter.'

'Cheerio, Andy, see and bring me a tin o' corn beef when ye come on Thursday!' she called.

'Cheerio!' Andy cried.

The Van moved away to the next street, but the women still stood talking. They dispersed gradually until only Dirty Minnie and Mrs. Moore were left, with Bessie and Lily leaning against the railings, listening to them.

'Well, I must go,' Mrs. Moore said at last. 'I want to go up the town this afternoon and buy masel' a new pair o' shoes. The ones I've got the now are near worn through to the uppers. Cheerio, Minnie! See and be good!'

'Take that advice to yersel'!' Minnie cried, moving off majestically like a large and grimy ship, her bust sticking out in front of her. 'Cheerio, Bessie! Cheerio, Lily!'

'Cheerio!' they cried.

'I'll come in and see ye the night, hen, after tea,' Mrs.

Moore said to Bessie. 'Ye'll know by that time what the Doctor thinks o' the baby.'

'Well, I suppose I'd better get inside,' Bessie said, shifting her position reluctantly. 'I expect the kids 'll have murdered the baby by this time.'

'Ach well, why worry!' Lily grinned. 'Are ye doin' anythin' the night, Ferret?'

'How?'

'I was wonderin' if ye wouldnie come to the picters with me?'

'Oh, I'd love to go, but——' Bessie screwed up her face. 'I cannie. I have thae bloody kids to look after. No, I cannie go the night. But some other night . . .'

'Okay,' Lily said. 'That's a date. I'll keep ye in mind o' it. Cheeribye the now!'

6

THE first sound Bessie heard as she went in was the wailing of the baby. 'That damned kid again,' she muttered. 'What's wrong with it now?'

'I thought I told ye to look after the baby?' she said to Jenny.

'But I did!' Jenny's eyes widened with injured innocence. 'I did, but he wouldnie be good. I think ye should smack his wee bottom, Bessie.'

Bessie did her utmost to soothe the child, but he kept on wailing. She sighed with exasperation. The next thing would be that her father would be yelling from the room, complaining that he couldn't get his nap. And she would have to take the rap for it, of course. As if she could help the bloody kid having something wrong with it and yelling its head off like this. . . . She shuddered when she remembered what she had nearly done before dinner-time. And furtively she made the sign of the Cross.

'What are ye doin' that for again, Bessie? Show me how ye do it.'

'Aw shuttup, Jenny! Leave me alone for God's sake!'

'If you tell me a story.'

'I will not tell you a story,' Bessie cried. 'I've enough to do without tellin' you stories. Now get away outside, out of here! Where's Billy?'

'He's down in the back-green, playin'.'

'Well, you go and play with him.'

'But I don't want to play wis him,' Jenny said. 'I want to stay here wis you. I want to see you washin' your bosies.'

'Well, I'm not goin' to wash ma bosies just now, so there!' Bessie took her by the shoulder and gave her a little push towards the door. 'Away you go outside and play!'

'I'll say a Bad Word if ye don't let me stay!'

'I don't care how many bad words ye say,' Bessie cried. 'Away ye go and play!'

Jenny scowled and wandered slowly into the lobby. Bessie pushed the pram into the kitchenette and prepared to wash the dishes. The baby was still whimpering. She listened, but she did not hear Jenny open the front door. What's she up to now? she thought. But she did not have time to go and investigate. She filled the sink with hot water and began to wash the dishes. Occasionally she reached out with her foot and gave the pram a rock.

If only she had been able to say to Lily that she would go to the pictures with her tonight! Wouldn't that have been swell! It was funny that Lily had asked her, wasn't it? You'd have thought she would have been going with that sailor she'd been capering about with for the last three days. Wonder what's happened to him? . . . He looked nice. Wonder if I went out with Lily if I could get a sailor, too?

She looked at herself in the mirror hanging above the sink. She could see her reflection only dimly through the steam that covered it. Not bad! She looked a bit ghost-like. The lady in the veils . . .

Madame Royale leaned back in the corner of her limousine. Dove grey tulle swathed her head. 'You are like a grey tulip,

76

my dove,' whispered the Prince in naval uniform, who sat
close beside her on the white silk cushions. 'You are like a
slender grey cloud. . . .'

'Bessie!'

She started at the sibilant whisper and let a plate slide
through her fingers back into the greasy water.

'Well, what is it now?' she snapped. 'I thought ye were away
outside to play.'

'When are ye goin' to wash yersel', Bessie?'

'In a wee while,' she said. 'As soon as I get thur dishes
washed. I'll not get myself washed any quicker if you're goin'
to keep on botherin' me. Away ye go outside and play!'

But Jenny leaned against the door. She looked down at a
piece of string she was twisting, her small face serious. Then
she looked up at Bessie.

'Would you like to be left alone, Bessie?'

'You bet I would!'

'Who else would like to be left alone?'

Bessie pulled out the plug, then as the water began to run
away she swirled a cloth round the sink, wiping away the ring
of grease. 'Oh, I don't know,' she said, wringing out the cloth
and hanging it on a pipe below the sink. 'Greta Garbo maybe.
She aye wants to be left alone.'

'But I wouldnie leave her alone,' Jenny said.

'I ken ye wouldnie.' Bessie shook her head with exasperation.
'But maybe Garbo would be able to deal wi' ye better than I
can!'

She started to wipe the dishes. 'Let me help!' Jenny cried.

'No, ye might break them.'

'I wanna dry them!' Jenny yelled, tugging at the towel.

'Well, you're not goin' to dry them,' Bessie said, pulling the
towel away. 'So that's that!'

'I'll say a Bad Word in two ticks,' Jenny said, glowering.
'Mind, I will! I'll say a Bad Word, then I'll say anuzzer Bad
Word.'

'Out ye go!' Bessie cried, shoving her through the door.

'I'll hit the baby if you don't watch out!'

'G'out of here,' Bessie cried, shutting the kitchenette-door on

77

her and locking it. She grinned when Jenny started to kick the
door and rattle the handle. If this woke up the old man, what
would he say to his beloved wee pet that he thought could do
no wrong? Maybe it would give him a wee idea of what she
had to put up with.

'Stop it!' she called. 'If ye don't stop it, I'll come out and
rattle yer lugs!'

But Jenny went on kicking at the door. Bessie dried the
dishes and put them away. The kicking still went on. 'Let me
in, you buggis!' Jenny shouted every few seconds.

'Now, Jenny, Bessie doesnie like to hear you say thae bad
words.'

'Well, let me in!'

'No, run away and be good, you're wakenin' the baby. And
you'll wake Daddy and then what will he say?'

There was silence for a few seconds. Bessie stood with her
head cocked to the side, then thinking that Jenny had at last
given up, she started to peel off her frock. She'd just wash herself in here; she couldn't be bothered going to the bathroom,
and anyway if she unlocked that door there would sure to be
another row with Jenny. She glanced at the small blue alarm-
clock on the shelf. Almost half-past two. The Doctor couldn't
possibly be here for another half-hour yet; his consulting
hour didn't finish until three. The baby had stopped crying,
though he still gave an occasional whimper and tossed about
in his pram. Now, if he would just settle himself until she got
herself washed . . .

'Bessie!'

Bessie turned the hot water tap and did not answer.

'Bessie!'

She bared her teeth in a snarl at the closed door. 'Ay, what
is it now?'

'Bessie, I can see your bosies! I can see them through the
keyhole!'

'Run away and play,' Bessie cried, soaping her hands and
beginning to wash herself. 'If ye dinnie run away I winnie tell
ye a story at bedtime.'

But all the time Bessie was washing herself, Jenny kept shouting through the keyhole at her. Finally, after she had dried herself, Bessie hung her frock over the door-knob, effectively shutting out her little sister's view. Then she struck a match and allowed it to burn for a few seconds before blowing it out. She looked at the door to see that the keyhole was still blocked, then she stood on her toes and got her face as close to the mirror as she could. Gently does it now. Not too thick. What you want is a fine dark thin line like Marlene Dietrich's. . . . Wonder if I should make it curl up a wee thing at the ends like hers?

But she decided not to. People would notice that too much. It would only be drawing attention to them. She contented herself with making an ordinary fine line. Then she stood back to eye the effect. It wasn't too bad. She could hardly have done any better if she'd had a real eyebrow pencil. She must remember and get one, though. Now, her lips . . . but this wasn't going to be so simple. She wished she'd bought a lipstick out of Woolworth's. That was another thing she must remember to buy the next time she was in Leith. She stood, her bare arms akimbo, considering. . . .

'I've got it!' she said, snapping her fingers.

'What have you got, Bessie?'

Bessie blew angrily through clenched teeth. 'Nothin',' she cried. 'It was just a flea!'

She draped the towel around her shoulders and unlocked the door. 'Now, get out o' my way,' she cried, pushing past Jenny, who was crouching on the floor. And she ran along to the bedroom where her clothes were mixed up with those of the children. As she rummaged in the communal wardrobe, she wished again that she could get a bedroom of her own. It was a nuisance having to sleep on the put-u-up in the living-room and having to keep her clothes in the kids' room. Oh, if only she could get a room of her own . . . a room with pale pink walls and a huge ivory and gold bed with pink silk drapery and a thick pink velvet carpet that her feet would sink into. Her little bare pink-toed feet that Ferdinand would say were like petals of roses. 'Oh, thou art lovely, Rose of Bourbon, lovelier than all your Bourbon lilies. . . . '

She put on her best frock. It was a simple grey frock that her mother had chosen for her, and it had been bought on the big side so that as she grew the hem could be let down. After her mother died, she and Mrs. Moore had sewn black cuffs and a black collar on it. Bessie stood in front of the mirror now, considering it. . . . She had wanted to buy a black dress, but Mrs. Moore had overruled her. 'Ye cannie afford it, lassie,' she had said. 'And this one will do fine. Yer puir ma wouldnie hae wanted ye to spend money uselessly.' Really, Mrs. Moore was the bloody limit. There hadn't been any question of expense the other day when she'd wanted to buy a kilt for Billy. It was a good job her father had put his foot down good and hard. 'There's no kilts comin' into this house,' he'd said. 'A kilt for Billy indeed! There's lots of things he'll need to get before he gets a kilt. Time enough for that when he joins the sodgers when his time comes.'

If only it had been a black frock . . . a slinky black velvet, cut low at the neck and without sleeves . . . or she could have had long floating black net sleeves over her bare white arms, and she could have had fine black tulle wound around her head and shoulders, and a diamond clip on her shoulder and diamond-clip ear-rings . . . just like Norma Shearer in yon picture . . . oh, it would have been lovely! She put one hand on her breast and half-closed her eyes, and she started to walk with a swaying motion from the dressing-table to the mirror of the wardrobe. It was just too bad she couldn't see her feet. That was the worst of this mirror, it wasn't long enough. When they went to Paris she would see that all the rooms had huge full-length mirrors on the walls so that you could see every bit of yourself. . . . She entered the throne-room, swaying voluptuously, her lips parted in a sensuous smile (or was it sensual? She wasn't very sure of the right word). 'Madame Royale de France!' The heralds blew their trumpets. And all the courtiers bowed low as she swept past them. . . .

'What are ye walkin' like that for, Bessie?'

Bessie sighed impatiently. 'Is that you again?'

'What are ye walkin' like that for?' Jenny sidled into the

room. 'Show me, Bessie, show me how to walk like that. See, is this the way?'

'No, it's not the way,' Bessie snapped. 'Here, get out o' ma road and let me get on wi' ma dressin'. The Doctor 'll be here any minute.'

She brushed her hair and then she combed it, trying to get it to lie as much like Greta Garbo's as possible. 'Damn!' she muttered, and she took the comb again and combed it a different way. Maybe if she put it the way Alice Faye had hers in *Alexander's Rag-Time Band*. . . . No, that wouldn't do. It was better like this.

Och to hell, that would just have to do! It looked better than it had been before, anyway. She put down the brush and comb and rushed into the living-room. She started to rummage among the pile of old papers that Jenny had been playing with that forenoon. It had been here this morning. Where could it have got to?

'Here, Jenny!' she cried. 'Did you see ma auld red exercise-book here when ye were playin' amongst thur papers?'

'What excise-book?'

'A school book,' Bessie said. 'The one I sometimes draw in for you.'

'Oh, are you goin' to draw me somesing, Bessie?'

'No, I'm not. I've got more to do.'

'Well, I'll not tell you where it is.'

'Where is it?' Bessie demanded, shaking Jenny's shoulder. 'Come on! Tell me where it is, quick!'

'I'll tell ye if ye draw me somesing,' Jenny said, putting out her lower lip in a determined way.

Bessie gave her an impatient shake. 'All right,' she said. 'I'll draw ye somethin' after—after the Doctor's been. But hurry up and get me the book first. I'm in a hurry.'

'Promise!' Jenny said, hanging back.

'All right, it's a promise.' Bessie put her hands on her hips and glared angrily at her. 'You little shithawk, I'd like to cuff yer ears for ye.'

But Jenny was quite undaunted. 'Cross your heart and hope you're dead if ye tell a lie?' she said.

81

'All right,' Bessie said. 'All *right*.'

Jenny wiped her nose on her sleeve and went behind the sofa. 'I hided it,' she said. 'I hided it from Billy.'

'Oh, hurry up!' Bessie cried. 'What are ye scufflin' about at down there?'

'It's not here,' Jenny wailed. 'I hided it here and it's no' here now. Billy must 'a' taken it. The wee buggis that he is.'

'Here, let me look.' Bessie flopped down beside the sofa and looked under it. 'You stupid wee tawpie!' she cried, reaching under the sofa. 'Here it is! Now, run away outside and play and I'll draw ye somethin' when ye come in.'

'No, draw me somesing right now.'

'When ye come in.'

'No, right now!'

Bessie flung the exercise-book on the table and swooped upon Jenny. 'I'll draw somethin' for you after you've been out to play,' she cried, seizing her by the shoulders and propelling her violently towards the door. 'If ye don't go out and play quietly I'll no' draw nothin'. I'll draw my hand across yer lug. So there!'

She banged the door behind Jenny, then heedless of the kicking and yelling that went on behind it, she picked up the exercise-book and went into the kitchenette. She glanced at the baby. He was still whimpering slightly, but it was nothing to worry about. She took hold of one corner of the book and tore off a good-sized piece of the red cover. The yelling from behind the outer door made her stop. Better close the kitchenette door in case that hulabaloo wakened the old man. . . .

Furtively she moistened the red cover with water, then she dabbed it quickly on her lips. She pushed her face close to the mirror. Ummm, it showed all right! She rubbed her upper lip with her forefinger. It wasn't as good as lipstick, still it did the trick a wee bit. . . .

She stood back to look at the effect. Not bad, Bessie, not bad! If that old cow of a District Nurse saw you now she wouldn't go about saying that the Hipkiss girl was just a slut. She'd see what kind of trick she took with the Doctor!

She picked up the exercise-book, and she began to turn the

pages slowly, reading little bits of the essays she'd written at school. 'If I were a Famous Actress' . . . Now, that was a good one! Miss Aitchison had read that out to the class. 'It shows a wealth of imagination. It has something that no other essay here has got. I wish you other girls would take an example from Bessie. . . .' But they hadn't—the bitches!— they'd just laughed at her and yelled after her: 'How long will it be now before we see yer name up in electric-lights, Ferret?' And then somebody had chalked on the walls of the girls' lavatory: The Whole Town's Talking About Bessie Kiss My Arse Who Is Starring In If You Know Of A Better Ole. . . .

7

'O H, it's you! I thought it was the Doctor!'

Bessie pulled open the door, and the weedy-looking young man in the blue suit hurried past her, saying: 'No, it's just the Insurance Man! I'm a day earlier than usual. I'm goin' to my brother's weddin' tomorrow, so I can't come then. And how's your health today, Miss Hipkiss?' he said, laying his note-book on the table and pulling out a pencil.

'Aw, I'm fine,' Bessie said, blushing.

'You're a great swell today! What are you all dolled up for? Goin' to a weddin', too?'

'No bloomin' fear,' she said. 'I wish I was.'

'One of these days, Miss Hipkiss! One of these days! Some lucky man 'll be leadin' you up to the altar one of these days!'

'Ach away!' Bessie giggled and went to the little red tin on the mantelpiece where she kept her insurance money.

'You never know your luck!' he laughed. 'Until a dead horse kicks you!'

'Ach away!' Bessie said.

'And how are the kiddies? And the baby?' He was writing quickly in the book all the time. And he scooped up the money she laid on the table, counted it rapidly and shoved it into his pocket, talking all the time. 'Baby gettin' any better? It's tough luck on you, Miss Hipkiss, having all those kids to look after. Still, you're thriving on it! You're blooming like a rose!'

'Ach away!' Bessie said.

'But you are,' he said. 'My word, you're getting more like Loretta Young every day! If I wasn't so busy runnin' round, takin' folk's money offen them, I'd ask ye out to the pictures!'

'Ach away!' Bessie giggled.

'We must go to the pictures some night!' He winked. 'If you can get somebody to look after the kids for you. That's a date now! I'll keep you in mind of it. Well, I must run, Miss Hipkiss, I've a lot to do today. See you next week!'

As he ran downstairs he shouted: 'Mind about that date for the pictures!'

'Ach away!' Bessie shouted.

She went to the mirror as soon as she'd closed the door. This was the first time the Insurance Man had ever called her 'Miss Hipkiss'. Gee, things were looking up! He wasn't a bad-like fellow either. Those pimples on his forehead spoiled him a wee bit, but for all that he wasn't bad. And he was nice and cheery. Always on the go, and with something funny to say to everybody.

She pursed her lips and patted her cheeks with her finger-tips. Really, she was looking quite fetching! It was wonderful what a bit of touching-up did. She must remember to get that lipstick and eyebrow pencil out of Woolies, and some powder. . . .

'Damn! This must be the Doctor this time!'

Doctor Henderson was not pleased with the baby at all. 'If he isn't any better by Saturday,' he said, 'I'm afraid we'll have to send him to the Sick Children's Hospital. I'll send the Nurse in tonight again, Mr. Hipkiss,' he said. 'There's something far wrong with the child. Of course, it was a premature birth . . .'

'Still,' he said as he went away, 'I wouldn't worry too much. We'll pull the little man through all right.'

8

BUT the baby did not get any better, and the following
Saturday it was taken to the Sick Children's Hospital where
it died on the Tuesday. 'Oh, the poor wee baby!' Bessie wailed.
'Oh, the poor wee thing!'

'Now, ye mustnie take on like that, Bessie,' Mrs. Moore
said. 'You cannie help the bairn bein' no' well and dyin'. It's
God's will.'

But Bessie wept and carried on hysterically. 'Oh, the poor
wee lamb!' she cried. 'Whatever would ma mother have said?
Oh, Ma, Ma, I didnie mean to do it. I tried to be kind to it.
Oh, Ma! Ma!'

'Now, Bessie, snap out o' it,' Mrs. Moore said briskly. 'It's
no' good for the other bairns to hear ye takin' on like this. Ye
couldnie help the bairn bein' no' well, and that's an end o' it.
Remember it was a Higher Hand. And remember the poor
wee bairn 'll be with your Ma now, up there in Heaven.'

That was the only comfort Bessie had; that the baby would
now be lying in her mother's arms away up there beyond the
clouds. It would be smiling happily, and her mother would be
looking down fondly at it the way she used to look at her. . . .

'Oh, Ma, I didnie mean to do it! Honest, I didnie, Ma. It
was just for a minute that I thought . . .'

Mrs. Moore said to Mrs. Finlayson: 'It's a good thing
Bessie has thae other bairns to take up her attention, otherwise I think she'd go clean daft. I'm surprised at her. I never
thought she was so fond o' the bairn. I aye felt that she didnie
like it. You'd hae thought she'd be pleased to get rid o' it,
wouldn't you?'

'Ah, but folk are funny,' Mrs. Finlayson said. 'You never
know what they're thinkin'. In fact, sometimes ye dinnie
know what ye're goin' to think yersel' until ye think it, and
then ye get a shock!'

'Ay, too true!' Mrs. Moore said. 'But mind, I'm awful glad Bessie has thae other two bairns to take up her attention.'

Bessie wasn't glad, however. Jenny and Billy were a great trial to her during the days before and after the funeral. They were intensely interested in the small white coffin, and Jenny howled with temper because she could not have one, too. 'I want to be put in a wee box like that and go and be an angel!' she screamed. Yet for all their questions about where the baby had gone, and their questions about Heaven and their wish to go there also, they acted as if the baby was still a member of the household. They kept referring to it, and occasionally Bessie would discover Jenny rocking the empty pram and saying to her, finger on lips: 'Shush now, Bessie, or ye'll waken the baby!'

Every time they mentioned it, Bessie felt guilty. She got into the habit of crossing herself whenever she thought of the dead child. She was so upset that she completely forgot all her plans to buy cosmetics out of Woolworth's, and her face became thinner and she had dark circles under her eyes. At nights she lay in bed, thinking of it, and she would enact the poisoning scene to herself again and again, widening and changing the background and her own personality every time. She was Lucrezia Borgia and she was Marguerite de Valois, and she was Madame de Maintenon, and she was Madame de Pompadour visiting Cagliostro . . . until finally she fell asleep, and then almost always she had nightmares. . . .

One of them kept recurring for weeks afterwards. In it she was standing at the living-room window, looking out at the street. But it was no longer the street as it normally was. The houses opposite had gone further away and had grown taller and wider. They looked now like enormous tombs. Processions of people were coming out of the entries, all clothed in long white robes and carrying harps and palm-branches. A high, thin tower had appeared in the centre of the street. There was an empty throne on top of it: a golden throne that glistened in the sunlight. The people were all moving towards this tower, singing and waving their arms. They crowded around the base, looking up in expectation. And all the time they sang hymns and cried 'Hallelujah!' Before long the square around the tower was crowded, and there was no room for anybody else. Suddenly the crowd became silent, gazing upwards. The golden throne gleamed even more brightly, but it remained empty. Bessie turned to go out and downstairs to join the throng. But she found Mrs. Moore standing beside her, blocking her way. 'I want to go down to the crowd,' Bessie said. But Mrs. Moore put her arms around her and held her back. 'No, Bessie, you can't go. You can't join that crowd. You've got to stay here and watch.' Mrs. Moore drew Bessie to the window again, and they stood there and looked down. Suddenly the crowd gave a tremendous shout, then they all fell on their knees, gazing upwards and crying with joy. Bessie looked up at the golden throne towering far above her and the grey roofs of the tenements. Jesus had appeared and was holding out his arms, blessing the people, before he sat down. Bessie turned again to go out. But Mrs. Moore held her back. 'No, Bessie, m'dear,' she said, 'you cannie go down there. You've got to stay here. You're too bad to go amongst all these people and listen to Jesus. You've got to stay here and watch. You're a sinner. . . .'

And as she struggled with Mrs. Moore, crying: 'Let me go! Let me go!' Bessie always awoke, weeping. . . .

PART III

1

ONE night about the middle of August Bert Hipkiss said:
'Bessie—er—I'm bringing a lady to tea on Sunday. She was
a great friend of your mother's—oh, years and years ago.
You've never seen her, and I don't expect you would ever 've
heard your mother speak about her. But they were great
friends years and years ago. She wants to see you and the
bairns. Her name's Miss Stevens, but you'd better call her
Auntie Mabel.'

'What time's she comin' at?' Bessie said.

'I'll bring her,' he said. 'About four o'clock, I expect.
You'd better tell the bairns she's comin'.'

'All right,' she said.

A great friend of my mother's, she said to herself. The chorus
is, believe it if you like. I bet Ma never saw her. Mabel Stevens
—I never heard Ma speak about her. No, you can't fool me,
my man.

'Yer Auntie Mabel's comin' on Sunday,' she said to Jenny
the following afternoon.

'Will she bring sweeties?' Jenny said.

'How should I know? Now, you stop playin' with the fringe
o' that table-cover! If you don't watch, ye'll have that vase
knocked over.'

'I will nut,' Jenny said, giving the table-cover a little tug to
show that everything was safe.

'What did I tell ye!' Bessie cried, darting forward and grabbing at the vase of flowers just too late to prevent it from
toppling over. 'Ye meddlesome wee brat! Why can ye no'
leave things alone? Ye're like yer faither; ye cannie leave well
alone. Away and get me a dish-cloot.

'Now,' she said, mopping up the water that was sopping into the table-cover. 'Away ye go outside and don't let me see yer ugly wee face until tea-time.'

But Jenny sat down on the little stool beside the fire. 'Tell me a story, Bessie, and I'll be good. I'll be as good as gold,' she said solemnly.

'Ach, yer granny!' Bessie said, wringing the wet cloth into a basin and carrying it into the kitchenette. 'I've heard that story before. I can't be bothered. I'm tired.'

'What are ye tired for, Bessie?'

'God knows,' Bessie said, filling the kettle and putting it on the gas-cooker. 'I'm tired, that's all.'

'Are ye goin' to make a fly-cup, Bessie?'

'Ay,' she said, picking up a book.

'Well, while you're waitin' on the kettle to boil you could tell me a story,' Jenny said. 'Just a wee story, Bessie hen.'

'No,' Bessie said, opening her book with determination. 'I'll tell you a story before you go to bed, and that's all.'

Jenny wheedled and whimpered, but Bessie stuck to her point. 'No story until bedtime,' she said. 'Now away ye go outside and let me read ma book in peace.'

Seeing that Bessie was quite determined, Jenny walked slowly to the door. She hovered there for two or three minutes with her hand on the handle. 'Well, can I get a cup o' tea first?' she said. 'If ye don't give me a cup o' tea, I'll tell Daddy you was makin' fly-cups, and then he'll give you what's what.'

'All right,' Bessie said, infusing the tea. 'I'll give ye a fly-cup, but if there's one sound out o' you—out you go on your ear!'

They sat for a while in silence, sipping their tea. Bessie skimmed quickly through the pages of *A Great Court Scandal* by William Le Queux. Boy, this was the life and no mistake! If only she had diamonds and jewels she could pawn after she ran away from her Royal husband. . . .

'Bessie!'

'Ay, what is it now?' she said irritably.

'I'll play at Auntie Mabel comin' to tea, and you've to ask me things. Ask me how my little girl is.'

'Auntie Mabel hasn't got a little girl,' Bessie said. 'Now, shuttup!'

There was silence again for two or three minutes. Then Jenny said: 'Is that your third cup, Bessie?'

'Ay,' she said. 'And what if it is?'

'Oh!' Jenny raised her eyebrows until they disappeared under her thick fringe of hair. 'Oh, you'll be doin' wizzies on yer breeks!'

'Tell me a story, Bessie,' she said after another interval. 'On and on and on with the story!'

'Look here,' Bessie said, laying down her book with a bang. 'What did I tell you? Didn't I say that if there was one more word about stories from you, out you'd go on your ear?'

'Just a wee story, Bessie!'

'Not even a wee story!'

Jenny pouted. 'Tell me a story,' she threatened. 'Or I'll break the windows!'

'Aw, you wouldnie do that, would ye?'

'I would sut,' Jenny said. 'I'll go outside and I'll pick up stones and I'll pick up bricks and I'll throw them up and they'll break the glass and hit ye on the head and you'll get your face all cut. So there!'

'All right.' Bessie sighed and she reached into the cupboard beside the fireplace for a picture-book.

'I dinnie want ye to read it,' Jenny cried. 'I want a story out of your mouth.'

'I'm tired. I'll tell ye a story out of my mouth at bedtime. I'll read one just now.'

'No,' Jenny said. 'Out of your mouth.'

'You're a wee pest.' Bessie put away the book with resignation. 'What kind o' story do ye want?'

Jenny lay on her stomach on the rug. 'About a witch. About a witch that steals little girls and boils them in a pot. Only, not me! Not me!'

'Ach, the witches are all away their holidays,' Bessie said. 'They're all away to Leven to see the pierrots like Dirty Minnie and her pal, Big Maggie Burns. I'll tell ye a story about somethin' else.

91

'Once upon a time,' she said, before Jenny could say any more, 'there was a good little girl called Evangeline, and Evangeline had beautiful fair hair and blue eyes and she had a white white skin without any freckles and she was terribly pretty. Well, one day Evangeline was asked to a party at Mrs. Moore's. She got a new pink dress for the occasion, and——'

'What's an occasion, Bessie?'

'Ach, shuttup and lissen to the story,' Bessie said. 'She got a new pink dress—no, it was blue to match her eyes, and she went to the party at seven o'clock. She knocked at the door and waited, but nobody came. And she knocked and knocked. But nobody came. That's funny, she said to herself, Mrs. Moore said the party was tonight at seven o'clock, what can have happened to her, I wonder? But just then she noticed the bell, so she rung it, and almost immediately Mrs. Moore came to the door. And Mrs. Moore was dressed in a red velvet frock with a string of pearls round her neck, and she had on a diamond tiara.'

'Our Mrs. Moore?' Jenny asked.

'Ay, of course. What Mrs. Moore do ye think it could be? Well, Mrs. Moore came to the door and she said in an awful posh voice: "Ah, Evangeline, there you are! The Duke was just asking if you weren't coming to the party." '

'What duke?' Jenny said.

'The Duke,' Bessie said. 'The Duke of—oh, the Duke of Windsor. If ye dinnie stop interruptin', I'll no' tell ye the story; I'll pack ye right down the stairs. "The Duke is expecting you in the anteroom," Mrs. Moore said, and she sailed away in front of Evangeline, sailing just like a duchess herself. So Evangeline went into the party, and there were crowds and crowds of folk there. . . . Little Jack Horner and Clark Gable and Tommy Tucker and Jack and Jill and Greta Garbo and Joan Crawford and Lily McGillivray and Lily McGillivray's sailor and the Insurance Man and . . . Jack the Ripper and Hitler and Mr. Churchill and President Roosevelt and Dirty Minnie and Big Maggie Burns and . . . who else? Oh, yes, Henry Hall and Rusty and Dusty Brown and Mr. Chamberlain and Joe Stalin and . . . and Mr. Chamberlain's Umbrella.

And almost at once Mr. Chamberlain asked Evangeline to dance with him, and they danced and danced, and then she danced with Mr. Chamberlain's Umbrella.'

'Did she?' Jenny opened her eyes wide.

'They danced and danced, and the band played *Umbrella, Umbrella, toorleayeay*. . . . And then Mrs. Moore presented prizes for the best dancers, and Mr. Chamberlain's Umbrella and Evangeline got the first prizes. They were fair away with themselves. And the Umbrella bowed and kissed Mrs. Moore's hand and said: "Thank you very much, madam, from the bottom of our hearts we thank you." '

'And from Henry's bottom, too!' Jenny cried.

'That 'll do ye now,' Bessie said in a shocked voice. 'Ye're not goin' to get to listen to Henry Hall's Band again if ye say things like that. That Oliver Wakefield should be shot!'

'On and on with the story,' Jenny said.

'So then Evangeline danced with Hitler. And what do ye think he said to her?'

'I don't know,' Jenny said. 'It's you that's tellin' the story.'

'He said: "I want peace, peace, peace!" ' Bessie did her best to impersonate a popular radio comedian's impersonation of the Führer. ' "I want a piece of this, I want a piece of that." '

'Bessie,' the little girl said solemnly. 'I want a piece, too. If you give me a piece I'll tell you a story.'

'No, you're not gettin' a piece. You're gettin' nothin' to eat until tea-time. You're just a wee Hitler, that's what you are.'

'I am nut!' Jenny opened her mouth wide. 'I'll scream if you say I am, and I'll waken the baby.'

Bessie sighed and looked at the clock. Half-past three. It was too late now to send Jenny to the matinée at the nearest cinema. 'Well, let me think,' she said. 'Evangeline danced with Winston Churchill and then she danced with Jack the Ripper and then they all went in to supper, and they had pink icecream and jellies and——'

'Sweeties!' Jenny cried.

'Ay, sweeties,' Bessie said. 'Lots and lots o' sweeties. And meringues and cream-cookies and—oh, lots of other things.'

'And then they played games,' Jenny said, gazing into the

93

fire. 'They played hide the thimble and blind man's buff and—what else did they play, Bessie?'

'You tell me,' Bessie said.

'No, you!'

'They all went home,' Bessie said.

She rose and took her purse from the drawer of the living-room table. 'Here's a penny,' she said. 'Away ye go and buy some sweeties for yersel'. And if ye tell Billy I'll—I don't know what I'll do to ye!'

Jenny took the penny, but she hung back at the door. 'If you give me twopence, that would be better,' she said. 'I could buy choklit then.'

'Away ye go!' Bessie cried. 'Leave me in peace for any favour!'

And she took Jenny by the shoulders and thrust her out.

She went back to the fire and picked up her book, but after a few lines she stopped reading. The runaway Archduchess and her jewellery had ceased to charm her for the moment. She crouched on her stool, gazing into the fire, wondering what this Mabel Stevens woman would be like. . . .

2

MARIE-ELISABETH DE FRANCE, Duchess de Bourbon-Parma, Princess de Cleves, sat in her sitting-room in the Palace of the Louvre. She tapped the ivory floor impatiently with one slender foot. She looked at a small ivory and gold clock on the table beside her, then she held up one aristocratic white wrist and examined her diamond wristlet-watch. Ten past seven . . .

There was a knock at the door, and her Lady-in-Waiting, Countess Lili de Gillivray, entered and curtsied. 'Milady Stevens, your Royal Highness,' she announced.

'You are late, milady,' Madame Royale said, without rising from her chair.

The foreign courtesan flushed as she curtsied. She was a bold-looking woman of about forty, with sleek dark hair and a pale oval face. Marie-Elisabeth glanced at her swinging ear-rings, and her lips twisted sarcastically. How like a gipsy this woman was! And how like her poor, weak father to fall for the cheap charms of such a woman!

'I sent for you, madame,' she said languidly. 'I wish you to leave France immediately.'

Milady Stevens blanched. 'But, your Royal Highness, why —what have I done?'

'This affair has gone on long enough, milady,' said Madame Royale. 'It is time to stop. You will leave Paris tonight.'

'Oh, will I?' The courtesan suddenly showed her true colours. 'Will I? We'll see what your father has to say about that!'

'His Majesty will not be consulted,' Madame Royale said with dignity. 'Everything is arranged, milady. Here is your passport and the necessary visas. You will be taken straight from here to the Gare du Nord. You can choose whether you wish to return to England or whether you care to go to Switzerland or any other country. But you will certainly not be allowed to set foot on the soil of France again.'

'You little bitch!' Milady's face mottled with fury. 'You scheming little bitch! Don't think you can get away with this! I'll go straight to the King just now, and I'll tell him everything.'

'La! La!' Marie-Elisabeth de France laughed. 'So the gipsy is still a gipsy under the skin! Set a beggar on horseback, milady, and she will ride to the devil! Be careful, milady! Remember you are speaking to a Princess of the Blood Royal and not to one of your companions in a brothel.'

Madame Royale rose and pressed a bell. 'The car is waiting at the side entrance, milady. You will be conducted there by the Swiss Guards. I shall make all arrangements for sending your baggage after you. Perhaps you will be good enough to leave me an address? No doubt you do not wish your effects to be sent to that dive in Marseilles that you came from!'

Milady broke into a torrent of oaths. Her sallow fingers plucked at the skirts of her gaudy dress. Marie-Elisabeth watched her, smiling triumphantly. 'Enough, madame!' she cried, when the courtesan's fury was beginning to abate. 'Any more of your vile language and I shall have you committed to the Bastille. You had better choose between a cold, damp cell there and a safe conduct to another country.'

The Countess Lili de Gillivray entered. 'The car awaits, your Royal Highness.'

Milady Stevens' face twisted with rage and fear when she saw the guard of soldiers waiting in the corridor behind the Lady-in-Waiting. 'Your Royal Highness,' she said in a pleading tone. 'Your Royal Highness, don't . . .'

'Go, madame!' Marie-Elisabeth pointed majestically to the door. 'Your day in France is over!'

The courtesan staggered for a second, then she drew herself up and hissed through clenched teeth: 'You win, Madame Royale, but I will repay!' Then she turned and walked rapidly from the room.

Marie-Elisabeth de France gave a low, mocking laugh. She watched the door close behind the Modern Pompadour, then she sighed with relief and turned to the window. Below her, the gardens of Versailles stretched as far as eye could see. A lily pond gleamed in the twilight, its surface like green glass in the sheen of the rising moon. Marie-Elisabeth threw back her shoulders proudly. She walked slowly to the mirror and stood for a long time, looking at her reflection. She saw a tall, slender girl dressed in black velvet trimmed with silver lamé, looking back serenely at her. She crossed herself, and the girl in the mirror crossed herself also. And she smiled, conscious of having done a good evening's work. The name of Marie-Elisabeth de Bourbon would go down into History. She had saved France.

3

MISS MABEL STEVENS was a bit like Glenda Farrell on the pictures, only not so good-looking. She was an old woman, about thirty: not just as old as Bessie had imagined, but old enough. She wore a checked costume, and she had a pair of cute, green, clip ear-rings and a green necklace to match. Bessie would have liked to examine them closely, but she was determined not to look at Miss Stevens any more than she could help. She was furious at Billy and Jenny for the way they crowded around her, pawing her necklace and her handbag. Jenny swaggered about with the bag for a while, then she sat on the floor and opened it. 'Jenny!' cried Bessie. 'You leave Miss Stevens' bag alone or I'll—I'll hamstring you!'

'It's all right.' Miss Stevens' grin was like one of those advertisements for Have You Macleaned Your Teeth Today. 'She's not doing any harm. There's nothing in the bag she can break.'

'Still, she should leave it alone,' Bessie said. 'You heard what I told ye, Jenny Hipkiss!'

'Give Auntie Mabel back her bag, sweetheart,' Bert said cajolingly.

'I'm just playin' wis it,' Jenny said, opening her eyes very wide. 'I won't hurt it. Honest I winnie!'

'Give it back to Auntie Mabel, there's a nice wee girl,' Bert said. 'If you do—well, Daddy's got something for a good girl!'

'What?'

Jenny stopped rummaging in the bag, but she still held on to it. 'What have you got? Let me see,' she said cunningly.

'No, after you give Auntie Mabel back her bag.'

'Let me see first,' she said.

Bert laughed and pulled several bars of chocolate out of his pocket. Jenny dropped the bag and swooped upon him. 'I want a whole bar!' she yelled.

Bessie frowned with exasperation. The soft cratur' that he was, letting that kid take a loan of him. He was just spoiling her, that was what he was doing; and it was she who had to bear the brunt of it. He did not know what a little bitch Jenny could be sometimes. He saw her only occasionally, and then she was aye as sweet as honey to him. It was a pity he wasn't forced to look after her for a whole week and have to put up with her tantrums. That would learn you, my man! I just wish I could be ill and have to take to my bed, and then you'd see how you'd get on! I wonder if you'd be as sweet and nice-auntie then! Of course, he was just showing off before Miss Stevens. Doing the gentle parent act. He'd been as nice as ninepence to them all ever since he'd come in.

As for this Auntie Mabel stuff, it was getting on her nerves. Though it was fairly taking a trick with the bairns. Billy was sitting on Miss Stevens' knee, playing with her necklace, his head cooried in her flat bosom. 'Me would like a string of beads like this,' he lisped.

'What would you do with a string o' beads, you big jessie! All the other wee laddies would laugh at ye!' Bessie jeered, and she rattled the chairs towards the table, trying to vent her annoyance on something. 'Tea's ready. Sit in!'

'Will you sit here, Mabel?' Bert drew out the chair at the head of the table. 'You'd better pour out, and give Bessie a rest for once. I'm sure she's tired attending to us all!'

'No, I think we'll let Bessie be hostess as usual.' Miss Stevens smiled at the sulky girl.

But Bessie did not smile back. She sat down in her accustomed place at the head of the table without another word. So he thought he'd try that game, did he? Well, he wasn't going to get away with it if she could help it. There was time enough if he married this Stevens woman for her to give up her mother's place. She wasn't giving it up a minute sooner than she needed.

'Do you take sugar, Miss Stevens?' she said politely.

'Yes, please, dear.' Miss Stevens sat down beside Jenny, making a great fuss about helping her on to her chair and pushing it into the table. 'And remember—Auntie Mabel after this!' She smiled at Bessie as she took her cup.

'Billy, you put that bar o' choklit away until after tea,' Bessie snapped. 'Don't you dare take another bite! Look, Pa! Lookit him! He'll never be able to take his tea.'

'Billy!' Bert leaned forward, smiling. 'Put the chocolate away just now, like a good boy.'

'I'm just goin' to take one more bite.' Billy took an enormous mouthful, grinning from his father to Miss Stevens. Bert shrugged and sat back. 'Well, my wee doo!' he smiled at Jenny. 'Are you going to eat a big tea tonight? You'll show your Auntie Mabel what a good eater you are, won't you?'

He was lifting the plate of bread to offer it to Miss Stevens when Bessie said: 'Will you say the Grace, Pa?'

She bristled with triumph while her father muttered the Grace quickly. It wasn't the way she'd have liked to have had it said, but it was better than nothing. It let that Stevens woman see, anyway, that they'd been well brought up. I bet she's never heard a Grace in her life before, she thought. She looks a right fast-like piece.

'You'd think Daddy was tellin' God a secret, wouldn't ye, from the way he says the Grace?' Billy cried, and he sniggered, as if being modest at his own cleverness.

Normally Bessie would have felt like hitting him a clump on the side of the head, but today she was glad of his comment. So he'd remembered what their mother had once said, had he? That was a good thing. She herself would never forget how her mother had always upbraided her father about the way he mumbled the Grace and about the quarrels there had always been when he'd had to say it.

All through tea Auntie Mabel did her best to bring Bessie into conversation, but the girl held back. She wasn't having any, thank you! Maybe Miss Stevens could take a trick with Jenny and Billy, but she couldn't with her. There were no flies on her, no sir! She knew fine that her father had only brought this woman here to show her his family before proposing to her. All this pretending that Miss Stevens had been a friend of their mother's when she was young and that she was anxious to see poor Margaret's children. . . . No, it wouldn't wash! She knew better, or her name wasn't Bessie Hipkiss.

And I wish to God it wasn't, she said fiercely to herself, watching her father take a sup of tea to wash down an enormous mouthful. She clenched her teeth on the edge of her cup and looked into her tea in order not to show her annoyance. If Miss Stevens still felt romantic about him after seeing the way he behaved at a meal—well, she was welcome to him! He ate

99

like a pig. Though honest to goodness a pig would have had better manners.

Mind you, he wasn't bad-looking. All dolled up in his Sunday sports-jacket and grey flannels he looked a bit like Ronald Colman, only a lot more common-like than Ronald, of course. Ronald was a gentleman. After all, her father was only thirty-five. Lots of people would consider him to be still a young man, she supposed.

Bert belched, then he grinned and said: 'Excuse me!'

Bessie clenched her hands under the tablecloth. He was that common! Fancy, if he was to do that at a dinner-party in the Louvre when Hitler and Mr. Chamberlain and the King of Spain were there! She leaned forward and hissed: 'Jenny, if you don't stop making such a mess with your bread, you won't get a cake.'

After tea, Bert switched on the radio, saying: 'It's nearly time for the six o'clock news. I wonder if the war's any nearer. Things are looking gey bad. I doubt we're in for it before very long now.'

'Surely not, Bert,' Miss Stevens said. 'Hitler would never dare go to war.'

'It's not Hitler we've to depend upon,' Bert said, lighting a cigarette. 'There are a lot of Hitlers in this country. A lot of greasy auld money-grubbers that don't need to go and fight themselves but are willing to send others to fight for them. For King and Country!'

The News started, but nobody could hear the radio because of the noise the children were making. Billy and Jenny were scrambling all over Miss Stevens, fighting to sit on her lap. Eventually Jenny won, and she said:

'Do you have a little girl, Auntie Mabel?'

'No, dear.' Miss Stevens smiled down at her. 'Your poor Auntie Mabel has no little girl. Would you like to be my little girl?'

Jenny drew her brows together meditatively. 'Do you know any stories?' she said.

Miss Stevens smiled across at Bert. 'Yes, I know a lot of stories!'

'Tell me one,' Jenny commanded, nestling against Miss Stevens. 'Tell me a story about a witch.'

'No, tell us a story about lions and tigers and cowboys,' Billy said, sitting on the arm of her chair and burrowing his head into her shoulder.

'I'll tell you a story after I've helped Bessie to wash the dishes,' Miss Stevens said.

'That's all right,' Bessie said quickly. 'I'll manage the dishes fine myself.'

'No, I'll help you, dear.'

'No, you tell the bairns a story,' Bessie said. 'It 'll be a treat for me not to have to tell them one.'

Miss Stevens protested, but Bessie was firm. She wasn't having this woman plaistering about in her kitchenette. Let her entertain the bairns. Let them see what a bad story-teller she was, and then they wouldn't be so keen on her! Emptying Rinso into the water and swirling it round until she got a nice lacy lather, Bessie listened through the half-open door to Miss Stevens begin the story of Goldilocks and the Three Bears. She smiled sarcastically. No, you'll need to go one better than this, dear Auntie Mabel, if you want to get them to like you! Bessie looked at herself in the mirror above the sink, and slowly she closed one eye. . . .

La! La! Milady Stevens, you are a veree clever woman, but you are not as clever as Anne-Marie, Duchess de Bourbon-Braganza! The children of the Blood Royal are not such fools as to be taken in by your cheap fairy stories. They 'ave ze intelligence, madame!

She swept one lace-covered arm contemptuously in the air. 'Your stories will not win them, madame! They are not such fools as their poor deluded father!'

'Hell!' Bessie whispered, and she took the dish-cloth and wiped the froth of soap-suds off the mirror.

4

AFTER her father had gone to escort Miss Stevens home, Bessie started to get the children ready for bed.

'I dinnie want to go to ma bed!' Jenny wailed. 'I want a story first.'

'Ye've already had a story,' Bessie cried. 'Miss Stevens tellt ye a lot o' stories.'

'Ach her!' Billy said.

'I want one of your stories, Bessie,' cried Jenny. 'I want a *real* story.'

Bessie tried not to look triumphant. 'But Miss Stevens told ye a lot of stories,' she said. 'What's wrong with her stories? Haven't ye had enough for one day?'

'Ach, her stories were daft,' Billy said. 'They were just stories for kids. I want a real story.'

'So do I,' Jenny said.

'Well then,' Bessie said, pretending to sigh with exasperation, although she felt elated. 'What kind o' story do ye want?'

'About an elyphunt,' Billy said.

'All right then.' Bessie considered for a moment. 'Once upon a time there was an elyphunt, a wee pink elyphunt, and his name was Pompo Prettybum.'

'What a funny name!' Billy sniggered. 'Prettybum!'

'Yes, it's a funny name,' Bessie said, 'and poor wee Pompo didn't like it at all. But it was his father's name, so he just had to like it or lump it. Poor wee Pompo's Mammy was dead, and Pompo's Daddy wanted to marry a witch. Oh, she was a terrible bad witch, but Pompo's Daddy was that blind that he couldn't see how bad she was. She was a wicked, wicked witch and she wore green ear-rings and a green necklace——'

'Like Auntie Mabel?' Jenny cried.

'Ay, just like Auntie Mabel,' Bessie said, and she went to a drawer in the dresser and took out a bag of sweets. 'I was

goin' to keep these until the morn—I thought ye'd had plenty
o' sweeties for one day—but seein' ye're such good wee bairns
I'll let ye have some tonight.'

'Well,' she continued, 'this witch didn't like poor wee
Pompo at all. All she wanted was Pompo's Daddy, and as
soon as she had got married to him, she put poor wee Pompo
out into the cold. She shut the door on him. Poor wee Pompo
stood and shivered, and then he ran into the jungle to see if
he could get warm there. Poor wee Pompo wasn't any bigger
than Jenny here, and he had great big red eyes. They were like
saucers and they used to gleam at nights like motor-car lights
when he went through the jungle. He lived in the middle of
a great big jungle, in the middle of a great big forest, in a wee,
wee cave. And every night he used to go through the forest,
looking for food. And it was aye that dark in the jungle that
nobody could see Pompo. Except his eyes. They gleamed and
gleamed like great big red rubies.'

'What's a ruby, Bessie?' asked Jenny.

'Be quiet and lissen to the story,' Bessie said. 'Well, one
night when Pompo was crawling through the jungle the witch
saw him. The witch was sitting on top of a tree, waiting for
something to turn up. You see, by this time the wicked, wicked
witch had given Pompo's Daddy the go-by. She had killed
him with a big nail—she'd driven it right through the poor
silly man's skull. And she was on her own again. She was
sitting on top of this tree. And she saw Pompo's red eyes
coming towards her, and at first she thought it was a motor-
car, but she remembered that there was a practice blackout
that night and that all motor-car lights had to be shaded, so
she wondered what it could be. And she fair got the wind up,
I can tell you. But she sat tight and waited. And when Pompo
was underneath her she saw that it was nothing but a wee
elephant. So she jumped right down on top of Pompo's back,
and she hit him a crack with her broomstick and cried "Gee
up!" Poor Pompo was that amazed that he didn't know what
to do. He just stood. Then when the witch went on whacking
him he began to gallop. And he galloped and galloped until
he was fair out of breath. Then he stopped. The witch hit him

another crack and cried "Gee up," but poor wee Pompo was that tired that he couldn't gee up. So the witch jumped offen his back and she said a few magic words to her broomstick. Tiddletiddleeedeedee! And then she grabbed Pompo by one of his big lugs and the broomstick soared away up in the air with the witch on its back and trailing poor Pompo after it. Pompo was fair terrified. He didnie like sailing through the air at all. But he just had to put up with it, for the witch had a hold of him. They flew on and on and on, then they came to a big white cloud, and the broomstick landed on the cloud. And there was a high silver castle—all silver towers and gleaming red windows—in the middle of the cloud, and the broomstick flew right up to it and landed at the foot of the silver stairs. And the witch jumped off and hauled poor Pompo right up the silver stairs, bumpetty-bump, bumpetty-bump, singing *Here Comes the Galloping Major*. And his poor wee bottom was all black and blue as though somebody had leathered him. And the witch pulled him through the high silver door and they went into a great long hall, and away at the far end of the hall there was an ogre sitting at a table, counting his money. A great big ogre with orange hair and blue eyes, taller than this tenement. He was twice as tall as this tenement. And when he saw the witch he laughed like anything and said: "What have you brought me this time, Witch Blacknose? I hope you've brought me something good, for I'm awful wanting something good to eat." But when he saw the wee pink elephant he stopped laughing and roared: "What's this you've brought me? What kind of meal do you think this 'll make for any giant? A wee skinny thing like this. I could swallow it in one bite." But the witch laughed and said: "You can easy fatten it up if you keep it long enough. It's the best thing I could get. I couldn't get any wee boys or girls now that most of them are getting so clever, like that wee Jenny and Billy McSquirt. You'll just have to put up with this. And now I want my pay!" And she held out her long claws for the money. But the giant argued and argued with her because she hadn't delivered the goods. At last, however, he gave in. He gave her three pounds, and she put it in her pouch. "Well, ta-ta the now," she said. "I'll be back next week. I hope I'll have something better for you then." And she gave poor wee Pompo a dig in the ribs with her long skinny fingers and went away laughing. Then the giant lifted Pompo up on the palm of his great muckle hand and looked at him and said: "What a wee shaver ye are! I could swallow ye in one bite. I must put ye in a cage and fatten ye up before I eat ye." And he did. It was a great big cage, and poor wee Pompo was awful lonely in it, and every day the giant shoved in beef and tatties and stuff for Pompo to eat, and every day he took him out on the palm of his hand to see if he was getting any fatter. And Pompo was getting a bit fatter. Soon the giant had to hold him on his two palms, and he said: "Another week and you'll be almost big enough for me to eat." So poor Pompo got more and more worried, and he wished he was safely back in his wee cave in the jungle.'

The children were gazing at her, too intent to make any sound. Bessie herself was a bit carried away by the story. Her voice rose and fell. She roared like the giant, and she spoke in a weak, trembling voice when she was trying to get under the skin of the little elephant.

'Then one day,' she whispered dramatically, 'the giant forgot to lock the door of poor Pompo's cage. Pompo discovered it when he was searching round the bars with his trunk, trying to see if he could squeeze through. He was fair excited. He looked to see what the giant was doing, and he saw that he was in the other room, fast asleep. Pompo could just see one of his great big feet sticking out. So very, very quietly Pompo opened the cage-door and he stepped out on to the table. It was an awful big table. It would stretch from here to Harrisfield Pier. It must have been a mile wide. Pompo ran across it, and when he came to the edge and looked over he saw that the floor was miles and miles below him. He walked all round the table, but he couldn't see any way of getting down, and he began to get sadder and sadder. "Oh, what am I going to do?" he cried. "I want to go home." Just then he saw a fly crawling on the table, so he said: "Could you please help me, Mr. Fly? Tell me how I'll get down from this horrible table."

The fly was a good fly, and he said: "Well, if you like I'll give you some of the glue offen my wings." So he did, and Pompo smeared it on his paws, and then he found he was able to crawl down the table-leg just like the fly. He was terrible pleased. He ran as fast as he could across the great hall and out of the high door and down the silver steps, aye looking back to see if the giant had wakened and was following him. But the giant was still sleeping, and Pompo scampered across the great white cloud until he came to the edge. And then he stopped at the edge of the cloud and wondered how he was ever going to get down. It was all very well getting on to it. He had come on the witch's broomstick. But getting off it again was another matter!'

'What did he do, Bessie?' Billy whispered. 'Did an airyplane come for him?'

'Just a minit till I think,' Bessie snapped. 'Is it you or me that's tellin' the story?'

She rose and put some more coals on the fire. 'Well then,' she said. 'We'll go back to the forest. Down in the forest something stirred! And do you know what it was that stirred? It was wee Pompo's pal, Jeremiah the tiger. He was creeping through the jungle, wondering what had happened to Pompo. He was awful, awful sad, for he missed Pompo like anything. He had nobody else to play dominoes with. And as he was crawling along, something hit him on the head! And do you know what it was? It was a great chunk of white cloud, and on it was printed *HELP, I am stranded on this cloud, your pal Pompo.* Jeremiah looked up and he saw the great big white cloud high up above the forest, and right at the edge of it there was a wee pink dot, and the wee pink dot seemed to be waving. So Jeremiah took out his telescope and when he put it to his eye he saw Pompo waving down to him like anything. Jeremiah scratched his head with his tail, wondering what he should do. And then he minded there was an aerodrome at the edge of the jungle, so he ran towards it as fast as he could. There was a plane just getting ready to take off, so Jeremiah jumped into it and sat down behind the pilot. And when the pilot looked round and saw a tiger just behind him he near fainted. But Jeremiah said: "Dinnie be feared. I winnie hurt ye. I just want ye to fly up to that big white cloud and rescue my wee chum, Pompo Prettybum. He seems to be stranded." And so the pilot did as he was bid, for it wasn't safe to argue with a real live tiger.'

'And so they rescued poor wee Pompo,' Bessie said, looking at the clock. 'And they lived happily ever after, him and Jeremiah playin' in the jungle.'

'And now it's time for yer beds,' she said.

'No, no,' Jenny cried. 'On and on with the story!'

'I'm goin' out to play with Jackie McGillivray,' Billy cried, rising and making for the door.

'You are nut,' Bessie cried, rushing between him and the door. 'It's half-past eight. You're goin' straight to yer bed, my man.'

'I am nut,' he yelled. 'Get out o' ma road, Ferret-face! Scram!'

'I'll scram ye!' Bessie cried, catching him by the shoulders and shaking him. 'Come on, away to yer beds at once!'

'Who do ye think you're givin' orders to?' he roared in a man-like voice. 'I'm no takin' orders from you.'

'I'm no' goin' to ma bed till I get another story,' Jenny screamed. 'If you don't tell us another story I'll yell and yell and yell till I wake the baby. Then I'll hit the baby! I'll hit it on the head and kill it. I'll stick pins in its eyes.'

'Aw, ye wouldnie do that to the poor wee baby,' Bessie said plaintively. 'A nice wee lassie like you.'

'I'm no' a nice wee lassie,' Jenny yelled. 'I want to be bad. I'm goin' to be BAD!'

'Well, ye can be as bad as ye like in yer bed, ye wee bitch!' Bessie cried, seizing her and rushing her towards the bathroom. 'I've had enough of both of ye for one day. I want some peace now.'

5

IT was not until after the children were asleep and she was lying in bed reading that Bessie remembered Jenny's threat to hit the baby. Consciously dramatic, she laid aside her book and crossed herself. Then she stared for several minutes, her eyes stretched widely, at the ceiling, muttering: 'Oh, the poor wee baby, the poor wee thing . . .'

Whether it was due to the unnatural contraction of her eyelids or to genuine emotion, in a little while tears formed and began to trickle down her cheeks. She turned abruptly and buried her face in the pillow. 'Oh, the poor wee baby,' she whispered, clenching her fists and beating the pillow.

For about ten minutes she abandoned herself to an orgy of sobbing, then as if a film-director had shouted 'Cut!' she stopped and dried her eyes and cheeks.

Princesses don't cry, you muckle gowk, she told herself. The baby's dead and that's an end of it. The poor wee thing's better away. If it were still here, that would just be an added excuse for him to marry that woman. He'd play the motherless bairns angle to death then. But seeing the baby's away, it's not so easy for him. Or for her either! The painted bitch with her green ear-rings. They don't need to think they took me in with all their soft soap. I know fine she was just here to see what way the land lies. But she's not coming here if I can help it. If she comes—well, that 'll be my cue to get out. . . . But she'll not come. She wouldn't dare. Or if *she* dares, he wouldn't dare bring her. He's got me to contend with. And Elisabeth-Marie de Bourbon is a pretty hefty obstacle, believe me. So you think, mon cher Papa, that you will sweep aside your family and your government and marry this cocotte from the Paris gutters? La, la! I'll have you certified first, you fool.

'Yes, I'll have you certified, you fool!' she hissed, bending

108

over his chair, her eyes blazing as brightly as the diamonds on her black velvet gown. 'The Prime Minister and the Archbishop of Paris are on my side. We can easily force you to abdicate in favour of Guillaume. And then I shall be virtually Queen of France!'

Robert de Bourbon squirmed in his chair as he looked up at this termagant of a daughter. 'You would not dare, Marie,' he whispered, gnawing at his finger-tips. 'You would not dare.'

'Would I not?' she hissed. And she folded her arms tightly across her bosom, her long white fingers gripping the black elbows of her dress, tapping an impatient tattoo (like Greta Garbo in yon picture, what was it called, something about South America, that I saw her in years and years ago). 'Would I not?' Madame Royale repeated. 'Remember, my dear papa, that I am a descendant of Catherine de Medici and Marguerite de Valois. What they dared, I would dare too. Only I would dare more, for I have more to gain. And the Archbishop and the Prime Minister would help me. Remember what happened to Edward VIII of England—he who was so secure and so well-beloved—yes, remember him! And what happened to him when he wanted to marry a commoner! And Madame Simpson, remember, was a lady in comparison with this cocotte!'

'That is the Archbishop's car arriving now,' she said. 'Do you want to renounce this woman, or do you want to make a declaration of abdication from the steps of Notre Dame?'

She blew a cloud of cigarette-smoke towards the ceiling. 'Make up your mind quickly, cherie. His Eminence will be mounting the great staircase at this moment.'

Robert de Bourbon gripped the arms of his chair. His head was sunk on his breast, his face pale and haggard. 'You unnatural daughter!' he groaned.

Marie de France twisted her mouth sarcastically. 'No, Papa, I am not an unnatural daughter. It is you who are an unnatural father. Years ago in Edinburgh when we were still in exile, after my poor mamma died, you sacrificed me then to your ambitions. You are not going to sacrifice me a second time. I know what would happen if you married Milady

Stevens. France would rise and drive us out again. I will not have that. You must abdicate first in favour of Guillaume. I shall rule France until he comes of age.'

'And then I shall poison him,' she said to herself.

'What do you mean, girl? When have I ever sacrificed you?'

Marie leaned against the small inlaid table and looked contemptuously at her scarlet finger-nails. 'You have a conveniently short memory, mon Papa,' she hissed. 'Do you not remember that when my poor mother died you took me away from school and tried to make a servant out of me? You are a true Bourbon, Papa! You are like the others; you 'ave forgotten nothing and learned nothing! You were like Abraham then, Papa—you sacrificed your daughter! Although it was his son Abraham sacrificed, it comes to the same thing. Son or daughter, what does it matter, the sacrifice is still the same. And the victim is a human being. You must be like Abraham in another thing now, Papa, you must really and truly become the Father of your People.'

Ay . . . and Abraham sacrificed his son Isaac . . . just in the same way as her father had sacrificed her. She was Abraham's daughter right enough. But she wasn't going to go on being Abraham's daughter. Not pygmalion likely! She was going to get out of here. She was right fed up cooking and washing dirty dishes and taking care of those brats of bairns. She was going to light out, or her name wasn't—well, it wasn't Bessie Hipkiss, anyway. Or if it was, it wouldn't be for long. She was right fed up with her name and with everything else.

By this time real tears were streaming down her face, and she buried her head in the pillow, carried away by the emotions her imagination had conjured.

She was still sobbing when she heard her father's key in the door. Hurriedly she dried her eyes on the sheets and pulled them over her head. But she could not restrain a sniff as her father came into the kitchen. He came over and pulled the clothes back gently from her face. 'You'll smother yourself, lassie,' he said.

'Hello,' he said, looking at her swollen eyelids. 'Been greeting? What's wrong?'

'I—I've got the toothache,' she muttered.

'Awful bad?'

'Terrible,' she said.

He patted her shoulder. 'We must get somethin' for it. A wee thing whisky should help it.'

He went into the kitchenette and returned in a few seconds with some whisky and hot water in a tumbler. 'Drink this now,' he said. 'Joogle it over into your tooth and see if that 'll not help it. I doubt you'd better go to the dentist.'

'No,' she said quickly. 'No, it 'll be all right by mornin'.'

He stood back, watching her as she sipped the toddy. 'That any better?' he said.

'Uhuh.' She handed back the glass and snuggled down again.

He stood awkwardly, playing with the glass. 'I hope it 'll not bother ye through the night,' he said. 'Well—good night, Bessie!'

'Good night, Da,' she said.

6

'I SEE that Hipkiss is courtin' again,' Mrs. Moore said to the other women at the Store Van.

'He's not waited long, has he?' Mrs. Finlayson said.

'Och, hot blood!' Mrs. Moore tittered.

'Still, it's the best thing that could happen,' she said, placing her Store Book on the counter at the back of the van. 'Thae bairns need some woman-body to look after them. Mind you, I'm sorry for Bessie—she's a willin' cratur'—but she's not able to manage them. They just take a loan o' her.'

'Ay, she's aye been a bit soft,' Mrs. Finlayson said. 'With that vacant stare.'

'She's aye such a ticket, too,' Mrs. Stout said. 'She's got no pride in her appearance at all.'

'Well, she's not been so bad lately, I've noticed,' Mrs. Moore said. 'No, no, give the lassie her due. I must say she's been tittivatin' hersel' up a bit. Not that it was afore time, and she's still got a long way to go!'

'Whisht, here she comes now!' Dirty Minnie whispered.

They watched Bessie come out of the entry and saunter aimlessly down the path towards them. 'Hurry up, hen!' Mrs. Moore called. 'Or ye'll lose yer place in the queue.'

'There's no danger of you doin' that, anyway,' the Vanman said. 'B'God, I hardly get my horn tooted afore ye're fleein' out the door as if a pack o' wolves was after ye!'

'I've aye been an early bird!' she guffawed.

'I bet ye never tellt yer man that,' he said. 'Or he'd 'a' had somethin' to say to ye!'

'Less o' yer impiddence,' she said. 'My man's not a worm, whatever else he is!'

Bessie leaned lackadaisically on the railing, swinging her basket against her leg, while she waited for her turn to be served. She was right fed up. She'd just been having a terrible time with Jenny. The little bitch had knocked over a pail of water in the kitchenette, then she'd danced about in it. Bessie had cuffed her ears, and then there had been a howling match. And of course, their pa had taken Jenny's part and had bawled at Bessie. Och, she was right fed up with him. She wished he'd go and drown himself or go away to the war or something—if there was going to be a war.

'Well, things look bad, don't they?' Andy was saying. 'It said on the seven o'clock news this morning that Hitler is still wanting the Polish Corridor.'

'I'd polish corridor him!' Mrs. Moore cried. 'If he wants a corridor to polish, let him come along and polish mine!' She laughed as heartily as if the joke was a new one.

'Christ, I wish I had a pound for every time I've heard ye say that,' Andy said.

'Och well, a guid joke's worth repeatin',' Mrs. Moore said. 'My gum, wouldn't I like to get him down on his bended sparrabils with a pail o' water beside him and a muckle scrubbin' brush in his hand! My word, Adolf, if I catch you bendin'!' She chuckled bawdily. 'What a fine chance it would be!'

'I doubt there would be a queue waitin' for their turn,' Andy said.

'I tell ye another one I'd like to catch bendin',' Mrs. Moore said. 'And that's auld Neville Chamberlain. He's a silly auld geezer if ever there was one.'

'He's a very nice old gentleman,' Mrs. Finlayson said sharply. 'By jings, I just wish they were all like him. He's out for peace. He's a gentleman if ever there was one, and British for by, and I lift my hat to him.'

'Gentleman my—my granny!' Mrs. Moore snapped. 'What right had an auld done cove like him to speak about peace in our time? He's as bad as the rest o' them, British or no British. Out to feather his ain nest like a' the rest.'

'Well, ye can't say that he didn't do his best to stop war last year at Munich,' Mrs. Finlayson said huffily.

'Ay, and look where it's landed us now!' Mrs. Moore said. 'The guns are goin' to start boomin' at any minit. It said on the one o'clock news that the evacuation o' bairns from Paris had started.'

('Ah, ma belle Paris,' Bessie said to herself, and it was only by an effort that she refrained from crossing herself.)

'What regiment are you goin' into, Andy?' Dirty Minnie said.

'I'm goin' in an airyplane, lady!' Andy said, taking her Store Book and beginning to write down her messages. 'I'm no' footsloggin' if I can help it. Besides, ma varicose veins are bad!'

'What regiment are you goin' to join yersel', Minnie?' Mrs. Moore laughed. 'Us women 'll have to go and fight in this war, too. I think I'll be like Andy and gang up in an airyplane. You'll be joinin' the Women's Navy, I suppose, seein' ye're so fond o' sailors!'

'Not me! I never was very fond o' water!'

'You're tellin' us!' Mrs. Moore nudged Mrs. Stout.

'As long as they dinnie use gas,' Mrs. Finlayson whined. 'It would be terrible if they used gas.'

'That Hitler wouldn't dare,' Mrs. Stout said.

'Talkin' of gas,' Dirty Minnie said. 'Where's Mrs. Winter the day? She's aye out long afore this, feared she'll miss her turn in the queue.'

'Och, did ye no' hear?' Mrs. Moore said, laughing. 'There's no so much gas about her the day. She's got a quinsy throat and she can hardly speak.'

'Has she, poor thing,' Mrs. Finlayson said.

'Ach, it's a fine hammahuddy,' Mrs. Moore said. 'She's a greetin'-faced bitch. There's aye somethin' wrong wi' her. She's aye lookin' for sympathy.'

'It's a pity she wouldnie lose her voice all thegither,' Dirty Minnie said. 'That would keep her from complainin'.'

'Oh, Minnie, what a like thing to say!' Mrs. Finlayson cried.

'Well, I'm right fed up wi' her,' Minnie said. 'She's aye like a washing hangin' out on a wet day. It would be wicer-like if she thought less about her troubles and looked after her man and bairns better. I was in the chemist's the other day when she came in, and she was buyin' as many different kinds o' medicine. She wanted me to try one o' the bottles. What would I want to try it for? I said. There's nothin' wrong wi' me. I was fair tickled to death at her. It was some medicine that she'd tried hersel' and it didnie agree wi' her. "Isn't that the one that gave ye jip?" I said. "Ay," she said, "it was fair hellish." "Well, what do ye want me to try it for?" I said. "If it didnie agree wi' you, how do ye think it's goin' to agree any better wi' me?"'

'The trouble wi' her is that she's hippycondrick,' Mrs. Moore said. 'We all have our aches and pains, but we dinnie go about tellin' everybody about them like her. She's like the man in the advertisement for Doan's Kidney Pills. Every picter tells a story! I often have a sore back, too, but I dinnie tell the world about it.'

'Ach, I have a sore back just now,' Minnie said. 'But I'm no' tellin' other folk about it.'

'Ah, but ye should, Minnie!' Mrs. Moore laughed. 'Put on a greetin' face and get sympathy. Every picter tells a story!'

'Ah, but it's two stories that mine's is tellin',' Minnie said with a guffaw.

'All the same, it's no laughin' matter,' Mrs. Finlayson sniffed. 'Poor Mrs. Winter losin' her voice. My goodness, it must be a terrible thing to be dumb.'

'Ach, I think it would be worse to be deaf,' Mrs. Moore said. 'Just think! You wouldnie be able to hear things. Just think o' the tasty bits o' scandal you'd miss.'

'I'd rather be dumb,' she said.

'But you couldnie tear folk to bits if you were dumb,' Dirty Minnie objected.

'Could I no'!' Mrs. Moore laughed. 'I'd soon learn the Deaf and Dumb Alphabet and then I'd wear my fingers to the bone.'

'Come on, Bessie,' she shouted. 'Take yer turn afore Aggie Renton comes. I see her comin' out her entry now. Hurry up, hen, it won't be long now! Ye'll no' have many more days left to stand at this van—ye'll soon be awa' with a uniform on, and a rifle ower yer shoother!'

7

THE Bourbon children had gone into exile again. They called it Evacuation, but it was exile for all that. Madame Royale stood and watched the train disappear out of the Waverley Station. She showed no sign of emotion on her pale, proud face. The other people on the platform looked curiously at her, but none of them made any sign of recognition.

'Come on, hen,' Mrs. Moore said, taking her arm. 'There isnie any sense in greetin' about it. The bairns 'll be all right. It 'll just last for two-three days. It 'll be a nice wee holiday for them.'

Madame Royale turned abruptly and began to walk slowly up the platform, gazing straight into the distance. She knew what they were saying—that High and Low, they all had to come to this, the children of the Poor and the children of the

Blood Royal, all had to go into exile because of the Shadow of War.

She settled herself in the black limousine with the gold Bourbon crest. 'To the Palais, Alphonse.'

'Two tuppenny yins, dear,' Mrs. Moore said to the tram-conductor.

Soon—alas! too soon—her father and she would have to follow the children into exile. . . . Leaning on the rail of the great ship that was taking them to South America, Madame Royale leant her face on her black-gloved hand and thought sadly of the past . . . wondering about the future. . . .

The quay was seething with newspapermen when they docked at Buenos Aires. But their Aides-de-Camp steered them safely through. 'His Majesty will hold a press conference later.' And there was Ferdinand waiting for them. 'Ma belle,' he whispered. 'Ma chere belle Elisabetta!'

That night he took them to a cabaret. There was polite but enthusiastic applause from the other diners as the Royal exiles went to their table. Marie-Elisabeth arranged her black tulle veil around her shoulders and touched the diamond stars in her shell-like ears. 'Champagne,' she said without glancing at the Wine List the waiter was holding deferentially in front of her. She looked over the foaming liquid, straight into Ferdinand's dark, smouldering eyes. 'To the future, cherie! Let us eat, drink and be merry, for tomorrow we die!'

'Apres nous la deluge,' he answered.

The lights were dimmed. A spotlight shone on the tiny stage. Invisible bagpipes began to wail. Marie de France stiffened, and a shiver ran down her spine. Ma belle Scotland, she whispered to herself. A handsome negress dressed in white came on the stage. She wore a tartan scarf around her shoulders in honour of the Royal diners, and she swept them a curtsy before she started to sing.

'*Hame o' mine, hame o' mine that I dwelt in lang lang syne. That's where my heart and my thoughts are forever. . . .*'

Marie-Elisabeth de Braganza was unable to control the tears that ran down her cheeks . . . remembering the little thatched cottage where she had been so happy as a child, and the burn that tinkled amongst the heather at the foot of the brae . . . the bonnie purple heather . . . far, far away in dear auld Scotland. . . .

She raised her glass again and said to Ferdinand: 'To the future, cherie!'

'Ye'll have to snap out o' it, Bessie,' Mrs. Moore said briskly. 'Goin' about there as if you'd lost a shilling and found a sixpence! We cannie help the war and the bairns havin' to be evacuated. They'll be all right. It 'll be all ower in two-three months, anyway. C'mon, ye'd better get up yer blackout or we'll have auld Nebby Finlayson on our tracks!'

Listlessly, Bessie went to the cupboard and pulled out the blackout-curtains that they'd made for the Test Blackout several months before. 'It's a damned nuisance,' she said peevishly.

'I ken it's a damned nuisance, but we'll just hae to make the best o' it,' Mrs. Moore said, hoisting herself on to a chair beside the window. 'But it 'll no' make any difference folk like us sayin' anythin' about it. The war's started, and we'll just hae to put up with it. Ours not to reason why, ours just to do and die, as ma auld man keeps sayin'.'

'Here, gie me an end o' it,' she said.

Bessie gave her one end of the curtain-rod and stood on a chair, holding the other end. 'A wee bit your way, Mrs. Moore,' she said.

Mrs. Moore gave the curtain a tug. 'That seems all right,' she said, cocking her head to the side and putting her hands on her hips. 'Ay, that looks all right,' she said, and she stepped back.

'Oh, hell!'

'Did ye hurt yersel', Mrs. Moore?' Bessie cried anxiously, helping her up.

'No, I'm all right. I just got a fright. I forgot I was standin' on a chair.' Mrs. Moore rubbed her bottom. 'It's a guid job I'm well padded!'

She grinned ruefully and gave the blackout a twitch.

'Bugger auld Hitler!' she said.

PART IV

1

BESSIE was hurrying out of the entry when Lily McGillivray shouted from the opposite side of the street: 'Where are you tearin' to, Hippy?'

'Goin' to the picters,' Bessie cried.

'The Rialto?'

'Ay.'

'Want a chum?'

Bessie halted. 'If ye like. I was just goin' myself. Have you nothin' else on the night?'

'No,' Lily said, teetering on to the pavement with her high heels and cleeking her arm through Bessie's. 'The latest boy-friend's given me the heave.'

'Och, what a pity!' Bessie said.

'Aw, what does it matter?' Lily laughed raucously. 'He wasnie a great catch, anyway. We'll maybe pick up somethin' better at the picters.'

Bessie felt her stomach turn slightly with excitement. Gee, if they did! She always hoped when she went to the pictures alone that she'd click with somebody, but somehow she never did. Maybe tonight with Lily it would be different. . . . Lily knew her onions all right. It would be fine going with Lily. She'd feel more adventurous. . . .

'Och, dinnie let's go to there,' Lily said as they reached the top of the street where the Rialto lay. 'Let's go up the town to the Playhouse. There's an awful good picter there. *All This and Heaven Too*. Bette Davis and Charles Boyer. Oh, it should be guid! Bette Davis is lovely. And Charles . . . mmmmm, he's gorgeous! I could go for that man in a big way.'

'All right,' Bessie said.

On the way to Granton Road Station to get a tram, Lily talked about her work and her various boy-friends. Bessie felt very proud to be seen walking along beside her, and she shoved out her behind the way Lily shoved out hers, and she wished she had higher heels so that she could prance as Lily was prancing. Her gas-mask, in its new bright blue case, kept bumping against her bottom. She resolved to do her hair differently; to try to arrange it in a high sweep off her forehead like Lily's.

'Are your kids still evacuated?' Lily said.

'Ay, they've been away a month now,' Bessie said.

'Fancy! A month already since the war started! Ye'd hardly credit it, would ye? I expect ye'll miss them.'

'Not me!' Bessie giggled. 'I'm glad to get rid o' the wee brats.'

'Mind you, I missed them at first,' she said. 'I didnie ken what was wrong wi' the hoose—it was that quiet. I kept thinkin' they'd be in yellin' their heads off for pieces at any minute, but I've got ower it now. Och, it's fine to have the hoose to myself and nobody to worry me except my da.'

'I hear he's courtin' again,' Lily said. 'Are ye goin' to get a stepmother?'

'I don't know,' Bessie said stiffly.

'Well, if you do, you take my advice and get a job,' Lily said. 'Lookit the fun you would get in a job. You'd have a far better time than bein' cooped away in that dump, cookin' and dustin' and aye havin' your father on your track if his meals arenie ready in time.'

'There's an Eight!' Bessie cried. 'Will we run for it?'

When they got on the tram Lily's attention was taken up with a sailor from the Naval Base at Harrisfield. She kept eyeing him and she did not say much beyond meaningless mutters and giggles to Bessie, so all the way to the Playhouse Bessie was able to sit and brood over what Lily had just said. Her father had never brought Miss Stevens to the house again, but she knew that he still saw her several nights a week. In a way Bessie did not mind this. She saw less of him and, therefore, was less irritated by him. And it gave her more time to herself to read and daydream. She had read a great deal since

the war started. Mrs. Moore had said to her one day: 'Ye're
never away frae the Public Library. Every time I see ye, ye
have great muckle bundles o' books under yer arm. Ye're
gettin' as bad as my man! Goodness me, if ye take in all the
stuff ye read, yer noddle 'll be gettin' to be a fair encyclopaedia!'
Her father had also spoken about the amount she read. He had
said: 'You're just wastin' your time readin' such trash. By
God, if you weren't so big, I'd belt you. Can you not read
something decent for a change? All this muck about kings and
queens!' And he had thrown Marjorie Bowen's *Glen O' Weeping*
to the other side of the kitchenette, and the binding had come
away a bit, and she'd had a terrible job trying to explain it
away to the girl in the Library.

When the girls got off the tram they found a long queue
stretching up Leith Walk on either side of the Playhouse. 'Aw,
hell!' Lily said.

They took their places at the end of the queue for the ninepenny seats. People were hurrying towards it from all directions, and the girls had been standing only a few minutes before
there were two or three dozen people behind them. Lily stood
out from the queue and looked up and down. 'Lookin' to see
if there's any decent talent,' she whispered, nudging Bessie.
'Oh, say, lookit this!'

Two soldiers had joined the end of the ninepenny queue.
Lily gave them a quick look-over, then she grabbed Bessie by
the arm. 'Aw, we'll not wait any longer then,' she said in a
loud voice. 'We'll see it another night. Come on!'

And before Bessie could protest she had yanked her away
from the queue, and those behind them had moved up.

'What are ye playin' at?' Bessie said.

'Shuttup,' Lily hissed.

'Oh well, if you think we should,' she said loudly. 'I suppose
we'd better just wait.'

She shoved Bessie into the queue just behind the soldiers.
One of them turned and smiled: 'Missed your place, sister!'

'Oh, what does it matter?' Lily simpered. 'My friend wanted
to go, and then she changed her mind. Really, Betty, it was
awfully stupid of you.'

'Still, what does it matter?' she said to the soldier before Bessie could say anything. 'We've got the whole night in front of us to wait.'

'Colder tonight, isn't it?' the soldier said.

'Yes, it's getting very chilly,' Lily said.

At first Bessie was unable to say anything; she was so amazed at the classy tone Lily was putting on. But when the other soldier, a small, stocky, fair-haired fellow of nineteen or so, said: 'Howya, toots!' she smiled and said: 'Howya!'

'Does your Old Lady know you've escaped from your pram?' he grinned.

'Of course,' she said indignantly; then she swallowed and lied bravely: 'I'm sixteen past.'

'And the band played!' he said.

'The band played nothing,' she said, copying Lily's classy tone as well as she could. 'I was sixteen my last birthday, and I'm perfectly capable of looking after myself, amn't I, Lily?'

'Of course, dear, you've been around.' Lily coyly rearranged the mane of curls lying on her shoulders, then she put her hands back in her coat-pockets and pulled it more tightly around her behind. She half-turned round to let the soldiers get an eyeful of the effect.

'Let's see your identity card!' the fair-haired soldier grinned.

'I'll let you see the toe of my boot!' Bessie said.

'I'll hold him so that you won't miss the target!' The other soldier swung his pal around and held him in position.

'I wouldn't soil my foot!' Bessie said, and she touched her hair, copying Lily.

'Honest, though, what's your name?' the stocky soldier grinned.

'What's yours?'

He pulled himself away from his pal's embrace and said: 'Lord Haw-Haw.'

'And the band played!' she giggled.

He sprang to attention and saluted: '136574 Gunner McNab, George.

'Now, what's yours?' he said.

'Betty,' she said, and she blushed. 'Betty—er—Betty

Bourbon.' And she looked back and rearranged her gas-mask over her shoulder to avoid meeting Lily's eye.

The soldiers insisted on paying them into the cinema. Lily made a great show of protesting, but when it looked as though the soldiers might take her at her word she suddenly gave in. She manœuvred so that she and Bessie sat between the two soldiers in the back row of the ninepennies.

The News Reel was on. Bessie giggled when Gunner McNab took her hand, and she said: 'Ach away and not be daft!' but she let him hold it. But when *All This and Heaven Too* started and he put his arm around her shoulders she wriggled a little. She wanted to enjoy the film. But she saw that Lily and her soldier had their heads on each other's shoulders and were not looking at the film at all, and so she resigned herself to the inevitable.

2

'THEY were real nice chaps, weren't they?' Bessie said as she and Lily climbed to the top of the last tram going to Harris-field Square.

'Aw, not bad,' Lily said. She prodded Bessie in the back. 'There's a couple of seats away at the front, Ferret. Grab them!—Betty, I should say,' she said in her classy voice as they sat down. 'Betty—what was it? Betty Bonbon! I help my God, Ferret, what made you pick on a name like that to tell them? I know Hipkiss isn't a world-breaker, but it's hardly as daft as Bonbon.'

'Bonbon!' she shrieked, and she held on to the seat in front of her, giggling. 'Betty Bonbon!'

'I didn't say Bonbon at all,' Bessie said. 'I said Bourbon. It's a famous . . .'

'Boorbon! Christ, that's worse still!'

Bessie turned and looked out of the window, though she could see nothing for the blackout. Really, Lily was terrible. They went to see a lovely picture like *All This and Heaven Too*, and all the time Lily sat and necked with a soldier. Of course, Lily would say that she had sat and necked with a soldier, too, but she *had* managed to see some of the picture. She had held George off not too badly on the whole.

'Gee, Bette Davis was lovely, wasn't she?' she said.

'Och, she wasn't bad,' Lily said.

Bessie sighed, wishing that she'd been in Bette Davis' place. The part would have suited her just down to the ground, being French and all that. Ah, ma belle France! She pressed her forehead against the steamy window of the tram, wishing that it had been Charles Boyer who'd had his arm around her. It was just her luck to get landed with a common gunner when she might have had a Duc de Praslin to take her to balls and concerts. I'll go back and see it again myself tomorrow, she said to herself, I've still got my ninepence.

'Bonbon!' Lily began to splutter again. 'Honest to God, Ferret, you take the cake! I can see that you and me are goin' to have some fun before this war's lasted much longer.'

'Hey, what are you two makin' all the noise about?' Somebody poked them in the backs. They turned round and saw Mrs. Moore beaming at them. She was so broad that she took up almost the entire seat, and she was overlapping her husband, who sat, smiling in an embarrassed way, on the edge.

'Hello,' Bessie said. 'Been to the picters?'

'Ay, we were at the Playhouse.' Mrs. Moore puffed out her fat cheeks with exasperation. 'But it 'll be the last time I'll go to the picters while this war lasts. What wi' the blackout outside and the blackout in the picters—och, it's a right scunner! We couldnie see a step in front o' us when we went in. The lassie wi' the torch was away showin' some other folk to their seats, and afore we knew where we were we went bang into a petition. My word, I didnie half sing out, I can tell ye! I says to him, I'm not as feared as I used to be, I'll let them know that I'm here. "You might shine your torch along here, please," I cried. Oh, my goodness, I fair put on the posh tone for them —doin' the ladidah! "I can't see one step in front of me," I cries. "Shine your torch along here, please." So she put on the flashie. A piece of nonsense! She was just tryin' to save the battery, but I sorted her. Of course, even when she did put it on full blast His Nabs here couldnie see—but I soon gave him the right-about-wheel into the seat!'

'It was terrible dark,' Mr. Moore said apologetically.

'Och, they should have a better system o' lightin' picter-hooses,' Mrs. Moore said. 'But I'm the boy for them! "You might shine your torch along here, please," I cries. Jings, I was just thinkin' if the folk at Calderburn had heard me they'd 'a' been sayin' there's Mrs. Moore tryin' to put on the High Pan! Ye ken, I was almost glad to come back out into the blackout.'

'Still, I wish the war was finished,' she said. 'It's no' natural, all this darkness and creepin' about wi' torches in your hands and bumpin' into sandbags and havin' to take your gas-masks wi' you everywhere you go.'

She bounced the offending gas-mask up and down on her knee. 'It's a wonder to me they dinnie tell you to take it to the lavvy wi' you,' she said.

3

BESSIE and Lily were to meet the two soldiers the following night at seven o'clock at the Wellington Monument at the east end of Princes Street. But when Bessie went for Lily at half-past six she found that she wasn't ready. Bessie leaned impatiently against the bed, watching Lily rouge her cheeks. 'Aw, hurry up, Lily!' she cried. 'You'd think we'd all night in front o' us. If we dinnie hurry up, George and Eddie 'll not wait.'

'They'll not be there,' Lily said calmly, reaching for her powder-puff.

'What?' Bessie stopped drawing her forefinger along the top of the end of the bed. 'What are you talkin' about?'

'They'll not be there,' Lily said. 'And even if they are, we're not.'

'But George said——'

'We're not goin',' Lily said, humming *September in the Rain*

125

as she fluffed up the ends of her hair. 'They'll not be there either. It's just a gag. They don't expect us, and if they do—well, it's their lookout! They can just stand at the Wellington Monument till they die or get another click.'

'But George said——'

'Aw, don't be so green, Ferret!'

'But, Lily!' Bessie went to the window and beat a tattoo with her fingers on the pane She had seen somebody do this on the films, and she felt it was the right thing to do at such a moment.

'We'll take a walk down to the Base at Harrisfield,' Lily said, picking up her bag and her gas-mask. 'There's something about sailors that gets me!'

'But, Lily——' Bessie was turning away from the window when she paused and said: 'Oh, there's Nessie Porteous! My goodness, I havenie seen her for ages. My, what a toff she is!'

Lily peered over her shoulder. 'Ay, she's got up like a fizzing abdine all right! You used to run around wi' her and that Mabel Brown, didn't you? What's happened to them lately?'

'Och, I never had time to go out wi' them,' Bessie whined. 'After my ma died I was kept that busy wi' the bairns. I never had a minute to myself for tellin' them stories.'

'You're well rid of them,' Lily said. 'Bairns are just a curse. I ken this has been a happier hoose since our Jackie was evacuated. Come on! Where are yours evacuated to?' she said, as they clattered downstairs.

'They're at a farm near Peebles. I'm goin' to see them on Sunday. Would ye like to chum me?'

'Okay,' Lily said. 'If I have nothin' else on. It depends on what we pick up the night.'

All the way to Harrisfield Square Lily talked about the prospects of picking up something good, but when they got there and began to parade backwards and forwards in front of the big gates that shut off the Harbour, there was nothing doing. 'I guess all the talent's away up town,' Lily said. 'Isn't it hellish! Maybe we should 'a' gone up there after all.'

'Maybe we should just have gone and met George and Eddie,' Bessie said.

'Och them!' Lily looked supercilious. 'They're just small fry. I'm not wastin' my time on the likes o' them.'

'Och, I suppose we'll just have to go to the picters,' she said. 'There's nothin' for it but the Rialto now.'

'I cannie go,' Bessie said, blushing. 'I—er—I spent all my money this afternoon, and I cannie take any more out the housekeepin' money or my faither 'll raise hell. I went to see *All This and Heaven Too* again.'

'Well, for cryin' out loud!' Lily said. 'What was the idea of goin' to see it again? I'm sure once was enough for me.'

'Och, I liked it,' Bessie said. 'I could go back and see it again the night—if I had the money.'

'Well, we're not goin' there,' Lily said. 'C'mon, we'll go to the Rialto. I'll pay ye in.'

But whether it was because Lily paid her in or whether it was the film's fault, Bessie did not enjoy the show. Half of the time anyway she kept watching Lily, who was carrying on with a young chap next her. And she was not surprised when Lily whispered towards the end of the film that she was going out with him.

'Okay,' Bessie said. And she added: 'Be good!'

'Be good yersel'!' Lily giggled and followed the young man out.

On her way home Bessie stopped to buy some chips at Alfie's van. 'So ye're still here, Alfie?' she said, taking the greasy bags from him. 'I thought you'd 'a' been away to the war by this time.'

'Ay, I'm still here,' he said. 'But I doubt it winnie be long now. My Age Group 'll soon be gettin' called up at the rate they're gettin' through us! They'll be takin' the very grandfathers before very long and shovin' a rifle across their shoothers! Ay, but there have been a queer lot o' changes in Calderburn this last month. What about yersel'?' he said. 'Are ye no' for joinin' the A.T.S.?'

'I wish I was,' she said. 'Though it's the W.R.N.S. I fancy. But I'm no' auld enough yet.'

She was opening her bag to pay him when she remembered

she had no money. 'Aw, ye'll have to gie me thur on tick, Alfie,' she said.

'You and your bloody tick,' Alfie said, opening a small, greasy accounts-book. 'That's seven and ninepence you owe me now. High time you were gettin' it paid.'

'Ach, I'll pay you some Sunday through the week !' she said. 'Cheeribye!'

She walked slowly towards home, eating the chips moodily. Ay, there was a lot of changes like Alfie said, but mind you there wasn't such a lot of changes as you'd have thought. At first everybody had thought the Jerries would be over here like a flash, raining down bombs and knocking everything to hell, but it hadn't turned out like that after all. The sirens went sometimes, and then everybody dived for their shelters. But nothing very bad ever seemed to happen. The most exciting thing had been that first Sunday when war was declared and the sirens had gone no sooner than auld Chamberlain had stopped speaking. By gum, everybody had flown quick enough to their shelters then. But, of course, nothing had happened. It had just been a false alarm. And now when the sirens went everybody seemed to think it was something of the same kind and they all went about as usual, except some silly auld women like Mrs. Moore and Dirty Minnie and Mrs. Winter. If they'd go to the shelters themselves and let other folk go their own way, it wouldn't be so bad, but they were aye trying to get other folk to go with them. Silly auld bitches, they were aye diving to their shelters. Of course, they were aye glad of a chance to take some bottles with them and have a drink!

Her hands were so filled with the bags of chips that she could not use her torch, but she didn't mind that. She knew her way home blindfolded, she told herself proudly. Catch her needing to use a torch! Of course, she aye took one with her in case. You never knew when you might need it in some of those dark corners where you weren't very well acquaint. But really some folk were terrible the way they couldn't go the length of themselves without their flashies. They kept them on the whole time they walked along, even though the moon was shining.

They were just a damned nuisance, for they flashed them in other folk's eyes and blinded them. Look at that couple at the other side of the street just now. Both of them with a torch, as if one wouldn't do between them, and flashing them about as if they were signalling to somebody. Christ, they wouldn't need to be in some places or they'd get a crowd after them. It was a wonder somebody wasn't shouting: *Lower thae bloody torches. Do ye want to let Jerry ken where ye are?*

She had a good mind to shout to them herself, and she was halting, wondering what she should do, when somebody bumped into her. She managed to keep a grip of her chips, but she was so intent on saving them that she almost fell herself. But a man's arms grabbed her and a very English voice said: 'Easy there, mate, easy!'

'Can ye not use yer torch?' she said angrily when she had recovered her balance.

'Why can't you use your own?' He laughed.

'I couldn't for thur chips,' she snapped. 'Anyway, I ken my way about here blindfolded.'

'You're telling me!' he said.

'Ay, I'm tellin' you,' she said. 'I've lived here for years, so if I don't know my way about, who should?'

She had been peering at him in the darkness, and she saw that he was a sailor. 'Oh, you're lodgin' with Dirty Minnie, aren't you?'

'I'm lodging with Miss Nimmo,' he said.

'Miss Nimmo!' Bessie giggled. 'Gosh, I never knew Minnie's Sunday name afore!'

'Well, I'll get on,' she said after a pause. 'Thanks for bumpin' into me'!

'I'll walk along to your door with you,' he said. 'In case somebody else bumps into you!'

'Okay.'

She felt far more excited than she had felt last night when George had put his arm around her in the pictures. She had seen Minnie's lodger going out and in, and she had thought how good-looking he was. He was a tall bloke with curly brown hair and a clean, sunburned neck. She tried to think of something to say, but couldn't. She wished in a way that Lily was here to back her up, though if she had been Lily would have been sure to have tried to bag him for herself.

'It's late for a kid like you to be out,' the sailor said.

'It's no' late at all,' she said. 'I've been to the picters.'

'Well, you should go earlier and come home earlier,' he said. 'There are so many queer customers moving around in the blackout.'

'Och, yer granny!' she giggled.

Really, he had a right good cheek talking to her like that. He wasn't much older than her. He would be only nineteen or twenty. 'Talking to me like a grandfather!' she said. 'You'd think ye were a hundred! How auld are ye?'

'Twenty.'

'Well, here we are,' she said, stopping at the entry.

'Okay,' he said. 'In you go, and don't let me catch you out so late again!'

'Or else?' she giggled.

'I'll put the police on your track!' he said. 'Cheerio!'

'Cheeribye!' she cried. 'I'll be seein' you!'

But he didn't take up the challenge; he cried 'Cheerio' again and disappeared into the blackout. Bessie went into the entry feeling disappointed. It hadn't turned out as exciting as she'd hoped—though it had been exciting enough, mind you! It was always a beginning, anyway. After this, when she met him, she'd be able to speak to him. Gosh, she'd have some tale to tell Lily when she saw her tomorrow night.

He kissed me at the door, cherie! I ran up the grand staircase of the Louvre, and when I turned at the top, there he was still standing at the foot, looking after me. The moonlight was shining on his bright curls and on the gold braid on his shoulders.

Elisabeth-Charlotte d'Angouleme drew her white ermine cloak tightly around her bare satiny shoulders and began to ascend the next staircase. La, la, what would Papa say if he knew that his daughter was carrying on a flirtation with a junior admiral of the French fleet? She flitted silently along the dimly-lit corridor, watching carefully for any of the footmen.

She was congratulating herself that she was safely past Madame Deluzy-Desportes' door when it opened silently, and her governess whispered: 'Is that you, Elisabeth?'

So!

'You 'ave trapped me, cherie!' She giggled softly and allowed Bette Davis Deluzy-Desportes to draw her into her boudoir.

''Ow I love heem, cherie, 'ow I love heem!' she exclaimed at the end of her story. 'But he is charmant!'

Bette Davis smiled and drew her pupil against her breast. 'I am so glad you 'ave found love at last, ma petite,' she murmured.

'Will you ask Charles—I mean Monsieur le Duc de Praslin to make an assignment with him for me?' Elisabeth said. 'You and he are the only people I could trust at court with my secret.'

'I shall ask him,' Bette promised. 'Where did you meet him?'

'We clicked in a cabaret in Montparnasse,' Elisabeth said, and she walked to the window and drummed her fingers against the pane.

'A cabaret in Montparnasse!' Bette's large eyes opened even wider than usual. 'Madame! Are you mad? The King's eldest daughter to go to a squalid cabaret! Were you not recognized?'

'No, I 'ad on ze mask!' Elisabeth drew a black velvet mask from her corsage. 'So! Ze Woman in ze Iron Mask! Zat ees what he said to me when we clicked! Ah, but 'e is lovelee, lovelee, lovelee. . . .'

And she waltzed towards the door, her white tulle draperies billowing around her. . . .

4

'WHERE have you been?' her father said when she went in. 'What are you doin' out gallivantin' at this time of night?'

'I was at the picters,' Bessie whined. 'And then I stopped at

Alfie's for chips for yer supper. There was such a crowd at his van that I had to wait ages and ages.'

'Well, hurry up and get them heated up,' Bert said, picking up his paper again. 'I'm fair famishing. But another night after this see and have somethin' more substantial than chips for my supper. Chips, chips, chips! I hate the sight of them. The staple diet of the British Working Class! No wonder they're such a stupid lot of buggers! Give them chips and the pictures and they'll let you do whatever you damned well like with them. My God, if I was in Parliament I'd draw up a Bill for the extermination of cinemas and fish and chip shops.'

Bessie tried not to listen to him as she put on the kettle and laid the table. She saw that he'd had a drink or two and was in an argumentative mood. He was aye on the subject of politics when he'd had more to drink than he should have had. Him and his auld politics and what he would do if he was ever in Parliament. A fat chance he had of ever being in Parliament. They wanted gentlemen in Parliament.

Christ! there he was putting on the wireless. 'Let's have a wee tune to cheer us up!' he said. Him and his wee tunes to cheer him up. She was sick and tired of the wireless. It was all right through the day when she was in alone and could have on whatever programmes she liked. But it was a different story at nights when she had to listen to whatever he put on. I'll go batty soon if I don't get out of this.

'Supper's ready, Da,' she said.

They were halfway through the meal when the sirens began to wail. 'Hello, hello!' Bert said. 'Are we goin' to get visitors!'

Bessie crossed herself quickly without thinking what she was doing. She saw her father look at her, and, to hide her embarrassment, she reached for the teapot.

'Here, don't you let me see you doing that again,' Bert said quietly. 'You'd think you were a bloody Papist. I've noticed you at it once or twice lately, and I've been going to check you before. We'll have no more of it, see?'

'I was just doin' it for fun,' she whined. 'I saw them doin' it on the picters.'

'Well, if that's the kind of thing you see at the pictures it's high time you stopped goin'. I've aye said the pictures were a menace.'

'Will we go to the shelter?' she said, anxious to change the subject.

'You can go if you like,' he said. 'But I'm staying right here. There 'll be nothing, anyway. It's just one of those nuisance raids to make us think there's a war on. It's almost twelve o'clock. I'm goin' to listen to the News and see what more lies they've got to tell us about this phoney war.'

5

THE next afternoon Bessie watched out of the window for Lily McGillivray coming home from work. When she saw her she leaned out and yelled: 'Hey, Lily, how did ye get on last night?'

'Aw, he's just an apprentice engineer in Bruce Peebles,' Lily shouted. 'Not much of a catch!'

'Are you comin' up?' Bessie called.

'Naw, I'll see ye at night,' Lily screamed. 'I've got my stockings to darn the now. Cheerio!'

Bessie leaned on the window-sill for a while, watching the people passing up and down the street. On the opposite side Dirty Minnie was doing the same. Bessie could see her passing remarks to somebody in the room behind her. She wondered if it was the young sailor. Or was it one of Minnie's other lodgers?

She waved to Minnie, then she drew in her head and pulled down the window. She had just remembered that it was about time for the Insurance Man to come.

She and the Insurance Man had been getting on not too badly lately. Of course, there was nothing in it. He was far too auld for her. Still, it was aye a bit of fun. He was a right cheery go-ahead fellow, and you could always get a laugh with him.

She did her hair, trying to get it as near Lily's hair-style as possible, then she put on some lipstick and powdered her face. There, that was better! Maybe she wasn't as glamorous as Bette Davis, but the Insurance Man wouldn't know any better.

She took the Insurance Books from the drawer of the dresser and put the money on top of them on the table. Now she was ready! He could come whenever he liked.

6

THE Insurance Man was pushing his bicycle up the hill from Harrisfield Harbour when he heard the sirens. A woman who was gossiping at the door of an entry let out a yell, and she scuttled across the street like a frightened rabbit and dis-. appeared into another entry. The Insurance Man wheeled his bike into Goldengreen Street and made straight for Number Nine. He was determined to get Mrs. Lyons in before she went out and got lost in one of the shelters. The noise of many windows being pushed up made him look upwards. Heads were shoved out like mops being withdrawn from pails of water.

'It's an air-raid!' The words were shouted from window to window, flying backwards and forwards across the street: reed instruments against the dull fury of the sirens in the background. 'Get thae bairns inside!'

The Insurance Man hesitated for a minute, then he placed his bicycle against the railings and went into the doorway of Number Nine. Air-raid or no air-raid he was determined to get the money Mrs. Lyons was due him. She had been out the last four times he'd called. He must get what was due him to-day or his boss would want to know the reason why. He was going up the first flight of stairs when he was almost knocked over by a number of women rushing down. They were carrying the cardboard boxes containing their gas-masks.

'It's the Insurance Man!' Dirty Minnie cried. 'Are ye here

to see that we all get killed properly? Our men 'll no' have so much bother to get the insurance!'

'I never knew ye had a man, Minnie!' Mrs. Stout giggled. 'Which o' yer lodgers is it?'

'That's enough o' yer sauce!' Dirty Minnie laughed.

'Come on,' she said to the Insurance Man. 'Ye'd better come down to the shelter.'

He was enveloped in their rush, and before he knew where he was he was in the back garden. A woman with a number of children clustered around her was weeping mournfully as she placed their gas-masks over their heads. 'Get yer gas-masks on,' she was crying. 'Ye never ken what's in the air now.'

'Ach, Mrs. Winter, dinnie be daft,' Minnie cried. 'There's no gas yet. Ye dinnie need to put on yer mask until ye hear the hand-bells.'

'It's her own fault for bringin' her bairns back so soon,' Mrs. Stout said sharply. 'She should 'a' left them evacuated like other sensible folk. My word, if I'd had ony wee ones I'd 'a' seen that they were left safe in the country.'

'What's she doin' in our shelter, anyway?' another woman said. 'Comin' rushin' across the street to ours when she's got a good enough shelter o' her ain.'

'Ach, hers is flooded,' Mrs. Stout said.

Mrs. Winter was too busy putting the masks over the heads of her struggling children to pay any attention to what the other women were saying. Then with the help of Dirty Minnie she herded them into the shelter. The Insurance Man stood at the opening and looked up at the sky. He could hear the drone of planes, but he could see nothing. The sky was a clear bright blue with small cream-coloured clouds clustered over it like a pattern of flowers.

'Come away inside, Mr. Rankin,' pleaded Mrs. Stout. 'You'll get hit if you stand there.'

People were pouring from the tenements into the shelters in the neighbouring gardens. Rankin wondered which shelter Mrs. Lyons had gone to. Some painters in white overalls ran from an entry and made for the shelter next to that at which

135

Rankin was standing. They jumped in, and immediately there were shouts. One of them popped out his head and grinned: 'The bloody place is flooded! My pal's near drowned!'

Rankin went over and helped them out. They were soaking up to the thighs. 'Painter Drowned in Air Raid Shelter,' one of them said cheerfully. 'Boy, that 'd make a good headline, wouldn't it? What a story you'll have to tell to your grand-children, Jimmie!'

'If I ever get any grandchildren to tell stories to!' Jimmie laughed.

'See anything yet, mate?' the other painter asked. And he and Rankin squinted up at the sky. 'Oh, boy, yes, there's a plane! See, away over there, towards Leith!'

'Wonder if it's a Jerry?' Jimmie said, wringing the water from his trousers.

'Come inside, you three!' Dirty Minnie cried. 'Come inside and get a wee somethin' to cheer ye up!' And she held a pint bottle of whisky enticingly in the air.

'Whoopee!' Jimmie cried, swooping into the shelter. 'This is the stuff the doctor ordered!'

'We're havin' a Bottle Party,' Minnie chuckled. 'I dinnie see why we shouldnie. Thae society folk have their Bottle Parties and take their gas-masks along wi' them. So it's up to us to keep the war democratic! What's sauce for the goose is sauce for the gander!'

'Ach, the smell of the cork would knock some o' you women flat on your backs!' Jimmie jeered.

'That's all you ken,' Minnie said.

'Do ye see anythin' yet?' A dust-capped head poked over Minnie's fat shoulder and gazed anxiously at the sky.

'Nothing but Mrs. Moore and Miss Hipkiss,' said Rankin. 'Come on, Mrs. Moore, hurry up or you'll be late for the Bottle Party!'

'Oh dear,' Mrs. Moore panted, handing an enormous bag to one of the women in the shelter. 'What an awkward time thae Germans aye come at! I wish they'd gie folk mair warnin'. The other day I was in the middle o' makin' the dinner when the sirens went. And the day I was busy washin'.

Talk about hangin' out yer washin' on the Seefreed Line or whatever they call it! Ye cannie get peace!'

'Come awa' in,' Dirty Minnie said, helping her neighbour into the dugout. 'Upsadaisy! Easy now, easy!'

'Eh, but I wish I was a bit thinner,' Mrs. Moore grumbled. 'It's fine for thae young ones like Bessie here, they can scramble out and in shelters as much as they like. But you and me are gettin' ower auld for thur kind o' capers.'

'I don't know,' Mrs. Stout said. 'Bein' thin didnie prevent me from checking my finger in the scullery door when I heard the alarm.'

'What did ye do in the Great War, Mummy!' Mrs. Moore giggled. 'You'll be able to show yer bairns yer war-wounds!'

'Ay, but I'll need to get the bairns first,' Mrs. Stout sniffed.

'Come on, Minnie, gie's a dram out yer bottle,' Mrs. Moore said. 'And you, Bessie,' she yelled. 'You come in here at once! Standin' up there like the lost sheep on the mountain! Ye'll no' stand very long if ye get a bit shrapnel in yer napper.'

'I had to go and fetch her', she whispered to the other women. 'That's what put off my time. She wasnie for movin', mind you. Really, I dinnie ken what to make o' the lassie sometimes. She's that vacant. Whiles I think she's really no' all there.'

Bessie was giggling at something Rankin had just said to Jimmie. She leaned against the side of the shelter, hugging her folded arms tightly across her thin chest. 'He's a right scream, isn't he?' she said to Jimmie.

'Ay, and how's your health today, Miss Hipkiss?' Rankin said. 'I haven't had time to ask you yet, there's been so much excitement.'

'I'm fine,' Bessie simpered.

'I hope you're keepin' that date for me,' he said. 'You promised you and me'd go to the pictures one of these fine nights.'

'Och away!' Bessie giggled.

'You're a great toff today, Miss Hipkiss!' he said. 'Isn't she?' He winked at Jimmie.

'Ay, are you expectin' your boy-friend?' Jimmie laughed.

'Och away!' Bessie giggled.

'Bessie!' Mrs. Moore popped her head out of the shelter. 'Did you hear me yellin' to ye? You come into this shelter at once when I tell you. I dinnie want yer poor da to find a corpse when he comes hame frae his work.'

'A' right,' Bessie said sulkily.

She clambered into the shelter, and Rankin and the painter followed. The droning of the planes had faded away, and there was no sign of any aircraft in the sky. 'It'll be a reconnaissance plane very likely,' Rankin said. 'I don't think there's any danger.'

'Ay, take off thae gas-masks now, Mrs. Winter,' said Minnie. 'The bairns 'll be suffocated.'

But Mrs. Winter refused to take off the masks. She crouched in a corner of the shelter with her children clustered around her. Rankin and the painters stood at the door and looked up at the empty sky. Bessie stood just behind them, looking at Rankin's neck and ears. He wasn't a bad-looking fellow at all, mind you, even though his ears were a wee thing big.

'This is just a waste of time,' Rankin said. 'I could 've been at half a dozen customers by this time.'

'That's right,' the oldest painter said. 'Here, Jimmie, pop over and get those patterns. These women might as well choose the patterns for their living-room wallpaper while they're here.'

When Jimmie returned there was a great deal of hilarity among the women as they started to choose their patterns. 'I'll be able to tell folk I picked it in an air-raid,' Mrs. Stout cried jubilantly.

'Ay, if it ever gets the length of bein' put on yer livin'-room wall,' Mrs. Winter wailed.

'It's no' improvin' yer taste, onyway,' Mrs. Moore said. 'That's an awful-like pattern you're lookin' at the now. Ye'd have nightmares every time ye looked at it!'

'Och, it's not bad,' Mrs. Stout said.

'Please yersel',' Mrs. Moore said, leaning back and folding

her arms. 'But I'm warnin' ye. If ye pick that, yer man 'll go up in smoke. It would be guid grounds for a divorce!'

'I think I'll go,' Rankin said. 'I want to get a hold of Mrs. Lyons. I'm just wasting time standing here.'

'So am I,' Bessie said. 'I'll come with you.'

'Ye'll do no such thing, Bessie Hipkiss,' cried Mrs. Moore. 'You're bidin' here till the all-clear goes.'

'Och away!' Bessie said.

'You're bidin' here,' Mrs. Moore said.

'Yes, you'd be better to stay here, Miss Hipkiss,' said Rankin. 'You never know when something might happen.'

Bessie glowered sulkily as she watched him scramble out of the shelter. It was just her luck to be saddled with an interfering auld bitch like Mrs. Moore. Dragging her here to the shelter when she didn't want to come and then holding her back when she wanted to go. Really, some folk had a right nerve! Could they not mind their own business? After all, it was her own lookout if she got killed.

Just then the wailing of the All Clear was heard in the distance. Bessie did not wait to help Mrs. Moore or anybody else out of the shelter; she was out and running across the back-green before the sirens closer at hand could take up and intensify the signal. She rushed into the nearest back-door and along the passage and out into the street. She was halfway up the stairs in her own tenement when she halted in amazement. There was the warning again!

Cries of unbelief came from some women who were coming upstairs. 'There must be a mistake somewhere,' one of them cried. 'The bloke that sounds the siren must have been sleeping!'

Everybody turned and made again for the shelters. Bessie stood, clinging to the stair-railing. She wondered if she should go straight up to her house or if she should go back to the shelter. Maybe Mrs. Moore was right. Maybe a bomb might drop one of these fine days, and then where would she be?

She was trying to make up her mind when she heard footsteps hurrying along the ground-passage. She looked down the well of the stairs and saw the Insurance Man. Without waiting to think, she began to rush downstairs.

'Oh, it's you, Miss Hipkiss!' he cried. 'You'd better stay here now. You're as safe on the ground floor here as you'd be in a shelter.'

'D'ye think so?' she cried. 'Oh, I'm scared stiff!'

'It's all right,' he said. 'I think it's a false alarm. But you'd better stay here in any case. I think the people at the controls must have made a mistake. There's no sign of any aircraft.'

Just then Mrs. Abbott opened her door and looked out. .

'Is that you, Mr. Rankin? If you come in a minute, I'll give you your money.'

'You'd better come in, too, Bessie,' she said. 'You'll be safer in here than in that passage.'

'It'll save you callin' on Saturday, Mr. Rankin,' she said as they followed her in.

'Do you expect to see Saturday?' Rankin laughed.

'Of course, what's to hinder us?' Mrs. Abbott slapped him jocularly on the arm. 'I'm no' expectin' to die yet. Are you? I've got a long life-line!'

'Well, I don't know. They've certainly not been very near today so far, but the other day—Whew! I don't fancy bein' machine-gunned.'

'Ay, it was a close thing. It was sad about that puir man that got a bullet in his leg in the Ferry Road, wasn't it? I just said to my mother it might 'a' been any of us.' Mrs. Abbott opened her purse, then she put it down impatiently. 'Did ye ever see the like o' that?' She nodded at her mother, an old woman of eighty-two. The old woman had the window raised, and she was leaning out. 'Really, mother!' Mrs. Abbott cried. 'D'ye want to get killed?'

'No, but I want to see all that I can while I'm still able,' the old woman snapped. She chuckled and beckoned them to the window. 'See that wife over there!'

'I help my God!' Mrs. Abbott cried. 'Look at her! Roarin' and laughin'! Fancy anybody roarin' and laughin' on a day like this!'

'Ay, it's no' a laughin' matter,' Bessie said.

She and Rankin stood beside the old woman and looked out of the window while Mrs. Abbott went to the drawer of the table in the kitchenette where she kept a box with coppers for the gas-meter. 'Thur air-raids are just comin' too often,' she shouted to them. 'Somethin' will have to be done about it or folk will be complainin'.'

'And who are they goin' to complain to?' The old woman chuckled and nudged Rankin.

'I ken who I'd complain to,' Mrs. Abbott cried, tugging at the drawer, which was stiff. 'When the first warnin' went I was standin' with a rotten egg in my hand, and I just wished *That Hitler* had been here so that I could 'a' thrown it at him.'

She tugged so impatiently at the drawer that it came out unexpectedly and fell on the floor. The cutlery in it made a terrific din.

Bessie and Rankin jumped at the noise, but the old woman turned calmly from the window and said: 'Was that a bomb, Sairey?'

7

'was that a bomb, Sairey?' Bessie giggled, telling the story to Lily McGillivray that evening. 'Honest to God, Lil, you'd 'a' died if you'd heard her. Was that a bomb, Sairey! Gosh, it takes thae auld ones, doesn't it?'

'I guess so.' Lily patted her hair and squinted at herself in the mirror. 'Well, what happened next?'

'Me and Mr. Rankin went and stood in the entry-door,' Bessie said. 'He was terrible anxious to catch Mrs. Lyons. Fancy, she hasnie paid him for weeks and weeks. What a bad limmer, eh? So we stood there to watch for her comin' in from whatever shelter she was hidin' in. We were standin' there talkin' when a plane came swoopin' ower the roofs. My God, it was right low down, I can tell you! We fairly ducked back into the entry.'

Bessie shivered at the remembrance. The plane had been low all right. Rankin had craned his neck, trying to make out the markings on it. And then suddenly he had jumped and yelled 'Ow!' clapping his hand to the back of his neck. His cigarette fell out of his mouth. 'I'm hit!' he cried.

'Let's see,' Bessie said, grabbing his shoulder.

There was a roar of laughter above them. They looked up and saw Jimmie the painter laughing down at them from a window. 'Caught you that time, mate!' he called.

Rankin grinned with relief and bent down to pick up a small piece of wood. 'I'd better keep this as a souvenir,' he cried, tossing it in the palm of his hand.

'Ay, maybe it 'll help you to get a War Pension!' Jimmie shouted.

'The All Clear went just then,' Bessie said to Lily. 'So of course Mr. Rankin had to leave me. I was right annoyed. We were gettin' on that fine! We saw Mrs. Lyons comin' out a shelter, so Mr. Rankin made a bee-line for her. But as soon as she saw him comin' she stepped back and—*plonk*! Honest to God, Lil, you'd 'a' died! Doon she went! Gosh, she must 'a' got a right tumble. Mrs. Moore cried: "Oh, the puir dear's slipped. Just a minit, hen, and I'll help ye." But Dirty Minnie says: "Ach awa', ye couldnie help yersel' far less her. Get oot ma road and I'll get her out!" '

Bessie giggled. 'It was right funny in a way. Ye should 'a' seen the two of them tryin' to help her out. The blind helpin' the blind! Poor Mr. Rankin,' she said. 'He didnie ken what to do. He just stood there like a stooky, and Mrs. Moore says: "I doubt ye'd better not bother her the now, poor hen, she's had such a shock." And so he didnie. But he said to me he'd watch Mrs. Lyons after this. I should jolly well think so, too! She's right cute. Fancy owin' him the Insurance Money for weeks and weeks and weeks.'

'And then to crown all,' Bessie said, and she started to giggle again. 'Really, it's not fair,' she said. 'It's no' a laughin' matter, but I can't help it. It was that funny! And then to crown all, when he went for his bike—it wasn't there! Somebody had pinched it!'

'Fancy,' Lily said.

She patted her hair again and stood up. 'You've never said how you liked my hair, Hippy.'

Bessie stood up and looked critically at her. 'I thought there was somethin',' she said. 'What have ye been doin' to it? Dyin' it?'

'Peroxide,' Lily said, turning round on her tiptoes and looking at herself in the mirror. 'It's not too bad, is it?'

''S lovely,' Bessie said. 'Really, it looks gorgeous.'

'I just took the notion this afternoon,' Lily said. 'I was in the middle of it when the sirens went, but I just said Och to hell, I might as well get bombed dyin' my hair as sittin' in a shelter amongst a lot of stinkin' auld women.'

'That's what I thought, too,' Bessie said. 'I'd never have gone to the shelter, but that auld bitch Mrs. Moore came rushin' in for me and dragged me with her. Really, what a cheek she had! As if I wasnie perfectly capable of lookin' after myself.'

'I just saw the peroxide bottle in the bathroom,' Lily said. 'My auld man had bought it for somethin'—he had a cut hand or somethin'—I cannie mind what it was that he bought it for—but I thought I might as well take it. So I did!'

She pirouetted again and went to the mirror to look more closely at it. 'It's not bad, although I say it myself.'

'What about doin' yours, Hippy?' she said.

'Oh, I wouldnie dare,' Bessie said. 'My faither would kill me.'

'Och, what about him!' Lily said. 'Once the deed's done he can do nothin' about it. C'mon, I'll do it for you.'

'I'd better not,' Bessie said.

She bit her lip and looked at herself in the mirror over Lily's shoulder. Her hair certainly needed something done to it. It was a helluva shade of red. It fairly showed up her freckles.

'Aw, c'mon,' Lily said. 'Here's the bottle.'

Bessie looked at it, then she looked at her reflection. 'Well, I dunno,' she said.

'Come on,' Lily said. 'It'll make all the difference in the

143

world. The Insurance Man 'll fall like a ton of bricks for you the next time he comes.'

'He's fallen already,' Bessie said tartly. 'And not only him!'

She put her hand on her hip and walked to the window, swaying her buttocks. 'He's not the only pebble on the beach!' she said.

'Honest to God, Hippy, you take the cake!' Lily laughed raucously. 'You'd think you had a string of men after you. How auld are you, anyway?'

'I was fifteen last month,' Bessie said.

'Fifteen! Christ, you're just a bairn yet!'

'You're no' much aulder yoursel',' Bessie said.

'Ay, but I know what I'm doin',' Lily said.

'Still, if you stick around with me, you never know what you might land!' she said

'I think I've landed somethin' already,' Bessie said.

'Och, the Insurance Man!' Lily snapped her fingers. 'That's not a catch. You've got to aim for higher things than that.'

'I'm not talkin' about the Insurance Man. I'm talkin' about that sailor that lodges with Dirty Minnie.'

Lily whistled and leaned forward. 'The young one with the curly hair?' she said. 'Oh boy, where did you fall in with him?'

'It was last night,' Bessie said as casually as she could. 'When I was comin' hame from the picters myself. I bumped into him in the blackout.'

'Boy, I wish it had been me!' Lily rolled her eyes. 'It would 'a' been some bump!'

'C'mon,' she said, lifting the bottle. 'If you're goin' to land this sailor, you've got to do a bit of camouflagin'. Are you game?'

'Okay,' Bessie said.

8

FOR at least an hour before the Store Van was due to arrive
the next day Bessie was in a state of trepidation. Her father
had raised such a row about her hair that she was in absolute
terror about what the women in the street would say. 'You'll
be the laughing-stock of the whole place,' Bert said. 'Making
a mug of yourself like that! God Almighty, have you looked
at yourself in the mirror? D'you mean to stand there and tell
me you think it's bonnie? *Bonnie!*'

'I don't see anythin' wrong with it,' she whined. 'And after
all, it's my hair.'

'Ah well, please yourself, please yourself,' he said. 'I wipe
my hands off it. But let me tell you, my lassie, that you're a
bonnie-like ticket for soup, and the quicker you let your hair
grow back to its natural colour the better I'll like it.'

'However, please yourself,' he said, picking up his newspaper. 'Just you wait and see what kind of reception you get
outside! You'll not be long, my lassie, in wishing you'd left
your hair the colour nature intended. Just you wait until some
of those women get started on you!'

As if she cared for what the street thought. The canaille!
As if Marie-Charlotte de Bourbon cared what the knitting-
women of the Place de la Guillotine thought and said about
her!

All the same, she was very nervous as she went out of the
entry and saw the crowd she had to face. Courage, mon
enfant! Allons! She pushed out her behind and swayed her
hips like Lily did. You have the blood of Marie Antoinette in
your veins. If she could face the crowd around the guillotine
. . .

'Hello there, hen!' Mrs. Moore cried. A spasm shimmered
across her jolly, fat face. 'Michty me, hen!' she exclaimed.
'What have ye been doin' to yersel'?'

'Another suicide blonde!' Dirty Minnie laughed. 'Dyed by my own hand!'

Bessie giggled nervously and leaned against the side of the van.

'It's a bit patchy, hen.' Mrs. Moore eyed her critically. 'Ye've surely been ower sparin' wi' the peroxide. Or did the bottle run done afore ye'd finished?'

'Ay.' Bessie giggled and looked down at the pattern she was tracing with her toe in the dust.

'Ye'll just hae to get another bottle then,' Mrs. Moore said. 'A wee ticky more should work the oracle! It'll take awa' that streakiness. It's ower-like streaky-bacon for ma taste the now!'

'Still, it's not too bad, Bessie,' said Dirty Minnie. 'It suits ye. It's a big improvement.'

'Ay, it should look very nice once she's given it a second coat,' Mrs. Moore said. 'My word, we'll soon no' be able to recognize her! We'll be sayin' to each other: What glamour girl's this comin'!'

'Come on, glamour girl, less o' yer lip and gie's yer order,' Andy the vanman cried. 'Ay, I mean you,' he said to Mrs. Moore. 'Or am I makin' a mistake? Maybe your time for bein' a glamour girl's long past!'

'Ach no, I still have my moments!' she laughed, handing him her Store Book. 'Ye must come up and see me sometime —when ma auld man's out!'

'She'd gar ye hop, Andy!' Minnie nudged Mrs. Moore, and they laughed boisterously.

'Or do ye fancy me, Andy?' Minnie said. 'I could maybe get my hair peroxided, too. I doot I'll hae to get it done or I'll no' stand a chance wi' thur young ones when this rationin' starts.'

'When's it goin' to start, Andy?' asked Mrs. Moore.

'Search me, lady!' he said.

'Come on then!' she said. 'Will I come into the van, or will ye come up to ma hoose?'

'Seriously though,' she said. 'When's it goin' to start?'

'You ken as much about it as I do,' Andy said. 'All I ken is

146

that ration books have been given out. But when they're goin'
to start workin' God knows. I ken I'm no' lookin' forrit to
them, anyway. They'll be a right headache for shopkeepers.'

'Huh, and what aboot the headache they're goin' to gie us?'
Mrs. Moore said. 'I ken I cannie make head nor tail o' mine.
All thae letters and numbers and wee coupons! It would take
a Phillydelphy lawyer to understand them.'

'They'll gie more than you a sore head, Andy,' Dirty Minnie
said. 'They've gien the postman gey sore feet for a start. He
was boogerin' and swearin' when he delivered ours. Sendin'
thur things through the post, he says. So I just said to him: "If
there wasnie the likes o' them for you to deliver," I says, "there
wouldnie be ony use for the likes o' you. What d'ye think ye
get your salary for?" I says. "D'ye expect to get it for doin'
nothin'?" '

'Thae civil servants!' Andy said.

'Ay, I just wish I'd been like Bessie here wi' ma hair done
up to the nines,' Minnie said. 'Maybe he'd 'a' been a bit more
pleasant then! I'll hae to do the Mae West act on him and see
what happens!—Though maybe I should try it on ma lodgers
first,' she said.

'I was speakin' to your lodger the other night, Minnie,'
Bessie said.

'Which one, m'dear?' Minnie began to shove her purchases
into her shabby black oilcloth bag. 'I've got four, ye ken!'

'The one wi' the curly hair,' Bessie said, giggling.

'Young Albert,' Minnie said. 'Ye'd better watch yersel' with
him, hen!' She gave Bessie a dig in the ribs. 'Albert's a regular
lady-killer! He's English, ye ken!'

'What about ma tatties, Andy?' she said.

'Here you are!' He hoisted a half-sackful of potatoes over the
counter. Minnie staggered a little as she caught it and cried:
'I help ma kilt, Andy, I'm no' Samson! How do ye expect me
to carry this up all thae stairs?'

'You'd better vamp one o' yer lodgers into carryin' it for
you, Delilah!' he grinned. 'It'll be guid practice for gettin' to
work on the postman!'

'I'll take it up for you, Minnie,' Bessie said.

147

'Dinnie haver, hen! You could never manage to carry this, a wee shaver like you. No, no, I'll manage it fine masel'.'

'Och, I'll take it,' Bessie said, trying to take it from Minnie.

'Havers!' Minnie exclaimed. 'And three hefty able-bodied sailors sittin' up there on their fat arses doin' nothin'! No, no, I'll soon get one o' them to take it up. HOY!' she screamed at the pitch of her voice. 'Toots! George! Albert! I want ye!'

Bessie wrestled the sack from Minnie and slung it on her back. 'Och, it's nothing',' she said. 'I'll soon take it up for ye, Minnie.'

'Keep ma place for me, Mrs. Moore!' she called, setting off towards the entry of Number Nine.

Minnie made no move to follow her. Although she'd got all her messages she would stand until the van went away. Such a collection of women gathered together at one time was too great a temptation to miss.

'Hoy!' she screamed again.

Bessie was shifting the sack into a more comfortable position on her back when two of the sailors pushed their heads out of Minnie's window. 'What's all the fuss, Minnie the Moocher?' one shouted.

'Come on, ye lazy boogers, and carry up that bag o' tatties!'

Bessie was beginning to feel the weight of the potatoes by the time she was halfway along the passage, and she stopped thankfully when she heard some one rushing downstairs.

'You shouldn't of bothered to bring it in, kid,' Albert said. 'I'd of come all the way out for it.'

'Och, it's all right,' she simpered.

She leaned against the wall and exhaled noisily. 'Gee, it doesn't half take the puff outen you!'

'You've said it!' The sailor tested the weight of the sack. 'I know this little boy wouldn't like to carry it very far, anyway!'

'Och away!' Bessie giggled.

'Gospel truth!' He grinned and leaned against the wall opposite. God, he did look nice! He looked even better than she'd thought. He was wearing nothing but a vest and his bell-bottom trousers. His firm muscular arms were sun-burned.

'Smoke?' He pulled a crumpled packet of Woodbines out of his vest.

'Thanks.' Bessie took one.

'You shouldn't, y'know!' he said, striking a match. 'It'll stunt your growth.'

'Och away!' she giggled, then she began to cough as the smoke went into her lungs.

'What did I tell you?' he said. 'You're far too young to smoke.'

'And you're far too young to encourage me!' She giggled and took another puff. 'Listen to grandfather talkin'!'

'What's Minnie doing out there, standing all this time?' he said, going to the entry-door.

While his back was turned, Bessie got herself into as good a posture as she could manage; she put the sole of her foot against the wall, bending her knee into what she hoped would be an artistic pose. And she put her hands behind her, trying to thrust out her breasts. Gee, if she could only put on a wee bit more weight in the right places. . . . She must mind to ask Lily about these false busts she'd read about. Lily might know where to buy them.

'Och, Minnie 'll stay out there to the last gasp,' she said. 'She won't be in a hurry to come in.'

'You'll be losing your place in the queue,' he said, coming back and lifting the sack. 'Better get a move on, kid. Thanks a lot for bringing this in for Minnie.'

'Mrs. Moore's going to keep my place for me,' she said, not shifting.

'Is she?' He settled the sack on his back and moved towards the stairs. 'Well if you lose it—it's your funeral! Tell Minnie to hurry up,' he said, his foot on the first step. 'Tell her if she doesn't hurry up, Toots and me won't take her to the pictures. That should fetch her!'

'Okay,' Bessie said. She took a step towards the door. 'What pictures are you goin' to?' she cried.

'The Rialto.'

149

'Aw, it should be guid,' she said. 'Madeleine Carroll and Ronald Colman in *The Prisoner of Zenda*. 'S lovely. I've seen it three times, but I wouldnie mind seein' it again.' She waited expectantly, but there was no response. 'Well, see and enjoy yersel',' she shouted.

'Sure thing!' His voice seemed to come from a great distance. 'Bye-bye, kid!'

9

THE following Sunday Bessie and Lily McGillivray went by bus to the farm near Peebles where the Hipkiss children were evacuated. Bessie had bought another bottle of peroxide and redone her hair. It was now a bright white-gold. She kept glancing at her reflection in the windows of the bus, touching her hair every now and then.

'Aw, for God's sake, Ferret!' Lily cried at last in exasperation. 'Leave it alone! You'd think you were Jean Harlow and that nobody had ever turned platinum before.'

Bessie pouted sulkily. Really, Lily was an impudent bitch sometimes. As if she had any room to talk. Her own hair was platinum, too—and it didn't look half as good as hers, either! She thought she was the whole cheese because she'd got off with a Petty Officer at the Rialto last night. As if anybody else with any sense would have had him. A wee skinny cratur with watery blue eyes and a long coat near tripping him. His ears were that big that they were holding up his hat. Lily was welcome to him. Just because he'd got some gold braid on his sleeves she thought he was It! But he was nothing like as good a catch as Albert. . . .

A guardsman sprang forward and opened the door of her limousine as it drew up in front of Buckingham Palace. Marie-Elisabeth de France barely glanced at him as she stepped from the car and ran lightly up the steps.

'It is rumoured that the French princess is in London for

more than a shopping expedition. Yesterday Her Royal Highness had lunch with their Majesties the King and Queen. Rumour has it that a Royal Alliance between this country and France . . .'

'Her Imperial Highness, Elisabeth, Madame Royale of France, Duchess de Brabant, Princess of Zenda.'

The slim young man in the naval uniform hurried forward to greet her as the heralds shouted her name.

'Hello, kid!' He grinned boyishly.

Marie-Elisabeth lowered her lashes and smiled mockingly as she swept him a deep curtsy.

'I am honairred, your Royal 'Ighness,' she said.

Albert Edward, Prince of Wales gave her his arm gallantly. 'You are beautiful today, Elisabeth,' he murmured.

'Hey, is it no' about time we were gettin' off?' Lily jabbed her with her elbow. 'I'm gettin' right fed up sittin' in this bus. If I sit much longer I'll be gettin' corns on my behind!'

'I don't think it should be far now,' Bessie said. 'The conductress said she'd put us off at the right place. I've never been there, ye ken. It's aye been my da that's been to see the kids since they were evacuated.'

She wondered if there would be much change in the children. It was nearly six weeks since she'd seen them. Poor wee souls, too, shut away here in the country, far from home and everybody that loved them. . . . You never knew what kind of folks they were amongst and what kind of ill treatment they might be getting. You bet they'd be glad to see her and Lily. She just hoped they wouldn't set up a hue and cry and want to come home with them. 'No, Jenny dear, I cannie take ye home. Ye'll have to wait till the war's over, pet. Ye'll have to wait till that bad Hitler's dead and done for.' She'd better practise saying that. Goodness me, it would be terrible if Jenny created a scene. Jenny was that sensitive. Poor little soul. Such a loving bairn, and she had such a nice sunny nature. . . .

It was starting to rain when Lily and Bessie got off the bus at the end of the narrow road leading to the farm where the children were evacuated. They hunched their shoulders and tried to lower their bare heads inside their coat collars against the cold east wind.

'It would have to rain!' Lily muttered. 'Jesus Christ and General Jackson!' she said as her high heels caught in a deep cart-rut. 'What roads! If this is the delights of country life, anybody that likes can have my share of it. It's heart-breaking, positively heart-breaking.'

But despite the bad road and the cold wind, they pushed out their behinds jauntily as they approached the farm buildings. You never knew who might be watching them! Some farm-labourers were terribly handsome fellows. After all, Henry Fonda had been a farm-hand in a picture they'd just seen—and Henry Fonda was the tops—yes, sir!

A dog rushed towards them, barking. 'Ge'away, ye brute!' Lily cried, trying to shoo it off. 'Ge'away! Mind ma stockin's! What for do they aye have to have yelping dogs at farms?' she said angrily, pushing open the gate of the farm-house and closing it quickly before the dog could follow them. 'Tearin' decent folk's stockin's with their claws. There should be a law against it!'

Mrs. Hood, the farmer's wife, met them at the door. She was quite an old woman about thirty-five; stoutish, with her brown hair done in earphones. 'The children are out playing somewhere,' she said, leading them into a pleasantly furnished sitting-room with comfortable easy chairs. 'They know you're coming—but where they've disappeared to, I don't know! Jenny was here two or three minutes ago. I expect she's in the byre. She's crazy about the cows.'

'I'm laying your lunch in here,' she said. 'I thought you would like that. The children usually have theirs with my husband and me; but I thought today as it was a sort of family reunion that you might like to have it by yourselves. I hope you don't mind.'

'Not at all,' Lily said, touching her hair and looking at the ceiling.

'Thank you very much,' Bessie said, thinking that Lily was putting on the City Lady act just too much. 'Dinnie be so high

and mighty, Lil,' she said after Mrs. Hood had left them alone.
'You're over-doin' the Garbo stuff a bit!'

'Aw, we might as well let her see life!' Lily said. 'Poor
bitch, stuck away here in the country. She'll never see anything.'

They sat down on either side of the fire and looked around.
'Not too bad a room,' Lily said in an offhand way. 'I wonder
if Her Nabs would kick up a dust if we smoked?'

'Oh, Lily, we'd better not!' Bessie looked around guiltily in
case she'd been overheard. She sat on the edge of the easy-
chair, wishing she could be as nonchalant and appear as much
at home as Lily. Gee, it took Lily to carry off an act.

'We'd better not,' she said again.

'Oh, Christ, all right!' Lily put her cigarettes back in her
handbag. 'I'm beginnin' to wish I'd never come to this dump.'

Mrs. Hood bustled in, carrying a tray. 'This is my maid's
Sunday off,' she said. 'So I'm kind of busy! You'll excuse me,
won't you? Oh, would you like a cigarette?' she said, taking a
packet from her apron-pocket.

'There's Jenny!' she exclaimed, as she struck a match.
'Jenny!' she called. 'Jenny!'

Jenny rushed in, her hair tumbling over her eyes. She
glanced at Bessie and Lily, then she rushed to Mrs. Hood and
threw her arms around her, crying: 'What's for the dinner?'

Mrs. Hood blew a cloud of smoke in the air, then she smiled
at Bessie. 'Here's your big sister to see you, dear! Aren't you
going to say hello?'

'What's for the dinner?' Jenny cried.

Mrs. Hood sighed smilingly. 'Rice soup and——'

'I don't want soup,' Jenny cried. 'I don't like soup.'

Mrs. Hood gave her a little push. 'Go and say hello to
Bessie like a good girl.'

'Hello, stinky Bessie!' Jenny said without moving. 'Did you
bring ony sweeties? Auntie Mabel aye brings sweeties, doesn't
she, Auntie Grace?'

'Yes dear, Auntie Mabel always brings sweeties.' Mrs. Hood
smoothed back Jenny's hair. 'What've you been playing at?
Tell Bessie about the cows and the tractors.'

'Come 'ere and tell me what ye've been doin', hen,' Bessie cajoled, leaning forward.

Jenny scowled. 'I will not. I'll throw a stone at you,' she said, retreating behind Mrs. Hood. 'I'll throw two stones at you!'

'Now, Jenny,' Mrs. Hood said. 'That's not the way to speak to your sister. Your big sister that's come a long way to see you. You must be nice to her.'

'I don't want to be nice,' Jenny said. 'I want to be bad.'

A door banged, there was a clatter of iron-shod boots and Billy ran in. He stopped and stared. 'H'ya, Ferret! What are *you* doin' here? I hope you havenie come to bide.'

'She hasnie come to bide here, Auntie Grace, has she?' he asked.

'No, dear, she's come on a visit.'

'That's all right then,' Billy said, sticking his hands in his pockets and striding forward manfully. 'As long as she's not comin' here to interfere. She'd just cramp my style. What have ye been doin' to yer hair, Ferret?' he said.

'Have ye bought new hair, Bessie?' Jenny came from behind Mrs. Hood and looked at her with wide eyes. 'It's nice,' she said. 'Could I buy hair like that?'

'You're fine as you are, dear,' Mrs. Hood said. 'Now be a good girl and speak to Bessie while I lay the table.'

Bessie wondered if she should offer to help, but as Lily made no move, neither did she. She envied the way Lily was leaning back in the chair with her legs crossed. She pulled Jenny towards her, saying: 'Come on, ma wee hen, tell Bessie what ye've been doin' with yoursel'.'

'We were at the Fair, weren't we, Billy?' Jenny looked at her brother, but he had lifted the lid of the cabinet-gramophone and had his head poked inside it.

'I want to put on a record, Auntie Grace,' he shouted.

'Violin!' Jenny screamed. 'Violin!'

Mrs. Hood laughed. 'All right, you can put it on, but if you break anything, Billy, I'll—I'll break your neck for you!'

'Violin!' Jenny screamed. 'Put on Violin!'

'Jenny's favourite record,' Mrs. Hood said. 'Put it on first, Billy, and that'll keep her quiet.'

Jenny leaned against Bessie's knees and listened to the music. 'It was so long agoooo, violin,' she joined in with the crooner. 'When the café lights were gleaming . . . sweet and low da di da . . . and your song goes on forever . . .'

'What did you do at the Fair?' Bessie said.

Jenny was gazing into vacancy, singing. 'It wasn't me that went to the Fair,' she said. 'It was Jenny McSquirt that went. She went there on a cow's back, and the cow had a ring in its nose. And when they got to the fair there was a lot of pigs, and the cow jumped on the pigses backs, and a witch came waving her broomstick and chased the cow away. The witch was awful angry, and she shouted a lot of Bad Words, and she had a long rope and she threw it at the cow and caught it round the neck. Then the witch jumped on her broomstick and took Jenny McSquirt away with her. She took her to her cottage and gave her tea and cookies, and then when they'd eated their tea they went into the garden, and a tractor came and runned over the witch.'

Jenny paused, fingering Bessie's skirt. 'That was a good story, wasn't it, Bessie? Now you tell me a story!'

'After dinner,' Bessie said.

'If you tell me a story I'll tell you anuzzer story.'

'No, after dinner.'

Jenny scowled, then she said: 'Let's play at visiting. I'll be Auntie Mabel visiting you. No, I'll be Auntie Mabel at a dance. I've just been dancing with Hitler,' she said.

'Have you?' Bessie said. 'Did you see Daddy at the dance?'

Jenny nodded solemnly.

'Who was he dancing with?' Bessie said, smoothing back Jenny's hair. There was no getting away from it, the kid was looking well. She'd aye been pale and peely-wally, but now she had some colour and her cheeks were a lot fatter.

'He was dancing with an elyphunt,' Jenny said, gazing out of the window as if in a trance. 'He danced with a big elyphunt, then he took the elyphunt on a cloud, and then a witch came and blowed them right off the cloud.'

'Play this one, Billy,' Lily said, holding out a record.

'I will nut.'

'Aw, go on! Play this one! It's my favourite tune. *Night and Day.*'

'I don't care,' he said. 'Who do you think you are, anyway, McGillivray? You're not the boss o' this house.'

'Lunch is ready,' Mrs. Hood cried.

'C'mon, Jenny, and I'll wash your face and hands before lunch,' Bessie said.

'I dinnie want my face washed,' Jenny screamed. 'It's not needin' washed.'

'Oh yes, it does.' Bessie took her by the arm.

'My hands are not dirty!' Jenny screamed.

Mrs. Hood laughed. 'Och yes, they're a wee bit dirty, pet. Let Bessie wash them for you. Show her the way to the bathroom like a good girl.'

'Okay,' Jenny said.

She insisted on washing her hands herself. She dabbled in the water, crooning over it. 'It was so long agooo, Violin. . . . It was so long ago that I lost my penny. . . .'

'See's your face,' Bessie said brusquely, grabbing her chin and rubbing her face with a wet flannel. 'Now there! That's a much cleaner wee lassie!'

Lily sat at one end of the table, and Bessie sat at the other, the children on either side. 'Who's goin' to say the Grace?' Bessie cried.

'Aw, for God's sake, Hippy!' Lily leaned her head on her hand and looked at the ceiling.

'We don't say Grace here, Ferret,' Billy said. 'C'mon, hurry up and gie's ma soup.'

'We're sayin' Grace,' Bessie said. 'Remember that Mammy liked us to say the Grace. Jenny, are you goin' to say it?'

'Not me, kid!' Jenny grinned across the table at Billy.

'Dish out the soup and let's get on with it,' Lily said, pretending to yawn.

'I'll say it myself,' Bessie said, and she closed her eyes and said it slowly, conscious all the time that Lily and the children were grinning at her. It was high time the kids were home again. They'd been evacuated long enough. They were just learning a lot of bad habits. It was true that they looked well enough, but health wasn't everything. That Mrs. Hood was just spoiling them.

'I don't want soup,' Jenny said.

Bessie placed a plateful in front of her and said: 'You'll eat this before it eats you.' Jenny took a few spoonfuls, then she leaned her elbow on the table, playing with the soup, lifting a spoonful high and letting it splash down into the plate.

'Stop doin' that!' Bessie shouted. 'Eat up your soup at once. Look how good Billy is! He's eaten all his.'

'I dinnie care.' Jenny lifted another spoonful high and let it splash. 'I dinnie like this soup. It's poisoned.'

'I want Billy to die,' she said suddenly. 'To die of hunger!' And she smiled like a malevolent old woman, crinkling up her face.

'It's you that'll be dying of hunger,' Bessie said. 'Eat up your soup, or a black dog 'll come and sit on your back.'

This was a fantasy their mother had invented, and it usually worked when Jenny was unmanageable. It worked now. 'No, a white dog!' she screamed. 'I dinnie like black dogs.'

'All right then, a white dog,' Bessie said. 'It's at the door now. It'll come and sit on yer back if ye eat up yer soup.'

Jenny looked round. 'I see it!' She took a few spoonfuls. 'It's a nice wee dog, isn't it, Bessie? Is it sittin' on my back now?'

They were in the middle of eating chicken and potatoes and vegetables when Billy said: 'I don't like the school here, Ferret-face. The teacher 'll no' let me go to the lavvy when I want.'

'Och, nonsense!' Bessie said. 'Of course, she will.'

'I'm surprised at you tellin' such fibs, Billy Hipkiss,' Lily said sanctimoniously.

'It's not a fib at all, McGillivray,' he shouted. 'You shuttup! Who asked you to come here, anyway? Tryin' to boss the show!'

'Keep your hair on,' Lily said. 'I'm sure if I'd known it was to be such a wash-out I'd never of come.'

'Of course the teacher 'll let you out if you ask her,' Bessie said. 'Just ask her nicely to get outside.'

'I dinnie like,' he said. 'I'm feared.'

'But it'll be all right,' she said. 'The teacher kens what ye want. She needs to go to the lavvy hersel'.'

'But I dinnie like,' Billy said.

'Ach, dinnie be daft,' she said. 'Just you say "Excuse me, please," and it'll be all right. Then you can run outside.'

Jenny had been listening in silence. She started to slip off her chair. 'Excuse me, please.'

'Here, you sit still and eat yer dinner,' Bessie said, reaching out and pushing her back on to the chair.

'But I'm goin' to do a wizzy,' Jenny said, opening her eyes wide and putting on a reproachful face.

'So ye've been takin' it in, have ye?' Bessie smiled. 'A' right, away ye go to the bathroom.'

'Can I go outside?' Jenny asked.

'Of course no'. What would ye want to go outside for?'

'But you said to Billy he could go outside.'

'But that was different. He's a little boy.'

'But nobody'll see me. I'll go round the corner.'

'No, away to the bathroom.'

'I'll go to the byre, Bessie. The cows 'll not see me.'

'Go to the bathroom when you're told.'

'No.' Jenny stuck out her lower lip and bent her head until her nose almost touched her plate. 'I'm no' goin' now.'

'A' right,' Bessie sighed. 'But mind, if ye wet yer breeks . . .'

Jenny shoved a spoonful of potatoes in her mouth, then she pushed them in further with her forefinger. She glowered at Bessie. 'Shuttup,' she said, taking a gulp of milk. She rammed another spoonful of potatoes into her mouth. 'Shuttup, you buggis!'

10

AFTER lunch Bessie helped Mrs. Hood wash the dishes while Lily played the gramophone and quarrelled with Billy. 'Has

Auntie—has Auntie Mabel been here often, Mrs. Hood?'
Bessie said, frowning at the plate she was drying.

'She comes every Sunday with your father,' Mrs. Hood said.
'She's an awful nice woman, isn't she? The bairns fair adore
her.'

'Ay, she's all right,' Bessie said.

Mrs. Hood swilled out the sink. 'You know, I think it would
be a good thing, if your father and she got married. Of course,
it's none of my business—but I'm very fond of the bairns, and
I'm sure it would be a good thing for them. Little Jenny needs
a mother,' she said, wringing out the dish-cloth. 'She's such
an affectionate bairn—she needs somebody.'

She struck a match briskly and lit cigarettes for herself and
Bessie. 'Now away you go!' she said. 'Get the bairns to show
you and your friend round the farm. I must do some baking
for the tea.'

'We'll go and see the tractors first,' Billy said.

'No, the cows!' Jenny cried.

'The byre's nearest, Billy,' Mrs. Hood said. 'You can go
there on your way to the tractor-shed.'

The children took Bessie's hands. Lily followed, picking her
way moodily through the muddy farm-yard. 'Jees, what a
stink in here!' she cried as they entered the byre. She peered
into the semi-darkness, at the rumps of the cows and their
swishing tails. 'I'm no' comin' any further,' she said. 'I've
seen enough.'

Bessie would fain have stayed with her friend at the door,
but Jenny pulled her on. 'Come and see Shirley Temple,' she
cried. 'She's ma favourite cow, isn't she, Billy?'

'Look, she knows me!' she cried, letting go of Bessie's hand
and running into the stall beside the cow, rubbing her cheek
against the beast's neck. 'See, she likes me! She's goin' to lick
ma face!'

'Come out of that, Jenny Hipkiss!' Bessie cried, terrified.
'Come out of that at once afore ye get killed!'

'Aw, nuts!' Billy said.

He strode into another cow's stall, giving her a smack on
the rump. 'Hup there, Marigold! Hup there, lassie!'

Bessie hovered anxiously near the wall, keeping as far from the cows as she could get. 'C'mon outside, both of you!' she cried. 'I thought ye were goin' to show us the tractors, Billy?'

'A' right.' Billy gave the cow another smack and swaggered manfully towards the door. 'What are ye so feared at, Ferret-face? The cows 'll no' touch ye. They're far more feared at you than you are at them. And no wonder wi' that hair o' yours! Have ye looked in a mirror?'

'Well, glamour girl!' he said to Lily. 'It's a guid job *you* didnie go in there. There would 'a' been a riot if the cows had seen you!'

'I'll glamour girl you!' Lily aimed a kick at him. 'I'm for less of your lip, Billy Hipkiss. I've a good mind to give you a scud on the jaw.'

Two tractor-men were working on the engine of a tractor when the girls and the children entered the shed. The younger one, a lad of about nineteen, looked up and said: 'Uhuh!'

Billy swaggered up to them and shoved his head under the bonnet of the tractor. 'What's wrong with it, man?' he said.

'Somethin' wrong with the magneto, Billy lad!' The young man grinned and winked at the girls. 'But don't worry, sir, we'll get it ready in time for you to drive the morn!'

Lily and Bessie hovered inside the doorway, but Jenny joined Billy and glowered into the dismantled engine. 'We had chicken for our dinner, Sandy,' she said to the young man.

'Had ye? God, but ye're a lucky wee lassie! Is this yer big sister?'

'Ay, this is stinky Bessie!' Jenny grinned. 'Do you know this,' she said solemnly. 'She didnie bring me any sweeties. My Auntie Mabel aye brings me sweeties.'

'Ach, that's not fair,' Sandy said.

He winked again at the girls. But they stood at the door. 'Come on, you two,' Lily said. 'I thought you were going to take us for a walk?'

'No sense in wastin' our time with the likes o' him,' she said as they went through a gate into a field. 'He's just small fry.'

Bessie nodded. Too true, he was nothing patent. Now, if Albert had just winked at her like that. . . . But he would! Just give him time, and he would. He was shy, that was what was wrong with him. If only he had some of that tractor-bloke's gumption . . .

'Aw, I'm fed up to the back teeth,' Lily said after they'd walked about a hundred yards through the field. 'This is not my idea of pleasure at all. Let's get back to the house and play the gramophone.'

'Have we seen everything, Billy?' she said when they returned to the steading. 'Are there no other men working?'

'They dinnie work on a Sunday,' he jeered. 'It's just thae twa tractor-lads that are workin' the day.'

Jenny ran ahead and scrambled on top of an empty stone horse-trough. 'Let's sit down here,' she cried. 'And you'll tell us all a story, Bessie!'

'I'll certainly do nothin' of the kind.'

'You promised!' Jenny shouted. 'You promised!'

'Och, I'm tired.'

'Just a wee story, Bessie! Just one wee story!'

'A' right.' Bessie sat on the edge of the trough. 'It's warm enough here, Lil, as long as the sun stays out.'

'Not for me, thank you,' Lily said. 'If you don't mind, I'll go into the house and play the gramophone.'

Bessie sighed, watching her friend teeter across the tractor-tracks towards the house. True enough, there was a coldish wind. Maybe they'd be better in the house. But when she rose to follow Lily, Jenny pulled her down, crying: 'On and on and on with the story, Bessie!'

Bessie sighed. 'Well, once upon a time there was a witch and her name was Witch Blacknose. And she was a wicked, wicked witch and wore green ear-rings and a green necklace. And there was a good wee fairy called Jenetta McSquirt.'

'Me! Me!' Jenny cried rapturously. 'Am I a good wee fairy, Bessie?'

'Sometimes,' Bessie said.

She watched some hens scratching on top of a midden, wishing she'd found out what Miss Stevens had been wearing when she visited the farm. Likely enough she hadn't had on either her green ear-rings or her necklace.

'Did Auntie Mabel wear pretty clothes?' she asked.

'Ay,' Jenny said. She tugged impatiently at Bessie's arm. 'On and on with the story!'

'Well, there was a princess imprisoned in a castle, and they called her the prisoner of Zenda, and she was a beautiful princess with fair, fair hair. And she kept standing at the window, waiting for a handsome prince to come and rescue her. And one day she saw a boat coming up the river towards the castle, and when the boat stopped a handsome sailor jumped out. Oh, but he was a handsome sailor with brown curly hair, and his name was Albert Edward. He waved up to the princess and shouted: "Half a mo, kid, I'll rescue you in a trice." But the door of the castle was locked, and a wicked man called Rupert of Hentzau had the key. Oh, but he was a wicked man, and he was in league with the wicked witch. However, Albert Edward looked around to see what he could do. And while he was looking, the wicked witch flew up on her broomstick and caught hold of him by the curly hair and carried him off.'

Bessie looked again at the hens scratching so industriously. She felt a vague uneasiness. The setting was so unfamiliar that she could not put the heart she usually put into her stories into this one. She stood up; the cold stone of the trough was seeping through her thin skirt.

'Ach, let's play at witches,' she said. 'I'll be Witch Green-nose, and Billy 'll be Witch Blacknose. And you'll be a good wee fairy,' she said to Jenny, who had run towards the byre-door and was playing with two small kittens.

She contorted her face and, pointing her finger dramatically in the air, she cried: 'I'll turn you into a rock, Witch Black-nose, unless you come away from that plough. Are you comin' away from it, Witch Blacknose, or do ye want me to put a spell on ye?'

'It's no' a plough,' Witch Blacknose said. 'It's a harrow.'

'Well, whatever it is, you come away from it,' Bessie cried. 'Do ye want to cut yoursel', ye bad boy?'

162

'Blethers!' Billy said.

'A' right,' she said. 'I'll turn ye into a rock. I've still got this good wee fairy beside me, so I'm no' needin' ye.'

'I'll kick yer bloody arse,' the wee fairy said.

'Aw, but ye wouldnie do that, would ye?' Bessie smiled and pushed back Jenny's straggling hair.

Jenny stared at her. 'I'll kill you,' she said solemnly.

'Aw, but ye wouldnie do that, would ye?'

'I'll kill you, you buggis,' Jenny said. 'Then I'll kill thur kittens. I'll bash their heads in with big big stones.'

'Aw, the poor wee kittens!' Bessie cried. 'What would Mrs. Hood say if ye did that?'

'I'd kill her, too. But I'll kill you first,' Jenny added.

'But what if I killed you first?'

'I'd run away.'

'But if I ran after ye?'

'I'd run away to Mrs. Baxter's.'

'But I'd follow ye.'

'But I'd lock the door.'

'Then I'd come in the windy.'

'But I'd shut the windy.'

'But I'd break the glass.'

'But I'd. . . . Aw, shuttup, you buggis,' Jenny said, and she turned away, tired of the game. 'I'll kill you,' she said again. But she said it listlessly, and she yawned. 'I want my tea,' she said.

11

AS soon as they got on the bus Lily slumped on a seat and said: 'Jesus Christ and General Jackson, what a wash-out of a day!'

Bessie slouched sulkily beside her. Lily was a right pest sometimes. All she ever thought about was men. As if she could help it because there weren't any nice-looking fellows

163

at the farm. The whole day had been a wash-out as far as she was concerned, too. Jenny and Billy had disappeared after tea and they'd had to look for them to say good-bye before she and Lily left. Jenny had been in the byre, sitting on some straw beside a cow. She'd just looked up and said: 'See and bring sweeties the next time you come.' As for Billy, they hadn't been able to find him at all. Mrs. Hood had said that probably he'd be at one of the cottar houses and that they'd see him on the way to the bus. But they'd seen neither hunt nor hare of him. It was high time they were both home again, so that she could keep her eye on them. They were just growing wild. Turning into real country jossers. Not saying Grace or anything. I don't suppose that Mrs. Hood bothers about making them say their prayers. After all the bother her mother had had teaching them, too. It was scandalous. But what was more scandalous was her father taking That Woman to see them. Auntie Mabel this and Auntie Mabel that. They'd been more taken up with Auntie Mabel than they'd been with her and Lily. It was high time it was put a stop to. Auntie Mabel —the painted dyed-haired bitch—was probably at Goldengreen Street today, having tea with her father and kidding herself on the house was hers already. But she didn't need to bother. She's not coming here as long as I'm alive. Over my dead body, Miss Stevens! You think you're awful clever, but you're not.

'I have arranged for you to be put on board a destroyer, Milady.' Marie-Elisabeth de France leaned back in her chair and looked scornfully at the trembling courtesan. 'His Royal Highness, the Princes of Wales, will himself conduct you aboard. . . .'

'What a hell of a slow bus!' Lily muttered. 'Crawlin' along here like the dead march. And you can see nothin' in this bloody blackout. Christ, but I wish the war was finished!'

Lily didn't need to complain about the blackout. Lily, like lots of other people, had a damned fine time in the blackout. She was beginning to have quite a good time in the blackout herself, if it came to that! After all, if it hadn't been for the blackout she might never have got the chance to speak to

164

Albert. Of course, the war was terrible and all that—but well, nobody had been killed yet (or not many, anyway) and it might all be over soon. Everybody said it couldn't last more than a month or two. She might as well make hay while the sun shone—or while the moon shone, anyway! *Moon at sea, tell me that my love's a true love. . . . Wait for me. Keep on shining on high as he goes sailing by. . . . Moon at sea . . . Tell me there'll be no new love, that he sails away with my heart . . . Moon at sea. . . .* Oh, but he was lovely! If only he was sitting beside her just now, instead of Lily, with his arm round her, pressing her tight against him. . . . Jees, it was almost painful the way she felt about him. She'd *never* felt like this about anybody before. There was a kind of lump or something in her breast. Like something trying to get out that couldn't. Almost as if she were going to be sick. Oh, Ma, I love him that much. Oh, Ma, I just wish you were here so that I could talk to you about him. I just want to hug him and keep on hugging him. It's funny, isn't it, Ma? Or is it funny? Did you ever feel like this, Ma, about Da? You couldn't have, Ma, could you? No, nobody could feel like this, the way I feel about Albert. I feel I'd like to crush him to death. I don't want anybody else to touch him. Jees, wouldn't it be terrible if he had to go away to sea again soon. . . . She must get to talk to him. She must. . .

But Bessie, you're just fifteen. He thinks you're just a bairn. He doesn't realize how old you really are, how experienced you are. He doesn't know how you feel about him. You'll have to show him. You'll have to make some excuse to go up to Dirty Minnie's tomorrow and get a chance to talk to him. To show him . . .

Fifteen's not ower-young to marry, is it, Ma? How old were you when you married my Da? I'm not a bad girl, am I, Ma, for thinking things like this? Tell me I'm not a bad girl, Ma. I say my prayers every night, Ma, like you learned me. Oh, Ma, if you just knew how crazy I feel about him. Oh, Ma, I just wish I could marry him and get away from my Da. I'd do anything to get away from my Da. . . .

'You know, Lily,' she said. 'I'm beginnin' to think I'll maybe take a job.'

12

THE next day Bessie left the midday meal preparing on the gas-cooker and ran across the street to Dirty Minnie's. One of the lodgers, the tall sailor called Toots, opened the door for her. 'Oh, I wondered if Minnie—er, I mean Miss Nimmo, could lend me a wee ticky semolina?' she said. 'I was just goin' to make a puddin' and I discovered . . .'

'Is that you, Bessie?' Dirty Minnie called. 'Come awa' in, hen. We're just havin' a fly-cup!'

Minnie was sitting at the table, her fat elbows spread out amongst a collection of different-shaped and coloured cups. 'Bring another cup for Bessie,' she said to the ginger-headed sailor who was sprawling beside the fire.

'You get it, Toots,' he said. 'I can't be bothered rising.'

'Ye're a right lazy devil, George!' Minnie laughed. 'You wouldn't do a hands-turn if you could help it.'

'Well, neither would you,' he said. 'Lookit that table! There's still bits of yesterday's breakfast sticking to it!'

'Ay, it's hellish, kind friends!' Minnie laughed boisterously. 'Never heed him, Bessie,' she said, pouring tea into a cup for Bessie. 'He's browned off because the Old Man or the C.O. or whatever they ca' him wouldnie give him ten days' leave.'

'You'd be browned off yourself if you was me,' George said. 'What would you do if you saw other folk gettin' leave that hadn't as much right to it as you? You'd squeal, too, I bet. And you'd squeal hard!'

'Ay, I guess I'd gie him a piece o' my mind,' Minnie said. 'For I'm no' one for takin' things lying' down as you know! But never mind, son,' she said, stretching out for his empty cup. 'Ye'll get over it.'

'I will not,' he said. 'I'll get even with the Old Man for this if I have to swing for it. I'm sick and tired of the graft there is down at that Base.'

'There he goes again!' Minnie cried. 'The balloon's away up! Ye never saw such a bloke for arguin' as George here,' she said to Bessie. 'He'd argue the backside out a wheelbarrow. Everythin' must be just so! If George had the runnin' o' the world, it would be a better place.'

'Or a worse,' Toots said laconically.

'I like a square deal for everybody,' George said. 'The way this war's being run would sicken a kangaroo. It's a case of money, money, money all the time. What's the war about, anyway? It didn't start because a bloke called Hitler wanted a bit of Poland. No, sir, it started because the money-bags in this country were terrified the money-bags in Germany would cut them out in the world's markets. It's all a question of graft—but the thing is that the buggers that want the money and the big business won't go and fight for it themselves. They send a lot of poor sods like us to do all the dirty work for them.'

'Ay, it's a hard life, son,' Minnie said. 'But cheer up! We'll soon be dead and away from it all! Drink up yer tea afore it gets cauld. All the hot air you let out winnie make one bit o' difference.'

Bessie leaned against the dresser and sipped her tea. George was just like her father. Politics! Politics! Politics! They were aye shooting out their necks about something. They never agreed with what was in the papers, and they said the wireless was a lot of lies. It was a good job everybody in the world wasn't like them. She wondered where Albert was. It was funny he wasn't here drinking tea with the others.

'Is that somebody at the door?' Minnie cried, cutting into the middle of a long harangue by George, who was denouncing the Government, mixing it up with descriptions of the graft at the Naval Base, trying to prove various points.

'See who it is, Toots,' she said. 'And, George, for God's sake shuttup in case it's the polis! We've enough stuff from the Base in this very hoose to hang us all!'

It was Mrs. Moore. She was a bit breathless, and she was very red in the face as she preceded Toots into the living-room, clutching a large shopping-bag to her ample bosom. She dumped the bag on the table and sank thankfully into a chair.

'Thae stairs'll be the death o' me yet!' she exclaimed.

'Never mind, hen, have a cup o' tea!' Minnie cried. 'We're right thankful to see ye! We thought it was the bobbies!'

'I'm kind o' heavy on the feet,' Mrs. Moore giggled. 'But I dinnie think I'm as heavy as all that yet!'

'I was just gettin' ready to hide a' the boys' Winnings—a' the meat and fags and stuff they brought up frae the Base this mornin',' Minnie said.

'Where were you goin' to hide it, Minnie?' George winked at the others.

'God knows!' she said. 'Every hole and corner in the hoose is filled already. Even under the very beds! There's nae room under mine even for a jerry! It's a guid job I dinnie need one!'

'Where have you been stravaigin' the day?' she said to Mrs. Moore. 'Ye surely got up wi' the lark!'

'I've been awa' to Leith. I went to Woollies to see if I could get some rubber soles.' Mrs. Moore sighed. 'Ye ken, it's gettin' to be a bit of a job. Shoemakers 'll no' take yer shoes to mend. So I just says to ma auld man: "Ye can hae a shot at tryin' to sole them yersel'. It'll be wicer-like," I says, "than sittin' there by the fire wi' yer head buried in a book." Books, books, books! I'm fed up wi' the sight o' them. He's never awa' frae that Public Library—comes hame every time wi' a muckle bundle o' books under his arm. I'd burn the whole jing-bang o' them if I had ma way.'

'You're as bad as Hitler,' George said. 'He ordered a lot of the books in Germany to be burned, and look where it's landed us!'

'That was a different matter entirely,' Mrs. Moore said. And she added quickly before George could say anything further: 'Then after I was at Woollies I went up to Princes Street and had a dander along it to see all the sights.'

'Ye're a right auld trail-the-wallets!' Minnie laughed, pouring out more tea.

'Well, ye'll no' see nothin' if ye sit by the fire all the time,' Mrs. Moore said. 'I'm a great believer in goin' out and seein' and bein' seen. And that reminds me, Bessie Hipkiss,' she said. 'Where were you trailin' to yesterday? I saw ye go away in the mornin' wi' that Lily McGillivray.'

'I was doon near Peebles to see the bairns,' Bessie said.

'Oh, of course, I forgot! I saw ye goin' away wi' Lily, and I wondered where ye could be goin'. I'm glad to hear it was just to see the bairns. I thought maybe you and Lilly were up to some dodge. I must say I'm surprised at ye makin' such a pal o' Lily.'

'What's wrong with her?' Bessie said belligerently.

'Oh, she's maybe right enough,' Mrs. Moore said. 'But she's not a pal for you, Bessie. Oh no, she's not a pal for you, is she, Minnie?'

'Och, the lassie's well enough,' Minnie said.

'But she's no' a pal for Bessie,' Mrs. Moore said. 'No, no. I dinnie ken what yer puir mother would have said, Bessie. She wouldnie have liked to see ye gallivantin' aboot the streets to all hours o' the night with that Lily McGillivray. Lily's a right bad little egg.'

'I dinnie care,' Bessie said. 'I like her—and that's the main thing.'

'What will yer puir da think?'

'Ach, him! He doesnie care what happens to me. He's that taken up with his Mabel.'

'She was here yesterday, I see,' Mrs. Moore said. 'I saw them both goin' out after tea. My goodness, but yer da did look spruce! I could 'a' taken a fancy to him masel'!'

'But you mind what I say,' she said. 'Dinnie you have too much truck wi' Lily—or ye'll be finding yersel' in the soup.'

'Well, who else am I goin' to go out wi'?' Bessie whined.

'Get a lad!' Mrs. Moore laughed. 'Look, there's plenty o' sailors here!'

'D'you want us to get taken up for cradle-snatchin'?' Toots grinned.

'Albert would 'a' been the one for her,' Minnie said with a bawdy giggle. 'Ay, Albert would 'a' been the right one! It's a pity he's awa'.'

'Albert awa'?' Mrs. Moore said.

'Ay, he went yesterday. Did I no' tell ye? Of course, I havenie seen ye since. I must say it was a right surprise to us, too. He's got shifted to Devonport.'

'D—Devonport?' Bessie said.

'Ay, he got leave, and was told to report back to Devonport, so he just packed a' his gear and up tail and awa'.' Dirty Minnie sighed and raised herself slowly from the table, leaning heavily on her hands. 'He was a nice laddie, Albert, and we'll miss him.'

'Maybe you will,' George said. 'But there'll be plenty of other dry eyes in the house. The little twirp! He got the leave I should of got. It was my turn for it.'

'Ach well, what does it matter?' Minnie patted him on the shoulder. 'If you'd gotten the leave, maybe you'd 'a' been shifted to Devonport instead o' him—and we couldnie have had that! Dinnie look on the black side, George. Every cloud has a silver lining. We can spare Albert easy enough, but this house couldnie do wantin' you.'

'Bring through that butter frae the kitchenette, Toots,' she said. 'I must gie Mrs. Moore and Bessie a wee bit to help them grease their wizzens. Only—if ony o' ye as much as gie a whisper aboot it to anybody else in the street, it's the last ye'll get!'

Bessie accepted the lump of butter and accompanied Mrs. Moore downstairs in a daze. She nodded mechanically to the old woman's chatter, saying 'Ay, that's right' every now and then. But she heard nothing.

It was only after she was in her own house and had been standing in front of the mirror for some time that she remembered she'd never got the semolina she'd gone to borrow. 'Imbecile!' she cried to her reflection. And she crossed herself and went to the jar where she kept her own semolina. It was practically full. As she poured some of it into a bowl, she said to herself: 'Aw well, there's as many good fish left in the sea as ever came out of it.'

PART V

1

'MAKE way for the jam tarts, ladies!'

In the despatch department of Andrews' Bakery there was continuous noise and bustle. Girls clad in bright blue overalls rushed hither and thither, pushing trolleys of cakes, pies, biscuits and bread. The floor was littered with paper and shavings. Cakes and cookies fell continually off the trolleys and counters and were trodden unheeded amongst the rubbish on the floor. The girls did not take time to walk; they ran as if the Devil were behind them, chasing them on with a big stick. 'Take yer behind out o' the way, Annie!' one was shouting. 'I don't want yer big dock to squash thur meringues!'

Bessie Hipkiss was counting pies at her counter. A few feet from her, Lily McGillivray was piling up rounds of shortbread. Miss Christie, the forewoman, in her black sateen overall, was standing with her notebook a few feet beyond, writing down what Ginny Smiles and May M'Queen were shouting out.

'Eleven dozen Bath Buns,' Ginny shouted.

'Eleven?' Miss Christie looked up from her note-book. 'There should be twelve.'

'Oh ay, so there should.' Ginny grinned. 'Sorry! I forgot that Jim had taken a dozen o' them.'

'Well, you shouldn't forget,' Miss Christie said. 'What do you think you're here for? What did Jim do with them?'

'I dinnie ken,' Ginny said. 'Honest, I dinnie.'

'Jim!' Miss Christie shouted to a youth in shirt-sleeves and white apron who was edging his way through the trolleys, pushing girls aside, with a baker's board on his head. 'Jim, what did you do with that dozen Bath Buns?'

He stopped, grinning sheepishly. 'I gave them to the East Trinity vanman.'

'Did he sign a chit for them?'

Jim looked apologetic. 'No, Miss Christie, he said he'd sign it when he came back. He was in a hurry.'

'You know perfectly well not to let him take stuff out without signing a chit,' Miss Christie snapped. 'He might swear black was white that he'd never got it. I've told you about this before, Jim.'

'But he was in a hurry——'

'That doesn't matter. He could easily have taken time to sign the chit. If this happens again I'll report it to Mr. Wilson.'

Miss Christie moved away majestically to speak to another woman in a black overall who had cried: 'Could you spare a minute, please, Miss Christie? You're wanted in the front shop.'

'It's heart-breaking the way that dame Christie gives herself all the airs, isn't it?' Lily muttered to Bessie. 'Positively heart-breaking.'

'Aw, she's daft,' Bessie said without looking up. 'Never let on ye hear her, Jim,' she said.

'I'm not givin' tuppence for her,' he said. 'She can rant and rave as much as she likes for all I care.'

'Get out o' my road, love!' a girl with a trolley shouted behind him.

He moved nearer Bessie, and he leaned towards her, putting up a hand to steady the board on his head. 'Is it all right for tonight?'

'Ay, the Playhouse at six o'clock,' she said.

He moved away, and she watched him as he threaded his way through the girls and the piled trolleys of tea-bread and cakes. Gee, she was for Jim in a big way. She'd *never* felt like this about anyone before. She loved him so much she could eat him.

'Quit dreamin', Ferret!' Lily gave her a jab with her elbow. 'Christie'll be back the now, and if she sees you lookin' like that she'll be on yer top like a ton o' bricks.'

But Bessie continued to dream as she counted the pies and

watched for Miss Christie. Already in the three weeks she'd
been here she'd become an adept at this. Counting pies was
a mechanical thing. La, la, it was like playing cards. . . . Or
dominoes. Remember the time she'd played dominoes with
the Mexican ambassador?

Tiens! That had been a time! She had sat with a poker face,
watching the diamonds on her hands as they moved the black
and ivory counters. She was playing for higher stakes than
the pile of chips between her and Señor Juarez. Little did the
poor man realize that. He might be a great politician in his
own country, but he was no match for a princess of the Blood
Royal of France. She knew that he had come to Paris to give
her and her husband the once-over, to see if they'd make a
suitable Emperor and Empress for his uncivilized Mexico.
His mission was supposed to be secret, but Madame Royale
of France had her own Gestapo. . . . *Eh bien,* she would go.
But only at a price. She must have complete sovereignty.
Neither she nor Jim were to be used as catspaws in the way
an earlier Mexican government had used Maximilien of
Austria and poor Bette Davis. She didn't want Jim to end his
life facing a firing-squad on the Hill of Bells like Brian Aherne.
'No, Señor Juarez, my 'usband and me—ve moost 'ave ze
complete power. Vat I say shall be law—I, Elisabeth
Carlotta de Bourbon, Princess of France and Empress of
Mexico.'

Of course, her father raised quite a stink when she told him
she'd accepted Juarez' invitation. 'Look here, Bessie,' the
King cried, putting his glass of beer down with a bang on the
golden table, 'we can't have this. You're taking too much upon
yourself, my girl. First of all you insist on marrying this common boy from a tenement in the back streets of Abbeyhill.
Then you force me to make him Duke de Guise. And now
you want me to help you make him Emperor of Mexico. We
cannot 'ave eet, Elisabeth. Your place is here in la belle
France beside me. Remember that I am the King and that
my word is law.'

But Papa was no match for her. She had won her way then,
and she would go on winning her way. She was Elisabeth

de Bourbon. Indomitable, overbearing, proud and ambitious —one of the great women of History. . . .

'Did I hear ye say to Jim ye'd meet him at the Playhouse?' Lily said.

'Ay.' Bessie did not look up from counting the pies.

'But ye've seen the picter! You and me saw it last week. It's *Juarez* with Bette Davis and Paul Muni.'

'I ken,' Bessie said. 'I want to see it again.'

'Christ, you're the limit, Ferret!' Lily said. 'I wouldnie waste time and money on goin' to see any picter twice.'

2

MOLLY in the Staff Canteen had adenoids. She was a tall, thin woman in her early thirties with lank fair hair cut à la Garbo. A soiled chef's cap was stuck on the back of her head, and it looked as if it were always on the point of falling off. Molly's face was woebegone, and she talked all the time in a complaining, nasal tone.

'Well, hen, how are ye the day?' she said when Bessie went to the counter for lunch. 'Ye're still here, I see. Jethuth God, if I was you I'd lift ma books and get while the gointh good. Thith is no place for a minister's daughter! Ye'll never get on in thith place. Lookit me! I wath a tattie-peeler and now I'm a cook. But not a penny extra!'

'Dinnie take the mince, hen,' she whispered. 'It's no' guid. Try some o' this meat pie.'

'Okay,' Bessie said.

'I'm just givin' the mince to folk I dinnie like,' Molly winked. 'Ay, I wath a tattie-peeler,' she went on. 'When I took thith job I dinnie ken what I was lettin' masel' in for. Miss Lindsay said to me when I applied: "You're not afraid of work, are you?" And I thaid I wasnie. For honest to goodness, I'm not. I love work. That's what I thaid to her. "I love work," I thaid. "Ethpecially scrubbin'. I'm just fair daft about scrubbin'.'' But devil a bit o' scrubbin' have I had to dae since I came. She put me to work in thith bloomin' canteen right away, peelin' tatties. Jethuth God, the amount of tatties I've peeled in ma time! They would thretch frae here to Jeruthalem! But now that Chrithmuth ith comin' on, I've got a change. I wath a tattie-peeler and now I'm a cook. And not a penny extra. A pound a week and all found. All found! Huh, the workth found for ye all right. Ye never need to go out and look for it. I tell ye, hen, Mith Lindsay would like ye to bring yer bed here wi' ye. I'm fair pushed frae potht to pillar.'

'Och, ye'll get a rest in Heaven,' Bessie said.

'Will I hell!' Molly moaned. 'There'th never any rest for poor thouls like me.'

'All right, I'm comin',' she shrieked to a girl at the other end of the counter.

Bessie took her plate of meat pie to the large table and sat down between Ginny Smiles and Miss Matheson from the office. Opposite her sat Mrs. Irvine, the Canteen Cook, who had just finished her lunch. She stopped talking to Mrs. Woods from the Grocery Department to say: 'Hello, Bessie, how are you today, m'dear?'

Bessie grinned and mumbled: 'Fine, thanks.'

She liked Mrs. Irvine, and evidently Mrs. Irvine had taken a fancy to her. Mrs. Irvine was an ardent spiritualist, and the first time she'd seen Bessie she'd said: 'You're psychic, m'dear. I know it!'

She was a very stout woman with an enormous bust. A large cameo brooch held her white silk blouse in place, but it always appeared to be playing a losing battle. Mrs. Irvine kept toying genteelly with it.

'Ay, just a minute, just a minute!' Molly shouted to Lily McGillivray who had rushed in and was banging a plate, knife and fork on the counter. 'I hear ye all right. I'm not deaf. But I've only got one pair o' handth. I'm fair pushed frae potht to pillar.'

Bessie gobbled her meat pie, listening to Miss Matheson tell Ginny about an Oratorio she was going to sing in that

175

evening. 'It's *Elijah*,' Miss Matheson said. 'And oh boy, is it first class! Really, it's lovely, Ginny. You should join a choir.'

'Ach, what good would I be in a choir?' Ginny grinned. 'I dinnie ken one note from another—unless they're pound notes!'

Miss Matheson pushed her rimless glasses more firmly on her little snub nose and leaned past Bessie. 'Oh, but that doesn't matter,' she cried. 'As long as you can sing in tune. What are you, anyway, Ginny? A soprano?'

'Naw, I think I'm an alto!' Ginny winked at Bessie. 'All to hell!'

But Miss Matheson was above sarcasm, even as pointed as this. 'You've no idea how grand it is, Ginny. What a wonderful roar you get! Really, it's gorgeous. If you like, I'll speak to Mr. Sands, our choirmaster, about you.'

'Ach, choirs are for auld women,' Ginny said. 'No thanks, love, I'm no' havin' any!'

But Miss Matheson went on about the glory of singing in a choir and what a wonderful feeling it gave you. 'It fair uplifts you, Ginny,' she cried. 'Really, you have no idea the gorgeous feeling you get at some of those top-notes.'

Ginny gathered up her empty plate, knife and fork and rose, shouting: 'What's next on the Me and You, Molly?'

'Cuthtard and prunes, or themolina and figs?'

'I'll try some o' yer custard,' Ginny said.

'I'm fair pushed frae potht to pillar,' Molly lamented, following Ginny to the table with her own lunch. 'That'th what I said to the Head Chef just now. I was down in the bathement for somethin' for ma dinner. I thought there might be somethin' good goin' frae the big restaurant. But the greedy Bee followed me into the frig. "What are ye wantin' here?" he thays. "I want thomethin' for the morn's thoup," I says. "Ye're far ower early," he thays. "Come back in the mornin' and I'll give ye thome scraps. They're guid enough for the workers." Didya ever hear the like? That'th a felly-worker for ye! Jethuth God, if there's ever a revolution I ken yin I'll help to thtring up on a lamp-post.'

'But I did him,' Molly said, reaching for the staff tea-pot

176

which was larger than the kettles in most households. 'I did the Bee all right. I thlipped thith bit o' meat when he wasnie lookin'.'

'You should 'a' slipped some for us when ye were at it,' Lily cried. 'This mince is terrible.'

'Ach you, ye're ower fancy-mouthed,' Molly said. 'If ye want to complain, ye'd better complain to Mrs. Irvine.'

'What's that?' Mrs. Irvine said, twisting her huge bulk towards Lily. 'I'll have you know, Miss McGillivray, that there's nothing wrong with the mince. It's the person that's eating it that's at fault.'

'It's got a funny taste,' Lily said.

'It's your mouth that's got the funny taste,' Mrs. Irvine snapped. 'It's the after-effects of all you drank in that pub last night. Don't think I didn't see you, my girl, trying to hide behind that sailor! I saw you all right. I'm not blind.'

'I've as much right to go into a pub as you,' Lily said defiantly.

'I'm a much older woman than you, Lily McGillivray,' Mrs. Irvine said. 'I've earned my right to go into pubs in broad daylight. My godfathers, I don't need to hide behind sailors!'

'It would need a pretty hefty sailor to hide you!' Lily laughed derisively, but nobody echoed her laughter, and she shrank back into her seat, pushing moodily at her mince.

'I was thpeakin' to wee Jeannie in the Grocery,' Molly said, 'and she thays there's a strange thailor been hangin' about the back entrance these last two-three nights. He pounced on her and May M'Queen last night in the blackout. Didya ever hear the like? If he doesnie watch out he'll get nabbit.'

'I just hope he does,' Miss Matheson said.

Bessie listened, shivering with apprehension. A sailor in the blackout! Jees, if he would just pounce on her. . . . But this was her early week; she'd be finished at three o'clock before the blackout started. It was just her luck. Anyway, she was going to the pictures tonight with Jim. . . .

Oh, Jim! Jim, you're worth twenty sailors. The way your

head's shaped and the way your hair curls on top. . . . Oh, Jim, Jim. . . .

'I'd sentence people like that to the Cat,' Miss Matheson said. 'Frightening the life out of decent girls.'

'Och, Mith Mathethon!' Molly giggled. 'The girlth like it fine!'

'I don't believe it.'

'But——' Molly giggled. Bessie knew from the look on her face that she'd been going to say Miss Matheson was no girl; she'd never see forty again.

'Well, here'th one that would!' Molly said. 'Only I never get the chance. Nobody ever thinks o' pouncin' on me.'

'I just hope the police get him,' Miss Matheson said. 'It would serve him jolly well right. A good dose of prison would settle his hash.'

'Och, don't thay that, Mith Mathethon,' Molly said. 'Poor thoul, if he had to go to jail. Still,' she said, perking up at the thought, 'I'd be able to wave to him from my windy then! Oor hoose is right opposite Saughton Jail, ye ken. I often thee them lookin' oot the windies or marchin' round the yard. There wath one standin' at a windy the other day, and I shouted up to him: "How long are ye in for?" And he put hith hand through the barth like thith——'

Molly held up five fingers, closing and unclosing them while she intoned dramatically: 'Five, ten, fifteen, twenty, twenty-five, thirty—— Oh Chritht!' she cried. 'I wondered whether it wath thirty days or thirty years!'

She sighed. 'There wath yin standin' at oor entry the other mornin' when I wath comin' away to ma work. They had just let him oot. I mutht thay they let them oot terribly early in the mornin'. It's no' fair on the poor thouls. They might let them have a nice long lie on their last mornin'. This yin looked that cauld and bedraggled like, I felt real thorry for him. He thays to me: "Mithith, could ye gie me tuppence for a pint?" '

'Tuppence!' she cried. 'Tuppence! Jethuth God, it's a long time since beer was as cheap as that. Poor thoul, I just wondered how long he'd been in there.'

'Whatever he was in for I'm sure he richly deserved it,' Miss Matheson said, rising.

178

'Jutht a minute, Miss Mathethon!' Molly cried. 'Will ye read ma cup afore ye go?'

Miss Matheson bridled with pleasure. 'Well, if you like, Molly——'

'Ach, I'm surprised at ye, Molly!' Ginny Smiles giggled. 'It's just a lot o' havers!'

'I ken fine it's a lot o' haverth,' Molly said lugubriously. 'But I like to get it read all the same. I might hear some bit o' bad news I hadnie thuthpected for masel'.'

'Oh, but there's good news in this cup,' Miss Matheson said, holding it up and squinting over her glasses into it. 'You're going to get a surprise! Oh boy, yes, you're going to get a big surprise.'

'Huh, that'll be a bomb fallin' on our tenement very likely,' Molly said. 'It's aye guid folk like me that gets bombed, no' bad folk like you, Ginny Smiles! You're the kind that aye comes off without a thcratch. But puir folk like me get it in the neck every time. But I thuppose we'll just have to let it come. We cannie do anythin' aboot it.'

'You're going on a journey, Molly,' Miss Matheson said. 'Yes, you're going on quite a long journey.'

'Huh, I could 'a' tellt ye that,' Molly said with a sniff. 'I'm goin' on a journey all right. I'm goin' oot o' here at six o'clock, and I'm goin' on a tram, and I'll likely hae to stand all the way because nobody ever thinks o' offerin' the likes o' me a seat. If I was a bright young thing wi' painted nails— gloriouth technicolour in tooth and claw!—now *that* would be different. But I've aye got to stand. And then I'm goin' to walk aboot half a mile, and then go in to a dead fire and three hungry bairns. Ay, I ken I'm goin' on a journey all right!'

'Never mind, Molly,' Miss Matheson said, putting down the cup. 'Here's something to cheer you up. You're going to get a letter.'

'Huh, it'll be the rent bill,' Molly sighed. 'Or maybe it'll be a letter from ma man. It's about time he wrote. It'th thix weeks thince I had a letter. It'th all very well for him bein' away in Egypt enjoyin' himsel' in the thands o' the dethert, but I have the three bairns to look after. He kent what he was

179

doin' all right when he joined the sodgers. Jethuth God, but it gets me down sometimes.'

Bessie had been listening eagerly to the cup-reading. She leaned forward and cried: 'Will you read my cup now, Miss Matheson, please!'

'Sorry, Bessie, not today.' Miss Matheson gathered up her handbag and her spectacle-case in a flurry. 'Goodness, I must rush! I'm late!'

'Yes, I doubt we've all taken more than our official half-hour,' Mrs. Irvine said, placing the palms of her hands on the table and heaving herself up.

'C'mon, Bessie, or we'll be gettin' Lady Christie on our tracks,' Ginny cried.

'Ay, get to hell out o' here, the whole jing-bang o' ye,' Molly said, leaning her head on her hands and gazing mournfully into her empty cup. 'Away back to yer work and let me get thome peace. Dinnie let me thee yer ugly faces again before tea-time.' She drew the tea-pot towards her. 'Jethuth God, I mutht have another cup o' tea to thuthtain me. Then I think I'll away oot and thee if I cannie get a hold o' that thailor!'

3

BESSIE was at the top of the stairs when Mrs. Irvine called her back and said: 'We're having a little Circle tonight, m'dear. Would you like to come?'

'I cannie,' Bessie said. 'I'd like to, but—but I promised I'd go to the picters wi' somebody.'

Mrs. Irvine smiled. 'Ah well, it can't be helped. See and enjoy yourself! Maybe you'll come to a Circle some other night? Next week maybe?'

'I'd love to,' Bessie said. 'Can I really?'

'Of course, m'dear. You can come any night you like.'

Mrs. Irvine smiled and waved her on. Bessie hummed gaily

as she ran downstairs after Ginny Smiles. Mrs. Irvine was a real nice body. She knew fine it was Jim she was going to the pictures with, but she was too much of a lady to say anything. Now, if it had been any of the others they'd have chaffed the life out of her. Even as it was, she couldn't be seen talking to Jim but one or other of them would make raffish remarks. But Mrs. Irvine wasn't like that at all. Mrs. Irvine was a cut above everybody else in the place. Not in the least bit common. Of course, she talked broad sometimes, but only when she got annoyed and forgot herself. Usually she was very genteel.

In a way Bessie wished she'd been able to go to the Circle tonight. She'd been wanting to go ever since Mrs. Irvine had told her about them. 'We have one every week, m'dear,' she'd said, and she had told Bessie a lot of the things that happened. She had told her all about her Arabian guide, Ali Ben Hassim, who advised her about everything she did. 'I consult him about everything, m'dear,' Mrs. Irvine said. 'I never even go the length of my sister's at Portobello without asking him if it's propitious.'

Mrs. Irvine didn't really need to work. She had a boarding-house for students in one of the streets off Nicholson Square. She had taken this job as Staff Canteen Cook in Andrews' just for the Christmas rush. 'I thought it would be a nice wee change, m'dear,' she said. 'My boarders are all on holiday. And it always helps the War Effort a bit, doesn't it?'

This was Bessie's early week, and she finished at three o'clock. She had just got home and was cutting some meat into pieces to make a stew when her father came in. 'Well, how's the World's Worker?' he said. 'You haven't got the sack yet, have you!'

'No' yet,' Bessie grinned.

'I suppose you think Andrews'll not be able to get on without you now!' he said. 'Now that you've wormed your way in you'll be well on your way to becomin' a mainstay of the firm!'

'Aw, I dinnie ken,' Bessie giggled.

'Still, it can't go on much longer, m'lassie,' he said, settling himself on the sofa and opening his newspaper. 'It's high time you gave up this daft nonsense about havin' a job, and settled down again at home. I'm gettin' bonnie and tired of havin' most of my meals in restaurants.'

Bessie sighed, but she said nothing. She and her father had been over and over the same ground countless times in the past three weeks. He had raised the roof that first day when she had said: 'I've got a job!' And when he had heard that she'd got it through Lily McGillivray he'd been angrier than ever. 'It's bad enough you're bein' chummy with that little bitch,' he'd cried. 'But it's a bloody sight worse to go and work beside her. It's not as if you needed to take a job, anyway. Your place is at home here with me.'

'But I'll hae to take a job sooner or later,' Bessie said. 'Lassies are goin' to get called up to do war work as well as men.'

'Well, there's time enough to bother about that when the time comes,' he said.

'I cannie help it,' she snivelled. 'I've taken the job now, and I'm goin' to start on Monday. D'ye want me to ask Mrs. Moore to come in and make your dinner for you every day, or would you like to go to her place for dinner? Or would ye rather go to a restaurant?'

'So you've got it all cut and dried already,. have you?' he said. 'By God, you're a sleekit bitch, too. You're like your mother. I'll bloody well go to a restaurant. And if I die of food poisonin', heaven help you, m'lady!'

'And how's everybody in Andrews' today?' Bert said now. 'How's that daft bitch, Mrs. Irvine? Has she been spoutin' spiritualism to you today again?'

'She's not daft,' Bessie said. 'She's a very nice woman.'

'She's a daft skate,' he said. 'And the less you have to do with her the better. Has she been gettin' elevated again?'

'I dinnie ken,' Bessie said huffily.

'Elevated!' He laughed ribaldly. 'I know the kind of elevation she goes in for. Though I must say I haven't seen her in our bar lately. She must 'a' changed her haunts.'

Bessie said nothing. She regretted ever having told her father about Mrs. Irvine. And she was terrified Mrs. Irvine would find out that her father was a barman in a pub that she often went to near the McEwan Hall. She had been very careful not to tell Mrs. Irvine anything about her home life. That first day she had just simpered when Mrs. Irvine said: 'You're different from the other girls here, m'dear. I sensed that as soon as I saw you. It's not only because you're psychic. There's something about you that makes you stand out.' Bessie hadn't told Mrs. Irvine yet about being an exiled Bourbon, but she'd made up her mind that she would when she went to her first Circle.

'How's Molly?' Bert said. 'Now, there's somebody with both feet on the ground! Molly's not the kind that would get elevated at any bloody spiritualist meeting. Molly's too down to earth for that. It's a hard life and she knows it.'

'Aw, Molly's a pain in the neck sometimes,' Bessie said. 'She's like a bloomin' Christmas card, she's aye greetin'!'

'Christmas,' Bert said, lighting a cigarette. 'Ay, it'll soon be Christmas.' He took two or three puffs, then he said: 'I was wonderin' if maybe we shouldn't have the bairns home for Christmas.'

'Aw, Pa, we can't,' Bessie cried.

'Och, why not? I don't like the idea of the poor wee souls bein' away from home at Christmas.'

'But the bombs, Pa! There might be an air-raid. You said yourself they were better to stay evacuated.'

'An air-raid your Granny!' He laughed. 'Talk about Molly aye lookin' on the black side! If you only knew it, my lassie, you're as bad as her every bit.'

'There'll be no air-raid,' he said. 'When did we last hear a siren? This war gets phonier and phonier. I shouldn't be surprised if it just fizzled out.'

Bert continued to talk like this for a while. 'The balloon's away up again!' Bessie said to herself, beginning to chop onions. The war and the way it was being run was one of her father's favourite themes. She never listened to him.

'There's a complete deadlock,' he said at last. 'There we are, sittin' on our arses at one side of the Maginot Line, and there are the Germans sittin' on theirs at the other. And it's all a question of who's goin' to give in first. Is it goin' to be British Big Business? Or German Big Business?'

'In any case,' he said, 'they're so inter-mixed that it must be difficult for them whiles to know which side they're on. I bet there are a lot of folk in this country with shares in I. G. Farben shittin' their pants in case Jerry has to give in.'

'And then there are the Americans,' he said. 'Sittin' back and wonderin' which side they'll put their shirts on. And all the time they're rakin' in as much of the world's trade as they can get.'

Bessie went on making her stew. She wasn't interested in the war. She was driving in a high-powered Rolls Royce towards the Hill of Bells, clutching Juarez' pardon for Jim in her slender white hand when she heard her father say: 'I think I'll write to Mrs. Hood and say we'll have the bairns home for a fortnight.'

'Aw, Pa, we cannie,' she wailed. 'I cannie look after them. Christmas and New Year weeks 'll be our busiest time at Andrews'. I'll likely have to work overtime.'

'There's nobody asking you to look after them,' he said. 'Your Auntie Mabel'll be delighted to come here and see to them. I wouldn't dream of deprivin' you of the pleasure of workin', my girl, seein' your heart's so set on it!'

Bessie lit the gas-cooker and put on her stew. She gave it a few vicious stirs. When you thought of the fuss her father had made when she wanted to bring the bairns home before, really this was too much. She didn't want Miss Stevens here, but at the same time she didn't want to give up her job. Her father had got her in a cleft stick.

'What do ye want for yer tea?' she said. 'We'll have this stew at supper-time.'

4

s o Milady Stevens is to reign supreme in France, to Queen it in the Louvre, is she, mon pere, while you send your daughter to barbarious Mexico! Madame Royale bit her lips as she paced angrily up and down the long gallery hung with portraits of her ancestors. Eh bien, so be it! She would go, she would say farewell to Europe, and she and Jim would sail for Mexico and whatever awaited them under its hot, pitiless sun. If need be, they'd stand on the Hill of Bells together, facing the firing-squad. She would disdain the handkerchief for her eyes that the General in command of the firing-party held out to her. Imperial and proud, she, Elisabeth Carlotta, would stand with her handsome young husband, facing their death —pitiful pawns in the game of power politics. And in France the bells would toll, and there would be a service of remembrance in Notre Dame, and the flags would fly at half-mast. And on their way to the funeral service the Parisian crowds would hoot and boo at Robert I and his black-veiled companion—the courtesan who had driven Madame Royale the Well Beloved to her tragic end.

'Well, where are you gallivantin' to the night?' Bert said when she went into the living-room.

'Goin' to the picters,' she said.

'With Lily McGillivray?'

'No, she's goin' out with somebody else.'

'Huh,' Bert said sarcastically. 'I'm damned glad to hear it. Did you know that she had the nerve to come into our bar the other night with a sailor? He ordered whisky for her. Whisky! I just said to him: "That girl's gettin' no whisky here, sailor," and I gave him a lemonade. He was goin' to cut up rough about it, but I just told him. I said: "I know that girl, sailor. I know she's under eighteen. She's gettin' no whisky here." If I ever hear of you goin' into a pub with her, my girl,' he said, 'I'll skin the hide offen you.'

'But I've never been in a pub with her,' Bessie whined. I've never——'

'Or with anybody else,' Bert said.

'Who're you goin' to the pictures with?' he said.

'With Jim,' she said.

'Jim? Oh ay, that's the laddie in the despatch.' Bert grinned. 'You're a bit young yet, m'lady, to start courtin'.'

'But I'm not——'

'Okay, okay!' Bert grinned and shoved his hand in his pocket. 'Forget it! I was just jokin'. Here's half a crown. That'll help to pay you in. I don't expect your precious Jim 'll be able to afford it off the wee pay he's bound to get from Andrews'.'

'Better ask him to come to tea on Sunday,' he shouted as she went out. 'Your Auntie Mabel 'll be here, and she'll help to entertain him!'

5

I WILL not ask him to tea on Sunday, Bessie said fiercely to herself as she ran downstairs. The idea! I'd never ask Jim to come here and meet that painted bitch of a woman. And I'll take damned good care that I'm out myself when she comes. What a cheek he's got asking her to come here and look after the bairns at Christmas. I've a bloody good mind to leave and go to lodgings.

But even as she thought it, Bessie wondered if she would have the courage to make this final step.

When she got out of the entry she stood for a second to allow her eyes to get accustomed to the blackout. A black mass was waddling towards her.

'Hello there, Mrs. Moore!' she cried. 'I havenie seen ye for weeks.'

'My, is that you, Bessie! What a stranger ye are!' Mrs. Moore was panting with exertion. 'Ye're such a busy wee shaver these days that I never see ye. Ye must come up and see me some time, like Mae West!'

'Ay, I will,' Bessie said, edging past her.

'I'm fair scunnered wi' this blackout,' Mrs. Moore said. 'I cannie get hangin' out my window at night like I used to. I've got to come down into the streets at night to see what's doin'. It's hard lines on an auld body like me. But it's all right for you

186

young ones,' she said. 'My, I wish I was your age again. There'd be no holdin' me back! Ye must have a lot o' high jinks!'

'Ay, it's not bad,' Bessie giggled.

'Is this you away on the ran-dan again!' Mrs. Moore laughed. 'See and be guid! Dinnie do anythin' I wouldnie do!'

'No bloody fear!' Bessie laughed and cried: 'Cheerio!'

Now there was Mrs. Moore, she thought, running down the hill to Harrisfield Square to catch a tram, she could look after the bairns if he insisted on bringing them home for Christmas. Ay, there was Mrs. Moore . . . She'd suggest that to him when she got home. She'd far rather have Mrs. Moore nosing about the house than Auntie Mabel. She'd never have any peace of mind if she thought yon woman was raking about among her mother's stuff. Ay, that was an idea. Wonder what he'll say to that?

She felt more cheerful at the thought, and by the time she had reached the Playhouse she'd forgotten all about Auntie Mabel. Jim was waiting for her on the steps of the cinema, and she put her hands into the pockets of her short jigger coat, drawing it tight and thrusting out her bottom as she pranced towards him.

'Hya!' Jim said.

'Hya!' she said.

How nice he looked, she thought. It was a fine change not to see him in his white apron. He suited his navy blue double-breaster. Although it was a cold night, he had his overcoat pushed open and his hands in the pockets of his grey flannel trousers.

'What have you been doin' to your hair?' she said.

'Nothin'.' Jim put up his hand and smoothed his fair hair. 'Just put some oil on it.'

'Aw, it's far nicer without it,' she said. 'My goodness, if I had waves like yours I wouldnie try to plaster them down with any old oil.'

'Ach, it looks so sissy,' he said.

'Don't be daft!' she giggled.

'And anyway, it makes it look darker,' she said.

187

'Ach, what do I care!' he said.

'Well, what seats are we goin' to?' she asked.

Jim balanced himself on the edge of the steps, hands in pockets, looking down at the toes of his pointed black shoes. '"There's nothin' but three and sixpennies left,' he said. 'I guess we'll have to wait in the queue.'

'Ach, let's go to the three and sixpennies,' she said. 'My dad gien me a half a crown. That'll pay the extra.'

'Ach!' Jim frowned.

'No, I'd rather wait in the queue,' he said. 'There should be seats soon.'

'Aw, come on!' she said.

'But——' He glowered.

'I've got some money,' she said.

'But I——' He flushed. 'I dinnie like.'

'Aw, don't be daft!' she said. 'C'mon!'

Prancing into the entrance hall, she hoped there was somebody in the queue who knew her. It was a pity it was so dark. She would just like them to say in Calderburn: Fancy, that lassie Hipkiss goes to the three and sixpenny seats in the Playhouse! It takes her, doesn't it!

'Have ye enough money?' she whispered to Jim. 'If ye havenie . . .'

'Naw, I've got enough,' he whispered. 'I'll get it after.'

Bessie put up. her hand and fluffed out her hair over her shoulders while she waited for him to get the tickets. My, but Jim did look nice. So nice and clean. He didn't have pimples or anything like that. Not like a lot of fellows of his age.

As they went upstairs to the Circle she took five shillings from her bag and, looking round to see that nobody was watching, she slipped it into his hand.

'Ach!' He frowned, but he put it in his pocket.

Gee, but she was for Jim in a big way, Bessie thought, sinking into a seat. She'd never felt like this about anybody before. It was funny, wasn't it, when you came to think about it. Three weeks ago she hadn't known he existed. And yet now . . . She knew far more about him than she knew about anybody else. And he knew far more about her. He was the first person she'd ever met who understood her. Not that he talked much. He just talked about football and the bakery and what he did when he went out with his pals. But oh gee—he was lovely!

She put out her hand and touched his knee, and he took her hand and held it tightly. She snuggled her shoulder against his and gave herself up to watching the film.

Juarez was almost ending. Bessie sat, mouth slightly open, watching the scene on the Hill of Bells. God, how she hated Paul Muni. If she'd been Bette Davis she'd have scratched his eyes out. Christ, but she'd like to rip open that stolid Mexican face. But poor Bette, she just moaned and stared with those big eyes of hers, and she didn't seem able to realize it when they told her Maximilien had been shot. She just rushed out into the darkness of the garden. Out into the darkness, disappearing in her white dress, disappearing until nothing but the frill of her crinoline could be seen, disappearing out into the darkness . . . going mad . . .

Bessie gave a deep sigh as The End was flashed on the screen and the net-like curtains drew across it with a swish. She looked at Jim and smiled. 'It was guid, wasn't it?'

'Ach, I don't know,' he said. 'You can't tell what a picter's like when you see it like this. I don't like to see the end first. It spoils the beginning when you know what's goin' to happen.'

The lights went up, and for a few minutes hidden gramophone records played while the audience looked about them, changed seats, or went out. Bessie leaned against Jim, humming with the music. Bing Crosby was singing *Love In Bloom*. 'Can it be the trees that fill the breeze with rare and magic perfume . . .' The honey-husky voice dripped into every corner of the vast building, and numerous couples like Bessie and Jim sat, hand in hand, lapping it up. 'No, it isn't the trees . . . It's love in bloom!'

All through the News and the Disney cartoon Bessie thought about what she would say to her father. 'Mrs. Moore would be awful offended, Pa, if you didn't ask her to look after the bairns. After all, she was a great friend o' Mammy's . . .' But when *Juarez* started again she gave herself up to watching Bette

Davis and to dreaming about what she would do when she found herself in the same position.

'Will we go for a walk?' Jim said, when they came out of the cinema.

'No, I'll have to catch a tram,' she said. 'I cannie leave it ower-late. The trams are stoppin' that early thur days.'

'This war's a damned nuisance,' Jim said. 'The picture-houses come out that early that folk expect you to be home by ten o'clock. My old man raised Cain the other night because I was out till half-past ten. My God, he never used to say half as much when I came in at twelve before the war started.'

'My old man's the same,' she said.

'Parents are a damned nuisance,' he said.

'Too true!' she said, giggling, and she put her arm through his. 'But never mind, we'll get over it,' she said, as they began to walk towards the Theatre Royal where she would get her tram.

'That picture next week should be good,' she said. 'Merle Oberon and Laurence Olivier in *Wuthering Heights*. We must see it.'

'Ach, I don't like Laurence Olivier,' Jim said. 'He's soppy.'

'He is not,' Bessie cried. 'I think he's great. I think he's lovely. I could go for him in a big way.'

'Ach, I'd rather go for Merle Oberon,' Jim said, and he whistled. 'Boy, she's the goods!'

'Ach, I don't like her,' Bessie said. 'There's something . . . She's aye slinking about, and she looks that *fast*!'

'All the same I like her,' he said.

'We'll go anyway,' she said.

They had stopped in the dark empty doorway of a shop. Jim shuffled and mumbled something. 'I—er—I'll no' be able to manage,' he said.

'How?' she said.

'Well——' He grinned sheepishly. 'I'll likely be away to the Army by that time. I—I've just had my papers.'

'Aw, Jim, I didnie ken!' she wailed, gripping his arm.

'Ay, I had my Medical two-three weeks ago.'

'Aw, Jim!' she cried.

190

'I've been meanin' to tell you,' he said. 'But I—I didnie like.'

'Aw, Jim!' she cried, and suddenly she threw her arms around his neck and kissed him.

It was the first time they had kissed, and she bumped her nose against his chin. But she was unconscious of the bump as he put his arms around her and pressed her against him. 'You should 'a' told me,' she cried.

'Ach, I didnie want to worry you,' he mumbled.

She pressed her cheek against his. 'I never thought ye'd have to go yet,' she said. 'Ye're awful young to have to go.'

'I'm nineteen,' he said.

'Never mind,' he said. 'I won't be away for long likely. The war won't last. Jerry'll never be able to keep it up. We're far ower-strong for him. We won the last war and we'll win this one, too.'

'I hope so,' she said. 'But oh, Jim, I wish ye hadnie to go!'

'I'll write to you,' he said. 'You will write to me, won't you? Tell me all the news about the shop and Lily and Ginny Smiles and Molly and that Christie. Gee, but it'll be fine to get away from *her* for a while. She'll have to find somebody else to report to the manager for a change. Gee, but I think all women bosses should be sunk.'

'Well, there'll be no women bosses in the army,' she said.

'Ay, that's a consolation,' he said. 'Boy, am I goin' to have a whale of a time!'

'I'll write to you every day,' she said. 'But it'll not be the same, Jim, honest to God it winnie be the same.'

'Never mind, I won't be away for long,' he said, and he kissed her again. 'Oh, Bessie,' he murmured. 'I'm for you in a big way.'

'Even more than Merle Oberon?' she said.

'Anybody can have her that likes,' he said.

'Bessie,' he said, and he kissed her again, hugging her tightly. 'Bessie, will you—will you wait for me, Bessie?'

'Of course, I will, silly!' she giggled.

'Of course, we're a bit young to get married yet,' he said. 'But maybe—maybe we could get engaged when I get my first leave.'

'Aw, my dad wouldnie let me,' she cried. 'I'm ower-young. He'd take the back o' his hand across my jaw if I dared mention it.'

'Ach, surely he wouldnie mind you gettin' engaged?' Jim said. 'We could have a long engagement.'

'You don't know my dad!' she said.

'Ach, you're auld enough to have a mind of your own, aren't you?' he said.

'I'll not be sixteen till next month,' she lied, adding ten months.

'Sixteen! Is that all? I thought you were seventeen anyway.'

Bessie bridled with pleasure and said: 'Did you really, Jim?'

'Uhuh.'

'I wish I *was* seventeen,' she said. 'Gee, if I was, I'd be away from home at the toot!'

'Well, we'll see if he'll let us get engaged when I come home on leave,' he said.

'Ay, we'll see,' she said.

'Aw, there's a car away past!' she cried. 'I hope it's not the last one. I don't want to have to walk all that length.'

'Och no, there'll surely be another one,' Jim said.

'Ye'd better take down my address,' he said. 'Ye can write to me at home at first. My old lady'll send me on your letters.'

'Have you a bit paper and a pencil?' she said.

It was funny, she thought while he searched his pockets, she'd known him for three weeks and she thought she knew everything about him. It was funny that she hadn't known his age or his name. She knew where he lived, and she knew all about his parents. She knew about his dad who bred canaries and his mother who was suffering from asthma. But it was funny that she didn't know his surname. Everybody in the Bakery called him Jim; he didn't seem to need another name.

She took the piece of paper he'd been writing on. She fished her flashlight out of her bag and flashed it on it.

'What's this?' she said. 'S—M—E. . . .'

'Smellie,' he said.

6

'WHAT am I goin' to do, Lil?' Bessie said the following morning in a tram on their way to work. 'I couldnie marry anybody wi' a name like that. My own name's bad enough, but I'm no' wantin' to change it for somethin' worse.'

'Aw, what are you botherin' your buckie about, Ferret?' Lily said, eyeing a sailor across the tram.

'But he asked me to marry him. . . .'

'Well, that doesnie mean you've got to marry every daft bugger that asks you,' Lily said. 'Don't be so bloody green, Ferret—if you'll excuse my French!'

'But I promised,' Bessie snivelled.

'What if you did! It doesnie mean anything.' Lily smiled at the sailor.

'But I said I would wait until he came back from the war.'

'Och, what does it matter what you said!' Lily let the cigarette-smoke exhale slowly from her nostrils, tilting her chin so that the sailor could get a better view of her profile. 'If Jim goes away to the war, I bet he'll not worry about it. I bet he'll get another girl as soon as he's landed in wherever he's goin'. You're a right mug, Ferret, to bother yourself.'

'But I promised,' Bessie said.

'What's in a promise!' Lily nudged her. 'Get a load of that gorgeous thing across the passage. Isn't it cute! Gee, but I could go for it in a big way.'

'I nearly died when he said Smellie,' Bessie said. 'I couldnie believe my ears at first. I said it's a funny kinda name, isn't it? And he said yes, I suppose it is, I'd never thought about it.'

'Fancy anybody with a name like that never thinkin' about it,' she said.

'Aw, why worry! Use sunlight!' Lily said, rising and beginning to sway towards the door. 'C'mon!'

But Bessie could not take Lily's advice. She wished she could adopt Lily's hard, carefree attitude, but it was hopeless.

And for the next few days, until Jim left the Bakery, she worried about it, wondering if she could pluck up enough courage to tell him that as far as she was concerned she could not attach herself to him in any way. But on his last night in Edinburgh, when they went to the cinema together, she still had said nothing.

They stood for a long time in a doorway near the tram-stop, huddling together for warmth and comfort. The few words they spoke were incoherent and meaningless.

'This is the end, mon cœur,' Marie-Elisabeth de France said. 'This must be the end. It cannot go on. You are a commoner and I am a Princess of the Blood Royal. Tonight we must say adieu—a long adieu.'

'God, it's cauld,' Jim said.

'Ay, isn't it?' Bessie shivered. 'I'll better no' miss the next tram. It'll likely be the last.'

'Ay, we'd better both get home,' he said. 'I'll have an early start the morn's mornin'. I've to report at Catterick.'

'Catterick,' she said. 'It's a long way away.'

'Ay,' he said.

'Well, here's a Nine,' Bessie said. 'I'd better make a dive for it.'

'Cheerio then!' Jim said. 'I'll be seein' you.'

'Ay, you bet!' Bessie giggled and started to run. 'Cheeribye!'

'Cheeribye!' he called. 'Mind and write!'

'You bet,' she yelled from the step of the tram. 'Mind and send me your address!'

Marie-Elisabeth de France swept up the stairs of the Louvre. Courtiers fell away from her, curtsying and bowing as she made her way through them. Her head was held high. None of them must suspect that she'd just said good-bye to her lover in the rose gardens. None of them must ever know that her pale, proud face was just a mask that hid a broken heart. Her lover had gone to the wars, and she was alone once more. *Alone, alone . . . alone with the stars up above, alone. . . .*

She swept through the crowded throne-room and took her place on the golden dais beside her father.

'It's easy seen this is the last car, hen.' An elderly workman

194

edged nearer the window to make more room for her. 'I dinnie think anybody else could get on without the help o' a shoehorn.'

'Too true!' she giggled.

'The blackout's bad enough,' he grumbled, 'without the Corporation makin' the cars stop earlier. I had to run for this yin at the Post Office. I thought I'd hae to send hame for ma runnin' pants!'

'Did ye?' Bessie giggled again.

'Ay did I!' He laughed. 'And now that I've got on, I'm squashed like a herrin' in a barrel. Oh, it's a great life sure enough, it's a great life!'

'Ay, isn't it!' she giggled.

'And it's a great war!' he said. 'The cars are that full o' sodgers and sailors that a puir auld hard-workin' felly like me can hardly get on. I doubt I'll hae to write to my Union about it!'

He nudged her. 'Lookit that, hen! Dinnie tell me that they're givin' guns to the women in this war, too!'

Bessie glanced at the girl in A.T.S. uniform who was carrying a rifle for the soldier with her. She had a momentary pang of envy. 'Aw well, why not!' she said. 'Some o' us women could maybe do more wi' them than the men.'

7

AS soon as Jim Smellie left Andrews', Bessie took Lily's advice and forgot all about him. Lily knew best. Lily was right. Jim was away to the war and he would take up with somebody else, so she might as well do the same. It solved the problem of his funny name perfectly. In any case, she had plenty more things on her mind at the moment. There was her father. He was still harping on the subject of bringing the children home for Christmas. 'I've written to Mrs. Hood,' he said. 'And your Auntie Mabel 'll be delighted to come here and look after them.'

Bessie was furious, but she could do nothing. To bring the bairns here now when he wouldn't bring them back before when she'd wanted them! 'A month ago I prigged and prigged at him to bring them hame,' she complained to Mrs. Moore. 'But do ye think he would! No' him. "They're better where they are," he says, "safely away in the country." ' But Mrs. Moore gave her no sympathy. All she said was: 'Well, it's all for the best, hen. It's God's will. A Higher Hand than ours has to decide thae things.' And it was hopeless to look to Lily for consolation. Lily was too much interested in her own affairs. She had taken up with yet another sailor at the Base at Harrisfield. 'I'm the boy for sailors, amn't I, Bess?' she said. 'I dunno what it is, but somethin' about their uniform aye gets me. They aye look that clean, don't they? Oh, and the way their troosers flap round their ankles, and the way they stretch across their arses. . . .'

'This is The One this time,' she said.

Apart from this, the Christmas rush was well under way in Andrews', and the entire staff was almost rushed off its feet. 'Jethuth God, I'm mair pushed frae potht to pillar than ever,' Canteen Molly complained. 'Chrithmath is bad enough at any time, but thith year it'th a hunner times worse, what wi' this war and one thing and another.'

For the Christmas rush a temporary staff of packers had been engaged to tie up parcels being sent by post. These men were stationed at a long table running along one side of the despatch department. In front of each man there was always a pile of stuff waiting to be packed: tins of shortbread, boxes of sweets, currant loaves, tins of oat cakes, jars of honey, tartan-covered boxes of biscuits: Christmas presents being sent to friends and relatives or to sons in the Forces.

All the girls in the despatch were interested in the packers. Most of them were young men, who were either unemployed or waiting to be called into the Armed Forces. Several were students who were trying to earn extra money during the Christmas vacation. Some of the students only played them-selves at tying up the parcels, and they were always ready to chaff and banter with the girls.

'I often thay I'll have to bring my bed in here,' Molly said.

'But Jethuth God, I wouldnie mind doin' it if I thought one o' thae fellies was goin' to share it with me!'

'What yin are ye goin' after, hen?' she asked Bessie. 'I fancy that big bloke wi' the red hair masel'.'

'Ach, him!' Bessie giggled. 'I think I'll play safe with auld Mr. Jamieson,' she said.

'Ay, Faither's a smasher, isn't he!' Molly guffawed. 'Really, Faither's the bloody limit,' she said. 'He comes in here every afternoon at tea-time and asks me if I havenie ony scraps for his wee dug.'

'Him and his wee dug!' she said.

'I never see you refusing him, Molly,' said Mrs. Irvine.

'Och ay, I aye gie him thomethin',' Molly said. 'Poor cratur', he's nice enough, ye ken, but just a wee thing thoft in the head.'

'He wouldn't need to hear you say that,' Mrs. Irvine said.

Mr. Jamieson was a consequential little man, who was always very natty in dark pin-striped trousers. He had been a clerk of some description, but had evidently been unemployed for some time. As he was much the oldest man there, he had been placed in charge of the temporary packers.

Two of them intrigued Bessie. They were students. One of them was the tall red-haired young man on whom Molly had her eye. The other was his pal, a slim dark youth who always wore a white polo-sweater and a brown Harris tweed sports jacket with huge leather patches on the elbows. His name was Eric. The red-headed one was called Pete.

Pete was very serious, and he talked all the time. All the girls were amused by him. His fingers would be tying up parcels, but he scarcely ever looked down to see what he was doing. He kept up a steady stream of words at Eric beside him. 'What's he aye talkin' about?' Lily McGillivray asked Bessie. 'I've listened to him two-three times and I can never follow it.'

'Neither can I,' Bessie said. 'As far as I can make out, it's all about poetry. I heard him reelin' off a string of names the other day, but I didnie ken any o' them. I think I've seen their books in the Library, but I'm no' sure. They're no' in my line. Somebody called Awden and Dyling Thomas and Stephen

197

Spender. I mind I once opened one o' his books, and I couldnie follow it at all. Ye never saw such poetry!'

'We'll have to get auld Mr. Moore up to them,' Lily said. 'He's a dab hand for poetry, isn't he?'

'So Mrs. Moore aye says.'

'It would be wicer-like if Pete kept his attention on tyin' up his parcels right,' Lily said. 'You should see some o' his parcels! They're no' half tied. Jesus Christ and General Jackson, I dunno how half o' them ever reach their destination.'

'It's a wonder some of them even get out of the shop without fallin' to bits,' Ginny Smiles said.

'I know,' May M'Queen said. 'If they just saw the rough handlin' the parcels got in the Post Office Lady Christie and Mr. Wilson would have heart failure. My brother worked in the G.P.O. last Christmas as a temporary sorter, and he tellt me they just bunged things about any old how.'

'Ah well, it's not the packers' faults,' Lily said. 'I'm sorry for them havin' to tie up some o' the things. I know I'd never manage to make a parcel of some of the things. Mr. Jamieson was showin' me one of the parcels he had to tie. Holy Moses, I dunno what I'd of done if it had been me that was to tie it. I'd of gone straight and lifted my Books! There was a tin of shortbread—one o' thae round flat ones—six chocolate biscuits, a wee bottle o' sweeties, one o' thae long round tins o' oat cakes and two mealy puddings. Christ, I just stood and watched him tryin' to get them into some kind o' order, and for the life o' me I dunno how he managed.'

'It's heart-breaking,' she said.

'That's right,' Ginny said. 'And what does it matter, anyway, if they ever get to the folk they're meant for? Half of them don't need the stuff, anyway. You wouldn't think there was a war on, would ye?'

Nobody would have thought there was a war on if they'd come into the despatch department sometimes, Bessie thought. There was so much rush and bustle that often things fell off the boards and lay unheeded on the floor, where they got tramped upon amongst the waste paper and shavings. 'There's

198

enough cakes and pies lyin' about this floor, all squashed to atoms, to feed a regiment,' she said to Lily. 'What a waste! And yet if That Christie as much as found ye slippin' a chocolate biscuit into yer overall-pocket there would be hell to pay.'

'I know,' Lily said. 'It's heart-breaking.'

'It's such a change from the big front shop,' she said. 'What a contrast! It's aye that clean and tidy. I bet if some o' thae gentry bodies that come in from Princes Street, doin' the laddie-dah, saw in the back here they wouldnie buy so much. I bet some o' them would have a right good spew!'

'Aw, it would serve the buggers right,' Bessie said. 'It would maybe teach them no' to be so classy.'

'I think I'm goin' to look for another job after the New Year,' Lily said. 'I'm gettin' right fed up with this. Especially wi' gettin' up at six o'clock thur dark cauld mornings and comin' up here in the blackout. I'm wantin' a job where there are better hours. There's plenty o' them goin' about beggin' just now what wi' folk goin' away to the war. I tell ye what it is, you'll soon be able to pick yer job and name yer own price.'

'Well, the sooner the better!' Ginny Smiles giggled.

'Are you goin' to try for another job, Ferret?' Lily said.

'I'll see,' Bessie said. 'I dinnie ken what's goin' to happen. This business of my faither bringin' the bairns hame for Christmas and the New Year is fair upsettin' me. I can see what'll happen all right. Once they're hame the kids 'll no' want to go back to bein' evacuated, and then my da 'll say I'll have to bide at hame and look after them again.'

'Aw, tell him to go and take a running-jump at himsel',' Lily said.

' It's all very well for you to talk,' Bessie said. 'You've got a mother at home to look after things, but I havenie. I ken fine that my faither 'll tell me to give up this job.'

'Well, why do ye no' leave hame and be independent?' Lily said. 'I ken that's what I'd do if I had any trouble with my old man. In fact,' she said, 'I'm thinkin' about doin' that, anyway.'

Bessie stared at her.

'Ay, dinnie stare at me with yer big goggle eyes,' Lily said. 'I'm gettin' right fed up with this kind o' life. I was thinkin' I'd maybe get married.'

'Married?' Bessie said.

'Ay, married!' Lily giggled. 'What's to hinder me? Other folk get married, don't they? Folk are aye gettin' married. So why shouldn't I? I havenie broached the subject to Teddy yet, but I was thinkin' we might as well get married and then I'd get an allowance when he goes away to sea.'

'But does Teddy . . .'

'Ach, Teddy doesnie ken his own mind,' Lily said. 'But I'll soon make it up for him. I don't see why I shouldnie get an allowance off the Government as well as other folk.'

'But, Lily, ye're only sixteen!'

'What does that matter?' Lily said. 'I'm auld enough to get married, amn't I? You'd better think about it yourself, Ferret,' she said. 'If ye're so anxious to get away from the bairns— here's your solution! Your father couldnie object.'

Seeing that Miss Christie was approaching, Bessie bent over the board of cakes in front of her, counting them rapidly. What Lily had just said was true enough. It was a mug's game to go on working yourself if you could get somebody else to work for you. But who was she going to get to marry her? That was the thing. After all, she was only fifteen and a bit. Even though her father didn't raise hell, there were other things to be considered. Would *they* allow somebody as young as her to get married? It looked a gey blue look-out. And anyway, even though her father and *they* were willing, who was she to get now that Jim was away to the War? She hadn't a fellow at all at the moment, and there was nobody else in the offing. Unless you counted Eric. . . .

Bessie was intensely interested in Eric with the white polosweater; she needed somebody on whom to fasten her attention. Eric looked romantic enough and had such animal vigour that she could not help noticing him. Most of the other girls were also attracted by him, however. So what chance had she? As for Eric himself, although he chaffed her the same as he chaffed the other girls, he never showed the slightest interest in her in any other way. He was a vain youth and he knew he was attractive, so he was determined to make the most of it.

And it was all very well for Lily to say airily: 'You should leave home and be independent.' How was she going to do that on her small wage? Of course, as Lily said, jobs were getting more plentiful now that so many people were getting called up, and employers were offering higher wages. But all the same, at her age she couldn't expect to earn enough to keep herself.

Oh God, I'm not looking forward to this Christmas with that Stevens woman being there bossing everything. I wish to God I knew what to do. . . .

8

'BESSIE,' Miss Christie said. 'I wonder if you'd take your lunch later today? Two extra vans have to go out on the Morningside run, and we've got to pack them. It's at a very awkward time when most of the girls are up for lunch, but really we can't help it. The vans have to go out on time. Our customers expect them. So do you think you could run up to the Canteen just now and get a cup of tea and a pie or something, and then you and Ginny could see to the vans while the other girls are at lunch.'

'All right, Miss Christie,' Bessie said.

'Tell Molly to keep your lunch,' Miss Christie said. 'You'll just be about an hour later than usual.'

'Does That Christie think I've nothin' else to do but ladle out cups o' tea?' Molly said to Bessie and Ginny Smiles. 'We're just in the middle o' gettin' lunch ready. I wish she'd come up here and take my job for a while. That 'd learn her! I wouldnie mind swappin' places wi' her. I could go about fine in a black thilk dress and a string of Woolworth's pearls, doin' the lahdidah!'

'But never mind,' she said. 'We'll all have a nice cup o' tea. It'll be a fine excuse for Mrs. Irvine and me to have one, too.'

'I could be doing with one,' Mrs. Irvine said, wiping the sweat-beads from her red forehead. 'My Godfathers, I don't think I'll take another job like this in a hurry.'

'I don't see why ye bother wi' it,' Molly said. 'Jethuth God, if I had all your money it's not a job in Andrews' I'd be takin'. I'd be away on the Riviera, bathkin' in the thunshine.'

'How do you know I've a lot of money?' Mrs. Irvine laughed.

'Did ye no' ken I wath thycic!' Molly giggled. 'I can thmell thae things a mile off!'

'Money! My godfathers!' Mrs. Irvine said. 'Money! . . .'

'Money,' she said, sipping her tea genteelly. 'Yes, if I had all that I should have had, I'd have plenty of money. For my father, you know, left me a good tocher. Oh ay, there was money in our family. But Gilbert Irvine soon ran through it all. There was no holding him. I couldn't keep his fingers off it. Drink, drink, drink! My godfathers! the money that man spent on drink. Mind you,' she said, handing round her packet of cigarettes, 'I had a good time, too, while it lasted. Gilbert and I fairly saw life. I mind we went to London on a trip soon after we were married. What a time we had! My poor old father would have turned in his grave and kept on turning if he'd seen the way we were making his money fly. There was a party of us. My mother was there, too. Poor old body! I remember she was all dressed in black. Proper widow's weeds. Black from head to foot, and she wasn't as old then as I am now. My godfathers, if *my* family saw me dragging along the way *she* did, they'd take the feet from me!'

'Ay, folk theemed to get aulder quicker in thae days,' Molly said. 'I mind my mother tellt me my auld granny used to wear a mutch when she was only about forty. I mind ——'

But Mrs. Irvine was determined to have none of Molly's reminiscences. She had got the floor and she was going to hold it. She smiled at Bessie and Ginny, who were sitting open-mouthed, and she went on:

'My family like me to keep up with them. Flora—that's my eldest daughter, the one that's in New York now, married to a very wealthy man, oh, a very wealthy man! They have an

202

apartment in New York and a little place on Long Island—
Flora would shoot me if she saw me dragging around the
way my mother dragged around. "Mother," she always says,
"Mother, you've got to keep as young as the rest of us. We
can't have you growing old and decrepit." '

'Families are an awfie trial,' Molly said, not to be outdone.
'My family'th the bloody limit. My mother——'

'My godfathers! but what a time we had in London that
time,' Mrs. Irvine said. 'I mind I was wearing a Merry Widow
hat and it got soaked, so I went out to buy myself another one
in Whitechapel. I didn't tell anybody where I was going, and
when they missed me the whole hotel got up to ninety. My poor
old mother was wringing her hands and carrying on like
Lilian Gish in *The Orphans of the Storm*. It was the time of the
Peter the Painter murders, and Whitechapel was no place for
a young woman to be wandering about in by herself. And I
had as much stuff on me, too! Two thick gold bangles and a
gold watch and chain and gold ear-rings. And money, of course,
to buy the hat. But I bought it. A great big straw thing like a
basket—just full of flowers! It was like one of those Mexican
sombrero things they wear nowadays, and it sat on top of my
head. My godfathers! I was a real dandy in it.'

'We spent a lot of money on that trip,' she went on, puffing
delicately at her cigarette. 'Sometimes I wish now that we'd
spent more. I'd have got my proper share of it then. For it
was just after we came home that Gilbert Irvine started to run
through it. It just flowed through his fingers like water. Or
ran down his throat, I should say. Really, I never saw such a
man to drink!'

'Ay, ye've had a hard life o' it, Mithith Irvine,' Molly
lamented.

'Yes, see and you girls pick men for yourselves that don't
drink,' Mrs. Irvine said to Bessie and Ginny. 'Ask to see their
Good Templar cards before you let them take you to the altar.
Drink's a terrible thing.'

'I don't know what I'd have done without my Faith,' she
said, gazing into her tea-cup. 'It's been a great relief to me in
my time. You wouldn't believe the comfort it's given me.

203

When Gilbert was drinking terrible bad one time I used to go every night to meetings of the Friends. Gilbert took on very bad about it and dared me to go. For you see he was an Unbeliever. But I defied him. You have your drink, I said to him, I have my Faith. I remember one night he said that if I went he would lock the door on me. I couldn't enjoy the meeting for thinking about it, wondering what would happen when I got home. Because really Gilbert Irvine was a terrible man when he got roused. I was in such a panic that I spoke to Mr. Thatcher, the Medium, about it. Mr. Thatcher was a wonderful man. He was a bricklayer in private life, and he had enormous hands on him—proper navvy's hands. But when he went into a trance he played the piano most beautifully—he played Bach and Mozart and all that stuff. Oh, it was really beautiful! You'd never have guessed he had such great big ham hands. Well, when I told him I was feared to go home, he said: "I'll get Varconi to take you home." '

Mrs. Irvine sighed and held out her cup for more tea. 'Varconi was a guide,' she said. 'A spirit guide. He'd been a doctor in this life, and so he kept the title when he went to another plane. He was an Italian, and when he was in control of Mr. Thatcher, Mr. Thatcher always spoke in broken English. We always knew when Varconi was in the room, for the table would begin to tap "yes-no-yes-no-yes-no" like nothing on earth. I used to go to the Circles with my friend, Mrs. Arbuthnott, but she wasn't there that night. Varconi always called her and me "the two pretty plump ladies". Well, that night when Mr. Thatcher asked him, Varconi saw me home. He saw me home often after that, but this was the first night, and it was some experience, I can tell you.'

Bessie sat with her mouth open. She never took her eyes from Mrs. Irvine's face. She felt Ginny Smiles nudging her occasionally, but she took no notice. She was gazing at Mrs. Irvine as she and the children used to gaze at their mother when she told them stories. There was something about Mrs. Irvine, which was reminiscent of her mother, that held her. No other woman she'd met had ever had quite the same effect on her. She couldn't put her finger on what it was exactly, but it was there. Something . . . And so she gazed in admiration, drinking in everything that Mrs. Irvine was saying.

'It was right queer to be walking along the street with a spirit guide,' Mrs. Irvine said. 'It took a wee bit getting used to. But long before we'd reached my house I was chatting away to Dr. Varconi. I saw folk that we passed looking at me as if I was mad, but I never heeded them. And so we reached the house.'

'The front door was locked, and Gilbert had pushed furniture against it,' she said. 'And the back door was locked, too. And all the windows were fastened tight. There seemed to be no way of getting in at all. But do you know, Varconi shifted all the stuff and opened the door and let me in!'

She looked round her circle of listeners and gave a firm nod. Molly's mouth was as wide open as Bessie's, and her chef's cap was hanging precariously over one ear. Only Ginny looked a bit sceptical, but she looked down hastily at her hands when Mrs. Irvine's eye fell upon her.

'Yes, he shifted all that stuff, opened the door and got me in,' Mrs. Irvine said triumphantly. 'And what was more, he saw me safely upstairs, safely past my husband's room where the drunken brute was lying in wait for me. And do you know, our stairs usually creaked, but that night they never creaked at all. So Gilbert never heard me, and neither did any of my daughters. Poor lassies, they were all huddled in their rooms, terrified of their father. They'd wanted to go downstairs and shift the stuff away from the doors and windows, but they'd been scared stiff of Gilbert Irvine. It was a right surprise to them when I went into their rooms to say good night. But it was a bigger surprise for Gilbert the next morning when I shouted to him that his breakfast was ready.'

'I told him I'd never been out of the house,' she said. 'Varconi took me home often after that, and he always got me into the house without Gilbert Irvine being one bit the wiser. My Godfathers, I can tell you I was sorry when he moved to a Higher Plane and didn't come to our Circle again.'

'But I thought ye had a guide,' Molly said. 'Yon felly wi' the funny name.'

'Oh yes, I have an Arabian guide now. His name's Ali Ben Hassim.'

'My guide's name ith Ally Thloper!' Molly giggled.

Mrs. Irvine drew herself up with dignity. 'It's no laughing matter, Molly. I must say I'm surprised at *you* making such a remark. I expected better from you.'

'I'm thorry, Mithith Irvine,' Molly moaned. 'I wath just tryin' to be funny. I didnie mean any harm.'

'Well, you shouldn't try to be funny about things like this,' Mrs. Irvine said. 'It's a good job I'm not like lots of people who'd have been mortally offended. But try not to let it happen again.'

'I won't, Mithith Irvine,' Molly said. 'Honeth to God, I'll keep as mum as a bloody mummy after thith.'

'Here, Bessie, d'ye see the time?' Ginny started up with a jerk, pulling Bessie after her. 'Crikey jings, but Lady Christie 'll fairly be on our track. She said ten minutes, not half an hour!'

Bessie took away her eyes unwillingly from Mrs. Irvine. 'Och, it's a right nuisance,' she whined.

'Never mind, Bessie.' Mrs. Irvine smiled and gave her a little pat on the arm. 'It won't be long before you're back for lunch. Molly 'll keep something extra-special for you both, won't you, Molly?'

'That'th right,' Molly said, resettling her chef's cap and giving her straggly hair a fluff up. 'A lunch fit for a Queen!'

'You're not looking very well, Bessie,' Mrs. Irvine said, following her to the top of the stairs. 'Are you feeling all right, m'dear?'

'Aw, I—I suppose so,' Bessie said listlessly.

'Something wrong, m'dear?' Mrs. Irvine gripped her arm affectionately.

Bessie had a sudden temptation to lay her head against Mrs. Irvine's deep bosom and burst into tears. But she sniffed and put her foot on the top step.

'It's—och, it's just things,' she said.

Mrs. Irvine nodded with understanding. 'I know, m'dear, I know. Things get like that sometimes for us all. I know, for

I've had more than my share in my time what with Gilbert Irvine and all.'

'You and I must have a little chat, m'dear,' she said. 'What about coming up to my house tomorrow night for tea? We'll get more peace to talk privately there. And more time.'

9

BESSIE went back to the despatch department with her heart singing. Not even the dirty looks which Miss Christie directed at her could dampen her spirits. She was going to Mrs. Irvine's tomorrow night!

She seized the trolley that Lily had standing ready for her, and giving it a push, she shouted: 'Hoy there, ladies, make way for the Morningside bus!' Pushing it towards the entrance where the Morningside vanman was waiting, she skirled: 'A-huntin' we will go! Ahuntin' we will go! We'll catch an auld fox and we'll put him in a box, and ahuntin' we will go!'

'I'm glad it's not me ye're huntin',' the vanman said, grinning. 'I wouldnie like ye to be after me wi' a gun!'

'Do ye no' wish ye had a gun yersel', Wattie?' May M'Queen giggled as she tried to manœuvre her trolley alongside Bessie's.

'Ay, I do that,' he said, lifting a trayful of pies on to his head. 'I've at least six customers I'd like to put a bullet through!'

'Hurry up there, Bessie!' Ginny Smiles shouted behind them. 'Take yer trolley out o' ma road! I've got extra-special cream cakes on it, and Lady Christie says the cream 'll get sour if they're not out o' here in the next five minutes.'

'Ach, the cakes 'll be sour already after one look at her dial!' Bessie cried.

'Have any of you ladies seen a box of jam tarts?' Jean Williamson cried, rushing up to them. 'There's a box to go on the Morningside van and it's disappeared.'

'Aw, look among the shavings on the floor, love,' Ginny

said. 'I bet there's enough tarts lyin' there as would fill half a dozen boxes.'

'Hell, I think I've got one o' them on ma foot the now,' Bessie said, bending down and taking a squashed tart off her high heel. 'Any offers?' she cried, holding it up.

'Bet ye tuppence ye havenie the nerve to throw it at Christie!' May giggled.

'I might if I had my pay-envelope in ma pouch and was goin' home for good!' Bessie laughed.

'Home, Home on the Range!' Ginny crooned in a nasal voice. 'Where the deeer and theeee antelope plaaay!'

'Home was never like this!' Wattie said, coming back and settling another tray on his head.

'Aw, there's nothin' wrong with home,' May said. 'It's just the folk in it!'

'Ours is a nice house, ours is!' Lily cried, pushing another full trolley into the midst of them.

'I'll have to find that box o' tarts or Christie 'll flay the hide offen me,' Jean said mournfully. 'Are ye sure ye havenie seen it, Wattie?'

'What would I be doin' with a box o' tarts when there are so many other tarts here!' Wattie said. 'Eh, hen?' And he nipped Lily's bottom.

'Hey, keep yer hands to yersel',' Lily shrieked in a good-humoured way, and she aimed a playful slap at him.

'Action Stations, ladies!' Ginny hissed.

Pushing back her empty trolley under Miss Christie's watchful eye, Bessie wished it was twenty-four hours hence. It's just wishing your life away, of course, she told herself as she began to pile more cookies, pies and cakes on to her trolley, but oh gee! . . .

Mrs. Irvine had asked her several times to go to a Circle, but so far these had been always on nights when Bessie couldn't manage. However, this was a different kind of invitation. This was a special occasion when there would be only Mrs. Irvine and herself. She was right honoured. Mrs. Irvine had said they would have a real cosy chat together. Wasn't it lovely. . . .

Mrs. Irvine was a right lady, and what an exciting life she'd had. In a way she was a wee thing like Ma; she'd married a drunkard, too. Only she'd been a lot luckier than poor Ma. She hadn't died when she was still young, died with overwork and having too many bairns. Poor Ma. . . . Aw, wouldn't it be fine if only it was Mrs. Irvine who was coming to look after the house and the bairns next week. If only her father had taken up with Mrs. Irvine and not with that stinking Miss Stevens. . . . Maybe if her da took up with Mrs. Irvine and married her and then went on drinking the way he did sometimes he'd kick the bucket like Gilbert Irvine, and then there would be only her and Mrs. Irvine and the bairns left. . . .

What a posh funeral it had been! All those kings and ambassadors and princes walking behind the gun-carriage with the coffin covered with the Fleurs de Lys . . . and the sailors pulling the gun-carriage . . . and herself and the Queen and the two bairns standing at a window of the palace looking down at the weeping crowds. . . .

'He has gone, Elisabeth ma chere,' said Mrs. Irvine, taking off her black kid gloves and smoothing them. 'Le roi est mort, vive le roi!'

'Mais oui, Maman,' Madame Royale murmured, resting her head against the Queen's soft black shoulder.

'You are King now, William,' the Queen said to Billy. 'You must be a good king. With Elisabeth's help, I shall do my best to make you a good king. . . . You must depend upon us, William. Together we will guide you in the true paths.'

'I am depending upon you, my daughter,' she said, patting Madame Royale's pale cheek.

'I am with you, Maman,' said Madame Royale, 'hook, line and sinker.'

'But first we must rid the country of that vile creature, Milady Stevens.' Mrs. Irvine touched a bell. 'Ask Monsieur D'Artagnan to come here for an audience,' she said to a footman.

And so in no time D'Artagnan had got Milady Stevens on board a frigate and the country was rid of her. And then she and Mrs. Irvine settled down to rule France, making Billy do just what they wanted. . . .

'I wonder what Mrs. Irvine's name is?' Bessie mused. 'I must mind and ask her. . . .'

She was so lost in her daydream that she was oblivious of the noise and bustle around her. She counted pies and cookies mechanically and piled them on her trolley. It was only when she started to push it once again towards the entrance that she became aware of her surroundings.

'Hey, Annie, get oot ma road!' she yelled. 'I never met onybody like you for aye gettin' in folk's way.'

'Well, here's my little friend Miss Bessie!' Mr. Jamieson cried, as she pushed her way slowly past the counter where the packers were busy with their parcels. 'And how are you today, Miss Bessie?'

'Och, I'm fine,' she giggled.

She took a quick look around to see that Miss Christie was not in sight, then she halted and leaned against her trolley.

'So ye're still at it!' she said.

'There's no rest for the wicked, Miss Bessie!' Mr. Jamieson gave his funny little laugh as he deftly arranged some articles into a pile and measured round them with a piece of cardboard. He reached for a knife and began to cut it to the required length.

'Workin' late the night, Mr. Jamieson?' Bessie said.

'We work late every night, Miss Bessie!' He gave his funny little laugh. 'I'm like our friend Molly upstairs, I'll have to bring my bed in here! My little dog's beginning to forget what I look like.'

'How is it the day?' Bessie said, not because she was at all interested in Jamieson's dog but because it gave her an excuse to stand longer and admire Eric, who had changed his white sweater today for one of mustard yellow.

Tommy, the boy who had succeeded Jim Smellie, was piling more stuff to be parcelled in front of each of the packers. As he moved away from Eric's part of the counter, Eric picked up a list, frowning as he checked the contents of the topmost parcel. 'Here, I'm a tin of shortbread short!' he cried, making a sudden move towards Tommy.

'Steady there, steady!' Mr. Jamieson cried, stepping back quickly. 'You nearly ran into my knife, young man!'

'Good job I didn't,' Eric laughed, and he winked at Bessie. 'There's a big enough mess here already without any blood!'

'Yes, it would have been a bloody mess!' Mr. Jamieson gave his little laugh. 'If you'll excuse my rudeness, Miss Bessie!'

'What were ye yellin' at me for?' Tommy said, coming back.

'There's a tin of shortbread short in this parcel,' Eric explained.

'Nothin' o' the sort,' Tommy snapped, and he rummaged further down the pile of stuff. 'There it is! I wish some o' youse blokes would use yer eyes. Is that a' they learn ye at the University?'

'Temper! Temper!' Mr. Jamieson cried jocularly. 'You should always count ten, Tommy m'lad!'

'Hoy there, Hippy, you're blockin' the traffic,' Lily yelled behind her.

Bessie glared at her. Really, Lily was a perfect bitch shouting out her name like that in front of them all. She just hoped to goodness Eric hadn't heard.

'A' right,' she said, preparing to push on her trolley.

'Dinnie break your neck,' Lily said sarcastically. 'I'm not in all that hurry.'

'Well, Mr. Jamieson!' Lily leaned against her trolley, smiling at him as she patted the curls over her ears. 'You're still busy!'

'Still busy, Miss Lily!' Mr. Jamieson beamed at her. 'I was just saying to Miss Bessie here that there's no rest for the wicked. I expect that includes you, too!'

'Naw, you can count me out!' Lily giggled.

'Ahah!' He waggled his forefinger quickly at her. 'I bet you don't say that in the blackout! No offence meant, Miss Lily,' he said. 'I must have my little joke! I like to give you young ladies a laugh. It brightens things for you. It's a poor heart that never rejoices!'

'Watch yourself, Faither!' one of the young packers cried, pushing his way past Mr. Jamieson with a bundle of parcels.

'Here, here, young man!' Mr. Jamieson shouted. 'Don't you speak to me like that. I'll soon show you who's boss here.'

'C'mon, Hippy, get a bloody move on or we'll have Christie down on us like a ton of bricks,' Lily said.

Bessie pushed on her trolley, gazing at Eric as she passed. But whether listening to what his pal, Pete, was saying or whether sunk in a reverie of his own, Bessie did not know, for he never looked up from the parcel he was tying.

It was a right pity Lily had come along just then, otherwise she might have managed to get on the talk with Eric. Gee, but she could go for that fellow in a big way. He was smashing. He had far more go in him than either Jim Smellie or yon sailor that used to lodge with Dirty Minnie. Now if she could just manage tò attract his attention when most of the other lassies were upstairs, when she didn't have any competition. . . .

But the afternoon went past and Bessie was unsuccessful in all her attempts to catch Eric's eye. It was her late week. Normally she was delighted when six o'clock came. But tonight it came too quickly. All too soon most of the girls began the rush to go home, but Bessie put off as long as she could, lingering near the door to see if Eric wasn't coming. She'd made up her mind to pretend to trip on the steps going out. He'd put out his hand and steady her, and then this would be a grand chance to get on the talk with him as he walked up the lane with her. . . .

'Are ye not comin', Bessie?' Ginny Smiles shouted. 'Crikey jings, you're surely awful fond o' the place when you're bidin' this long.'

'I'm not in a great hurry,' Bessie said. 'I'm no' goin' home. I'm goin' to the picters.'

'Well, I must fly!' Ginny cried, struggling into her coat. 'I've to meet the boy-friend. Oh, here's Miss Matheson!' she cried, as Miss Matheson and Mrs. Woods and two girls from the Grocery Department came out of the cloakroom. 'Where are ye bound for the night, Miss Matheson? Goin' out on the razzle-dazzle?'

'I'm going to my choir practice, Ginny,' Miss Matheson beamed. 'Don't you wish you were coming along with me?'

'Not on your life!' Ginny grinned, and she winked at Bessie

as Miss Matheson went out into the blackout. 'I'm full o' tricks, but that's not one o' them! Can you imagine me tellin' the boy-friend I was ditchin' him to go to a choir practice. He'd send me to a doctor's to get my head looked at!'

'I'm sorry for thae poor packers,' she said. 'I heard auld Wilson askin' them to work overtime. There's a shoal o' parcels to go out in a hurry. Faither was tellin' me they'd be here until ten o'clock.'

'Oh, will they?' Bessie said.

'Well, cheerio, love!' Ginny cried, and she clattered out, humming *Red Sails in the Sunset.*

Bessie stood at the door, buttoning her coat, peering into the blackout. It had started to snow. She screwed up her face as the cold flakes hit her.

'Hya, Bessie!'

She turned and saw Big Ginger, one of the vanmen, putting on his coat behind her.

'Hya, Ginger!' she giggled.

'Where're you makin' for?' he said.

'I'm goin' to the picters,' she said. 'Goin' to the Palace to see Victor McLaglan and Cary Grant in *Gunga Din.*'

'Oh, I'm goin' there, too. Funny, isn't it?'

'Ay, isn't it?' she giggled.

'Might as well go along together,' he said. 'I wouldn't mind a chum, would you?'

They walked along the back lane together into Rose Street. Bessie felt very small beside Big Ginger, but she took big strides and raised herself as much as she could with every step, in a prancing way, to try to lessen the difference between their sizes. Wasn't it just her luck! Here she'd been trying to get off with Eric and now she had landed Big Ginger. It was a funny world all right. Not that Big Ginger was a bad soul. He aye had a cheery word for all the girls. He was a bloke about thirty, big and burly, with a red face and sandy eyebrows that bushed out. His teeth were a bit uneven, and they were yellow with tobacco smoke.

'Ye're no' goin' straight to the picters, are ye?' he said as they turned into Rose Street. 'C'mon in here for a drink,' he said, stopping outside a public-house. 'It 'll warm ye up before ye go into the picters.'

'Och away!' Bessie giggled.

'What are ye feared at?' he said.

'Dinnie be daft,' she said. 'My old man would flay me if he saw me in a pub.'

'Well, he's not likely to see you in here,' Ginger said. 'But if you like we'll go to another pub. There are plenty in Rose Street. We've got either nineteen or twenty to choose from. I just forget the exact number, but there's mair pubs in this street than in any other street in Edinburry.'

'Dinnie be daft,' she said. 'I'm no' goin'. If you're wantin' a drink I'll wait here till ye come out.'

'Och, dinnie be daft,' he said. 'C'mon!'

And he took her arm and propelled her into the Public Bar in front of him. Bessie was horrified. Jees, what would her father say! She buried her head as much as she could in the upstanding collar of her coat, looking round quickly, terrified she'd see somebody she knew. But there were only two or three men in the Bar.

'What're you havin'?' Ginger said.

'I'm no' wantin' anythin',' she mumbled.

'Aw, c'mon, a drink 'll warm ye up,' he said, and without waiting for an answer he went to the counter and said: 'Two nips, please, Alex.'

'Here, drink that up,' he said, pushing the whisky in front of her. 'That 'll warm the cockles o' yer heart.'

'I dinnie want it, thanks,' she said.

'What are ye feared for?' he said. 'Dinnie tell me you're one o' the glidin' lights in the Girl Glides!'

'I—I——' She hesitated, then she reached and took the glass. Och, to hell, what did it matter? Who was to see her, anyway, and who was to know? And if she didn't take it, Big Ginger would soon spread the news all round Andrews' that she was a bit of a sap. She didn't want the other girls to think she was goody-goody. Look at the way Ginny Smiles was always trying to take a rise out of Miss Matheson.

She coughed and spluttered as the liquid burned her throat.

'Steady, steady!' Big Ginger cried, slapping her back. She was so busy trying to catch her breath that she didn't notice that he held his hand on her shoulder for longer than was necessary.

'Have another one to keep that company,' he said, and he shouted: 'Another two, Alex, please!'

As they walked along Princes Street to the Palace, Bessie felt a warm glow inside her. Jees, but it was fine to be walking along like this with Big Ginger. Folk would think he was her bloke. He was a fine-looking big fellow.

She demurred at the pay-box when Ginger bought the tickets, but when he wouldn't take her one and sixpence she put it back in her purse. It wouldn't do to create a fuss. And she followed him meekly to their seats.

She felt so warm that she unbuttoned her coat. 'Are ye goin' to take it off?' Ginger whispered, putting his hand on her shoulder, preparing to help her with it.

'No, I'll just keep it on,' she whispered.

Ginger did not take away his hand. He slid his arm along her shoulder and drew her against him. 'Nice and cosy in here, isn't it?' he said.

Bessie tried to edge away, but the whisky and the darkness defeated her. She reconciled herself to the pressure of Ginger's arm, wishing it was Eric. *Gunga Din* was halfway through, but she could not follow the thread of the story at all. She watched Douglas Fairbanks Junior and Cary Grant, but all the time she was conscious of Ginger's nearness and of his heaviness against her. All thought of Eric disappeared from her mind. She was incapable of thinking of two things at the one time. She could think only of Ginger, not sure whether she liked him or not. He wasn't such a bad soul . . . if only he would take his arm away and leave her in peace to watch the picture.

But instead of taking away his arm, Ginger began to get bolder. Bessie nearly shrieked when he placed his hand on her leg and began to fumble with her skirt. 'Stoppit!' she whispered.

'Aw, what's bitin' you, dear,' he said. 'What's wrong with a bit o' fun?'

215

'Stoppit,' she whispered again. Then, afraid she would cause any undue and unwelcome attention, she added: 'Not in here, anyway. Folk 'll see you.'

'Righto,' he said, but he kept his hand on her thigh. 'What about comin' along to my place for a cup o' tea? My wife and bairns are evacuated, so there'll be nobody to disturb us.'

10

BESSIE spent the next day in a state of agitation. Things were happening just a bit too fast. Goodness knows she'd aye wanted an exciting life, but she was getting a bit more than she'd bargained for. Things were coming in too much of a rush. She couldn't keep track of them all. She needed more time to think about each of them. She felt like a lost bairn standing at a cross-roads with dozens of roads to choose from and not knowing which one to go along. If only one thing would come at a time, so that she could give all her attention to it. But they didn't. They came rushing in from all directions, so that she was fair bombarded and didn't know which way to turn. Some new catastrophe was on top of her before she'd had proper time to think about the one before. There was her dad bringing the bairns home. There was Miss Stevens coming for Christmas and her not knowing yet what she was going to do about it. There was Lily and Teddy, her sailor, and all this talk about getting married. There was all the rush and bustle in Andrews'. There were Christmas presents to buy for the bairns. There was Eric. There was Jim Smellie, who'd sent her a letter this morning, saying he was thinking about her. And now on top of them all there was this business of Big Ginger.

Oh, God! she was fair bamboozled. She just wished she could speak to somebody about it. But there was nobody . . . except maybe Mrs. Irvine. Lily was no damned good; she was far too much taken up with her own affairs. In any case, she didn't dare say anything to Lily about Big Ginger. It would be all round Andrews' before you could cough.

Really, it was a terrible thing, Big Ginger behaving like that. Who would ever have imagined it? And him with a wife and three bairns. Really, it was terrible. It was a good thing she'd had the sense to rise and say: 'Well, I must get away home,' and that she'd gone before he could rise and follow her. But she'd been terrified to come to the shop this morning. She hadn't seen him yet, but she was keeping her eyes open so that she could jouk away somewhere and hide whenever he appeared. She should never have let him give her that whisky. She'd been soft to take it. Whatever would her mother have thought if she'd known? Poor Ma, she'd have been flabbergasted. She'd prayed about it last night, but it hadn't seemed to do much good. She couldn't forget it. Her legs still shook when she thought of it all. That muckle hand of his groping . . .

She just hoped to God Big Ginger hadn't said anything to anybody. What if the other lassies heard? Maybe they knew already and were sniggering about her behind her back. She tried to read double-meanings into everything they said to her. You couldn't tell what they knew. They were such a sleekit lot of bitches. They might easy be talking about her behind her back. Laughing up their sleeves at her. Saying to each other: 'Fancy Hippy and Big Ginger! She'll be landing herself in the soup, that one, if she doesn't watch her step.'

Oh, God, she just wished she could speak to somebody about it. Lily would be sure to know if the other girls knew anything. They'd have been sure to speak to Lily, knowing they were such pals. But she daren't ask Lily just in case there was nothing known. Surely to God Big Ginger wouldn't be such a fool as to say anything to anybody. After all, he had come off worst. But you never knew. You never knew what men might say amongst themselves. He might have told one of the other vanmen, and he might have passed the news on to somebody else. . . .

'Here, Bessie, you're mixing thae pies wi' thur cream cookies!' Lily shouted. 'What're ye dreamin' about?'

'N—nothin',' Bessie blushed.

'Keep yer mind on yer job,' Lily said. 'What's wrong wi' you, anyway? You'd think you'd pished in a bed of nettles this mornin'.'

'Aw, shuttup,' Bessie muttered.

'Has that great mind o' yours got too many things to think about?' Lily jeered. 'If ye dinnie watch, ye'll be overtaxin' it. Jesus Christ and General Jackson, but Miss Christie was right when she told auld Wilson you had just a one-track mind,' she giggled. 'I'll never forget the look on her face when she said: "Oh, Bessie's all right so long as you give her only one thing to do at a time."'

'Aw, shuttup!' Bessie cried.

'Aha!' Lily jeered. 'Keep yer hair on, pet!'

'I'll throw one o' thur bloody pies at you if you say another word,' Bessie cried. 'I'll ram it down your bloody throat and choke you, you whore!'

'Oho! Naughty, naughty!' Lily giggled. 'Ye might be one yersel' yet!'

'I'm sorry, Hippy,' she said. 'I didnie mean to rile ye. I was just jokin'. You know me, Hippy. You know I was just in fun.'

'Och, it's all right,' Bessie said.

There was always Mrs. Irvine, she thought, recounting the pies as she separated them from the cream cookies. She was going to Mrs. Irvine's tonight. She would speak to Mrs. Irvine about it. Mrs. Irvine wasn't the sort who'd be likely to gossip about it with the other people in the shop. Mrs. Irvine wouldn't lower herself by going in for clash of that kind. . . .

She brightened at the thought, and she winked cheerily at Eric as he passed with a pile of parcels. 'Are you not goin' to leave one for me?' she said.

11

'MY godfathers! a girl's not safe with a man like that,' Mrs. Irvine said. 'My word, I've a good mind to give him a damned good piece of my mind.'

'Aw, Mrs. Irvine, you mustnie do that,' Bessie cried. 'I dinnie want to make any trouble.'

'But you never get anywhere in this world if you don't make trouble,' Mrs. Irvine said. 'My godfathers! it's me that knows that. What would have happened to me I don't know if I'd just sat quietly and taken everything that came to me. There was Gilbert Irvine now—that man would just have sat on me if I hadn't battled for my own rights.'

'But it might mean me losing my job,' Bessie whined.

'Well, what does that matter?' Mrs. Irvine said. 'You've just been telling me, haven't you, that you're thinking about getting another one. You'd be better out of Andrews', anyway,' she said. 'It's no place for a nice well-brought-up girl like you, m'dear. I never met such a crowd of foul-mouthed girls.'

'Och, they're not bad,' Bessie said.

'Oh, they're well enough, I daresay,' Mrs. Irvine said. 'But I think you'd be better away from them. Now, how would you like to come here?' she said, handing Bessie another cigarette. 'I've been meaning to speak to you about this. I'm needing a little maid to help me with my students when they come back. I'll have two extra ones next term, and the work's getting a bit beyond me.'

'Oh, Mrs. Irvine!' Bessie cried. 'D'ye really mean it?'

'Of course I mean it. Do you think I'd suggest it if I didn't mean it?'

'Aw, it would be lovely,' Bessie said.

She looked around. Mrs. Irvine had a nice big old-fashioned flat, well furnished with good solid furniture of the Edwardian era. Everything was comfortable and clean. There was nothing shoddy or makeshift about it.

'Aw, it would be gorgeous,' Bessie said.

'But ach, my father would never let me,' she said. 'I know what 'll happen. He'll make me bide at home again and look after the bairns. They'll not want to go back to bein' evacuated after they've been home for a fortnight.'

'Well, you can think about it, Bessie,' Mrs. Irvine said, watching her cigarette-smoke evaporate. 'There's no hurry. I'm not giving up my job in Andrews' for a week or two yet, and my students don't come back until the end of the second week in January.'

'I don't want you to do anything against your father's wishes, m'dear,' she said. 'After all, a father's a father, and he should have some say in the running of his house. If he thinks your place is at home beside him and the bairns—well, you'll just have to grin and bear it.'

'Ach, my father doesnie bother about what happens to me,' Bessie said. 'He's too much taken up with his fancy Mabel.'

'Now, Bessie, that's not the way to talk,' Mrs. Irvine said. 'This Miss Whatsername, this Miss Stevens may be a very nice woman. Of course, I understand your attitude perfectly, m'dear. No girl likes to see another woman coming in to take her dead mother's place. I'd feel the same myself. And I'd have been bonnie and angry if I'd gone first and Gilbert Irvine had taken a second wife. I'd have expected my Flora and my Anna to have behaved exactly as you're behaving.'

'Though, mind you, I don't see what you're worrying about,' she said. 'I don't see that you've any reason to think your father's going to marry again. I'm sure he's just friendly with this Miss Whatsername. You'll likely find when you come to know her better that she's a very nice woman and that your father has no more intention of marrying her than flying in the air.'

'I dinnie ken,' Bessie said. 'I wouldnie put it past him.'

'Well, don't look on the black side,' Mrs. Irvine said. 'Just wait and see what turns up. You'll likely find that Christmas will pass very pleasantly. It 'll be nice for you to have your little brother and sister home again. Bairns are such a comfort. And Christmas is the time for children. I'm sure you'll have a very nice time helping them to enjoy themselves. And I'm sure you'll get on famously with Miss Whatsername.'

'But remember,' she said. 'My offer to come here is still open whenever you feel you want to take it. If your brother and sister go back to the farm after the New Year, which I'm sure they'll do, and you still want to change your job, which I think would be a good thing, don't hesitate to come here. That is, if you think you'd like to be a maid of all work in a boarding-house!'

'It won't be all honey, mind you,' she said. 'My godfathers! no, there'll be plenty of hard work! But you and me could get along fine together, I'm sure. We've lots of things in common.'

'Ay, too true,' Bessie simpered.

'We could have some rare times together at the Circles,' Mrs. Irvine said. 'I'd like fine to have a wee pal like yourself with me when I go to meetings of the Friends. I'm sure you'll be a great success with them, Bessie, for as I've always maintained, you're psychic, m'dear.'

'Och away!' Bessie giggled.

'I'm telling you, m'dear. I know! I haven't been going amongst people all those years without knowing who was what.'

'Well, I'm glad to see that our little chat has cheered you up a bit, anyway,' Mrs. Irvine said. 'I always maintain that a girl should always have some sensible middle-aged woman to confide in. Of course, a mother's the best pal a girl can have, but we aren't all lucky enough to have mothers. You'll just have to try to look upon me as one, m'dear.'

'You bet I will,' Bessie said.

'And you'll find there's a lot of comfort in spiritualism,' Mrs. Irvine said. 'I'm fair looking forward to taking you to your first Circle. You'll enjoy yourself, I know. My Faith has been a great comfort to me,' she said. 'And it's taught me a lot, not only about myself but my ancestors. My godfathers! the things I've learned. The things Dr. Varconi and Ali Ben Hassim have told me. Incredible things, m'dear, you'd hardly believe. I've learned more about my ancestors from my spirit friends than I've ever been able to discover on this side.'

'Really?' Bessie said, wide-eyed.

'Yes, the things I've heard,' Mrs. Irvine said. 'Did I tell you that one of my ancestors was a very famous English admiral? Oh, he was a great man in History. The school books are full of him. Well, I have some connexion with him—what it is exactly I don't know, but he's always turning up in spirit messages for me. But one of these days I'll find out definitely. Oh, I'm sure the world's in for a great surprise when it hears. One day you'll be glad to say you know me, m'dear. When I'm amongst the High and Mighty ones where I belong, you'll be able to say "I used to know her." '

Bessie was trying to find words to tell Mrs. Irvine about being an exiled Bourbon, but before she could open her mouth, Mrs. Irvine went on:

'My Faith was a great comfort to me when my own mother died. Of course, I was much older than you are now. I was a fully grown woman with two daughters of my own. But mind you, I missed my mother when she passed over. Oh yes, it was a great blow to me. The only consolation I had was that my mother shared my beliefs, and it wasn't long, I can tell you, before I managed to contact her on the other side.'

Mrs. Irvine sighed. 'My godfathers! I was going through a terrible time with Gilbert Irvine at the time. He was having a right session of drinking. He'd got his claws on some of the money my mother had left me. I was terrified out of my wits sometimes. He threatened to kill me two or three times and I went about in deadly fear of my life. The Friends were a great consolation to me. I remember one Sunday, just two or three weeks after my mother died. We hadn't got in touch with her yet, but I was hoping, and as a matter of fact it was only two or three days after that that we managed to get her. But this Sunday—my godfathers! Gilbert had got several bottles in the house and he was roaring fu'. Anna and Flora and me just locked ourselves in a room, and we never budged, though he kicked and banged on the door and shouted all the dreadful things he'd do when he got hold of us. We were scared stiff, m'dear. Well, by good luck he drank himself into a stupor, so the girls and me slipped out and went to a service of the

Friends in a house near the Gallowgate. We were staying in Glasgow at the time. Gilbert had got a fine job there, but of course he drank himself out of it as he drunk himself out of all the other good jobs he got. My godfathers! the jobs that man had and lost in his time!'

'Well, as I was saying,' she said, 'we went to this house in the Gallowgate. The meeting had started, so we slipped quietly into back seats. But as we went in I saw a funny wee woman give a tremendous start when she got her eye on me. She nearly jumped out of her seat. And all through the meeting she kept turning round and looking at me and looking at me. I was fair puzzled, wondering what she was wanting. For I knew she was wanting to speak to me. Several times she made to rise and come towards me, but something aye seemed to hold her back.'

Mrs. Irvine paused dramatically. 'Well, during the meeting this wee woman went into a trance, and she testified. Oh, she testified most beautifully. Several different spirit friends got into her and delivered messages. One of them was a very highborn lady who had passed over. And this wee woman, that you wouldn't have given twopence-halfpenny for, spoke in a number of different voices—oh, she spoke really beautifully, the most lovely tones. It was like poetry to listen to her. I never heard such lovely English.'

Mrs. Irvine paused again like a well-trained actress. Bessie was sitting with her mouth slightly open, leaning forward and drinking it all in.

'Well, when the meeting finished,' Mrs. Irvine said, 'this wee body hurried away quickly. She got off her mark at once, and was almost the first to go out. But I was determined not to lose track of her. Me and the girls rushed after her, for I was sure she had something to tell me. I was certain she must have some great news from my mother, and I was determined to speak to her. But when we got outside, she'd completely disappeared. We looked up and down the street, but there was no sign of her. Then suddenly Flora saw her disappearing round the corner of a side street, so we rushed after her. My godfathers! we fairly flew, as if the De'il himself was at our heels. And we caught up on her after quite a chase. I was fair panting. I could hardly get enough breath to say: "Excuse me, but I think you wanted to speak to me." Well, do you know, that wee woman was fair terrified. She denied that she'd ever been to any meeting. "I've never seen yeez before in ma life, lady," she says to me in the broadest Glasgow accent. Such a change from the voices she'd been using when she was under control. Oh, you never heard such a broad Gallowgate voice! But I was firm. My godfathers! yes, I was firm, m'dear. I said: "You know fine that you want to speak to me. You were wanting to speak to me all through that meeting." And finally, after I'd shoved some money in her hand, she told me what it was. "Oh, lady," she said. "Oh, lady, I wanted to speak to yeez all right. I wanted to speak to yeez all through the meeting, but I didnie dare. Somethin' seemed to be huddin' me back. I was scared stiff, because——" '

Mrs. Irvine paused dramatically. ' "Because," ' she said. ' "Oh, lady," she said, "oh, lady, when youse came in half a ship came in with ye." '

12

BESSIE joined the queue waiting for a tram opposite the Surgeons' Hall. Most of them were stamping their feet, muttering about the cold, huddling their heads in their collars against the snow swirling out of the blackout. But Bessie did not feel the cold; there was a warm glow of contentment inside her after her three hours' visit to Mrs. Irvine. Under her arm she held a book which Mrs. Irvine had loaned her. *Ten Great Courtesans of History*. She was fair looking forward to reading it, and she wished it wasn't the blackout, otherwise she could have looked at it while waiting. Mrs. Irvine had said she was sure she'd enjoy it. Mrs. Irvine's name was written in big bold writing on the fly-leaf. Senga Irvine. She had laughed when she'd seen Bessie look at it. 'Senga!' she had said. 'Ay, m'dear, it's a nice name right enough. I should know that, for I picked it myself.'

'My name's really Agnes, you know,' she said. 'Agnes! Really, it's a dreadful name. I fair hated it when I was a bairn. Especially when the other bairns called me Aggie. Aggie! Talk about Big Aggie's Man! But of course, you're too young to remember that, m'dear. That was a great catch-word after the last war. Sometime in the early nineteen-twenties it was. There were all sorts of stories and jokes about Big Aggie's Man. Of course, by that time I'd changed my name—long before that, I may say—so it didn't worry me. But I often wondered how I'd have managed to bear it if I'd still had the name my folks christened me. My godfathers! I mind the rows I had with my mother about that name. "Could you not have called me something wicer-like?" I often said. "Something I needn't be ashamed of. Margaret or Mary or something decent. But Agnes——" Oh, my godfathers! the trouble I had with that name when I was a bairn. Other bairns coming to the door and saying "Is Aggie comin' out to play?" So I changed it as soon as I was able to take the law into my own hands. It was simple enough. I just turned it backside foremost. It really isn't so bad that way.'

'It's lovely,' Bessie said.

'It's passable,' Mrs. Irvine said. 'It's got quite a bit of tone about it, too. Certainly a lot more tone than Agnes. Agnes! My godfathers! even though it's mine and was my mother's and my grandmother's before me, I'm glad I never saddled any of my daughters with it.'

'Folk should be prosecuted for giving bairns such terrible names,' she said.

'Too true!' Bessie said.

'There's a young couple I know,' Mrs. Irvine said. 'They've just had their first bairn, and do you know what they've called her? A really terrible mouthful. They've christened the poor brat Olga Mary.'

'Olga Mary!' she laughed. 'And do you know what they call her?—They call her Button!' she said.

Bessie touched the book under her arm, stroking its spine

with the tips of her fingers. Jees, but she wished the tram would come so that she could get on and get started to read it.

'What a time we're havin' to wait,' the man in front of her grumbled. 'Cars goin' everywhere but in the right direction.'

'Aw, there should be one just now,' his wife said.

'Ye've been sayin' that for the last ten minutes,' he groused. 'There've been twa Sixes, and twa Thirteens and a Seven and a Five. But not a damned sign o' an Eight yet.'

'I'm fair scunnered,' he said. 'And I'm cauld.'

'Ah well, you're no' the only one,' his wife said. 'Everybody in the queue's feelin' the cauld as much as you do. Dinnie think you've got it all to yoursel'. The world's ill-divided, but the cauld and this bloody blackout are twa things we all get a share o'.'

Bessie put a cigarette in her mouth and fumbled in her bag for matches. But there were none. And she had none in any of her pockets. She must have left them in Mrs. Irvine's.

'Could I get a light, please?' she said to the man in front.

He held out his cigarette, and she lit hers off it.

'Thanks a lot,' she said.

By the light from a passing torch she saw the man's wife glare at her. The woman muttered something to her man, but Bessie could make out only the words 'glaikit little bitches like that. They need their arses skelped.'

Does she think I was trying to click with him, she said to herself. Christ, she's welcome to him. I wouldnie be found dead beside him.

'Thank God, here's an Eight at last,' the man cried. 'It's no' before time. My puir bloody feet are near frozen to the pavement.'

The bulk of the queue who'd been waiting impatiently for this elusive Number Eight, belched forward as the tram drew up. All order of the queue was broken, and they tried to clamber on the step of the tram. 'Let the passengers off first, please!' the conductor shouted. But he was unheeded, and for a few seconds there was complete congestion. Bessie clutched her bag and her precious book with one hand while with the other she held on to the rail of the tram. 'There's one that's determined to get on, anyway,' she heard somebody behind her say. 'By Christ, it takes thae young lassies. They've the cheek o' the Devil's self.'

'Upstairs only, please!' the conductor was shouting.

Bessie headed the rush upstairs, her gas-mask bumping wildly against her hip. Clutching book and bag, cigarette stuck jauntily in mouth, she sank breathlessly into the first vacant seat. She was rearranging her cheap, flowered artificial-silk scarf over her head when the person next her said: 'Why, Bessie—it *is* Bessie Hipkiss, isn't it?'

'Aw, hello, Miss Aitchison, I didn't recognize you.' Bessie grinned at her old school-teacher. 'I was that busy lookin' for a seat I didn't notice who I was sittin' down beside.'

'I hardly recognized you at first either,' Miss Aitchison said, looking her up and down, taking in the peroxided hair, the overdose of lipstick, and the black-edged nails from which the blood-red varnish was chipping. 'My word, you've fairly grown into a young woman since I saw you last.'

'Really?' Bessie giggled, and as she giggled she became aware that Miss Aitchison was gazing with disapproval at the cigarette stuck in the corner of her mouth. She took it out hastily. 'Is there such a change?' she giggled.

'Yes, quite a big change, I must say,' Miss Aitchison said. 'And how are you, Bessie? Are you still keeping house for your father and the children?'

As the tram rumbled over the North and South Bridges towards Princes Street, Bessie told Miss Aitchison what she was doing, speaking in the polite 'Edinburgh English' voice she used for people in authority.

'What's the book?' Miss Aitchison pursed her mouth when she looked at the title. 'Hm, hardly a suitable book for you, Bessie. It's not the sort of book a young girl should read.'

'It's such a pity you didn't carry on with your schooling,' she said.

'I suppose so,' Bessie said, watching the people who were boarding the tram at the General Post Office. 'But it can't be helped now.'

'Yes, those things happen,' Miss Aitchison said. 'We seem to be powerless against them.'

A girl and a sailor brushed past Bessie, the girl crying: 'There's twa empty seats at the front!'

It was Lily McGillivray. Bessie reached out, but before she could touch her, Lily had swept to the other end of the tram. Bessie looked after her, vaguely uneasy. There was something wrong. Lily looked kind of funny.

'Whew, but that was a fine whiff o' whisky!' the man in the next seat said, turning round to Miss Aitchison. 'Makes me fair jealous!'

'The whole tram's reeking with it,' Miss Aitchison said.

Bessie shrank into her seat. She did not look at either Miss Aitchison or the man. She looked over the heads and shoulders of the other passengers at Lily and the sailor.

'Wasn't it lucky you spoke?' Lily was saying in such a loud voice that everybody on top of the tram could hear. 'I had my eye on you all night, but I couldnie do anythin' because o' that sodger.'

The sailor had his arm around Lily, and she was leaning drunkenly against him.

'I couldnie get away from that soldier,' she said. 'Jesus Christ and General Jackson, he got his eyes on me as soon as me and my friend went into the pub. And he kept givin' us sweeties, so we couldnie very well get away from him. But I got my eye on you as soon as we went in the door. "Oh, what a lovely blond sailor," I said to my friend. "Just take a decka at him!" I saw you were givin' me the eye, but d'you think I could get away from that sodger? Not on yer life! He kept fistin' that poke o' sweeties at me, and honest to God I kept sayin' No thanks, but he would persist. He was a right pain in the neck. I think he thought he was goin' to date me up, but I wasn't havin' any. No bloody thanks! Once I'd got my eye on you I was for nobody else in the pub.'

'I kept sayin' to my friend "Isn't that a lovely blond sailor," I kept sayin'.' Lily guffawed. 'Christ, but I was glad when you came up and said "Are you goin' my way, sister?"' '

228

'She's fairly tellin' the whole car about it, anyway,' the man in the next seat said.

'It's disgusting,' Miss Aitchison said.

'Ay, it's a pity to see a young lassie like that in such a state,' the man said.

'Wasn't it lucky I went into that pub?' Lily was saying. 'We hadnie meant to, but my friend dragged me in after her. "It 'll help you to forget Teddy," she says. Teddy's the boy I've been runnin' around with, but he didn't turn up tonight. Not that he's such a miss, the cheap skate! "Oh, isn't that a lovely blond sailor," I said to my friend.'

'This damned war's got a lot to answer for,' the man in the next seat said. 'It 'll just be the ruination of young lassies like that.'

'There's more than the war to blame,' Miss Aitchison said. 'It goes deeper than that. The whole social system's to blame.'

'You're right,' the man said. 'Still, the war's bringing it all out. Young lassies like that are fairly gettin' their horns out. If there hadnie been a war they wouldnie have got the excuse. Ay, it 'll break up many a home, this war.'

'It's disgusting,' Miss Aitchison said. 'Such a young girl, too. She can't be more than sixteen or seventeen.'

'She's needin' somebody to take her in hand,' the man said. 'A good firm leatherin' would do her a world of good.'

'I'm glad she's not my daughter,' he said.

'Yes, she'll bring shame on some poor souls,' Miss Aitchison said.

'I seem to know her face,' she said. 'I can't just place her, but I'm sure I've seen her before. Wasn't she at school with you, Bessie?'

'I don't think so,' Bessie said. 'I don't know who she is.'

'I should hope not,' Miss Aitchison said. 'I should hope you'll never know anybody like that.' She peered out of the window. 'We must be getting near East London Street,' she said.

'Ay, it 'll be the next stop,' the man said. 'This blackout's

229

a damned nuisance. It's not the first time I've been carried past my right stop.'

'Well, good night, Bessie,' Miss Aitchison said, rising.

'Good night, Miss Aitchison,' she said, and no sooner had her former teacher's head disappeared down the tram-stairs than she opened *Ten Great Courtesans of History*. Everybody else in the car was listening to Lily and the sailor, but Bessie bent her head over the book. She was glad Lily hadn't recognized her, and she hoped she wouldn't look round and spot her. Thank goodness, Miss Aitchison was away. It would have been terrible if Lily had said: 'Hya, Hippy!' All the same, it was a damned nuisance meeting Miss Aitchison like that. It was just her luck. She was such a nosey old bitch, asking all these daft questions. And did you see the way she kept looking you up and down? Taking in everything you had on in such a criticizing way. . . .

Bessie skimmed quickly through the pages, reading little bits here and there; too eager to swallow the whole book at one gulp to begin at the beginning and read it properly. She kept looking at the photographs of Cora Pearl and Lola Montez and other naughty ladies. She could still hear Lily's voice, but by the time the tram had reached Cannonmills she was oblivious of everything but the adventures of Lola Montez. And she jumped when somebody slapped her on the back and said: 'Ahoy there, mate!'

Bessie closed the book with a sigh. 'Hello, George,' she said.

Dirty Minnie's lodger sat down beside her, placing his sailor's cap on his knee. 'Late tonight as usual!' he said.

'Hello, there's our pal, Lily, up there with young Archie,' he said. 'Wonder where she's fallen in with him?'

But in a few seconds he knew by listening to Lily's reiterated: 'I saw this lovely blond sailor and I just said to my girl-friend: "Didya ever see anythin' so lovely?"'

George kept nudging Bessie, saying: 'Listen to that, mate!'

When the tram stopped at Harrisfield Square, Lily saw them. 'Hello, Hippy!' she shrieked. 'My, you missed yourself the night. I've had a whale of a time. Haven't I, Archie?'

The girls and the two sailors stood for a short time outside the Post Office at the corner of the Square. Lily talked all the time, telling them how Teddy hadn't turned up. George kept saying that probably Teddy's ship had sailed suddenly. But Lily said: 'I'm finished wi' him. He doesnie need to think he'll make a muggins out o' me.'

'I think we're all mugginses standin' here when we might be warm in our beds,' George said. 'It's time we were away up the hill.'

'Yeah, I guess it's time I got down to the ship,' Archie said.

'What fellies!' Lily cried. 'Feared for a wee bit cauld! And yet you call yoursel's sailors! It's heart-breakin'.'

'C'mon, you two dames,' George said. 'Up the hill with you!'

'Aw, it's early yet,' Lily said. 'Who do you think you're bossin' around? I'm not goin' home yet. Me and Archie are stayin' here for a while yet, aren't we, Archie?'

'Archie's goin' to his ship,' George said, taking her arm.

'Here, who d'you think you're bossin'?' Lily cried. 'D'you think I'm muggins?'

'No, I think we're all mugginses,' George said. 'We're a bloody soft collection of mugginses, too, to let them put up posters like that.'

'What poster?' Lily said.

'This poster here,' he said. 'Don't tell me you've missed seeing it! It's big enough. Shine your flashie on it, chum.'

Archie flashed his torch on the huge red Ministry of Information poster plastered on the wall of the Post Office. In large white letters they read:

YOUR CHEERFULNESS
YOUR COURAGE
YOUR RESOLUTION
WILL BRING
US
VICTORY

231

'*Your* courage, *your* cheerfulness, *your* resolution will bring *us* victory!' George said.

'Do you know who US is?' he said.

He laughed. 'It's not you and it's not me and it's not folk like us. No, we're supposed to have courage and cheerfulness and resolution while we muck around in the blackout and get bombed and killed, while the muckin' money-bags sit back on their fat arses and rake in the spoils of victory!'

'This muckin' war,' he said, and he spat into the centre of the poster. Then he took the girls by the elbows and propelled them up the hill to the blacked-out tenements of Calderburn.

13

ON the Friday before Christmas Bert Hipkiss took the day off work and went to Peebles to bring the children home. He arrived with them and Miss Stevens about eight o'clock.

Bessie was ironing on the living-room table. 'Goodness, are ye here already?' she cried. 'I wasn't expectin' ye till nine. If I'd thought ye were to be as quick I'd have had the supper set.'

'I told you we'd be here about eight,' Bert said.

'Never mind, Bessie,' Miss Stevens smiled. 'We won't be long in shifting this and getting the table laid. I'll put on the kettle.'

'It's all right, I'll manage,' Bessie said with a martyred air, quickly folding the shirt she'd been ironing and rolling up the ironing-blanket. 'Just you sit down, Miss Stevens. I'll easy manage.'

'Oh, but I must do something to help,' Miss Stevens said. 'After all, it's time I learned to find my way about the house, isn't it?' She laughed. 'Now, if you'll just tell me where the things are, I'll soon lay the table.'

'Don't bother,' Bessie said.

'I'll help you, Bessie,' Jenny cried. 'I'm a good wee help about the house. Auntie Grace said it!'

'I'll manage,' Bessie said, lifting the iron and placing the roll of blanket under her arm. 'You get your coat off and get out my way. That's the best way you can help, my lady.'

'Yes, come to Mammy and she'll take your things off, dear,' Miss Stevens said, sitting down and holding out her arms to Jenny.

Bessie stiffened. Was she hearing right?

'The place is like a pawn-shop,' Bert complained. 'I'm sure you might have done something about it, Bessie, before we came. You knew fine we weren't going to be late. I'm certain I told you we'd be home about eight.'

'What were you needing to iron for, anyway?' he said. 'You might have had all that done long ago.'

'I didnie get back from my work until after five,' Bessie said. 'Then I had the messages to go for. The shops are that crowded I wasnie back here until after six. I stood in the Store for ages and ages. If I hadnie stood in a queue there wouldnie have been anythin' for yer supper.'

'Oh, it's all right, it's all right,' Miss Stevens said. 'We're in no hurry for our supper, anyway. We all had a good tea before we left Peebles. I must say Mrs. Hood gave us a lovely spread. Home-made scones and home-made jelly and lovely wee cakes she had baked herself.'

'Well, ye'll not get anythin' like that here,' Bessie said. 'I brought a cake hame from my work, but it's a gey mouldy affair.'

And I hope you choke on it, she thought, clattering into the kitchenette and putting on the kettle. Coming here and up-setting everything. I know fine that Da said eight o'clock, but I just wasn't going to put myself about for you. I had my ironing to do, and my ironing comes before any old Auntie Mabel. Auntie Mabel . . .

Was I hearing right when I heard her say 'Mammy'?

'Where's the tablecloth, dear?' Miss Stevens said, standing in the kitchenette door. 'I'll put it on.'

'I'm just comin' with it,' Bessie said. 'You go and sit down. I'll manage fine.'

'But I must help, dear.' Miss Stevens smiled, showing a gold filling in one of her back teeth. 'After all, I'm here to help.'

Bessie did not answer. She went to a drawer of the dresser and took out the tablecloth. She unfolded it with a flourish over the table.

'God, what a draught you're causin',' Bert said, looking up from unbuttoning Billy's coat. 'What do you mean by flaffing that thing about like that?'

'I'm sure I wasnie flaffin' it any more than usual,' Bessie said.

'You were causin' a bloody fine draught,' Bert said. 'And take that look off your face. You look as if you'd taken a dose of castor-oil.'

'She near knocked me over, didn't she, Da?' Billy said, making a face at Bessie.

'Here are the cups, dear,' Miss Stevens said, laying them on the table.

'These arenie the right ones,' Bessie said. 'We'll use the ones wi' the yellow roses painted on them. My mother just used thur ones at breakfast-time.'

She was picking them up to take them back to the kitchenette when her father cried: 'Look here, what's all this fuss about, anyway? Those cups are damned fine. I don't remember that your mother was so particular about havin' different cups at different meals. It doesn't matter what we drink out of as long as we get some tea. Come on, cut the cackle and let's have something to eat. It's high time those bairns were in their beds.'

'But my mother didnie use thur cups when we had visitors,' Bessie said.

'Well, there are no visitors here tonight,' Bert said. 'So put these back on the table.'

'But——'

'Your Auntie Mabel's not a visitor,' he said. 'She's goin' to bide here after this. I'd better tell you right here and now. I was goin' to wait till after supper and the bairns were away in their bed. But seeing you're making such a mollygrant I'll tell you here and now. Your Auntie Mabel and I were married this morning in the Register Office.'

'Married?' Bessie's mouth gaped open.

'Ay, married,' Bert said. 'Any complaints?'

'Oh, I think we should use the cups with the yellow roses, Bert,' Mrs. Hipkiss said. 'Since Bessie's heart seems so set on them. After all, this is a kind of celebration, isn't it?'

'Queer kind of celebration with her goin' about with a face like a funeral,' Bert said. 'Oh, for God's sake, girl!' he cried. 'Take that greetin' look off your dial.'

'I—I——' Bessie opened her mouth wide and closed her eyes, trying to stop the flood of tears.

'There now, Bessie, there, there,' Mrs. Hipkiss said, putting her arm round her. 'I know it must be a surprise to you.'

'Really, Bert, you should have had a wee bit more tact,' she said. 'Springing it on the poor girl like that.'

Bessie shrugged off Mrs. Hipkiss' arm and groped for the edge of the table for support. 'Ye might 'a' told me,' she wailed. 'Ye might 'a' told me.'

'For Christ's sake!' Bert cried. 'Stop the waterworks. If you're goin' to greet, for God's sake away to your room and greet there.'

'I—I'm—goin',' Bessie snivelled, and she rushed to the door and made for the bathroom.

She hung on the edge of the bath, unable to stop the tears that gushed from her eyes. They were tears more of rage than anything else now: rage that she should have broken down before that woman. And rage at her father. What right had he to spring this upon her?

'Oh, Ma, Ma,' she wailed soundlessly. 'Oh, Ma, I wish ye were here.'

She looked up and stared at her tear-stained face in the mirror above the basin. Her face was puckered like a monkey's: white and blotched. Her hair was dishevelled. She could see the darkness at the roots. I'll have to get out the peroxide bottle again, she thought. But as soon as she'd thought it, she was panic-stricken. To think of such a thing at such a time. To bother about her appearance when she was having a crisis like this. Really, it's not canny, Bessie Hipkiss, you must be daft to think of such a thing.

Nevertheless, as she stared at her reflection, gradually she became as interested in how she looked as in what had led up to her looking like this. Madame Royale reeled, but quick as a flash she remembered that she was a princess of the Blood Royal. Princesses don't show their feelings, you fool, she hissed. Princesses are always cool and cold and imperturbable. *Voilà!* What can the vile machinations of a woman like Milady Stevens mean to Marie-Elisabeth de Bourbon, Duchess d'Angouleme? *Pouf!* I laugh at you, Milady Stevens. I spit on you. I shall thrust my aristocratic little foot upon your thick neck. *Canaille!*

Bessie wiped her face and eyes and smoothed her hair. So! A virago glared at her from the mirror. Eyes flashing, bosom heaving so that the diamonds on it flashed as fiercely as her eyes, Madame Royale threw back her shoulders and swept into the throne-room. A Bourbon was going to battle!

14

ON Christmas morning Bessie was awakened by the shouts of the children. Jenny rushed into the living-room, hugging an armful of toys. 'It's Christmas, Bessie!' she shrieked. 'Lookit what Sandy Claus has brought me.'

'My, ye're a lucky wee lassie,' Bessie said, rising in bed on her elbow.

'Look, Ferret!' Billy cried. 'He's brought me an engine. But I'd rather hae had some toy sodgers and a tank,' he said. 'I asked Sandy Claus to bring me a great big tank wi' guns, but the auld bugger must 'a' forgot.'

'Aw, Billy, you mustnie say thae Bad Words,' Bessie said. 'Ye ken that Mammy didnie like to hear ye say them.'

'Och, what does it matter,' he said. 'Mammy's wi' the angels now. She doesnie care. And Auntie Mabel doesnie mind.'

'It's not Auntie Mabel,' Jenny cried. 'It's Mammy!'

'Daddy said it,' she said.

Bessie sighed and prepared to get up.

'Oh, Bessie, I can see your bosies!' Jenny cried. 'Let me see them, Bessie.'

'You go and play wi' the nice doll Santa Claus has brought ye,' Bessie said, struggling into her frock, keeping her back to the children.

'I dinnie want to play wis my doll,' Jenny said. 'It's no' a nice doll. Draw me somesing, Bessie,' she said. 'Draw my bosies.'

'I'll clout yer ears for ye if ye dinnie get out my road,' Bessie shouted, rushing to the fire and beginning to rake the ashes.

'Auntie Grace used to let me see her bosies,' Jenny said, with a faraway look in her eyes. 'When are we goin' back to Auntie Grace's, Bessie?'

'I dinnie ken,' Bessie said.

The sooner the better, she said to herself. The sooner you're both out of here and away back to Mrs. Hood's farm the better. Though I suppose that would just be playing into that Stevens woman's barrow. She's not wanting to be bothered with another woman's bairns. She's got my da and that's all she's bothering about.

'Ach, I'm no' goin' back to bein' evacuated,' Billy said. 'It's just kids that are evacuated. There's ower-much fun here. I couldnie leave the Gang.'

'Get out ma road!' Bessie yelled, darting past him into the kitchenette. She seized the axe and began to chop kindling for the fire.

She had it lit and the breakfast laid when her father and his new bride appeared.

'What a bloody row you've been making, Bessie,' he said, warming his bottom in front of the fire. 'Can you not break sticks for the fire the night before? Instead of wakening the whole neighbourhood in the morning. The times I've told you about it.'

'Will you infuse the tea, Bessie, while I fry the sausages,' Mrs. Hipkiss said.

Bessie was placing the tea-cosy on top of the pot when Mrs. Hipkiss brought in a plate of sausages and placed it in front of Bert. 'Oh, don't use that cosy, Bessie,' she said. 'Put the pot down in front of the fire to keep warm.'

'But my mother aye used this cosy,' Bessie said.

'Well, yes,' Mrs. Hipkiss smiled. 'But I'd rather we didn't use it. I'm terrified one of the children bump against it and knock over the pot and scald themselves. I think the pot's better to be in front of the fire.'

Sulkily, Bessie did as she was told. Her father had started to wolf his sausages. 'Come on, Billy, sit in and eat your sausages like a good boy,' he said. 'Leave off playing with your engine until after.'

'There you are, Bessie, eat them up while they're hot,' Mrs. Hipkiss said, placing a plate in front of her stepdaughter.

Bessie bent her head over her plate and said Grace silently. Her heart was full of black hatred for Mrs. Hipkiss. What a change this was from last Christmas. . . .

All through the meal she had difficulty in keeping back the tears that pricked her eyelids. And she was almost at scream-ing-point by the time her father rose and said: 'Well, I suppose I'd better get away to my work. That's the worst of working in a pub, you never get a holiday.'

She made the beds, and she was dusting the bedrooms when somebody knocked at the door.

'Oh, it's you, Mr. Rankin,' she cried.

The Insurance Man slipped past her, grinning as he said: 'Ay, Miss Hipkiss, a Merry Christmas, Miss Hipkiss, and how's your health today?'

'Och, I'm all right,' she said. 'I suppose.'

'And how's Jenny?' the Insurance Man cried, tousling Jenny's hair. 'Did Santa Claus bring you a lot of toys? Well, Miss Hipkiss,' he said. 'This 'll be the last time you'll see me for a while. That's why I had to come today. I'm off tomorrow.'

'Off tomorrow?' she said.

'Ay, it's me for the High Jump!' he said. 'I've to report at the barracks at Elgin on Wednesday.'

'Aw, Mr. Rankin,' she said.

'Ay, it comes to us all, Miss Hipkiss,' he said, writing rapidly in her Insurance Books. 'Me for the foot-sloggin' and the Bully Beef Brigade!'

'Hello,' Mrs. Hipkiss said, coming in from the kitchenette.

'Hello,' Rankin said, eyeing her up and down in an appraising fashion. 'This your new mother?' he said to Bessie. 'A wee bird whispered that I'd be seeing her. Another customer for me, eh?'

'That's what I came through about,' Mrs. Hipkiss said. 'I want to take out a policy for myself.'

'Delighted, Mrs. Hipkiss, delighted!' he said, searching in his breast-pocket. 'Here we are! Don't say this isn't service! Here's the form to fill in. If you'll have it ready, my wife 'll collect it when she comes round next week.'

'Your wife?' Bessie said.

'Ay, my better half—she's going to take over my job when I go away to stick bayonets into Jerry!' Rankin laughed.

'There we are then, Miss Hipkiss,' he said, handing her the books and scooping up the money. 'That's the last transaction you and me'll do for a while, I guess.'

'Ay, it's too bad,' she said.

'Ah well, we'll just have to grin and bear it,' he said. 'Nobody's sorrier about it than I am. I'd like fine to be still comin' every week to get a bit chaff with you and Mrs. Hipkiss here.'

'Aw, it 'll soon be over,' Bessie said. 'You maybe won't need to stay long at Elgin.'

'That's right,' he said. 'Another two-three months and it 'll all be settled. Jerry can't last much longer. They'll have caved in before March, 1940. I'd lay my shirt on that.'

'I don't know,' Mrs. Hipkiss said. 'I wouldn't lay anything on it if I were you. My husband says this war's going to last a lot longer than people think.'

'Naw, it can't last,' he said.

239

'Well, we'll see,' she said. 'I'm not living in a fool's paradise, anyway. The future's blacker than folk think.'

'Well, we'll live in hope or die in despair,' Rankin said, making for the door. 'But you and me must have that date when I come back, Miss Hipkiss! We've aye been goin' to go to the pictures together, but we've never got round to it yet!'

'Too true!' Bessie giggled.

'Make a note of it,' he said. 'The 1st of April, 1940. I'll stand you into the best seats in the Rialto.'

'All right,' she giggled. 'It's a date.'

'Cheeribye then!' he said.

'Cheeribye!' she called.

She watched him rush downstairs, and she leaned for a few seconds against the door-post, thinking of the changes there had been in the past few months. This awful war . . . And now here was Mr. Rankin going away to it. . . .

'Tell me a story, Bessie,' Jenny said.

'I will nut,' she said.

She finished dusting the bedrooms, then she picked up *Ten Great Courtesans of History*. She'd never had time to read it properly yet. She'd just been able to dip into bits. There was such a stir in the house since the bairns had come back. What between them and That Woman she was near demented. . . .

'God, what a life and not a fag in the house!' Jenny exclaimed, putting her hand to her forehead.

'What's that?' Mrs. Hipkiss said.

'Nussing,' Jenny said, opening her eyes widely at her stepmother. 'I was just playin' at being Bessie.'

Mabel looked at Bessie and raised her eyebrows. 'Really, Bessie, you'll have to watch what you say in front of those children.'

'I cannie help it if they will repeat things,' Bessie said. 'Their lugs are ower-long.'

'Tell me a story, Bessie,' Jenny whined, tugging at her skirt. 'On and on and on with the story!'

'Ay, tell us a story, Ferret,' Billy said, kicking aside his engine. 'Tell us a story about a tiger.'

'Tell us a story about poor wee Jenny McSquirt and a witch,' Jenny said.

'No, no witches!' Mrs. Hipkiss smiled. 'You remember what Daddy said, Jenny. He said you were getting too old to hear about witches. The witches have all been killed in the war.'

'I dinnie care,' Jenny pouted. 'I want a story about Witch Rednose that boils wee girls in oil.'

'Witch Rednose is dead,' Mrs. Hipkiss said. 'If Bessie will peel the potatoes I'll tell you a story about a little boy and girl who worked in a factory and about the wicked boss who made them work for practically nothing.'

'Och, I'm fed up with that story,' Billy yelled. 'Who wants to hear about them, anyway? They were mugs. It served them right if they didnie get enough to eat.'

But Mrs. Hipkiss was firm, and she began: 'Once upon a time there was a little boy and girl who worked in a factory . . .'

Bessie stood for a moment, biting her lips. Then she went into the kitchenette and started to peel the potatoes. She would tell the bairns a Real Story tonight when she put them to bed after That Woman had gone out. It didn't matter a damn what her father had said. The bairns liked stories about witches and stories about witches they were going to get. As long as she was here, anyway. . . .

But would that be for much longer? She was still trying to make up her mind about Mrs. Irvine's offer. She wished she had somebody to talk to about it. Somebody sensible. She had spoken about it to Lily, and Lily had said she should jump at it like a shot. But after all, Lily was hardly the right person to ask. Lily wasn't much older than herself. . . . No, she'd take a run over to Mrs. Moore's this afternoon and ask her what she thought about it. Mrs. Moore had been a great pal of her mother's. . . .

15

MRS. MOORE had the door open for her. 'I saw ye comin' across the street, hen,' she said. 'I was just hopin' I'd have a visitor. I must say I like a visitor on Christmas Day. It makes it mair hamely like.'

'Put on the kettle, hen,' she said.

'Ay, and how are ye gettin' on wi' yer new mother?' she said, waddling to the window and sitting down.

Bessie began to pour out her troubles, and before she was halfway through she was in tears.

'Now, ye mustnie take on like that, Bessie,' Mrs. Moore said. 'Greetin' winnie help it. What's to be, will be, and nothing 'll make a better o' it. A Higher Hand than ours decides thae things.'

'But what did he need to go and get married for?' Bessie snivelled. 'I'm sure I did everythin' I could for him. I've slaved and slaved for him, cookin' his meals and lookin' after the bairns. I'm sure I did my best.'

'Ay, puir lassie, ye've never really had a chance to show what ye could really do,' Mrs. Moore said.

'Too true,' Bessie sniffed. 'I've never had a chance.'

'It's a funny world,' Mrs. Moore said, pouring the tea. 'I must say I expected better of yer father. I never thought he'd go and get married again. No, not for one moment did I ever think that. He aye seemed that fond o' your poor mother.'

'I mind the day o' the funeral,' she said, sipping her tea. 'He says to me: "My puir Margaret's awa', my puir puir lassie." And I mind fine the way he carried on, howlin' and greetin' like a lost dug. It was a fell carry on. I mind I said to ma auld man: "Bert Hipkiss is badly put about, I just hope he'll no' go to the bottle for consolation."'

'Have a bit cake, Bessie,' she said, handing over the cake-stand. 'Ay, it just shows ye,' she said. 'Them that yell the loudest aye get ower things quickest.'

'Do ye think I should go to Mrs. Irvine's?' Bessie said.

'Far be it from me to give advice,' Mrs. Moore said. 'I'm not one for stickin' my nose into other folk's business. I doubt ye'll have to make up yer mind about that yersel', my lassie.'

'But it seems a grand chance,' she said. 'Ay, it seems a grand chance to better yersel'. She sounds a sensible-like body, and she would look after you.'

'Ay, she's an awfie nice woman,' Bessie said.

'Still, we'd miss ye here,' Mrs. Moore said. 'Ay, we'd miss ye, Bessie. After all, this is yer home. And there's the bairns—what about the puir bairns? They'd miss ye.'

'Ay, I suppose so,' Bessie said.

'It's a problem.' Mrs. Moore leaned her elbows on the window-sill, pressing her fat face against the pane. 'It's a problem that a Higher Hand than ours will have to solve.'

'Oh, there's Dirty Minnie!' she cried. 'We'll ask her up and see what she thinks o' it.'

She opened the window with a bang and shouted: 'Hoy there, Minnie, where are ye bound for?'

'I'm comin' up,' Minnie shrieked.

'Well, here ye are, hen,' Mrs. Moore said when Minnie came in, panting. 'Are ye aye keepin' sober?'

'There's nothin' else for it,' Minnie said, sinking into a chair. 'Drink like everythin' else is beginnin' to get scarce. I dinnie ken what I'm goin' to do this New Year. I cannie get a bottle anywhere for love nor money.'

'Ta, Bessie,' she said, taking the cup of tea. 'There's a pal!'

'Ye're an awfie swell the day, Minnie,' said Mrs. Moore.

Dirty Minnie giggled. She wore a fawn skirt on which tea had been spilled, and a pink silk blouse which was too tight for her; it stretched across her enormous bust, gaping at the front, showing an unwashed chemise edged with lace. Her stockings were wrinkled at the knees and ankles, and bits of grey fluff were sticking to them. Her greasy, matted hair was done in a roll, and the ribbon from a sailor's cap was bound round her head. It had *H.M.S. Invincible* printed on it.

'I like yer new hair-do,' Mrs. Moore said. 'And yer ribbon! My, ye're upsides wi' the young lassies!'

'I took it offen one o' George's auld sailor hats,' Minnie said, touching it proudly. 'He was for throwin' out the hat, but I said I'll have that, I said. So then I had a bit rake through Toots' gear and I found a hat with *H.M.S. Provocative* on it, so I ripped it off, and I have that, too. It's a fine change. My jings, but Toots didnie half create a stink,' she laughed. 'Provocative, he says, do ye no' think ye're provocative enough already!'

'Ye'll be lookin' for a man now, Minnie,' Mrs. Moore said.

'Ay, it's all my chance,' Minnie giggled. 'It's a right pity yer faither didnie take up wi' me, Bessie!'

'Too true,' Bessie said.

And really, she thought, Minnie would have been a damned sight better than that Stevens woman. She'd have been able to deal with Minnie.

'Have a bit cake, Minnie.' Mrs. Moore held out the cake-stand.

'My, what a nice stand!' Minnie cried. 'Ye're awfie posh, Mrs. Moore. It must take a lot o' elbow grease to keep that clean. It's shinin' like a sow's ear.'

'It's real bonnie,' she said. 'But it's not the sort o' thing I could be bothered with masel'.'

'Oh, I must have my cake-stand,' Mrs. Moore said. 'It gies the table some guff!'

The idea really wasn't as daft as it sounded. She could have coped with Minnie. She'd known Minnie almost all her life. But this Stevens woman . . . Aw, why could her da not have taken up with Mrs. Irvine. . . .

Bessie watched Mrs. Moore and Dirty Minnie shuffle their chairs to the window, where they sat back, prepared to see all they could on the street. Now, if only she was sitting here with Mrs. Irvine. . . .

'I was up the town yesterday,' Dirty Minnie said. 'I was lookin' for a winter nightie. What a job I had tryin' to get one, too. I wanted a nice white winceyette one. I'm needin' somethin' to keep me warm thur cauld nights, seein' I cannie get a man and somebody else has nabbit Bert Hipkiss—but do ye think I could get one? Not on your life! I was in umpteen shops

244

and couldnie find anythin' to suit me. What awfie-like things they showed me. You could blow peas through some o' them. Thin dirt o' stuff that would rip as soon as ye looked at it.'

'Ay, things are no' what they were,' Mrs. Moore said.

'I wanted an outsize,' Minnie said. 'But none o' the shops had any. They dinnie seem to cater for folk like you and me, Mrs. Moore. The folk are a' that thin and jimpit nowadays.'

'Ay, it's all this dietin' and dirt nowadays.'

'However, at last when I was beginnin' to lose hope the lassie in one shop said she thought they had somethin' to suit me.' Minnie paused and gave a gusty laugh. 'Suit me! My jings, I just about died when she held it out to me. "Here," I says, "it's a nightgown I want," I says, "no' a tent!" '

'Ye could 'a' put a dozen Boy Scouts in it,' she said.

Mrs. Moore reached for a tin of toffees and held it out. 'Have a toffee, Minnie. I got them this mornin'. My auld man's niece in Aberdeen sent them.'

'Ta, hen,' Minnie said.

'Thanks,' Bessie said, and as she sucked the sweet she thought again of Mrs. Irvine. What a difference she was from Mrs. Moore and Dirty Minnie. They were right enough, you know, but there was something about Mrs. Irvine. . . . Oh, Mrs. Irvine had a touch of class all right.

'They came by the post this mornin',' Mrs. Moore said, sucking her toffee. 'I was just wonderin' if he'd bring me anythin'. Christmas Day isnie like Christmas Day if ye dinnie get a parcel. I'm as bad as the bairns!'

'Och ay, we all like to be remembered,' Minnie said.

'I watched him comin' down the other side of the street,' Mrs. Moore said, 'and I got my eye on a wee parcel tied in fancy paper. My, wouldn't it be fine, I said to myself, if that was just comin' for me. I wasnie carin' whether I got a big parcel or no'. I was just wantin' this wee parcel tied wi' fancy paper. It looked that bonnie. I could see it quite plain from the windy here. I saw the postie gang into Bessie's stair and I thought: My God, I'll be bonnie and angry if that parcel's for somebody else. And I had my eye on him like a hawk when he came out. But he was still carryin' the parcel. My God, but my heart was goin' out and in like a concertina. And when I saw him comin' into our stair . . .' Mrs. Moore was almost panting again at the remembrance. 'I went and stood ahint the door,' she said. 'And when I heard him comin' up the stair and stoppin' at the door—my God! I flung it open and I near kissed him when he handed me the parcel.'

'I gave him sixpence,' she said.

'I was that pleased to get it,' she said, taking a piece of holly-sprigged paper from behind a vase and smoothing it out. 'It's bonnie paper, isn't it? Govey Dick, I think I'm mair pleased wi' the paper than I am wi' the toffees.'

'They're nice toffees, though,' Minnie said, smacking loudly.

'Ay, they're the noisiest toffees I've ever heard,' Mrs. Moore laughed.

'I doubt mine's has stuck to my teeth,' she said, poking her finger into her mouth to dislodge it. 'There it is!' she said, and she gave a few more chews, then swallowed it.

Almost at once a look of alarm settled on her face.

'Christ!' she cried.

'I've swallowed one o' ma false-teeth,' she said.

Dirty Minnie giggled, then she leaned forward and said sympathetically: 'Never mind, hen, it'll soon come bitin' its way through at the other end.'

'Ye should take a dose o' castor-oil, Mrs. Moore,' Bessie said. 'That should do the trick.'

'When I want advice from you, Bessie Hipkiss, I'll ask for it,' Mrs. Moore said majestically. 'I'm ower-auld in the horn to take advice from a young limmer like you.'

But not too old to give advice when it's not wanted, Bessie said to herself. The trouble is you never give advice right when it's asked for. . . . Now, if she was just sitting here with Mrs. Irvine instead of these two fat old gossips. If you asked Mrs. Irvine for advice she gave you advice. Not like Mrs. Moore who gave it with one hand and took it away with the other. As for Dirty Minnie, she was too taken up with winter nighties and her lodgers and things to be able to give advice to anybody. The trouble with these two fat old geesers was that they knew nothing about Life. They just sat there on their bottoms and they couldn't see further than the corner of the street. They didn't realize that she was at a critical period in her history. They didn't know what emotions were going on inside her. They just looked at her and said: 'Och, it's just Bessie Hipkiss,' and went on with their gossip. It was heart-breaking, as Lily would say.

'Talkin' o' castor-oil,' Dirty Minnie said. 'I havenie seen Mrs. Winter for two-three days.'

'Did ye no' hear!' Mrs. Moore guffawed. 'She's no' able to get out the house because o' her sore feet. She had the nerve to ask me if I'd go over and bandage them for her,' she said. 'Askin' me that's got sore enough feet masel'. No thank you! I just tellt her I couldnie manage to bend to bandage ma own feet far less hers.'

'Ach, Mrs. Winter's aye in a peck o' troubles,' Minnie said. 'She should have lived twa thousand years ago. There was a man called J. Christ that would've been delighted to dae it for her. She was born at the wrong historical moment, as George my lodger aye says. Well, I must go,' she said, rising. 'I must fly. This 'll not get boots for the bairns.'

'And what bairns have you got, Minnie!' Mrs. Moore giggled. 'Where are ye bound for the night?' she said.

'I'm goin' to the picters wi' my sailors,' Minnie said. 'There's a good picter in the Rialto. One o' thae horror films about yon bloke Franky Steen. Boris Karloff is in it.'

'My, but I could go for Boris Karloff in a big way,' Mrs. Moore laughed. 'A big way in the opposite direction!'

'It should be guid,' Minnie said. 'It's got an H. certificate.'

'An H. certificate?'

'Ay, it means it's no' for bairns,' Minnie said.

'Huh. It's some o' the bairns that should hae H. certificates,' Mrs. Moore said.

'Like our Billy,' Bessie said. 'He's a limb o' Satan.'

'I must go, too,' she said. 'The bairns'll be wonderin' where I am. That Woman 'll maybe hae murdered them by this time.'

'If they havenie murdered her!' Minnie laughed.

'It would be a good riddance,' Bessie said.

247

'Ach, I wouldnie worry about her if I was you, Bessie,' Mrs. Moore said. 'Everything 'll come out right in the end.'

'Ay, it's sure to come out in the wash,' Dirty Minnie said. 'Like me!'

16

It was Hogmanay night, and Madame Royale sat alone in the great palace of the Louvre. Tonight was the end of the old year . . . tonight was the end of the old life. She'd made up her mind to leave. In another wing of the palace her little brother and sister were fast asleep. *Pauvres petits enfants* . . . Tomorrow when they awoke they would find that their father and his new queen, their false and cruel stepmother, were in charge of their destinies. . . .

'But not in charge of mine,' Madame Royale hissed into the dying fire. 'Never, never will Milady Stevens lord it over me. I shall kill myself first. Or go forth into exile. . . .'

Bessie shivered and drew her cardigan tighter around her thin chest. It was right cold in here, but she didn't feel like going to the coal-cellar for more coals.

She switched on the radio. Vera Lynn was singing *We'll Meet Again*.

'We'll meet again, don't know where, don't know when,' Bessie hummed, 'but I know we'll meet again some sunny day.'

She looked at the clock. It was time she got going. She'd told Mrs. Irvine she'd be there about ten to help her cut sandwiches for the people she was expecting for the New Year. She had known that she couldn't manage any earlier. Her father and his new wife hadn't gone out until about eight o'clock. They were away to a party. 'We're dependin' on you to keep your eye on the bairns, Bessie,' he had said.

Well, you can just depend, Bessie said to herself, going to the cupboard in the lobby and taking out an old suit-case. The house can go on fire now for all I care. It's just a pity that

248

your braw new wife isn't here to go up in smoke along with it, my man.

She had said nothing about Mrs. Irvine's offer to him. She had been on the point of doing so several times, but the trouble was that she'd never been able to make up her mind to take the decisive step.

Now, however, she had made up her mind. She had told Mrs. Irvine that afternoon; and since Mrs. Hipkiss and her father had gone out she had written a note to her father, telling him about it. It was stuck behind the tea-caddy on the mantelpiece.

She tiptoed into the children's room and began to carry her clothes into the living-room, packing them in the case. 'Keep smiling like you always do till the blue skies chase those dark clouds far awaaay,' she hummed.

She took her mother's photo from the top of the dresser and packed it carefully on top of her clothes. Then she picked up *Ten Great Courtesans of History*. She glanced through it and looked for a time at a photograph of Lola Montez before she put the book in the case. My, what a grand time Lola Montez had had! Wouldn't it be rare if she could just have a life like hers. . . . It would be fine to see it on the pictures. Bette Davis could do the part of Lola fine. . . .

Ten past nine. She had asked Mrs. Finlayson across the passage to keep her ears open in case the bairns made any sound. She had told her that she had to go out for a wee while. My, what a surprise Mrs. Finlayson and all the others would get when they heard what had really happened. She could just imagine Mrs. Finlayson saying to the other women at the Store Van: 'Ay, she asked me as cool as a cucumber if I'd keep an ear open for the bairns. "I'm just goin' out for a wee while," she said. A wee while! The sleekit wee bitch! I'd never have thought Bessie would do a thing like that. It just shows ye, thae quiet kind are aye the worst. . . .'

Bessie looked around. Was there anything else? She closed the suit-case and put on her coat. But still she lingered. It was kind of funny to be going away like this. . . .

She switched off the wireless, then she stood, gazing into

space. She felt that something was wrong. Something was lacking. . . . Girls leaving home surely didn't behave as calmly as all this. . . .

She picked up the *Evening News* and glanced through it as if seeking for inspiration. She read slowly through the columns of Births, Marriages and Deaths. Her mother had aye read these first in the paper. . . . And the *In Memoriams*.

Ay, it was well remembered. She knew there was something. As Mrs. Moore would have said, a Higher Hand had guided her. She took a pencil and began to copy one of the *In Memoriams* on to a piece of paper. It was lovely. She must see that she inserted it in good time. . . .

She read over what she had written:

In loving memory of my Mother, Margaret Hipkiss, who laid down the Cross to take up the Crown on 16th March, 1939.

A smile for all, a heart of gold,
One of the best this world did hold.
A loving mother true and kind,
A beautiful memory left behind.

Inserted by her loving daughter, Bessie.

Should she maybe put the bairns' names at it, too? She must insert it in good time. That would make her father and that tart, Mabel, sit up. That would make them hang their heads for shame. And folk would read it and say: 'Fancy, poor Mrs. Hipkiss, just dead a year and that Hipkiss married again for three months already. . . .'

Nine months. . . . You'd never credit it that it was just nine months since poor ma had died. Somehow it seemed longer than that. Of course, so much had happened since. There was the war and the bairns being evacuated. And there was her job in Andrews'. And there was Mrs. Irvine. And then there was the baby being ill and dying like that. Poor wee thing. . . .

Bessie remembered suddenly what she had once thought of doing to the baby. And at the thought she crossed herself quickly and furtively.

The poor wee baby. . . . 'Oh, love that will not let me go,' she began to sing. 'I rest my weary soul in theeee. . . .'

She went to the mirror and looked at herself, crossing herself again. Ay, she must remember and put an *In Memoriam* in for the baby, too, when the time came. . . .

There was a gorgeous one in tonight. She'd just copy it, and then she'd be prepared.

Out early one morning gathering flowers,
An angel stooped down and picked one of ours.

It was really lovely. Tears came into Bessie's eyes as she read through it and the one for her mother. Then she folded them quickly and put them in her pocket.

Oh, Ma, I'm not a bad lassie for doing this, am I? I cannie bear it any longer, Ma. I try to be good, but I cannie bear my da bringing that woman here. You'll forgive me, won't you, Ma? You'll tell me, won't you? You'll come and tell me it's all right when I go to my first Circle with Mrs. Irvine, won't you? Oh, it'll be lovely to hear your voice again, Ma. You'll be able to tell me everything about Heaven. . . .

Bessie dropped on her knees, and burying her head on the sofa, she began to pray. She knelt until the tears had dried on her cheeks, then she rose and powdered her face. There was no knowing who she might meet on her way to Mrs. Irvine's.

She looked round the living-room to see that everything was all right. The fire was rapidly going out. It would be dead by the time her da and that tart came home. And it would serve them bloody well right. They should have treated her better.

She picked up her case and went into the lobby. Cautiously, she opened the door of the children's room and peered in. They were sound asleep. Poor wee brats. . . .

She stood for a second, but as she felt the tears prick her eyelids again, she picked up her case and went out. Closing the door furtively behind her, eyes darting towards the Finlaysons' door in case they looked out and saw her suit-case, she began to tiptoe downstairs.

But by the time she had got to the bottom flight she was running, her heels clattering. *Allons, mon enfant,* you are going to start a new life. *Courage, cherie.* . . .

Bette Montez swept down the great staircase, her servants carrying her luggage behind her. The carriage was waiting at the entrance . . . the carriage that was to carry her to freedom, a new life, and greater triumphs. . . .

Lightning Source UK Ltd.
Milton Keynes UK
10 December 2010

164200UK00002B/17/P